I0831942

THE SPECIAL EDITION

COPYRIGHT DISCLAIMER

Cover by Shoutlines Design, Seattle, WA, USA www.shoutlines.com

www.facebook.com/shoutlinesdesign

10 9 8 7 6 5 4 3 2 1

ISBN-10: 0-9893773-8-5

ISBN-13: 978-0-9893773-8-6

Parchman's Press 2013.

ABOUT THE AUTHOR

When A.L. Mengel arrived on the scene and published *Ashes* in 2013, he broke new ground in supernatural storytelling. Readers worldwide have embraced the story, pulling out different themes and elements based on their own individual backgrounds. Blending realism with fiction, he weaves Catholicism, theology, the paranormal and superstition in a tapestry of horrific storytelling.

His protagonists are frequently angels and demons, and more often than not, are found on a journey – a search for purpose, for understanding, or a quest for survival.

Whether or not a reader is religious or not, A.L. Mengel's writing and characters invoke thought, take the reader on a philosophical journey, and present the oxymoron of dark and light.

A.L. Mengel welcomes interaction with his readers at

www.facebook.com/authoralmengel

and his website at www.almengel.com

Please also read his blog: www.eatlivewrite.blogspot.com

A NOTE ON THE SPECIAL EDITION

I have put together a special "Author's Edition" of *Ashes*, which, ironically, will be the first edition that I will release of the novel. This will be the only "Author's Edition" that I plan to make of this novel, at least in the foreseeable future. After this has been released, the novel will most likely be split into two volumes, but with some new material.

Ashes was initially formatted double spaced, with 11 point Garamond font in a 6x9 book format. That proved to be far too long to publish for a reasonable amount of money. Still, I wanted to put this masterpiece out untouched; for I know, in the future, it will most likely be split and the plot re-worked. Of course, that will give you a reason to read *Ashes* once again - since there is a lot of new material that will make up each planned volume of this story when it is revised with New York publishers.

So, please enjoy this special limited "Author's Edition" of *Ashes*. This novel offers both volumes in a single book. Also, an added bonus of this edition of *Ashes* is an Author's Notes page at the end of the book, which you may find interesting.

Enjoy reading *Ashes*. It's my personal masterpiece for you…and I hope you have as much fun reading it as I did writing it.

And as you read – keep turning the pages after the story ends. There's a little Easter egg for you hidden back there.

Always, A.L

I hear you.

I see you.

Glistening your smile, looking at me through wispy white;

I hear your call.

Path, yours not chosen, spoken you have not.

You close my eyes.

My dream turns black. My night turns dusty.

My vision – blurred.

And then you show me.

The dust settles.

And there you lay.

You turn your head and smile though fleeting quickly.

You say to me, "I once danced."

- poem by A.L. Mengel

SPECIAL EDITION

A NOVEL BY A.L. MENGEL

THE TALES OF TARTARUS

For Ty – the one who dusted the manuscript off and inspired me to finish it.

I also dedicate this special hardback edition of the novel to my Mother and my Father.

These three people have had the biggest influence on my writing and my life, and all have provided amazing amounts of support. And with this new edition of my debut novel, I would not be where I am today without these three wonderful people in my life.

FIRST PROLOGUE

MANHATTAN AT NIGHT

The hospital room was starting to feel like a coffin.

Gasping for air, Darius made a feeble attempt to sit up in the bed. His bedclothes were soaked with a cold and clammy sweat, and even the faded yellow blanket - which hardly kept him warm - had a damp feeling to it. A voice cut into the quiet hum of the machines; a deep yet piercing voice that spoke with a commanding tone:

Darius…

His head snapped to attention when he heard his name whispered lightly. It spoke again, now more insistent.

Darius…Darius!

Again.

He snapped the light on, which bathed the room in a faint glow. He scanned the pale green walls but saw no one. The chair in the far corner of the room cast a dark shadow on the floor, but nothing seemed amiss. He reached for the small white beeper, startling himself when the thick cord it was attached to knocked his plastic water pitcher over and sent it crashing to the floor

We've got you, you miserable fuck!

Darius fumbled with the beeper, and started smashing his palm on the giant blue button. Over and over he pressed it, wishing someone would come.

Because of the voice.

He breathed in and exhaled deeply, and closed his eyes. Concentrating on each breath he drew in and exhaled from his lungs, he sat and waited, listening to the silence.

That voice he knew.

Dariiiuuuuuuuuussssssssssss –

His eyes snapped open.

The veins bulged from his hands as he held the beeper tightly. He pressed the button again and again, and as he opened his eyes, he screamed.

The shadow behind the chair elongated, feeling its way up the wall, grayish arms branching out – reaching towards the ceiling, casting an aura of darkness throughout the room. The indistinct arms crept across the ceiling, the veil falling over his bed like a dark sheet filtering out the light.

Darius reached his arms up, covering his eyes with his forearms, pleading through tears. "I am no longer a sinner! I have my absolution! *I have my absolution*!"

Spiny fingers were reaching for him as he cowered closer to the headboard, ducking under the blanket like a child as the arms stretched down above the bed.

Too many times, Darius, you have you been on the path leading to us…so many years you have willed us to come…and now we are here to take you with us!

Another shadow, the one cast behind the open door, felt its way around the dim yellowish light coming from the exterior hallway. It felt its way across the dusty checkerboard floor, slowly crept up the side of the bed, fingered itself under the blanket, all while the ominous shadow that was hovering above him lowered itself on him and straddled his chest.

Darius attempted to sit up, pinned to the bed by an enormous weight, and struggled to breathe. "Help….me…." he gasped, craning his neck towards the hallway.

The shadow above him started to come into focus.

All your life we have watched you…we watched you as a boy, we watched you as a man, we watched you as the demon you became and the sick fuck you now are!

The shadow that slithered up the sheets started to wrap itself around him – squeezing his chest in vice, tightening around his legs, and he suddenly gasped. It became even more increasingly difficult to breathe. His chest heaved as white foam started pouring from his mouth.

He no longer could call for help; but he managed to turn his head to the right; he saw several blurry white figures enter the room. They seemed so out of focus that they resembled beams of light. But that did not deter the assault from the shadows.

Come with us, the shadow above him commanded. *We will rip you out of your reality! You must come!*

One of the shadow's thorny digits lengthened – so long it touched the ceiling – and it drew it down on Darius like a whip. Darius cowered back, and grunted. He looked down at the sheets and saw blood seeping out of his chest.

Another crack of the whip.

Your father has forsaken you!

Again.

In my hands you will commend your spirit!

Again, again and again the shadow whipped, as the glowing luminescent figures gathered around Darius' bedside.

"My God!" Darius called out. He sat up his bed, his dark hair mussed and dirty, his eyes wide as plates, sweat pouring down the sides of his sunken cheeks. His vision was blurred by blood and tears. "Have you forsaken me?! What have I become?!"

One last strike and Darius fell back on the bed and the demons retreated back into the shadows. He opened his eyes and saw the white figures standing over him.

He struggled to bring his vision into focus. One of the figures moved closer to him.

"Darius?" it said. "Do you hear me?"

He closed his eyes again and felt himself breathing. His throat felt like it was on fire. His head was pounding, like a ton of cinder blocks were resting on it.

"Darius," the voice said, this time more clearly. "Please speak if you can."

He opened his eyes again, and saw salt and pepper hair, combed over a wrinkled forehead, and then saw the tired face of a doctor. The white coat, the blue scrubs.

"We almost lost you there," the doctor said. "We were trying to revive you for the past ten minutes." Darius scanned the room. No shadows. No demons. The lights were burning above him. A team of doctors and nurses were huddled around his bed.

"The Dark Ones…" Darius mumbled. "It's The Dark Ones…they are here again…The Dark Ones…get…me a priest…"

And he closed his eyes again.

PART ONE:

THE TRANSFORMATION

…death will come swiftly to all those who enter here…

- Inscribed on the entrance to the Tomb of King Tut

CHAPTER ONE

Present Day.

Antoine gathered his equipment - a shovel, brown tarp, pickaxe (in order to pry open the casket) and a flame oil lantern; carefully and quietly he entered the graveyard through a layer of swirling, early morning mist - the type of white cloudy mist that would leave a layer of dewdrops on the earth like a cool, wet blanket. The plot Antoine headed toward, located in the center of the graveyard, housed Darius' casket, encased for two centuries now in layers of earth - sealed by six nails, and placed in a thick cement liner with a crest of a lion on the marble-topped cover.

It was Antoine who put Darius here two centuries ago, and Darius has been in this graveyard ever since. In this cemetery and dead, yes – Darius was dead. But Darius had been dead before Antoine had ever put him there. And when the coffin was nailed shut, when the darkness enveloped satin interior, there was more of changing a state of existence.

It was Darius who had heard the nails being pounded into the edges of the casket; he had felt the shaking as the coffin was picked up – most likely with ropes tied below the bottom, but he couldn't know for sure – and lowered into the deep, dark grave. He had felt the sides of the coffin scraping the cold, hard earthen walls. The dirt fell onto the lid of the casket – each shovel of earth inundating the coffin further with a deep clump.

Blackness.

The sounds from above now seemed more distant. The coffin had been buried. Darius knew that. He even felt the weight of the dirt above him, as if the entire casket would fall on top of him in a cascade of splintering wood and falling sand. But it held. The coffin was holding fast against the pressures of the earth, and would prove to be his holding place for…how long?

The stagnancy of the air inside the small confines grew more insistent, as the heat overtook the darkness and caused him to cough and choke on the thickness of the air that was so quickly fading. But Darius knew. He knew that no matter how fast the air would dissipate, no matter how faint the sounds of the earth above would be – no matter how *dead* he would be – he would be just that.

Dead.

But death is just a state of existence. And Darius knew - all too well - that his death had been many, many years ago – and not so recently in his foyer. His death had been much earlier when he was a very young man passing into his newfound immortality. Not at the hands of Antoine.

As time passed, he became more aware of his surroundings, although all he saw was total darkness. He could feel the softness and smoothness of the satin liner, the pillow at the head of the casket - which grew hard and cold over time and dusty with mold.

Above where he lay, Darius on occasion could hear the faint, muffled voices above the cold ground expressing words of condolence, the grating of a casket being lowered into a freshly dug grave, or the pitter patter of children's feet; ceremonial instruments would play from time to time, signifying the passing of a loved one. All this, he experienced, lying in the cold darkness of the casket, as time passed by above.

Time passed with an eternal slowness until Antoine returned.

At one point, Darius knew the time had come. He continued to lie in the casket as he felt and heard snippets of the outside world over time, but there was one quiet day when he heard those familiar footsteps; the methodic, determined stomps coming closer and closer to his unmarked resting place. The footsteps stopped, just above. Darius could sense it. He knew who it was. No one knew of his grave except one soul. Only one.

Antoine.

~~*

Topside, Antoine reached the grave.

It was the only unmarked grave in the entire cemetery. Located under a tree, the plot was not originally used as the caretaker had been afraid that the roots of the massive tree would grow to a size so immense as to unearth a coffin. But that did not deter Antoine. It had been the perfect resting place for Darius.

It had been Antoine who dug the grave, in the middle of the night, so many days ago. But even then, as he had been digging, Antoine knew that a day of resurrection would come. Even as Darius burned into ash, even as Antoine drove a dagger directly through his steadfast heart, he knew that the day would come that he would need to channel Darius once again and ask for his assistance...no, *expect* his assistance…and receive the help and guidance from the one who created him so long ago.

And now, deep in the night, Antoine set down his tools. The tools were just as dull and rusted as they had been the night he buried Darius. He paused to the left of the grave, and looked to the sky. Night held steady.

I have come for you, Darius. Yes, the day has finally come. The day has finally come when I need you, I need you by my side. But please, please don't come to me with malice or ill-will for putting you here. I love you, Darius.

The moon burned brightly and cast a blue glow on the headstones, illuminating them like tiny, square lights a dark, dank sea. Opening the brown cloth bag, Antoine grabbed the shovel, trying so desperately to pull the tools from the bag in silence. His head snapped towards the direction of the woods as the shovel clanked against the other tools in the bag.

But he rose to his feet and pointed the shovel towards the earth, shifting his weight and breaking the ground. He stopped for a moment as he tossed the first bit of dirt to the side.

Darius…will you ever forgive me?

And then he dug - he dug and dug, hoisting shovelfuls of earth, one after the next, to the right of the grave, next to the bag of tools. The digging continued for quite some time, as Antoine broke through roots and clay. Darius had been deeply buried.

Bury them deep, Darius had once told him. *If you are extinguishing an immortal, bury them deep.*

Antoine finally felt the scraping of the grave liner, the impenetrable cement beneath the thin layer of caked dirt and sand. A black snake slithered from the side of the earth, slinking across the grave liner and re-entered on the other side. Antoine stood above the grave for a moment and looked down at the liner, and then scanned the area around him. The sky began to show the faintest hints of light blue, signifying that he needed to hurry, hoist the casket out of the grave, and head to safety.

The swirling mist was subsiding as the night was ever so gradually waning and giving to the very first peeks of the eastern sun, which slowly yet surely revealing itself way on the far horizon. Antoine had been digging for the better part of the night. He estimated that he had another hour or so of semi-darkness, and then the sunrise would occur. The sky was surely awakening.

Antoine jumped down into the grave and stood on the liner. He just was able to see over the threshold of the earth, and reached out and grabbed the pickaxe. He swung it down into the hole and smacked it against the lock on the grave liner, with a loud *clank!* which reverberated against the quiet early morning silence. But the one assault had not been enough to break the seal of death. He had to break the silence and take another risk of possibly being discovered by a mortal, and again *clank!*

With the second rap, the lock gave. It amazed Antoine that it had still held so prominently after so many years, and despite it being covered in rust, dirt and grime.

Antoine tossed the pickaxe out of the grave, and winced as it clanked against the other tools in the bag. It was time to open the casket.

The grave liner was caked with dirt and mud, the insignia was rusted out, but overall it was still intact (as was the lock) and it held together like an expensive grave liner would be expected to. As Antoine shifted the lid with a deep grating and rumbling, the small, wooden casket slowly came into view – rotted from years of decay. And there, beneath the six nails, beneath the wood and satin, would be Darius.

~~*

Darius Savauge was truly the demon extraordinaire!

It was Darius, who spotted Antoine from a distance, Darius who followed and seduced Antoine into a life of darkness -drawing him away from his mortal life of misery. It was Antoine, the one who lived a life of debauchery, incest and thievery who had called to Darius. Antoine had called for Darius to come, sit at a table, to watch Antoine closely...and wait. It was Antoine who beckoned, not Darius. Darius heard the call – the call that was not of a spoken word, but a call of actions. Antoine made the call so many years ago like he was now. His sins, his life then, had made him chosen. His life now, made Antoine call Darius once again.

Why did Darius first come? It was in Darius' eyes that Antoine could see that look of a lover - the kind but mysteriously fascinating eyes that commanded attention and following. And beckoned his eyes did. While Darius' eyes were firmly locked on Antoine's, they pleaded for an introduction and conversation. Darius couldn't help but smile.

But there perhaps something deeper deep within that smile. Perhaps something evil.

Whatever it was, the transformation took place. Darius was the cocoon, Antoine became the butterfly. And then, Antoine was born again.

Yes, Darius, the artist that used his brush and canvas to mold Antoine into what he became. Darius the creator, Darius the web spinner. It was Darius all along – who watched and waited until the best, most precise moment in time to meet Antoine.

Darius, the lover and the warrior, who for so many years was what he was. Who had been chosen himself, who was visited in the early mornings by Tramos. It was always Darius, who probably would never change…and who never wanted to die, and might never choose to forgive.

Now, he lay in this exposed casket underneath a thin layer of sand and dirt that was caked on the top of the coffin.

But what was left of him? What was left here after years of burial? Would he still be the Darius that had been so beautiful and treasured and loved? Or would he just be a rotted corpse, or a pile of dusty bones?

Antoine dug through the bag for a hammer so he could find out.

He pried at the first nail in the coffin with the back end of the hammer, and easily glided the nail out of the rotting wood, with a bit of the corner of the coffin falling apart in his hand. Antoine began to tear away at the lid, and the wood gave way with ease. It continued to crumble in his hands. Faster and more frantically, he tore away at the lid. Gradually, the satin interior of the casket came into view, faded and gray against the early morning sky; more of the satin lining came into view as the wood tore away.

Darius, now I am finally about to see you again. I am finally about to set my eyes upon your beautiful body, lying here in this casket since I put you here. I plead with you again, I need your help, not your anger. I will let you out of this confinement. But you must be honest and true and loyal, do not fear me and do not come to me in anger. Is the anger still there? Are you still feeling malice after all these days?

Antoine paused for a moment, before he was to pull the largest, most concealing slab of wood that made up the lid. When this piece was pulled away, Darius would be revealed. Would he still be as beautiful, as he was in life? Or would he be a horrid, piling mass of rotted flesh? Either way, it was Antoine's job to resurrect him. Darius was needed. But when Darius would be resurrected, would he be become? Antoine had no choice. He could not dwell on such insignificant matters. It was risk that must be taken.

Antoine sat for a moment on the edge of the grave, amidst piles of freshly dug earth scattered about, thinking to himself, remembering days past.

I may be placed into this grave.

Yes, that was the reality.

Darius, and the type of fierce demonic personality that he possessed, would not be too happy at all at Antoine for placing him in the grave, for going against his maker, and rebelling. But now, perhaps Antoine could convince Darius to spare him, to restrain himself from attacking as a way of revenge, but rather to listen to what Antoine had to say.

Of course, Antoine was digging up Darius because he had something to say.

It was just simply one benefit of being an immortal. Humans, of course, die and their death is final. It is, ultimately, the last word. Once a person goes into the grave, there will be no more communication.

Now in the immortal world, death is simply a different state of existence. With keen senses that remain present and aware as the body decays and withers, there is the distinct possibility for reanimation.

Quite a difference.

Antoine, the fierce leader and healer, who has been respected in the mortal world as a figure of mystery and awe, has now been humbled at the grave of his creator.

It was time for Antoine to ask for help.

No longer would Antoine be able to control Miami alone. He needed some assistance, someone at his side to give him guidance, to continue instruction.

And Darius was the one to be there at his side.

Knowing Darius, he would take over, as he tended to do back in the days in Lyon, when Antoine had been newly transformed, still learning the ways of darkness.

Given Antoine's dominating personality, the personality that he had during his short time as a mortal in Sri Lanka and also in his current life in Miami as a well -respected city socialite and businessman - could again cause conflict between the two. Antoine may have to put Darius back in the grave.

But Antoine did not want to think that far ahead in the future. If Darius remained stubbornly dominant and refused to concede to Antoine's plan, then he would deal with it then. Now, Antoine needed to deal with the grave. He arose from his sitting position. And started to deal with that last piece of wood on top of the casket.

Taking a breath of air into his lungs and holding it steady, Antoine tore away the last piece of rotted wood from the wooden, dirt caked casket with a cracking and crumbling sound, as it came apart in his fingers. The wood fell into an empty satin-lined casket.

Empty it seemed, at first.

But underneath the wood pieces - in the dark corners - there was something. A presence. Antoine knew it.

Deep in the darkened crevices of the coffin, Darius was lurking.

Hoisting the coffin to the ground above, he set it there with a slight thud. He lifted himself out of the grave and bent down to his knees next to the coffin, and reverently lifted the remaining pieces of wood away, of all different sorts and sizes.

He piled up the pieces of wood on the ground next to the casket. With his eyes transfixed on the unexpected emptiness, Antoine replayed in his mind the night that Darius was buried.

~~*

It was not long after Darius had transformed Antoine that it happened. It was the evening that the two shared in the chateau with the soaring columns in front, reaching up to four small windows on the second level, nestled into the stone, which strangely peered down like eyes.

It was in the library on the first floor, at the end of a small hallway and a grandiose foyer, where the two had been discussing *Les Livre Des Vampires* when Antoine had realized where he had come to in his state of existence. Sitting at a small, wooden table overlooking a glass pane window, Antoine buried his head in his hands. He grabbed at his hair as tears streamed down his cheeks. He slapped his head multiple times. "I just can't understand this," he said, slapping his hands down on the table.

Darius came to the chair, placed his hand on Antoine's shoulder, and looked lovingly down into his eyes.

Darius - the long, flowing dark brown hair, framing a white, chiseled face; Antoine and all of his sexual trysts and selfishness brought him to Darius' keen eye, and the selection was made. During Antoine's short life, he became somewhat of a ladies man, despite being tender and young. It was Antoine's youth and beauty that women

- and men - both desired, and Antoine was no inhibitor of passion. He did not care what others thought of the taboo and forbidden, and he had indulged in them quite often.

And that is how Antoine was selected for immortality. Darius, an immortal for hundreds of years before he first laid eyes on Antoine, shared many of the same opinions and had a similar mortal history. As through the passage of time, and how society becomes more accepting of previously shunned activity as years progress, it was apparent that Antoine did indeed have a more scandalous life. But that did not mean that Darius was without a dark side.

"My dear Antoine," Darius said softly, as he bent down, and placed his arm around Antoine's shoulder as if a father. "Don't obsess over the obvious. Look at you, sitting there like a schoolboy studying for a test." He let out a laugh as he said this. "You will learn soon!"

It's not that Antoine did not like or appreciate the life of an immortal. He actually rather enjoyed it. In what other state of existence can one live forever? Shortly after his transformation, the pair attended the operas, shopped on the finest promenades, took trips across the sea and lived a life of opulence and indulgence.

Still, Darius' behavior began to eat away at Antoine gradually and methodically, like termites slowly disintegrating wood. Each outing, Darius would reveal his plans, speaking like an excited child, to form a secret society and overtake the world. Antoine was more rational, and scoffed at the plans regularly. To him, Darius seemed like a young and inexperienced novice at social matters despite the age of the two partners being the same.

~~*

Antoine had one more nail to pry away, and then he could lift the last piece off and see the remains. Partially he knew what to expect, but this was the first time that Antoine had silenced a member of his species, and he had only read about what would take place during a reanimation.

He also heard several accounts of immortals that had claimed to be present when a reanimation was taking place. Some said that Satan himself has been known to appear. But Antoine thought that a lot of what he had heard could have been hearsay, as the evening seemed to be progressing fairly well so far.

The last nail was pried out and splintered the wood. He held the hammer in front of his face, studying the bent nail, hanging from the giant teeth of the dulled, rusted hammer, pulling bits of dried and rotted wood wedged between the nail and hammer, letting it drop to the ground.

And then he stopped. He heard a rustling coming from the woods.

He snapped his head, following the sound. All he saw was the dark green forest canopy. Looking up, he saw the tree tops were blowing in a light breeze. He listened attentively but the rustling ceased.

Glancing back down at the casket, the rustling started again, and this time a small tree branch snapped. The rustling continued and grew louder; it most certainly was not the wind – branches snapped over and over – and the rustling became more methodic and more determined. It started to grow with bass and grumbling.

And it was getting closer and louder.

CHAPTER TWO

Antoine ducked inside the grave, and looked towards the woods from the side of the casket which was lying on the ground in front of him. He scanned the woods, and despite his youthful and keen sense of sight, he struggled to see what made the deafening noise in the forest. The noise was so loud he could feel the ground shake around him, so loud that bits of dirt on the side of the grave wall broke loose and fell to the watery mess at his feet.

At first, he did not believe it could be what he was thinking it was.

During the crash, Antoine jumped and ducked at first, but managed to see beyond the casket in time to see the leaves ruffling, branches and twigs snapping, and a cascade of leaves and branches falling towards the earth in a wave of dark green.

It was not just branches and twigs falling to the ground.

It was an entire tree.

Whatever it was in the woods, whatever or whomever was watching Antoine…was big. It was big enough to bring down an entire tree; a tree large enough to cause the ground to shake when it fell to the earth below.

Antoine had to reanimate Darius – and fast. Time was running out. Daylight was steadily approaching. The sky was growing deep blue to pale blue ever faster, and each time that Antoine looked above, it seemed the sky was significantly lighter than before.

Antoine would just go ahead and begin the process of reanimation, but the woods were demanding his immediate attention. And he was too close to the edge of the forest to run.

"Antoine…" hissed a steady voice, which Antoine first dismissed as the howling of the wind. But it rang above all other sounds. It came from the direction of the forest.

Antoine's breathing grew to a rapid pace. His heart beat rapidly against his chest. What seemed like the first time in his immortal life, he was out of breath. And he remained still, feet perched on the edge of the cement grave liner, this time ducking below the surface of the earth. He was afraid to speak.

The sounds in the wood organized into a deep, bass-filled booming sound – like quaking footsteps. Whatever was making the steps was big – and each step taken shook the ground – slightly, not like an earthquake – just enough to shake the dirt loose on the walls of Darius' grave.

Antoine settled further into the grave; quietly as if a cat huddling into the liner, and lay down in the watery mess. He struggled getting himself situated in the grave as whatever was making the footsteps was massive. With each step, the earth again broke away from the side of the grave wall, now raining sand and clay down onto Antoine's face and torso.

He closed his eyes, feeling the cold and damp dirt land on his eyes, so if he opened them they would be gritty and grainy. He felt more of the cold, clammy sand on his torso and legs – all with each booming step – the steps that grew more powerful…and closer.

The water that Antoine lay in smelled foul and of death. Like water that has been stagnant for a long period of time, that has developed an odor of decaying and rotting flesh – and a smell so pungent and overpowering it would cause a mortal to vomit. But Antoine tuned out the stench, and concentrated on the sounds coming from above.

The rustling and cracking of the trees ceased. And the footsteps stopped for a moment. Antoine assumed that whatever it was had reached the clearing from the woods. And now was standing at the edge of the cemetery…perhaps as close as ten feet away from where Antoine was laying in the grave.

The coffin was being moved.

He heard the sliding of the wood on dirt, as if someone were dragging the casket away from the grave. The coffin was most definitely being moved. Antoine was sure of that. The footsteps stopped just above the grave, right next to where the casket sat.

Something was breathing.

Deep, grating.

Raspy and wheezy.

He could tell that now. The breathing sounded congested and very nasal.

Through closed and sand covered eyes, Antoine pictured a horrible demon-like monster above the grave…with a wolf-like face, super muscular manlike body…down to a long spiked tail like that of the devil.

But that was just Antoine's speculation. He did not know with certainty who or what was standing above the grave. But he knew one thing. Whatever was up there had to know he was lying below. One look over the side and into the grave would reveal a dark skinned immortal lying in a lake of putrid water.

~~*

The dawn was coming fast.

But there was still plenty of time to resurrect an immortal. The process had already begun – it had been put into motion when Antoine's shovel first hit the hard earth, and the progression would not stop until Darius was reanimated. The graveyard was much more active since the appearance of The Protector who diligently stood guard at the gravesite.

Numerous other trees fell, but The Protector did not move. He was perched at the edge of the grave, wheezing deeply, each breath full of mucus, emitting a rotten gas from his nose and mouth into the air like a light smoke.

From the fallen trees came several other man-demons all with super-muscular bodies like The Protector, all with spiked tails and dog-like faces. Each was adorned with rusted, dirty steel armor – a shield and sword – and all ready for battle.

Each demon lined up beside the graves – the first stood at the foot of Darius' grave and so on down in a long line as if preparing for a battle standoff. The line grew and grew as again another demon emerged from the forest, until the line reached the entire stretch of the cemetery.

The Protector reached inside Darius' coffin, and saw that there was nothing inside except for a heart.

Darius.

Even deep inside the grave, Antoine could see what was happening.

The Resurrection.

The Protector raised the heart out of the casket and held it up to the sky. He chanted something that Antoine could not understand – and the voice was so deep and discordant if it had been in a human dialect he probably would not have been able to discern it either.

Chanting, over and over. He was repeating it.

The sky opened up. The pinks and blues that had began to creep through just a short while earlier were instantly covered with dark black swirling clouds. The clouds were so black they made it seem as if the night had returned in full force, and that there was no hope of daylight or a rising sun.

The wind raged in an instant. The storm was centered directly over the cemetery, and the dark black sky was illuminated by flashes of bright lightning and crashes of deep thunder. Fallen tree branches and leaves blew throughout the graveyard – everything from small twigs to large brushwood – but none of the demons left their posts.

The Protector set Darius' heart down on the ground reverently next to the casket, and spoke. "It is time!" he commanded the army of demons, voice raspy, wheezing and full of mucus – yet loud and powerful enough to be heard by the entire army above the wind and commotion.

The Protector raised his arms to the sky and instantly the winds stopped. His command froze the storm – froze it so instantly that branches and leaves hung in the sky in suspended animation – waiting for his command to continue. It was as if the entire scene had been put on pause.

He turned to the graveyard to his minions. Each demon, guarding a grave, looked towards The Protector. All faces turned towards Darius' grave.

"We have an immortal with us," his deep voice booming in a dialect that Antoine had never heard before. "He is in the grave below! *He is lying in his maker's grave*!"

The Protector gave another wave of his arms and all of the suspended branches and leaves fell to the ground. He stood directly over the grave, peering down into the blackness of the hole, so dark and dank that a human would see nothing. But The Protector saw.

"Rise up, Antoine. Rise now."

As Antoine slowly opened his eyes, the dirt that had caked on his face fell into his eyes and blurred his vision. He raised his arms from the water, as water dripped from his jacket, and brushed the dirt and mud away, he got his first glimpse of The Protector.

And Antoine stopped still – his hands were holding his cheeks, in the midst of cleaning dirt; hands still on either side of his face next to his eyes, drinking in the horrific vision.

The Protector stood peering from above the grave down at Antoine.

There was no hiding. The giant, towering man-beast was indeed how Antoine pictured him - stacked like a beast with muscles, with the face of a dog or even a wolf but most certainly a beast. From his snout emitted some noxious gas that looked like grey smoke which rose into the air, and the saliva that poured from his mouth fell down into the grave and dripped in the water below. With each drop, it emitted a hiss – like pressure being released from steam, and a small puff of smoke arose from where the drop fell.

The skin was scaly, green and brown and was covered with black lesions that looked like sores that wept profusely. The scales pulled taught over the powerful muscles, and The Protector looked to be a legendary fighter. A dirty and dented steel shield was strapped over the powerful chest, and a sword was tucked at his side in its sheath.

Antoine lay frozen, staring up at the beast.

The Protector.

Antoine had heard about The Protector in the past, rumors of what the demon looked like wafted through the immortal community from those who claimed to have fought him, saw him, or witnessed him resurrecting an immortal.

The Protector of everything evil.

Satan's right hand.

A former angel cast down from heaven, as was his mentor and chief Lucifer, The Protector, also known as Asmodai, was the embodiment of evil. He reigned in Hell with Satan, and went out beyond the inner realms of the Underworld to bring followers to Lucifer.

Asmodai – the Demon of Lust and the sins of the flesh.

And he was staring directly at Antoine.

Some salivate dripped from the snout of the demon, and he emitted a deep grunt. The drool fell downwards into the grave, and onto Antoine's leg.

Antoine sat up and grimaced at the searing pain that raced through his body, and stared in disbelief at the small trail of smoke rising from his leg.

"Rise Antoine!" Asmodai commanded. "*Rise out of your maker's grave*!"

Antoine looked up from his leg and saw the demon's eyes, staring him down intently. The eyes were deep red and the scowl was of pure evil.

~~*

Asmodai stood over the grave, and cast his glare down at Antoine, who had not moved from the murky water below. Asmodai turned his head for a moment and issued a command to his army in their own dialect.

The legion of demons began to dig with their arms at each of the graves they were guarding; a massive exhumation had begun.

Upon Asmodai's command, the storm resumed and raged with a greater intensity that it had before – all of the fallen branches and leaves were instantaneously scooped up by the ferocious winds instantly creating an almost blinding wall of debris.

Antoine cautiously stood, still keeping his head below the earth, but had to struggle to get out of the grave with the intense winds. Holding on to the thick roots, and climbing up the deep, damp grave wall, his arms finally reached the surface and he felt for the pickaxe. Grabbing it in his right hand and standing on the sides of the grave liner, he stood on his toes and dug the axe into the ground, giving him some leverage and dragged himself out of the grave.

He collapsed on the ground for a moment, and gathered his senses and then looked up, shielding his eyes from the offensive and biting winds. He peered through his fingers to protect his face from the debris, he saw many demons exhuming casket after casket – tossing dirt and throwing bits of wood, satin liners and body parts everywhere. All the caskets were old and full of rotted and decaying wood. A few, perhaps of the more wealthy dead, were made of stone or marble.

But the stone proved to be insignificant to the demons. One stone coffin was raised out of the ground at such a velocity it flew across the clearing and landed just feet away from where Antoine was huddling. It landed on the ground with a deep *thud* and the cement lid crashed against the body of the coffin and broke into pieces. It fell on its side, almost rolling on top of Antoine.

A rotted corpse that looked as if it was lying in the cemetery for years spilled out of the coffin. The skin on the face was sucked in revealing the cheek-bones, as if the skin had melted off the face. The teeth looked as if on a wolf as the gums and soft oral tissue had long rotted away and served as a feast for maggots and other larvae.

The hair was still there - but in patches and dark, blotchy mold spotted the skin throughout the skull. The corpse, Antoine saw, was a man. Fairly young, perhaps not that much different in age from himself or Darius.

"Rise," said Asmodai, extending his arm to the body.

Antoine's head had turned in the direction of the body when he heard the falling cement. His eyes remained fixed on the corpse.

The remnants of the lid crashed to the ground. The eyes on the body glowed orange and the head turned slowly; it looked over at Antoine and sat up It started to rise out of the coffin.

It took some time for the body to lift all of the giant, heavy slabs of stone off its legs and step up and out of the casket. Antoine snapped his head to where Asmodai was standing.

Time appeared to stand still, if only for a moment, the sky, which had seemed brighter before, was now darkening. The wind quieted significantly. Asmodai seemed for the moment to be the only one else in the cemetery, save Antoine.

"This will be the one," he said to Antoine.

Asmodai gestured to the legion of demons and barked at them to stop in their native tongue. He then turned back to where Darius' heart lay on the ground, and picked it up with care.

"Take this and make it part of you," he instructed. "And then make it part of that rotted piece of human flesh. *And raise your maker!*"

The wind resumed once again, although the debris of branches and leaves were gone. It was a harsh and biting cold wind, and did not howl like the winds before. It was much less intense. The sky remained dark as midnight and the clouds swirled, but the lightning and thunder subsided.

Antoine looked over to where the multitude of demons stood guard, as the storm subsided somewhat, and saw that the graveyard now looked as though it were untouched. The demons all stood in military fashion once again at the edge of the cemetery. There were no unearthed coffins; no piles of dirt; no evidence that anything had happened at all.

It was eerily quiet; only a light wind whistled in the background.

Antoine's attention returned to Asmodai.

The corpse was lying on the ground again. Placing the heart into Antoine's open hands, Asmodai commanded: "*Make it part of you!*"

Antoine held the heart in his hands, feeling the cold, meaty flesh, listening to a distant heartbeat, feeling a warmth inside, treasuring the pleasure that it brought to his fingertips. He clasped the heart in his hands, bringing it to his lips, and stared at the organ. It was pulsating, as if it were still beating.

Antoine chose to make it part of him the only way he knew how. He opened his mouth, and tore into the rotting piece of flesh, sucking the warmth from the inner chambers.

~~*

The loud clap and roar of the thunder struck just as Antoine's teeth sunk into the meaty red bloody mess of flesh of the heart. The storm returned, far stronger than before. The trees ripped apart and the branches and leaves again began to blow across the open air of the graveyard; the wind instantly roared like a hurricane.

Antoine drank as the sky turned from black to deep red. In time Darius would shortly be rising, rising from the putrid rotted corpse that now lay next to the broken stone coffin; it was time that Darius would transform into the body and change it to that of his own, and walk the earth again.

The corpse still lay dead on the ground, limbs sprawled across the grass.

Darius was near.

The extraordinaire. Lover of all fine things. And what a demon himself!

"Darius!"

This is the blood! The blood of my maker!

Antoine cringed as he drank in the hot, thick potion. His teeth remained locked in the muscle as the liquid poured into his mouth; the liquid was so hot that it felt like it burned…he felt it ooze down his throat and into his body, racing at lightning speed through his veins as if seeking to overtake every inch of his body.

Antoine's eyes shot open and stared at Asmodai.

Darius was back.

He slowly withdrew the heart from his teeth, drawing it further from his mouth like a child slowly taking candy from his mouth when discovered by his mother.

He threw it in the open casket.

Asmodai stepped forward towards Antoine, and started to speak.

Before he could say a word, Antoine opened his mouth and vomited the blood, spewing a sticky red mess all over the coffin, drenching Asmodai in Darius' mess of innards.

"Rise, Darius! Come to me now!" Antoine screamed at the top of his lungs, blood streaming down his mouth and dripping to the ground below.

"Make him part of you or you will not raise him up!" Asmodai said, drawing his sword. "*Make him part of you or I will put you in this ground*!"

Antoine stopped dead in his tracks.

Asmodai was covered in what was left of Darius' blood; only the heart remained. He could not succumb to Asmodai's commands. He needed to get past Asmodai and reanimate Darius himself soon, despite that it seemed that Asmodai made the night last eternally.

Poised with a flaming sword in a fighting stance and ready for battle, Asmodai spoke again: "You have chosen to drink the blood of your maker. But you did not make it part of you and resurrect this corpse. You know, as well as I know, that you summoned me. You summoned me…the moment that your shovel hit the dirt in this earth. If you do not go forth with the ritual *you will be exterminated*."

With his words, every demon that was standing guard drew their swords instantaneously.

Antoine did not have time to think. He knew that if he were to ritualize Darius' reanimation, he would be forever in debt with Asmodai. Asmodai would own his soul.

He had to get that heart and get out of the cemetery. He could still reanimate Darius with the heart. It would be hard and close to impossible without the blood, but it could happen. Antoine needed Darius, but he did not need Asmodai's rituals and the high price that came with it.

"Make your decision!" Asmodai boomed. "There is no turning back! Resurrect him or I will put you here *in this ground forever*!"

The thunder crashed the loudest that it ever had, as if the storm were directly above them. With the bright flash of the lightning and the roar of the wind the sky opened up again. A curtain of blinding rain began to fall and the dirt of the earth quickly turned to sloppy mud, and Asmodai took Antoine's silence as the answer.

He lunged forward with his sword and Antoine ducked swiftly to the left, towards the coffin, like a cat. Gracefully he bowed down to the coffin and swiped the heart, and placed it in his coat pocket. He had Darius with him, closer to him than ever before.

As he darted to rush towards the edge of the forest, Asmodai swung his sword again and clanked on the metal hard, sending a shower of sparks into the rain.

As if on cue, every demon soldier sprung into action with swords ready in a battle stance. They equally and steadfastly pursued Antoine, as he tried desperately to make it to the woods and the safety of a thick canopy.

He used his immortal gift and jumped to a thick branch on a tall tree at the edge of the cemetery. Looking down on the action, he saw a swarm of demons approaching the base of the tree like ants overtaking a piece of food.

Asmodai still stood at the grave, glaring up at Antoine, staring directly at him, as he perched himself up in the tree like a bird. Asmodai did not say a word. His eyes beckoned. The skin on his forehead scowled in deep ridges; and the eyes pierced their gaze up towards the tree; they were a deep red – an intense crimson blood, and they were menacing. They were the deepest blood red eyes that Antoine had ever seen in his entire life.

And the eyes were filled with fury.

CHAPTER THREE

Five Years Earlier.

The Astral, Ponce De Leon and Anastasia Avenue, Coral Gables, Florida.

The dark green file for Antoine Nagevesh hit the desk with a flop, sending a puff of air across the plane of the table and rustling the days work. There was a small, wallet-sized photo of Antoine attached with a paper clip to the edge of the file. To a casual glance, the photo seemed to be of a young, strikingly handsome dark skinned man with long, dark hair. Once the file hit the desk, it would have seemed lost at first glance in the mountains of paperwork. Sheldon Wilkes was not the most organized of Directors, but he was passionate about his work.

The office was cluttered and always in a state of disarray – just like Sheldon's appearance. A short, paunchy and balding older man with a large gut, and forever wearing three-pieced suits and horn rimmed glasses, he seemed to mirror his office a bit. His demeanor projected the complexity of clutter – and it showed in his surroundings. Besides the blanket of papers across the voluminous desk in the center of the room, the walls were lined with bookshelves that reached from the floor to the ceiling; they were stuffed with volume after volume of books of the Undead, the paranormal, demonology and handbooks of the Immortals.

On one corner of his desk, *Les Livre Des Vampires* was opened, bookmarked and underlined with blue ink as well as highlighted in yellow and had notes penciled in the margins.

For the past several years, Sheldon had been obsessed with immortals, the paranormal, supernatural occurrences and the afterlife. His forehead wrinkled as he stared at the photo of Antoine. Sheldon mopped some sweat from his brow and loosened his tie. A drop of perspiration dropped on the photo, directly over Antoine's photo. Sheldon wiped it away, taking notice to Antoine's face – a dark complexion from years of working under the hot sun in the coffee fields surrounding Badulla. Antoine's long, black hair was pulled back tightly.

Sheldon began to formulate questions in his mind that he would ask Antoine later that evening. He fished a pencil from a pile of writing utensils on the desk and scribbled another question on a yellow legal pad, scooped up the file, and walked out of the office.

~~*

The hot air enveloped Sheldon as he entered the humidity outside his office. His jacket was draped over his forearm, and he struggled with the file in his other arm. As the glass door swung open with a squeak – on which "The Astral: Integrating Immortals into Everyday Society" read in frosted lettering – the Director stepped out and promptly dropped Antoine's file all over the sidewalk on Ponce De Leon.

He bent over to pick up the papers, and as he was gathering the file contents, he stopped for a moment.

As he looked straight ahead, he saw a pair of black boots.

His eyes followed upwards as he slowly arose from his crouched position – long legs, black pants, long, flowing black coat – could it be?

Yes, it possibly could be.

He looked up and saw a silhouette in the sunlight – the wind caught the mysterious man's hair, and it blew lightly with the breeze. The sun shone brightly from behind the mysterious figure, and Sheldon had to shield his eyes.

"Hello Mr. Wilkes," the man said, looking down. The curves on the side of his cheeks indicated he was smiling. He crouched down to Sheldon's height and poked through the contents of the file. He picked up several papers, shifting through them. "I see that this is my file you are keeping on me." He picked up the page with his photo on the corner, and paused for a moment, and unconsciously smoothed his hair that had caught the wind. "Not bad looking, am I?" he said with a chuckle, and dropped the paper back down on the sidewalk.

Sheldon sat on his haunches for a moment. He laughed softly and shook his head gently back and forth. His salt and pepper hair was thin and reached from his head like threads from a mop, matted and sweaty from the afternoon humidity. He was dumbfounded. He could not believe he was right here with Antoine. He remembered when he first encountered a photo of the intriguing spiritual healer – in a reference book in 1965. But so many years ago, Antoine was not who he was today, and now, things were quite different, and here he was, in the flesh. Kneeling right beside him on the sidewalk of Ponce De Leon.

Later that afternoon, he had cursed himself for being so astounded – because all he had managed to reply to Antoine – at first – was a simple "Yes".

Sheldon stood and cleared his throat, and put on his horn-rimmed glasses. Brushing himself off and buttoning his jacket, he gathered the papers and made an attempt to compose himself. Antoine stood slowly, smiling as he looked Sheldon in the eye.

"Tell me Antoine," he said. "Do you normally walk around in mid-afternoon?" He fumbled with the file. The papers were going in every direction, as Sheldon hastily stuffed the contents back in the brown folder.

"There are many things I do during the day," Antoine replied. "I actually was coming to speak with one of your researchers…Anthony. But let me ask, to where are you going in such a hurry?"

"Anthony? What do you want with Anthony?" Sheldon asked inquisitively.

Antoine merely smiled, but did not give an answer. His tone was very seductive with every speaking word – which seemed ironic in that situation. Regardless, Antoine's charisma came across no matter whom he was speaking to. Certainly most would not understand, nor would they care to know, why someone so strikingly handsome would be so charming to a short, paunchy old man…but that was just Antoine. He carried himself in the same way, equally polite with everyone he encountered. He reached out and opened the door for the older man – as Antoine always remained a gentleman.

"I was actually coming to see you," Sheldon admitted, as he snapped the lights on in the reception area. "I was coming to get your take on all of this." He held up the mess of a file to accentuate what he was talking about.

"And I see many discs there," Antoine commented, pointing to his bag.

"Yes. I would like a record of the conversation, if that's alright."

"I don't see an issue with that. You explained to me, as well as Anthony, that your organization is supportive of us."

"Yes, that's true," Sheldon replied. He stepped inside and interior door, setting the contents of the file down on a waiting room chair that was just inside. "Why don't you come inside? I am the only one here today, so I guarantee privacy."

"Certainly."

Antoine followed Sheldon inside the offices; the door slammed shaking the glass and the shade was hastily drawn.

~~*

The Astral had offices that looked like any typical office. There were leather-bound chairs in the waiting area, vast floor-to-ceiling windows in the lobby that had heavy drapes and blinds, and a smattering of magazines on a large, glass coffee table. A reception desk, which looked like any other reception desk in any other office stood at the far wall, with another door, a brown door with frosted glass, covered by a white slatted blind, which led deeper into the offices.

Inside, there were more islands of desks in a sea of light blue carpet. Sheldon's office, located at the far wall, had windows overlooking the common area with smaller desks and cubicles. Yes, it was a generic looking office. It could be any office anywhere .

But what was practiced in this office, most certainly, was anything but typical. As Sheldon snapped the light on in his office, he plopped the file on his desk.

"Why are you so interested in me?" Antoine asked, as the two sat down. Antoine took a seat on the leather couch that was under a window overlooking the rest of the offices while Sheldon sat behind his desk.

"It goes back a while," Sheldon admitted. "I studied Theology at Boston College and now I am a licensed Paranormal Investigator. I work with an open mind. I believe. In you, and your kind."

"I see."

"And I've read the newspapers. I know what you have done."

Antoine's eyebrows raised, silently urging Sheldon to continue.

"You're regarded as a Spiritual Healer. You have really made a name for yourself over the years that you have been in Miami. That interests me."

The two sat in silence for a moment.

"And I don't want you to think that this is some sort of a club that kids talk about – everyone hears about groups of people that call themselves vampires on tabloid TV – that's clearly not what we are."

Antoine crossed his legs and folded his arms.

"We are much more than vampires, Antoine. We are everything about the paranormal – we are demons, the afterlife…ghosts, hauntings…" his voice trailed off as he placed the last of the contents in the file. Upon finishing, he banged the side on the desk several times to pack the papers, and stood up again.

"We are very well funded, Mr. Antoine," Sheldon said. "So if you are thinking I am looking for a donation, that is most certainly not the case."

Antoine uncrossed his arms and placed them on his knee. "Where does your funding come from, if I may ask?"

"Many sources," Sheldon replied, walking around the desk and taking a seat opposite Antoine. He placed the file on a smoked glass coffee table. "We are primarily supported by paranormal societies, educational institutions, even churches."

"Churches?" Antoine asked with interest. "That's interesting."

"Yes," Sheldon added. "A lot of our work involves demonology."

Antoine froze for a moment. "Demons? You involve yourself with that?"

Antoine was unsure of what to think. Normally suave and sophisticated, he now felt like a small, troubled boy in class on the first day of school when he heard that word: demon. For the first time since he was a mortal, he felt stirring in the pit of his stomach. He uncrossed his legs and sat forward, placing his elbows on his knees. He stared straight ahead, seeing nothing.

After several minutes of silence passed, Antoine spoke: "Demons…"

"It's an integral part of our work," Sheldon said. "The church is one of our biggest financiers. Demons are here, Mr. Nagevesh. They are all around us. They may spend most of their time existing in alternate dimensions…but every so often…they cross over."

For a moment, Antoine wasn't sitting in Sheldon's office. He wasn't spread out on the plush brown-leather sofa, admiring the book-laden shelves and paper-strewn tables.

He was lying in a grave.

He was lying in the cold water – shivering and beginning to turn numb, he closed his eyes. He closed them so tight that they hurt. He closed them so tight and he dared not open them because he knew that Asmodai was right above. He could feel the hot breath from above. His presence.

"Antoine?" Sheldon asked.

"I am very sorry, Mr. Wilkes," Antoine said, shaking his head for a moment and running his hands through his hair. "So please tell me again why you want to speak to me?"

"Haven't you determined the answer? My deep fascination comes from your past and your history. But even more so, your present. You are a very intriguing individual, Mr. Nagevesh. With your celebrity status, you could bring a significant amount of positive publicity to our firm."

"I am known as a Spiritual Healer, not a killer, Sheldon. Not a demon."

"I want you to tell me that, Sir."

Antoine stood. He walked over to the shelves that lined the opposite wall of the office. Running his fingers upon volumes and volumes of books relating to the paranormal, unknown entities, UFOs, exorcisms and demons, his finger stopped on a book published in Boston by Parchman's Press.

He closed his eyes and sighed.

"I have not seen this book in many years," Antoine admitted.

Before Sheldon could respond, Antoine moved over to the window behind the expansive desk. The sunlight warmed the room through the blinds. He slowly opened the blind, looking out at the shoppers crisscrossing Ponce and 5th. Antoine turned back around to face Sheldon.

"You will be opening yourself up, Sheldon," Antoine said. "If you get involved with me, you will be opening yourself up."

Rise Antoine. Rise out of your maker's grave!

"I fully understand that," Sheldon replied. "From all of the information I have gathered on you over the years. All that I have here – needs to be substantiated. Please Antoine."

Antoine walked over to the door signifying that he was going to leave, that it was time for the conversation to come to a close. He turned back to face Sheldon. "If you must open that door, you may. If it betters your cause – if it betters *my* cause – then so be it."

Sheldon followed Antoine towards the front of the complex. "And where shall I meet you?"

"Come to my home this evening. I suspect that given your proven abilities that you should know exactly where to go without my having to tell you."

Sheldon nodded. Antoine opened the door slowly as he exited the waiting room; the afternoon daylight shined in with a fierce brightness. Antoine put on a pair of dark blue sunglasses, and adjusted them slightly.

"And one more thing, Sheldon. Before you meet me and before you press record. Just keep in mind what you will be opening yourself up to."

"I know, sir, I know," Sheldon said, joining him at the door and waving his hand as if brushing off the comment.

"My life has been…full of…" Antoine seemed to be searching for what to say. "Full of sin. And I have been paying for it. Dearly. When you spoke earlier of demons, I cringed. Just remember what you are getting yourself into, Sheldon. You will hear of everything – I will be totally honest with you about my past and my present. But the picture will not be a pretty one."

"I understand that," Sheldon said.

"Just consider yourself warned. I was chosen for a reason – and it wasn't because of my nobility and generosity in life. You will see."

"So tonight then? What time?"

"Just consider yourself warned."

With those words, Antoine slipped outside the door and disappeared in a throng of afternoon Miracle Mile shoppers. Sheldon was left standing at the door considering the warning. What exactly did Antoine mean by that?

Certainly he was immortal, but how exactly is he involved with demons? Pondering the questions, he stepped out onto the sidewalk, completely oblivious to the people who were walking right in front of him. He cut off a harried young red haired female shopper who gave an exasperated sigh and darted around him. He paid her no mind. He was too busy to even notice her. He was looking ahead to the direction he believed Antoine went; scanning a group of ladies ahead on the next block, to see if a man dressed entirely in black were to stand out taller than the women, looking for Antoine.

Antoine was nowhere to be seen.

He had disappeared just as quickly as he had come. Sheldon turned around and dashed back into the office. Once inside, he sought to find Anthony and see how he had ties to Antoine. Sheldon left shortly thereafter; the door slammed behind him, and the windows rattled. He hastily locked the door and charged down the street.

Beneath the setting sun, clouds leaped across a sky that painted crimson orange and red hues against pale blue; the streets of Ponce de Leon appeared aflame. The small shops, with their dusty windows displaying everything from books to cakes to evening gowns and designer purses, seemed to glow in the auburn tint. The fingerling shadows of palm trees stood like an army of watchmen, which elongated and stretched, growing ever taller and larger against the stucco as the sun sank into the horizon.

The crowds had dwindled as the dinner hour was close at hand.

Padding his way block to block, Sheldon decided to confront Anthony later. After this afternoon, he needed a drink. But the words Antoine said kept on replaying in his mind:

Consider yourself warned.

CHAPTER FOUR

Miami is the crown jewel on the tip of the Atlantic Coast. Glittering skyscrapers rise from the land by the water; a pastel patchwork of stucco and stone, mirrored by beautiful bright blue majestic seas and palm trees. Immense ocean liners and yachts dot the blue watered bays in the shadows of giant skyscrapers and contemporary mansions that had a hint of style; and terra cotta buildings under palms adorn the landscape lending to a tropical feel.

Antoine saw it as the land of Sodom and Gomorrah.

No other city in the country could boast so much diversity – or such a distinction between the poor and those with money, power and class.

And so much open sensuality.

It is no wonder that Antoine, the sexual deviant he was during his mortal life, found his way to this city – the skin, the muscles, the leather, the sin.

Most of the population that interested Antoine seemed to find their way to the busy life of the glittering neon-rich lounges and nightclubs of South Beach. The flashy signs and palm trees in pink accented quaint little art-deco style hotels and apartment buildings. Thumping music, splashing pools and seashell colors stood proudly in front of gleaming beaches with crystal blue waters. But at night was when South Beach would truly come alive. After the sleepy mornings have passed along with the lazy beach-and-rollerblade afternoons. The nighttime on Miami Beach…that time was the time that Antoine loved.

Sometime in the middle of the evening, the nightclubs on Washington Avenue started opening their doors, the crowds would trickle in and liven, and Antoine could find plenty of mortals willing to become a minion or one that he could feed on in a dark alley, for the type of clientele that patronized these clubs were already far strayed from religion and anything Godly. South Beach was "The Land of Steroids and Silicone", and these mortals would show that.

The men, beautiful and all were fantastically built, with muscles only hours in the gym could create. And then the women, all beautifully curved and shaped with the hourglass figure, enormous bosoms brought on by numerous and expensive trips to the plastic surgeon. These mortals were truly vain - worshipping their bodies by and far – keeping a vast distance from anything religious, good or moral.

And then, there were the parks.

By day, playgrounds and swing-sets are in full use. At night, the parks served a different purpose. Located back in the residential areas west of Washington, one found the really questionable characters. Walking down the side of the park, one could see several people in parked cars waiting for that next sexual venture to arrive. If one listened closely, the leaves could be rustling in the bushes beside you.

Darius stood at the entrance to Flamingo Park, the giant wrought-iron entrance stood tall before him, lined with overgrown ivy and a cross in the middle giving the impression of a cemetery. He leaned against the side of the entrance, near some tall hedges; a passerby might assume he was looking for some company.

Darius noticed a young Hispanic man sitting in a blue sedan about thirty feet away. Looking through the corner of his eye, Darius did not indicate to the man that he was watching. Slipping back through the park entrance, he heard the click and creak of a car door against the silence of the night.

Darius knew what the man was intending to do. Patiently waiting against the ivy wall just inside the park, he closed his eyes and reveled in the cool night air.

"Hi," the man stammered quietly as he approached Darius. Darius opened his eyes and saw a young brown skinned man, he noticed the man's jet black, short cropped hair, and couldn't help but notice the small hole in the thigh of his blue sweatpants. The man stepped back cautiously.

Darius said nothing.

Darius slowly extended his hand, and placed it on the man's shoulder. "How old are you?" Darius asked, lightly squeezing the man's shoulder.

"I – I'm twenty five," he said, and his eyes looked down at Darius' hand. The veins engorged slightly against the pale skin as Darius tightened his grip.

"What do you think that I am standing here for?" Darius asked. "Do you think that I am standing here, calling to you with the intensity of my stare?"

The man said nothing and cautiously stepped back, but Darius' grip tightened further, holding him in his place. "I saw you sitting in your car over there. I know what you were waiting to do." Darius squeezed his shoulder so hard he cried out, taking both hands and grabbing Darius' forearm, desperately trying and failing to break free.

"Do you know that I called you?" Darius asked the man, who was making an effort to pull Darius' hand from his shoulder, with great effort but to no avail.

Darius took his free hand and grabbed the tuft of hair on the man's chin. He bent down and brought his face right up in front of the man's eyes, and then bent around to whisper in the man's ear: "You don't know why I called you…you stupid, silly man. You come here to sin and then when you find it…all you can do is stammer and stand like a stone…" Darius whispered in the man's ear, softly and with heated breath, as he bent down lower and tore a gash in the young man's neck.

Deep red blood poured from the pierced neck, and painted the bushes red in a shower of crimson as Darius drank and drank; he did not stop his drinking until the nameless man was a lifeless corpse – pale and dried. He held the limp body in his arms, peering down at his prey as the fresh, bright-red blood leaked out of his mouth and dripped on the man's white shirt.

Darius suddenly saw a beam of light, and turned his head to the left he was blinded by the intensity of the light. He shielded his eyes, and dropped the body to the ground with a thud.

"Hold it right there!" a deep voice commanded behind the light. A uniformed police officer emerged, pointing a gun through the bushes, with another cop right next to him. Shielding his eyes with his arms, Darius turned towards the cop.

He could feel his anger mounting and the devil within coming. He no longer was the immortal with a purpose of finding his latest minion; he no longer appeared to be the man waiting in the park.

The monster was coming.

He screamed from deep within his chest as he grew to a muscular beast and his clothes ripped to shreds and fell to the ground.

The cop dropped his flashlight in the grass, looking up at the monster Darius had become; for a moment, the cop froze, his eyes as wide as plates, and then he turned and ran. The cop's partner cautiously stepped forward, and then stopped; he stood still in frozen shock. The cop struggled to keep his gun still locked on Darius, as his hand shook.

"Hold it right there!" the cop said, but his voice was quivering.

It did not deter Darius.

With one swipe of his claw, the super muscular demon that Darius had become tore the gun out of the policeman's hand – ripping the limb off in a spray of blood that coated the bushes. The other cop returned to the scene, hanging back at the gate, pleading for backup in his walkie-talkie, over and over again, as his eyes nervously watched Darius tear his partner apart limb from limb.

Darius did not pay any attention to the frantic pleas for backup.

Darius dropped the cop's body in the bushes, as it continued to writhe and shake. He descended on the other and grabbed the radio and squeezed it to bits, the roping muscle taught against the green-brown skin as he destroyed the device, the veins pulsating with shreds of muscle. With one swift movement, he tore off the policeman's head with one swipe of the other arm.

Darius did not have time for something so bothersome like the local police.

Towering over the dead cop, he surveyed the situation.

He breathed deeply, hard and grating – but he was not out of breath. He watched the limbless cop writhe in pain like a spider stripped of its legs, wriggling about, his main arteries spewing blood, cascading in pools throughout the park, staining the bushes and grass bright red.

Deep and dark red.

Darius calmed and cursed himself.

Why was it so hard to control his demon within? Of course, in this situation, he needed to transform and take care of the situation. But it did not matter. They were plain and useless. But so much wasted blood. What a pity.

Back in form, he brushed himself off.

Looking down at the bodies below, he bent down and scooped up his prey. Such a young and beautiful mortal. The boy couldn't have been more than twenty-five. Well-tended, close cut dark hair, a neatly trimmed short moustache – certainly he was loved, and would be missed. What a shame he was now just a corpse. How he would love to drain him all over again!

It was time to end all this.

He dropped the body into the grass, the limbs splayed like a rag doll, and he ascended into the air, leaving the three bodies below, in a lake of blood, in the middle of the park in the dead of night.

And then he flew.

He rose up above the city, up so high that the park appeared as just a green spot on the landscape; lights dotted the darkness like diamonds, and the tall, majestic buildings, dressed in their pastels and pinks lined the edge of the ocean, cast blurry reflections on the waters of the dark blue Atlantic.

~~*

Antoine loved all the sinful mortals around every corner.

Miami Beach was always packed with people. The streets, the tropical feel, the numerous palm trees and the cute pastel two story motels lent a feeling of the island life. But looking upwards at the towering, glittery skyscrapers that rose above the small shops, restaurants and nightclubs reminded one that Miami Beach is truly a metropolis in its own right.

Day and night the sidewalks were filled with throngs of shoppers, beach revelers, sun worshippers and vacationers young and old – all their footsteps marching over the peeling maroon paint and sand covering the walkways that lined the busy, congested avenues.

But the people that Antoine sought ventured out after the sun went down.

All the flesh that he could taste and venture to at all hours of the night…the feeding was a smorgasbord, and it went on every night seven nights a week, until it was time for him to return to Coral Gables.

There were also some nights that Antoine did not venture to South Beach, but rather headed north to an area of Palm Beach that he so much loved to roam.

And no matter where he walked, Antoine always returned in his Mercedes to Coral Gables, the city in Miami that was most quintessentially Spanish and Southern – from the giant oak tree lined streets hanging Spanish moss over the passersby, to the street names that would attest to the town's uniqueness – Anastasia, Ponce De Leon, Andelusia. Home to the famous haunted Biltmore Hotel.

Coral Gables - truly an old, charming and stylish town of class and luxury. This is the area in Miami where the well-to-do would live, those who spent countless hours in their expensive cars commuting to lofty positions in downtown, or at Blue Lagoon, and then drive home - past the Miracle Mile and the coral colored fountains and palms, pulling into their gated driveways and enormous, expensive homes. All during this while, of course, they would look the other direction and put out of their heads that towns like Hialeah - with small, shoebox-like homes with beat up, rusted out late model cars sitting in driveways and police sirens wailing in the distance - lie just a few miles away from the opulence and old-time grandeur of Coral Gables.

Antoine's Mercedes typically pulled down Anastasia Avenue to First.

First Street is perpendicular to Anastasia, which Antoine takes off of South Dixie Highway from the beach or the Manors. It is lined with enormous weeping willow trees, palms and other tropical foliage. The houses are enormous, and the average home price on the street is in the millions. Of course, Antoine had to have the largest home by far, and the previous owner was quite tasty indeed! Each day, Antoine would pull his Mercedes through the massive wrought-iron gates into the largest home on the street.

Antoine acquired the house shortly after he came to Miami.

The house was owned by the late Hernan Perez, and was a Spanish mansion through and through. Tall, majestic windows overlooked a carefully manicured tropical garden, and a winding stone path led to the sidewalk. But what was really impressive were the soaring columns that framed the front porch. It made the house a cross between what would be a Spanish Style Southern Mansion and an estate plantation.

Antoine chose the house for a number of reasons. He would always tell people that it was the architecture, but most knew that it was somehow linked to Antoine's affair with the owner's son.

Prior to the acquisition, he lived in a condominium at the ocean, and after he fell in love with the city and saw it for what it was, he decided to pursue a Miami home to somewhat settle. And this house was perfect in a perfectly southern town that was always turned on and active.

The boy that Antoine became enamored with had a wonderful olive complexion and dark, close-cropped black hair and smooth clear skin.

Roberto was his name.

He once was a sophomore in college at the University of Miami studying to become a doctor.

His short, black hair was spiked and gelled like all of the young boys would do; he always wore stylish, silver rimmed glasses tinted blue to add a hint of mysteriousness.

Perhaps the mystery of Roberto is what drew Antoine closer to him.

Antoine had been walking down Washington Avenue late one weekend night - perhaps two or three in the morning. He had fed, and was satisfied, and was just enjoying the Miami night, not really looking in any direction. Of course, there was a crowd on the street, club goers of every different denomination, in all different styles of dress. Most were dressed to kill with the latest expensive button down shirts and slacks. Others wore faded jeans and t-shirts, but all boisterous and laughing, heading in every different direction. All darted through the stand-still traffic in front of the pulsating nightclubs on Washington Avenue…rushing to the lines snaking between velvet ropes on red carpet leading into smoky colorful palaces.

But then, Antoine set his eyes on Roberto – down the block from where Antoine had been standing that humid and still summer night.

A face in the crowd, smiling, nodding, but also looking.

Through the throngs of people, shining out and calling to him. Slowly, Antoine approached him. The young man looked like he was alone. He was a face in this crowd, and time, for a moment, stood still. It seemed as though the crowds stopped and quieted, and that Roberto caught Antoine's gaze, if just for a moment. Roberto was leaning against the side in the shadows of the buildings, crowds of people moving all around them as they remained transfixed on one another. Roberto's face jumped out to Antoine like a shiny penny in a sea full of dull, dirty ones.

This is him, he thought. *Now isn't that just beautiful…*

CHAPTER FIVE

The night sky glistened with stars, a dark blue velvet drape over the neon lit pastel pinks and yellows highlighting the terra cotta stone buildings of Miami; the crystalline city from above became smaller and smaller once ascending through the pillow of the clouds; the streetlights shone like small diamonds scattered in black sea of nothingness; the city became more pronounced in its borders, telescoping through a tunnel of darkness.

The clouds wafted past, as the night air grew cold and stark. Looking beyond, farther west to where the sky grew pink, towards the waters of the Gulf, the clouds leapt forward, seeking unexplored territory.

The jeweled city stood at the base of the land peninsula shining upwards, piercing the vast darkness of the night. Looking down through the clouds, Antoine descended. Down, closer and closer he fell, gracefully and with determination, his arms raised like an angel. Nowhere else would be the perfect place to embark on his mission.

Sacrafice.

It was the perfect lure, the perfect bait.

Descending quietly, the miniscule dots took shape, grew larger and transformed into buildings. The streets widened and the trees lined the avenues, as cars raced down the avenues, and finally people dotted the sidewalks scurrying in every different direction, all heading a different way, with a different agenda.

He glided between the low, brightly lit buildings of Miami Beach and landed on his feet almost silently in a dark alley, not far from the hubbub of activity, but far enough that the air was almost silent and stagnant. Straight ahead of him were the throngs of tourists visible between the tall buildings on either side of the alley, and Antoine studied each group of people, moving in, and then quickly out of frame, like they were walking across his own private cinema screen. The people darted in and out of the candlelit cafés lining Ocean Drive; at each one a young, smiling hostess standing in front – offering samples and menus.

But none of that interested Antoine.

What he saw from above is what interested him. And that wasn't on Ocean Drive.

It was back on Washington, two blocks to the west. As Antoine glided through the crowds, it seemed as if no one noticed him. Dressed in his signature black on black, he floated through the families, couples and all the others looking around dazzled at the fancy glistening boutique hotels of South Beach.

What interested Antoine was what was waiting for him two blocks away. And he was being called to it.

I am coming to you…I hear your call. Not since years ago, not since Luxor did I encounter you. I see you, I see you in the sands, I see you lying and waiting, waiting for me to come. I see you in the earthquake, in the fissures and the flames, waiting for me.

Waiting for me to return with what is yours.

Antoine stopped dead in his tracks.

He looked up.

Standing before him was the most gigantic, imposing cathedral he had ever laid his eyes upon. But it was not a cathedral that one may imagine. It was dark, sinister and gothic – and at the base was a large and daunting stone staircase that led to a pair of giant wooden doors framed by dark stone walls. There were small stained-glass windows scattered about making the building seem more like a medieval castle rather than an ornate place of worship. It stood out as a striking contrast to the lighter colored, pale pastel hotels and hostels with a gloomy presence.

But it was not a place of worship. It never was.

Built ten years earlier as the Cathedral night club, it used to be one of the hottest clubs on Miami Beach that attracted celebrities and starlets as well as massive crowds of partygoers who wanted to see and be seen. But it was short lived, and now was a dark skeleton of its former self.

Antoine stood at the base of the stairs, staring straight ahead at the daunting building. But it wasn't the cathedral that preyed on his mind. That was just a building. What he felt – the feeling that surrounded him as he stood before the doors – was her presence.

He knew she was here.

Looking for him. A puff of wind blew across his face, blowing his hair. He closed his eyes, and turned around.

There she was.

She was standing across Washington when Antoine saw her – and he knew that she saw him. But she gave no indication that she did. Through the sea of taxicabs and SUV's, past the throngs of tourists and clubbers alike – she stood. She leaned against a palm tree, smoking a cigarette – blending in to the crowds, seemingly undetectable.

That most certainly was Claret.

She hid behind large, dark stylish sunglasses, her face framed with straight auburn hair, styled to appear more like a model or stylist than an ancient mythical figure – but he knew it was her. She was looking the other direction, to the south, but he knew that she knew exactly where Antoine was standing across on the steps.

She exhaled a cloud of smoke and stubbed out her cigarette with a black stiletto boot, pressing it into the mulched ground that surrounded the base of the tree. She stepped back and brushed her black leather coat off, looking downwards, checking her purse, pulling out her phone, and blending in just perfectly.

And as she turned and started to walk away, her head turned back for a moment to Antoine's direction, seeming to stare right at him. She pulled her sunglasses down the ridge of her nose, looking across the street to the steps where Antoine had been standing, and Antoine froze for a moment.

Antoine ducked back slowly and carefully behind a large bush at the base of the steps to the Cathedral. Had she seen him? She knew he was there. Of course she had seen him.

Claret walked slowly yet with determination down the opposite side of Washington, and as Antoine slowly emerged from behind the bush he never stopped watching her.

What is she doing in Miami? Antoine thought, his mind racing. *And where is she going?*

He took his eyes off of her for a moment, and turned towards the wall. He placed his head in his hands, and leaned hard against the building. He closed his eyes, and a tear fell down his cheek.

The Chalice. *Oh good God, no.*

After a few minutes, he got up and regained his composure. There was no way that feeling sorry for himself would rectify the situation. He had to keep track of Claret - that was for certain. She was vengeful and clever, and would stop at nothing to regain what was once hers.

Antoine ducked past the shrub and headed down the steps, his eyes still frantically searching the crowd for Claret. He walked down Washington, desperate to catch up with her. Dodging the crowds, he spotted her once again, standing at the corner of Washington and 5th.

She checked her watch.

She certainly knew how to blend in.

Her head turned slowly, one more time, in Antoine's direction. She was standing before a large building that looked like a nightclub, with large imposing doors covered by black curtains and smoke that billowed out into the night air from below the curtains.

For a moment – just for a moment - she seemed to smile. It was small, waning smile, maybe really just a grin, but Antoine noticed it nonetheless. It was a smile that was meant for him to see and only him to notice, but it spoke to him.

It said: *I've got you!*

She ducked into the curtain and disappeared into the smoke.

And later on that evening, when Antoine replayed the events in his mind, he had thought that maybe he had imagined it. Had he?

But Antoine remained still as he stood across the street, staring at the door that Claret had disappeared into. Claret disappeared into the curtains, and for quite some time. He stared in disbelief at the building.

Was that really Claret?

It had to have been. And as he turned to finally leave, facing a sea of faces that fought past him, he stood in one place. Closing his eyes and raising his head to the sky, he cherished the cool night air.

Despite the relaxation of the calming aspect of the wind, he could not ease his anxiety. He felt the sweat still deep under his arms, he noticed the beating of his heart, and he knew that her presence was the foretelling of dark times to come. He knew that Claret only appeared under demonic persuasion and the only demon that Antoine could think of was a demon from his past that still consistently haunts his days and his nights.

And he knew, deep in his soul, that it *was* Claret – the demonic seductress that even Asmodai would cower and relent to - just walked through those doors.

He walked back in a daze, unfazed by the chaos and the crowds. Even when a hard-partying group of young, towering jocks almost knocked him over, he did not budge nor did he react.

Right now, he felt defeated.

Claret was here, she was in Miami, and she knew where he was. And it was too late. The damage had already been done.

And she was ready to take her revenge.

CHAPTER SIX

South Beach at night.

The light and dreamy reflection of the chic and trendy hotels that lined Ocean Avenue cast a warm glow – the blurry brightness shone atop the dark Atlantic waters, like a moving painting, alive and pulsating with the waves. The serenity of the waterline, bathed in cool pale blue moonlight, and the pleasant dull roar of the surf, served as a striking contrast to the noise and chaos that dominated the streets a short distance away. The towering palm trees did nothing to conceal the lines of expensive cars, the roller-bladers, boisterous night strollers, dog walkers and diners that crowded the sidewalks.

The packed cafes that lined the west side of Ocean bustled with the usual Saturday night crowds and activity; rambunctious barflies lined neon-lit clubs and stood around shiny tables overlooking crystalline pools as salsa music wailed over the chaos.

Yes, that was night time on South Beach, away from the cosmopolitan skyscrapers of Miami, far from the quaint serenity of the Coral Gables mansions, and so close to the serenity of the ocean, the darkness of the night sea that reached towards a perfect line; a point in the horizon where the sky met and touched the sea, where the stars shined lower, closer to the earth, where one could take their finger, and point, and even try to touch them.

So close to such calm waters, yet so far.

One could take a moment, stand on the edge of the sand, and drink in the beauty of the night time sky, tune out the thumping music, ignore the expensive cars and celebrities, and pay no attention to the throngs of tourists who were captivated by the people and the places. But there was one woman on South Beach who did not care about the sanctity of the evening sea, nor was she mesmerized by the glitterati; she was not looking at any of the passing celebrities or the showy cars, she didn't gawk at the fountains or the pink and orange buildings dotted with lights.

She just merely stepped out of a door on Washington Avenue, brushing her red hair away from her face as it caught in the night breeze. She pulled a pack of cigarettes from her black leather purse which matched her black leather jacket, and fished out a cigarette. Lighting it she leaned against the building for a moment, taking in the scene.

Approaching her slowly was a group of young men and women walking down the sidewalk, laughing and chatting noisily. They stood out in the crowd to her. She lifted the sunglasses off of her nose to get a better look at the approaching group.

They all looked to be dressed in the finest of clothes; their hair in tight and neat hairstyles, and the labels they were wearing suggested that they did not need of money. She held her stare until she made eye contact with the young man who was closest to the building, and as he approached her, his attention became transfixed on the mysterious woman standing against the building up ahead at the corner.

He did not pay any attention to the conversation that his friends were having which was filled with intermittent roaring laughter. He was drawn to the woman.

And then, when the group had reached the corner he disappeared into the building. His friends continued chatting and crossed the street, completely unaware that he wasn't with them anymore.

The door shut silently.

Inside the building they were in total blackness, except for the light of a solitary candle which sat on a table just inside the entryway.

The cherry red tip of her cigarette glowed, indicating she was still there. She tossed her cigarette on the floor, snubbed it out with her foot, exhaling a stream of smoke in the man's face. He coughed.

She did not hesitate as a spiny grey fingers ripped at the man's throat, sending a spray of blood throughout the foyer, coating the candle but failing to extinguish it.

The man clutched his throat and fell to the floor on his knees, his wide eyes staring up at his assailant. There was no longer a beautiful, mysterious red-haired woman.

He tried to scream but couldn't, choking on the blood that was quickly filling his mouth and lungs. The bright red liquid oozed from his mouth. The monster stepped into the faint glow of the candle light. And he cowered and screamed, falling backwards, his feet slipping in the oozing lake. He still clutched his neck as he fell on his back.

The look in the man's eyes – the forehead skin wrinkled up and the eyes wide open; the white iris pronounced and open; the eyes locked and trained on the monster. As the grey scaly arm reached down and lifted him up, and tossed his body against the wall as his eyes remained open, and his eyes remained transfixed on the demon; his body was slowly draining itself of blood and dying, as he felt himself slipping away. The arm picked him up again and pinned him against the wall, screaming to him, over and over, with fury of pure evil sending forth whispers of the forsaken.

"I have forsaken my maker!" The demon screamed again, as she pinned the man against the wall one last time, the grey cement now splattered with fresh blood. "I have forsaken him!"

The monster's free arm swung up and decapitated the man, sending a shower of blood in the room. The body dropped to the floor, convulsing and writhing.

The beast stood above the body as it lay in the lake of blood, dying, as the flame on the candle grew; the flame grew and felt its way across the foyer, dancing above the body, creating a warm glow and golden aura.

"I have forsaken my maker," it said, once again, now much quieter, calmer, and with more clarity.

The flame stood above the body for a moment as the man expired, and just for a moment, the beast thought that the man's spirit could be seen, captured by the flame, showing itself in snippets of blue and white, the entity buried in the bright hot orange fingers.

The beast stood for a moment, staring at its prey, staring at the body lying on the floor now lifeless in a bloody mess.

The man was most certainly dead.

The towering wooden door shook with a long and persistent knock.

The beast's head snapped to the direction of the door. The knocking became louder, more determined and insistent, stopping and starting again.

The beast exhaled, deep and slow.

The door opened to the three companions of the young man. Huddled outside the door, the looks on their faces were of great worry and concern.

"Excuse me miss," said the apparent leader of the group. He seemed to be the eldest, though he could not have been more than twenty or twenty two. He hooked his blonde hair around the back of his ear as he spoke cautiously. "Sorry to bother you…I see you aren't open right now."

The man stammered for a moment, then continued: "But we're missing our friend Rodney. He was walking with us, and then just vanished. It was right around here, and we thought maybe he had ducked in here, but I suppose not, because the door was locked."

A petite, busty redhead shoved the man aside, interrupting him and forcing her way to the threshold. "Wait a minute!" she said. "I saw you! You were standing right here! Smoking a cigarette!" The woman pointed down the street at the corner the three were standing on, as if accentuating her statement.

Claret took a step closer to the three visitors. She pursed her lips quietly. The redhead took a cautious step backwards.

"Yes…" Claret answered softly and slowly. "Yes, I was. I remember you walking by. Why do you ask?"

Claret's eyes looked past the group, if just for a moment, for such a fleeting moment that the three did not notice her drift in attention. She scanned the street, looking out over the heads of her visitors, for a moment. The sunlight was fading.

Perfect timing.

The group did not even notice that she had been scanning street beyond them, nor had they even noticed that her attention was diverted. They simply continued with their plea.

"Well," the blonde young man started again, "as I was saying, we thought our friend Rodney might have disappeared in here…but I doubt it since seems the door was locked."

"But it wouldn't have been locked when I was outside smoking, would it have?" Claret offered.

The young redhead affirmed the answer.

This mysterious red haired woman was absolutely correct, and she stood in the doorframe above them, seeming completely unbothered by their unexpected visit. Claret suddenly took a step back, and gestured out her arm.

"Where are my manners?!" she exclaimed. "Please, do come in. Come in and we can discuss where your friend might have gone!" She stepped back and ushered them into the foyer.

When inside, the three visitors scanned their surroundings, see a large table next to the door with a burning candle, stone floors and walls, and not much else.

Very grey. Very dark.

There was a small window above the table which let in a small amount of the fading daylight, casting a yellowish glow on the wooden table.

There was also no sign of Ronald's corpse.

And there was no sign of any blood, or scuffle. The floor was clean, in fact it was spectacularly clean.

Claret had exited the foyer for a moment, coming back with a flaming torch. The three visitors looked at each other with confused looks on their faces.

"Just kidding!" Claret joked, as an overhead chandelier snapped on, bathing the entire stone room in light. She had instantly appeared on the opposite wall, by a light switch. "Not everything is primitive around here," she offered. Walking back over to the front door, which was now closed, the three visitors were huddled just inside the door, not sure of what to make of this strange woman and this even stranger place. None of them had heard her move. She just simply appeared again before them.

"Do any of you know what this place is here?" Claret asked. "You silly simple little fools." She smiled. The three visitors looked at one another, perplexed. "Do you not know where you are?"

The young redhead turned around and tried the door. It was locked.

Claret dumped the torch in a small opening in the floor below. "Did you think that door would be unlocked?" She laughed. She walked over to the redhead and put her arm around the frightened girl. "Oh, you silly little girl," Claret said, running her hands on the side of the girl's red hair, smoothing it down. "You three are coming with me. And when you come with me, I will show you where your friend went. Rodney is here, he is right down that hallway." She pointed over to a large, shiny steel door. "We go through that door, we will find your friend."

"What type of place is this?" The lanky black boy asked. He held the redhead close, and his older blonde friend continued hooking the sides of his hair behind his ears, repeatedly.

"Come with me," Claret said, "and you will find out where your friend is, you will find out all you need to know. It doesn't matter what you have done in your previous life, I will not judge you."

The three visitors each exchanged confused glances, and the girl shook her head slightly. Her friend gave her a peck on the top of her head.

Claret walked over to the door, and pulled a large, shiny silver key out of her pocket. It was the kind of classic skeleton key that would be set to open any door. It caught the light and glistened brightly. "Come with me," she said again.

The three visitors remained standing in the doorway, still seemingly too frightened to move. They spoke under their breaths to each other, and all were in agreement that this strange woman was off the deep end. The redhead kept staring down at the floor.

"Look up Christy!" Claret said with a big, toothy smile. Her enthusiasm covered the three friends like a cold blanket. "And I need you both too!" she said to the two young men. "Come on Philip! Jeff! Let's go! Do you want to find your friend or not?"

Jeff removed his arms from around Christy. "Phil?" he asked, looking over at his friend expectantly. Phil was standing next to Jeff, staring right at Claret. Phil started playing with his hair, and hooked it once again behind his ear. "I think we can go," he said. He then turned back towards Claret. "Who are you, miss?" he asked. "Forgive me, but this is just a really strange situation for all of us. We don't even understand what this place is."

They reluctantly walked over – Christy leading the two boys in an apparent display of feminine courage, and the will to overcome her friends' fear. The trio finally reached where Claret was standing. "I am waiting for you!" she said, jingling her keys, still smiling widely, eagerly looking towards the trio with wide eyes and a peculiar bubbly demeanor. "Let's go! Rodney is waiting!"

They filed next to where Claret was standing and lined up next to her. Claret waited in the doorway with a smile. She held the key up, and it again caught the light, and reflected on the faces of her visitors.

"Whatever you see," Claret said, "please realize one thing: I will not judge you. I will not take anything into account of what you each have done in your past, in your lives. I will not hold you accountable for that. The only thing that I will hold you accountable for is from this point forward. Do you understand?"

She put the key to the lock in the door, but did not turn it yet.

"Just let me ask you one question," Claret said, "what is so special about this guy Rodney? What has he done to deserve this? You three are coming in here, have no idea who I am, and I have stood here making a mock of the situation! And yet, you follow me! Yes, I had locked the door. Yes, you don't have much of a choice. But then, you hardly resist! Fascinating! What a gentleman this Rodney must be!" She chuckled to herself, and turned the key.

The door opened with a deep grating sound, and opened up to total darkness. "I will lead you," Claret said. "And we will find your friend."

Claret disappeared into the darkness, calling back to them to hurry.

But the darkness was enveloping. Claret had quickly disappeared, and the call of her voice beckoning them to come sounded more distant.

"Should we follow her?" Jeff asked, breaking the silence. He towered over Christy as he held her tight, silence only interrupted by Christy's breathing and a fire burning somewhere quietly.

One by one, the three visitors, who were still a little perplexed that this woman knew their names, disappeared into the darkness.

And then the door slammed shut.

"Hey!!" Christy screamed, banging on the door urgently. "You can't trap us in here! Where are you?!?"

There was the sound of a fire roaring, causing all three to look in the same direction. They all saw Claret, now standing behind a ring of fire.

"Ah, thank you," Claret said, "Now that we are in here," she said, circling the fire, "permit me to introduce myself. I am Claret. I have been dead for thousands of years. I am here to tell you, as I said before, that you will only be held accountable for what you do from this point forward."

"Let us out of there!" Jeffrey pleaded.

"Oh, I cannot do that. It's too late. The door is closed. You came with me, you agreed."

"Agreed to what?" Jeffrey asked, moving forward.

"To join me."

Christy turned around from the door that she had been trying to pry open with Phillip. "Join you?!" she said, "why would we want to join you?!"

Claret smiled and moved in front of the fire. She had her hands behind her back and she had a grin on her face.

"Oh you already have," she said.

And all three of the visitors desperately tried to open the door, but the door would not budge. Where there once was an edge to the side of the door, there now simply was a stone and earthen wall. They were trapped. This was it.

Turning around, Christy stared in horror, looking up and ahead at the sight before her. She stopped and stared, paralyzed with fear. She took her hand and nudged Phillip, who was to her right, her eyes still fixated and staring in horror.

Phillip turned around and screamed, but it was too late. The flames became red.

CHAPTER SEVEN

The noise continued on the sultry night – the roar of the traffic and the occasional honking horn filled the air along with chattering, laughter and the clapping of high heels on pavement. The heaviness of the warm air permeated all those who dared out at the late hour that it was; even so, despite the stickiness, the smell of the car exhaust, and the occasional appearance of unkempt vagrants, the streets remained crowded and busy.

Antoine paused, stopping for a moment in his tracks.

His gaze locked upon the young man, drinking in the mulatto complexion, the finely cropped hair, and the tautness and tightness of the man's skin. The young man slowly started moving closer to the spot where Antoine stood, noticing Antoine noticing him. The noise and commotion of Washington Avenue seemed to fade away; all Antoine could see was the young man.

The young man looked up for a moment in Antoine's direction, and their eyes met. Time seemed to stand still. When they got closer, they both stopped, in a sea of people moving in all directions, they both stood, staring at each other but speaking no words, not noticing the activity around them, both of them tuning everything out except the other.

"Got 'ne weed?" the young man finally asked, leaning in quietly close to Antoine's ear, once the two were close.

Antoine's eyes widened slightly, raising his eyebrows as if he weren't expecting this question, but he was. At first the young man seemed typical – dressed in the latest designer jeans, overblown gold jewelry hanging down to his waist and too-white sneakers; Antoine also thought he was the type known for doing drugs such as G, ecstasy , and of course, weed.

But that didn't faze Antoine one bit.

He stared at the man's livery lips as he spoke, focusing on the finest details of his mouth, his thin moustache and how the hairs were so neatly trimmed and kept. Antoine knew this specimen could be his forever.

Antoine gaze turned to the young man's eyes, never relenting his piercing stare.

"You want to go find some?" he asked. "I'm here by myself anyway. Name's Roberto."

"Very good."

Antoine said nothing else, and turned around, his black coat-tails flailing out as he did so, brushing against the man, and started the opposite way down Washington Avenue. Roberto followed quickly behind him, and the two made the short walk to Antoine's car.

"You from around here, man?" Roberto asked, having to walk-run to keep up with Antoine. "Damn man! Why you walk so fast? It ain't no rush!"

"So many words…" Antoine said, mostly to himself and under his breath, shaking his head.

The two approached Antoine's silver Mercedes, parked at Washington and 7th. Antoine gestured his left hand towards the passenger door, and nodded to the boy. "Get in." And Antoine said nothing more, only walked around the front of the car to his seat, opened the door, and got inside.

Roberto followed, taking the cue he opened his door, and fell into the plush leather seat.

"Damn man!" he exclaimed, running his hands along the walnut trim console.

The interior of the car was very luxuriously appointed, dignified and fit for someone who accepted only the very best. Wood grain accented the tan leather interior, and the dashboard controls glowed a bright blue.

Antoine turned the ignition and the engine roared to life, and he sped away with a slight screech of the tires.

"Nice car, man," Roberto said, after about five minutes of driving. Antoine did not respond, but merely nodded and guided the car through the small, poorly maintained suburban side streets of South Beach, and further west several blocks towards Alton Road. Then, further west they drove across the MacArthur Causeway over the Biscayne Bay towards downtown Miami.

"Where are you taking me?" Roberto asked.

Antoine looked over at the young man, still taken aback by his youthful beauty, and chuckled softly. "We are going, like you said, to your home." Antoine's eyes pierced Roberto's. Antoine continued to stare in the boy's eyes, drawing him in closer, until Roberto spoke.

"You watchin' the road man?"

Antoine half smiled, and turned his attention back to the freeway. Roberto let his breath out slightly and gazed out the window, Antoine chucked softly.

Antoine's companion looked slightly perplexed, shaking his head back and forth. "Wait a min man…what about the weed?"

"Oh, but of course," said Antoine, smiling, bearing glistening white teeth that stood in contrast against the darkness of the car's interior. "Of course there will be weed for my boy."

The young man stared straight ahead into the night, falling into a short silence as his eyes remained wide and shifted around nervously - looking at Antoine and around the interior of the car.

The car charged west towards Coral Gables, as the two rode in silence for a bit.

"Yeah, I guess I did invite you to my house man. I must of. I mean, it's the least I can do with you if you're gonna smoke up with me."

Antoine looked straight ahead again, and smiled. "Very good".

Antoine knew exactly where to go.

After leaving the causeway and 395, he took 95 South to Dixie Highway, straight to the Gables. Not once did he ask Roberto where to turn, or if he was going the right way. He headed the right direction, to Roberto's amazement. And soon, the large and elegant Mercedes pulled on onto First Street, lined with the royal palms and large weeping willow trees with hanging Spanish moss - so quintessentially southern.

The Spanish tiled roofs served as coverings for the stucco and stone compounds; some with wrap-around porches, others not. All had wrought iron gates centered in large stone fences; some had tall and imposing windows and the homes reached almost as high as the forested canopy.

And then there was the Perez Residence, just like Antoine pictured it, with giant bay windows in the front that looked like giant eyes peering out into the world, or perhaps eyes peering in to the world inside. The soaring columns, four to be exact, reached up towards the roof and divided sections of smaller windows on several different levels.

This is it, Antoine thought.

The house was a work of art.

The gigantic bay windows offered a mysterious view of the inside - silhouettes of what looked like furniture were shielded by white shears and heavy looking drawn drapes pulled to the side. The giant columns framed the expansive front porch overlooking a well-tended and well-manicured lawn with palms and tropical foliage.

Roberto's family apparently was quite well off, and that made it all the better. Nothing but the best of surroundings for Antoine.

"And, we are here," Antoine said as the car pulled on the side of the street in front of the Perez house. Roberto looked up from staring at his lap.

Their eyes locked in a stare.

The young man retuned his gaze to his lap and started nervously playing with his fingers in his lap like someone who was desperately searching for something to say.

"So, do you want to just go at it, or should we smoke up first?" Roberto asked, looking up at Antoine expectantly, undoing the clasp on his belt.

Antoine cut the engine, and did not answer the question.

He opened the door and exited the car, closing the door quietly. He scanned the surroundings from one end of the street to the other, and smiled and nodded in approval of the sanctity of this street. The houses stood guard against a tropical palette – the owners rarely making an appearance except in confines of large and expensive cars.

Roberto sat in the passenger seat for a while, staring out the window at Antoine. He was somewhat confused that Antoine was not making any moves yet. He most certainly was picked up tonight by this man and he most definitely was used to getting picked up night after night, but there was something different about this man. He ascertained that this man was not someone who usually would pay for his services; generally Roberto's clientele was an anonymous drunken tourist who would hire him for a night of devilish passion while the wife was at home, assuming that her husband was on a business trip. In most cases it was true - but the increased consumption of inhibition-lowering alcohol, fueling curiosity, and meeting a lustful young Latino man on South Beach, where inhibitions typically ran low, would lead the evening into darker territories.

Antoine, however, was different.

Roberto continued staring at the beautiful, mysterious man who was patiently waiting for him outside the car, staring at the homes and looking around the area.

Someone so beautiful, and so young, certainly would not need Roberto.

Hell, this one will be for free, he thought to himself, opening the door and slowly rising from his seat to join him.

~~*

Roberto walked around the front of the car, as Antoine fished through his pocket. Seconds later, he withdrew his hand as Roberto stopped and stood before him in silence on the sidewalk.

"This is what you wanted, isn't it?" Antoine asked.

Roberto's eyes widened. "You had that the whole time?"

Antoine rose his hand, the back of his fingers, slowly and carefully, to Roberto's cheek. He did it lovingly, like a father caressing his son.

Roberto initially pulled back. But after a few minutes, he let Antoine touch him, and closed his eyes, and let out a faint sigh.

"Come with me," Antoine finally said, after a moment of silence.

Antoine started down the path towards the house, and guided him down the rosebush and orange tree-lined path to the majestic front door. Wall sconce lamps lit the area with gas-lamp posts rising and burning from the bushes, creating a warm glow. It was, to put in words, quite elegant.

"Come with me," Antoine said again.

They ascended the stairs to the entryway. Standing before each other, Antoine gave the rolled joint that he had in his pocket to Roberto, and smiled. Roberto looked into Antoine's eyes, and then down at the joint, reaching out for it, cautiously, as if it were something foreign and unknown; taking the joint, he started examining the drug quizzically and with wonder, like a child – as if he had never seen something like it ever before. He took it from Antoine's strong, gentle hand, and held it in his palm, staring at it for several minutes before placing it in his pocket.

"Thanks man," he said. He fumbled in his jeans pocket for his keys, and they jingled against the still, quiet night as he turned the lock and opened the door.

It was dark and quiet in the house. Very still.

"No one is home," he said. "My dad is out of town and my mother is dead."

He entered the foyer, stepping over a copper crest of a lion at the threshold.

The floors were marble, and there was a Persian Rug in the foyer, with a dark stained mahogany round table in the center adorned with fresh cut white roses on the top with another bronze crest of a lion on the center pedestal.

Ahead, there was a mirror on the right and a long hallway that led back into a dark mysterious existence. To the left was a grand set of winding stairs that gracefully hugged the rounded wall up to a second level of darkness. Looking up, Antoine noticed a grand crystal chandelier hanging majestically above them.

The interior of the mansion seemed very stately and had a southern feel to it – not the upscale contemporary motif that Antoine had been expecting.

It was perfect.

Roberto now took the lead, as Antoine was mentally noting all that would soon be his. Roberto disappeared into the black hallway before them. Shortly after, a light snapped on with the quiet click of a light switch, illuminating a hallway with walls the color of deep red maroon blood and lined with large potted palms and old black and white photos from years past.

Observing Roberto, Antoine followed as the young man disappeared in a white door at the end of the hallway which Antoine deduced was his bedroom. Antoine followed, arriving inside the room just as Roberto flicked on a small table lamp next to the bed.

The bedroom was like that of any young guy. The music discs that lined the wall were located next to an over-the-top stereo system - with giant, towering black speakers in each corner of the room and a subwoofer that most likely drove his father crazy. On the other wall, a large bed, a red and yellow lava lamp, and posters the plastered almost every square inch of the walls. The floor was covered in clothes. On the opposite wall of the stereo, a massive computer system atop a desk with a cluttered sea of papers and data discs.

It wasn't a moment after they entered the room and closed the door that Roberto peeled off his shirt. Antoine stood and observed, hands folded in front of him, studying the man. What a specimen! Underneath Roberto's shirt was a sleeveless white tank-top, which hugged him tightly, accentuating a very well developed and quite muscular chest. His arms were also quite muscular, and he gave a short flex of his bicep, pointing out the tattoo of a rose, and smiled.

Antoine sighed.

The poor young man was missing the point, but it was to be expected. The purpose of bringing him along and coming here to his room was not to bed the man, as Roberto seems to be so clearly expecting.

But Antoine continued his gaze nevertheless.

Roberto removed his undershirt, and Antoine began to drink and lap at the fountain of Roberto's sexual lustful aura. He was gorgeous and muscular, a perfect male specimen. The type of body that men would love to have, and that women love to be with. Top form, exquisite definition – clearly built like a god.

Perfect.

His pants came off and he stood there in tight, brilliantly white underwear that reached down his thighs.

He looked over to Antoine, who still was fully dressed. He did not come here for a sexual escapade. Roberto then walked over to him and put his arms around him, in a childlike embrace, as if he were hugging his father, and Antoine returned the affection.

He placed his head on Antoine's chest, closed his eyes, and sighed.

Not before long, Antoine could hear him softly crying.

They hugged tighter.

"I know what type of life you have led, Roberto," Antoine said, soothingly. He caressed Roberto's face, tousled his hair, and at those words, the young man cried a little harder, a little more audibly, knowing all too well what has been his childhood.

Antoine smoothed Roberto's hair. "I know how hard it has been."

Antoine knew.

He knew everything about Roberto.

In this elegant embrace, where Roberto felt so utterly the pain of his existence, of his past, he felt, at first and for the first time in his life, he could be in the arms of a savior.

He cried, and let it all go. All the pent up frustrations, all the pain, came out, pouring onto to Antoine's shirt – as he pressed his face deeper in his chest.

And the young man just cried, sniffling and sobbing and crying some more, as Antoine continued holding him, squeezing his back, running his hands through his hair, and along his cheek.

Antoine closed his eyes, held Roberto closer, continued lovingly caressing him, and all the pain of a mother that he lost far too soon, and a father that would not accept him as a son, as who his son was, wet the material on Antoine's shirt and coat.

Roberto felt so content in Antoine's arms, it was like everything would be okay.

The boy continued to cry, but now more softly, and Antoine got a better perspective of his past the longer he held Roberto.

He better understood the reasons for his tears.

He knew about Roberto's violent father - who dutifully provided for his son - but also who has recently scorned him. He saw the same father who beat his son after hours of questioning and drilling when Roberto would come back later than his curfew.

But, it was recently that things became worse.

Roberto had never been very close to his father, and he became more distant and reserved in recent times. Roberto also spent a lot of time away from his father and the house, because he knew that every time he came home the talking led to arguing, the arguing led to anger, and the anger led to a beating of some kind.

Antoine saw all of this as he held and caressed Roberto, letting his tears flow all down the front of the black coat, wetting it, but whispering into Roberto's ear that all will be okay and that no one will hurt him anymore.

Roberto hugged Antoine tighter, and Antoine thought he heard the boy whisper "I Love You" in his ear, barely audible through the tears.

And at the same time, Roberto bore his body down closer and pressed it against Antoine's, and Antoine could feel his hardness press up against him. Roberto started to kiss Antoine on the neck, causing an electricity to run through Antoine's body like nothing he had felt in a long time - not since he had been mortal.

It was such a wonderful feeling! Oh, it had been years since Antoine had felt this, and he was taken back to the blissful night in the clouds. It did not matter that Roberto had been so terribly misguided.

What a beautiful night it was, what a beautiful night it is.

What a beautiful night…

Roberto's kissing intensified and he started to move upward, moving towards Antoine's lips, and Antoine stopped him. Roberto opened his eyes and looked up, as if to ask why he was being stopped.

"What's wrong?" he asked. "Isn't this what you met me for?"

Antoine did not answer right away, but simply closed his eyes, and breathed a quiet sigh.

"Roberto," he finally spoke. "Is this what you want?"

"Yes!" he answered quickly and eagerly, shaking his head to reiterate his response. Roberto's eyes were so wide with pleading that he looked like a child to Antoine, staring up at his ebony face, desiring the intimacy that mortals crave.

But, Antoine knew that this was not the type of intimacy that Roberto was seeking.

He could tell, and see it in his mind, his past, where Roberto's experience was not that of a loving and caring intimacy, but rather that of forced sexual intercourse, not necessarily that of a raping but rather a situation that Roberto did not necessarily want to be in.

Perhaps he felt that way because of a suppressive father who physically and verbally abused him on many occasions, and that he was sinking into a rough, unforgiving, underground homosexual existence - where he was the pretty boy who was there to please all who beckoned.

"I don't think it is what you want, my dear son," Antoine said, drawing Roberto's face closer to his, and planting a kiss on his forehead, in a sweet, loving manner. "I know how it was for you. This is a cold, cruel and unforgiving world. You don't need to do that with me, because I know it is not something that you really want, deep down, inside your heart."

Roberto began to cry again, letting out the pain.

"You will never have to doing anything like that with anyone that you don't want to do anymore," Antoine said.

They hugged closer and tighter, and Roberto softly cried in Antoine's arms, but the more he sobbed and the more Antoine caressed him, the more the pain began to drift away. And a nice feeling of contentment began to overtake him, and soon, the tears started to fade away, a slight smile started to form on Roberto's face, a faint, content smile. And then, Antoine heard the three words this time, even as thunder rumbled in the distance at the exact moment the words were quietly and faintly spoken.

I love you, dark lover.

~~*

Antoine tightened his embrace; he now had his child.

It was ready and it was done.

Growing slowly out of his clothes, his limbs elongated, and increased to a monstrous muscularity; his fingers lengthened; spiny with black pointed tips. His skin turned a greenish black, was leathery and scaly, and his hair shortened and his head elongated and the crown spiked.

He opened his eyes – for a moment – and stared at the door.

He had the face of a wolf, a face which was that of a man and also of a demon, with razor sharp teeth and saliva dripping to the floor.

But Roberto did not cry out in fear, he did not falter nor did his embrace ever loosen.

Before Roberto it stood, a monster readying to create his one and only child.

CHAPTER EIGHT

"And there you have it. That is how I became what I am today."

The fire crackled once again, but it was dying slowly. It had not been stoked in a while. The rain, eased up a little from before, pelted gently across the windowpane as some thunder rumbled in the distance. Antoine arose from his chair, and walked back over to the window. He stared out into the night.

"It was truly a magnificent feeling, to change like that," he said, not breaking his stare. "It was nothing like I had ever experienced before, and nothing that I have ever experienced since."

"What did you feel?" Sheldon asked, leaning forward in his chair, straightening his notebook on his lap, clearly interested in what Antoine had to say.

"It really is hard to describe it in mortal terms," Antoine replied, pausing for a moment, stroking a small tuft of hair on the end of his chin, appearing as if searching for an analogy.

"I am trying to remember my mortal years, Sheldon. I am trying to give you…"

He stopped for a moment, removing his hand from his chin.

"Imagine the most intense pleasure you have ever had – and I am not referring to sexual pleasure, but rather a total body state of euphoria. Like being in heaven, in a state of pure bliss…like nothing else mattered in the world. Every organ, every muscle in your body experiencing the same things, the same pleasures."

"So when you made others like you didn't feel the same things?" Sheldon asked, beginning to pack up his bag, closing his notebook, and then swallowing the last of his whiskey. He stubbed out his cigarette.

"No. It's a totally different experience, which I will tell you about when we meet again. As you can see, it's getting late. I will let you live, since we have just begun my story."

When Antoine said 'I will let you live' Sheldon looked up from what he was doing, as if caught by those words. The thoughts that possibly he might not survive this endeavor began to run through his mind for the first time since he started this project.

Immortals lived secret, destructive lives untouched throughout time basically for all of eternity. And Sheldon Wilkes, Director of The Astral, chapter in Coral Gables, was ecstatic when he came across Antoine.

"Thank you for your hospitality Mr. Antoine," Sheldon said. "When shall we meet again to finish this story? It seems like such a cliché!"

"What does?"

"This. Us." Sheldon waved his legal pad back and forth in front of him as if to accentuate his comment. He continued: "My pursuit of your story."

"Your intentions are noble, Mr. Wilkes," Antoine replied flatly. "At least on the forefront they seem to be. And for that, I am granting you your wish. Your reasons are what I believe no mortal who has encountered an immortal has ever thought of – and then, extinguishes any hint of it being a cliché."

Sheldon followed Antoine into the foyer.

Antoine paused to think, head facing forward, hand on the door handle, ready to show Mr. Wilkes out.

"Tonight. Come over if you can, around 11, and I will let you know a little more about what it was like in my early days of immortality. But, it's pretty much cut and dry. It took me some time, but I got used to it. Now, I am a father."

"You are a Father?"

"Yes. But he has betrayed me. He has risen to a Dark Throne of power that I will never rise to or be able to conceive. When I first laid eyes upon him, I was merely seeking companionship. But now…there are my minions out there, as well. And he has his." As he was saying that, he gestured his open hand towards the rainy, humid Miami night.

"Good night, Antoine, take care."

Sheldon stepped out in to the night, and opened his umbrella, seeking his car keys. Thunder rumbled again, closer and louder, shaking the side of the house.

Sheldon peered up towards the sky, startled. A few seconds later, the sky lit up with lightning from an approaching storm.

Antoine leaned his head out the door, avoiding the coming rain and said, "It is you that needs to be careful, mere mortal one."

The door shut with a bang, causing the knocker to shake violently.

CHAPTER NINE

Deep in his ears, ringing in his head, were Antoine's words: *It is you who must be careful, mere mortal one.* Sheldon pulled his Honda up towards First Street, looking up through the windshield as he cut the engine. The keys jingled as he took them out of the ignition. He felt himself shivering with goose bumps and felt a chill in the air.

This evening, the weather was much cooler. For some reason, the weather in Coral Gables was growing colder each passing day since he had met Antoine.

Distant thunder rumbled, warning of an approaching storm. Sheldon peered towards the dark sky as the thunder growled; dark clouds were circling above, growing angrier and highlighted by the following illumination of the lightning.

He felt a drop on his face.

The sun had not shone in Coral Gables for three days. And for three nights, the thunder rumbled and the rain pelted the windowpanes. The winds always grew more intense once entering this section of town, and there always seemed to be a consistent state of depression and a storm.

Staring at the mansion, he pulled his briefcase up close and hugged it to his chest.

Antoine had invited him back, but he did not know the reason why.

That house, which sat in the pale moonlight, the palm trees rising in front of it; the oak trees to the side of the yard creating eerie arms that would protrude in front of the walls, created uninviting shadows.

That house, it stood high and commanding and peered down at him. It seemed to have a personality of its own. Or maybe a personality shared by its owner, Antoine Nagevesh.

Sheldon took a sip from his shiny flask of bourbon, treasuring the warmth down his throat, and opened the door to his car. He spilled into his seat and slammed the door, and pulled the brown folder out of his briefcase. On the side of the folder, it read:

THE ASTRAL – ANTOINE NAGEVESH.

Before Sheldon Wilkes, there was Anthony Peterson, who still is an active member of The Astral. Shortly after they discovered Antoine, Anthony immediately took the case, fascinated by immortals in general. He was the type of guy who bought the plastic fangs at Halloween, had more than one Ouija board at home, and went to nightclubs that catered to people who thought they were part of, or at least were fascinated by, the occult.

He started meeting with Antoine about two months ago, and two weeks into their speaking, it was rumored that the two began having a secret love affair, which seemed ironic to those at The Astral, given the fact that "people say" that immortals don't have sex – at least not in the way that humans do. But, that is what "people say".

Another member, Paula Tandy, had openly wanted to meet Antoine, and was begging and pleading with Anthony for three days to come with him one evening. Paula became very interested since Antoine became newsworthy as a local spiritual healer. It seemed he had the gift to take away pain – both emotional and physical. It eventually got to the point that citizens of Miami who were in all types of pain would seek out Antoine with the hopes that they too would be healed. But it rare someone could find him.

Paula, however, had an obsession.

Anthony promptly and quickly refused to take her along on any of his visits to Antoine, and even after endless pleading and cajoling, he still stood his ground. It seemed to make no sense to Paula that she could not accompany him on something as simple as data gathering.

But, given the type of woman Paula is, she decided that she was not going to take no for an answer. So, at 10:35pm, when Anthony exited the door to the parking garage and walked to his Jetta, Paula crept quietly out behind him, behind the brushes on the side of the brick building to the corner, and down the other side towards the back of the building where her car was parked. She parked it there earlier that day, planning this all along.

She waited for a few minutes, then heard the faint sound of an engine turning over, and when she heard loud thumping music blasting from the direction of the main parking area, she knew that it was safe to start her car because there would be no way that Anthony could hear her engine turning over when he had his music at such a loud volume.

Paula's Chevy crept towards the exit on the 11th avenue, which would lead to Anastasia, and First Street. She didn't have to worry about catching up to Anthony, because she knew the way already. She studied the case since The Astral picked it up. She had always wanted to be on it, but for some reason the Director gave it to Anthony over her, which she had been resenting.

She knew that Antoine claimed to be very old, yet seemed eternally youthful, and that he looked divine – almost heavenly, like an angel – and that his eyes were captivating and alluring. She knew he is rumored to be very beautiful, with long locks, a chiseled perfect face with eyes that seemed so loving, an intense personality and a killer body. Whenever she thought about him, about what he could potentially look like, she would feel the heat rising in her. She'd heard the stories. She'd read the file. The guy was a minx.

Paula had never seen Antoine in person, and that's what she aimed to do. Once her car set onto First Street, she could see Anthony's car already sitting there, and there no was sign of Anthony so she assumed that he had already gone inside. That worked out perfectly for Paula, because she just wanted to look inside the windows tonight to get a glimpse of this mysterious man who claimed to be immortal and perhaps see what kind of activity was going on between him and Anthony.

She parked her car and cut the engine about fifty yards down the street from Antoine's house, got out of the car, and very gently shut the door as the night was very quiet, and started to make her way down First Street. She walked down the sidewalk, and it was so silent, she couldn't even hear the hum of the cicadas. Just the quiet, dark thickness of a warm, tropical evening.

Turning into the Nagevesh residence, through the palms and foliage with its eerie arms reaching out for her, she went to the side of the house, past the grand columns, towards a window, with shears drawn, and a faint glow of light coming from it. She hoped that the curtains were open, so she could see what was happening inside.

When she got to the windows and raised her head up to look, standing on her toes, all she could see were two sets of legs, standing close to each other, as the rest of the view was blocked by a sitting chair, nestled in the corner by the window. The two pairs of legs got closer to one another, and she desperately had to see what was going on!

She stooped down and ran to the other side of the house, hoping that there would be another window, or a door that she could sneak into. There was.

On the back side of the house there was a large lanai, covered with large and heavy outdoor furniture, a large pool lit in a greenish glow, surrounded by Italian sculptures in stone, palm trees, flowers and shrubs. The lanai opened up into the kitchen area, and there was a set of French doors leading into the dining area and one door was open slightly. She could tell that no one was in the kitchen. Perfect. She took off her shoes, and entered, tip-toeing as quietly as she could, through the French doors and through the kitchen and closer to the Parlor where the two men were.

When she got to the end of the hallway that was next to the kitchen, there was a single door, a large, wooden door but with glass in the center with curtains on it, but they were curtains she could slightly draw back and peer through, and see the activity inside.

And when she reached the door, she let out a slight gasp, because what she saw was something that was expected, but not. She saw Antoine, and she saw Anthony. Antoine was holding Anthony close, looking as if they were in an embrace like that of a lover, but she could not tell what was going on. The back of Antoine's head was blocking her view.

Paula's breathing became very shallow, because the anger started to boil up inside of her. She didn't know whether to burst through the room and start yelling at the two or slip out quietly and act like none of this ever happened. Paula decided that if the two were having a scandalous affair, she did not want to witness it or be a part of it. So, she decided to slip out the back door, the way she came in, quietly and unnoticed. She backed down the hallway and into the kitchen without any noise, but still at that same moment, Antoine's eyes shot open – he turned his head around and glared at the door.

Paula crept quietly down the side of the house again, back out towards First Street, dumbfounded. She sat down on a bench that was on the sidewalk in front of the house, and shook her head, reeling at the thoughts in her head: Antoine was a fraud!

CHAPTER TEN

The storm raged and the winds roared like a hurricane, sending a cascade of leaves, twigs and tree limbs throughout the dark, black sky above the graveyard. The legion of demons stood guard beneath the tree on which Antoine was perched high in the branches, contemplating on what to do next.

Asmodai stood by the open grave, his stern gaze never breaking. The intense scowl accentuated his death grip, his fiery red eyes pierced Antoine's soul, the wrinkled face contorted in anger. Saliva dripped from his snout, and his clenched muscular fists indicated that there was unfinished business. He barked a harsh command in his dialect in a deep, grating voice, and the rotted corpse rose from the fallen casket. The eyes glowed a bright orange, piercing through the power and fury of the storm, finding Antoine perched high above.

Antoine looked down from the tree and saw the corpse staring straight at him, and looking into the eyes was like staring into an orange beam of light. Antoine shielded his eyes.

"Your soul is mine!" Asmodai boomed over the winds. "That was the way it was written! That is the way it shall be!"

Antoine parted the branches in front of him to get a better look at The Protector. The corpse kept searching in the trees, detecting Antoine's movement and zoning in on his location. A high-pitched wailing noise sounded from the direction of the decayed eyes, and before he knew it, Antoine dodged to the left just missing a giant ball of fire.

The force of the explosion caused the tree to buckle and the top loosened and fell, causing Antoine to lose his balance. He fell through the limbs, each snapping under his weight, Antoine landed with a hard *thud!* on the ground below.

As soon as he opened his eyes, he was lying on the ground and staring up at several demons, each looking down on him below, saliva dripping from their snouts, swords drawn and, faces contorted with anger and ready to strike. Antoine was quick to jump on his feet and just missed being sliced and diced - dodging several swords. As soon as he hopped two steps back on his feet, two of the demons' swords swung down and hit each other with a loud, metallic *clank!* sending bright yellow-orange sparks flying through the intense winds.

Antoine used his keen agility to dart along the edge of the woods, past the slow, lumbering demons to the south edge of the cemetery. He ducked in some thick forested trees.

From his new perspective, he peered at Asmodai between the branches and leaves of the trees, and saw the corpse sprinting his direction, apparently honed directly in on his location. Asmodai had his arms raised to the sky calling the winds.

This was it.

He had to get rid of this corpse. The demons he could outrun – they were too slow and moved too stupidly.

Asmodai, on the other hand, was much trickier. Antoine knew – he had read, and he had heard others speak of – what Asmodai was capable of. Asmodai knew that he did not need to move from where he was standing. The right hand of Satan, Asmodai was the Demon Asmodeus – the Demon of Lust. Everything blasphemous.

And Antoine knew that if Asmodai wanted to, he could end Antoine's existence right then and there. But he chose not to.

"So it is written so it shall be!" Asmodai boomed once again, extending his arm and pointing his finger towards the patch of trees where Antoine ducked.

The corpse jumped into the bushes and fell atop Antoine. It did not waste any time. Digging into Antoine's arm with what was left of its teeth, it started chewing and tearing like a hellhound would with a piece of fresh, bloody meat.

Antoine's blood shot out of his arm like a geyser. He screamed out in pain.

But his pain turned to anger as his eyes glowed crimson red and he mustered up his energy, ripping the throat out of the corpse. He spit out a dusty bite of old, decayed flesh and ripped the head off, tossing it into the bushes.

Asmodai laughed. "I can raise this entire cemetery!" he proclaimed. "And the sun will be up soon! Where will that leave you?"

Antoine stopped for a moment. The night was perpetual right now, the winds howled, the debris still flew, but time was stopped. He had been in this cemetery for hours, what seemed like over a day, but the night held fast.

He knew that Asmodai had stopped time. But he also knew that Asmodai could reinstate time – which would mean that instantly it could be high noon of the following day.

It did not mean anything to Asmodai or the demons – although naturally creatures of the night, they did their best work in the daytime. It was during light hours that the demons were able to perform most of their deception and trickery. They left their death and destruction for the night hours.

For Antoine, it was another story. He was much more a night creature. An immortal, he was quite different than the mythical vampire or demon. He was able to move about normally by day, but his powers were weakened. He could not jump nor fly. During daylight, he was much more like that of a regular mortal, but still very persuasive.

So he knew, when Asmodai warned about the sun, that he either had to flee or go through with the reanimation. He was trapped. If he ran, he could probably make it to the chateau before Asmodai called the sun. Maybe.

If he didn't he would be slowed down greatly – he wouldn't be able to move at the same lightning fast speeds that he had been accustomed to as an immortal. Asmodai would be unaffected by the sun, and would still be able to send the his legion of demons and fighting corpses after him and they were certainly could overtake him in the woods – or if he was able to outrun them and make it safely into his coffin, the demons and corpses would most certainly surround the chateau, break down the doors with splintering wood, crash through the windows and tear him out of his coffin, and rip him apart – limb from limb.

CHAPTER ELEVEN

"Welcome again, Mr. Wilkes." Antoine extended his hand in hospitality. Sheldon did not even have to knock on the door. Antoine knew that he was here, before he even shut off his Honda or took that swig from the flask.

"I see, Sheldon, have we been drinking tonight?" Sheldon did not respond, just let out a deep breath and stepped through the massive door as Antoine extended his hand gesturing into the foyer with the rounded staircase to the side, and the dark hallway behind it that led back to the bedrooms, the same bedroom where he had first been with Roberto, years earlier.

Antoine led Sheldon to the left to the parlor, where he and Anthony had their episodes, and Sheldon took a seat in the very chair that was blocking Paula's view on that night she was peering at the men inside.

"Care for another drink sir?" Antoine asked, raising his eyebrows and also raising the crystal bottle of whiskey with his right hand, looking over at Sheldon.

Sheldon shook his head accepting the drink, and also lit up a cigarette. Drawing the smoke in and then promptly setting the cigarette in the ashtray on the small table next to the chair, he opened up the file that said THE ASTRAL on the side to a page that read "Antoine Nagevesh – Time Line" across the top.

"Okay Antoine," he began. "Let me get a few facts straight here. Now, I know this is only our second meeting in person, but I need to know exactly what year you claim you were transformed."

"It's been so long since I have been a human, I honestly don't remember the exact year."

"Okay then." Sheldon scribbled some notes on his legal pad, took a draw from his cigarette, and looked for a moment towards the ceiling. "And when did you break free from your maker's tutorial?"

That question made Antoine flashback to his first vision after his mortal life, a vision that he still remembers to this day, and probably still will remember in several thousand more years: the face of his maker, Darius, the flowing, long, brown hair; silhouetted from the candle he was holding behind him, the coffin lid rising open to start a vision with my new eyes. Seeing from the eyes of an Immortal.

Wake up, sleepyhead.

"That's right," Sheldon said. "I need to know how long he was teaching you the ways of a vampire."

"My dear, sweet man," Antoine replied. "What do you take me for? A simple, silly vampire? Are you here to listen to my story or not?"

Sheldon gave his answer by closing the file, putting his pen down on the table, and reaching for the cigarette and taking a sip of whiskey. He leaned back.

"Very good, sir," he said. "Now put down your pen, and close that file."

~~*

Sheldon awoke with a start to a loud crash of lightning. His head was throbbing. His mouth was dry and parched, and his tongue felt swollen. He swung his legs onto the cold tiled floor. It was still dark outside – still raining with the occasional flash of lightning. Running his hands over his face and groaning deeply, he stopped for a moment, staring at the coffee table before him.

Hello, Sheldon. I am still here.

The silver recorder glistened before him, sitting amidst a sea of papers strewn about the coffee table from Antoine's file. Emerging from the kitchen with a glass of water, he picked up the recorder, snatched out the disc and flopped it down on the table. Drawing a second disc out of the clear plastic sleeve, with a "#2" hastily scribbled in blue ink on the label, he put it in the recorder and pressed play…

"The walk home took a bit. I was not in the position to have a horse, so I had to walk across town, through the village square, and then onto Beaumont to continue the long walk through the thickly forested paths to my home. The night was cold, dark and uninviting. The moon was new, but there was some light. Enough light to barely make out what was in front of me.

"I could see the sparkling of the New River ahead, through the trees. But I could barely see the ground in front of me, and walked slowly for fear of tripping on a twig or a stone and injuring myself.

"The wide path was lonely tonight. I stopped for a moment. Silence. I looked towards the sky and saw a shooting star. And when I brought my head back down, standing before me was the man in the black coat, glaring at me, staring at me with cold uninviting eyes. He stood several feet in front of me, and appeared misty. Looking at his feet, there was a white vapor swirling below him on the ground. My breath stopped in my throat.

"I could only stare back at him. I was still as a statue…unable to move - my muscles taught and tight and tense.

"How had the man followed me? It was such a silent night. There had been no rustling of leaves, no twigs snapping, no feet dragging on the earth. No rustling of the gravel except from my own feet. I stared at him, unable to speak, and I saw that he started to fade! I could just barely make out the trees and the water of the creek down the path behind him, ever so slightly.

"And then it happened.

"As he faded he grew brighter, so bright that it became blinding.

"My lungs became hot and crying for air, and I exhaled and my eyes began to blacken as my brain succumbed and I fell to the ground in an unconscious unmoving pile of a mortal.

"I do not know how long I had been out, but it was still dark when I awoke. I was breathing very heavily, as if I had been running and out of breath, but I had not moved anywhere. I was paralyzed with fear. I opened my mind to the terror of simply being alone.

"He was no longer there. I was alone.

"Where did the mysterious man go so quickly? Had it been that short of a time? How long had it been? I desperately had to find out, and find out where the man had gone. Or even, how he got before me in the first place without me knowing. Right now I hated so much to be alone.

"The ground was still covered with a light, white colored mist. The air was damp and cold. I shivered, and grasped my arms to myself to try to keep warm. I could not remember ever being so cold. And the woods! How they seemed to be alive, yet so dead at the same time.

"I stared into the thick, distant woods. Deep beyond my eyesight, I heard a slight rustling of the leaves. I stopped breathing for a moment, and stopped my arms from rubbing on my chest for warmth.

"Where was that sound coming from? Who was rustling in the woods? Was it him? No, it couldn't be.

"Probably just a deer.

"I wanted to go home, to be away from this desolate path covered in cold mist, to be warm in my bed, under the covers, and to forget this walk home ever even happened. But then the rustling came again.

"Louder. Closer.

"I started to breathe, but my breath was labored. I did not want to be out here alone any longer.

"I scanned the woods for anything – anything at all. I squinted, for I could not make out what I was trying to see through the limbs. I dared not move my feet. The rustle of the gravel would have drawn attention to me. The rustle in the woods seemed methodic in nature, and was not by chance, at least it seemed. Was there a pattern to it? Like someone or something was trying to intrigue me? To capture and keep my undivided attention?

"So I stayed still, in one spot, and dared not move. But I leaned forward, squinting still, and peered - the best I could - into the woods.

I shuddered and held my breath what I saw. My fists clenched. My skin started to crawl on my body.

"I was overcome with terror.

"I was staring into a pair of intense red eyes before me. Staring at me through the thick of the trees.

Staring right back at me."

CHAPTER TWELVE

…"I broke into a run. My coat flailed behind me, the strap flapping in the cool, damp wind. I did not want to find out how my hallucination had manifested itself. My heart started to beat faster, and I sprinted closer and closer to salvation. Yet at the same time it seemed so far and unattainable. As I turned to run, the rustling came closer and closer. Then it stopped. I heard a grinding, like gravel on sand.

"He is following me.

"Or who was it? The uncertainty of what or who was chasing me preyed on my mind like a wolf attacks a sheep who has wandered far off from the pasture at the edge of the meadow where it meets the dark, evil woods. The noise, the horrible sound – rustling, tree branches snapping and falling was coming at me from all directions.

"Something was pursuing me.

"I did not know what to do, or where to go, I just moved forward - running, sweating, with my eyes closed, wishing and praying that this night would be over, and wondering where this being was.

"But what was in the woods moved with me.

"I did not have time to stop and think. My legs did the thinking for me. Their muscles carried me down and back, back to where I longed to be, back into my bed and safety. But then, I had to stop. The grinding stopped. The rustling stopped.

"The night again became eerily silent.

"Was I still being followed? I stopped running just as I stopped breathing. All of a sudden, the night stood still. Even the water ahead made no sound. I was at a break in the woods, where the small brook ran through; I saw myself standing before a small wooden bridge that crossed the brook.

"A cricket sang in the distance.

"The moonlight shined through the clouds above and reflected across the brook, and it made it seem brighter than it actually was. I could hear my heart beating, and my breathing was low and labored."

"And then, a voice. 'Good evening, Antoine.'

"I could not bear to turn around. As soon as he greeted me, as soon as he said my name, I closed my eyes. But how did he know my name? Who was this?

"A luminescent hand that seemed to reflect the moonlight reached around and placed itself on my chest, right over my heart. The hand looked human, save for the fact that it was so incredibly pale and glowing.

"Your heart….' He said, slowly and passionately towards my left ear.

"I could feel his hot breath on the side of my face.

"Your heart is beating so fast my fine friend. Are you scared of me? Why don't you turn around and face me?'

"I let a deep breath release in a long, deep sigh. I turned, but I kept my eyes closed. His arm was reaching across the other side of my torso, the hand moving towards mine, down my forearm, settling on my hand, offering a great contrast to our color: his, white and pale, yet elegant; mine dark, and muscular. His fingers intertwined with mine, and held my hand as if he were my lover.

"And then I was facing him. And I opened my eyes.

"There he was, right before me.

"The man that came to me years before when I was living in Badulla - there before me on that still night. His eyes were blue and beautiful. Had he been the one who was following me?

"I have selected you…' he said slowly. I did not know what he meant, or what he meant to do by saying that. The night remained still and quiet. It was just he and I standing next to the water His lips, close to mine, so close as if he meant to kiss me and I could feel his hot breath on my face, as he uttered the five words that made my hold my breath inside of me: '*You will be my child*.'

"I did not know what to do or say.

"He had me under his seductive power. I could not object or even try or begin to struggle, even if I had wanted to.

"I opened my eyes, and looked down. The tree tops were far below. We were high in the sky, moving in the clouds. I could see the bridge and the brook where he came upon me, I saw the path where I saw the red eyes, where I was running from the sounds and the eyes which I could not determine where they were.

"We appeared to be traveling faster and faster. He was not looking ahead of us or down at all. His eyes were closed, and he seemed to be enjoying being with me.

"And then we went into the clouds to where I could see nothing. And I began to feel such exquisite pain, it overtook my senses.

"Every sensation was heightened. A darkness overtook my eyes, stars danced in front of me, with all the bright colors of the spectrum, and I breathed hard and shook. The pain was so wonderful, it was like a security that I had not known before, of something or someone who I always, always longed to be with and be a part of - now it was finally here.

"The pain felt good and reassuring.

"It was a pleasure so intense that I had not experienced its kind before. I grew hard and was harder and larger than I had ever been before. The clouds were all around us, and we were floating on the air.

"We spun around and around, high above the land, and time seemed to stand still. There was no one around but the two of us, and I was in such an illustrious state! How wonderful it was! To be in that position, was total and utter pure ecstasy, and I was reveling in it. I was taking the ultimate pleasure, gasping, constantly ready, knowing that of all the human pleasures I would partake of in my past, they could not compare to what I was experiencing in the clouds. Intertwining limbs, spinning a web of lust and passion, entangling in the rapture and passion of the moment.

"And then, soon as it may, before I could totally partake in all that I wanted to partake of in this wonderfully, deliciously fine moment, I began to see darkness. I was not closing my eyes, yet the darkness was taking over my vision as if I were. At least I did not think that I was closing my eyes. My faculties were with me, but only partially, and they were fading fast, like daylight when dusk takes over.

"And then there was total blackness.

"My mind began swimming with thoughts, thoughts like an ocean of information easing through my brain, love particles dancing in my head. I saw myself as a child, saw myself helping my father when I was a boy, a strapping young man.

"I saw myself taking care of my family and my sisters and my mother, helping when my father passed away and becoming the man of the family shortly thereafter, I saw when darkness began to overtake my life. I saw when I began to spiral downward into a sexual deviant that I have been today. When I began to live a life of lust. That is when the images became more vivid and more difficult to control.

"I saw what I did, and saw that what I did was such an abomination. And it was a lovely, treasured thing. And I saw it now. I saw why I was chosen. The things I did, the acts that I committed, was an abomination to God.

""'Yes, you are right', the voice said.

"I heard those words, somewhere, speaking to me in that blackness. The sweet echo of the beautiful male voice resounded in my head, mixing with the clatter of my thoughts and brainwaves. I could hear myself speak, but I did not know where it was coming from.

"I know now! *I know!*'

"I did not know where my body was, I could not see anything. But I was having this strange revelation.

"You will see when you are reborn in the demonic darkness.'

"Again, those words. That comforting male voice, singing into my ears, soothing and eloquent, like a father: 'What do you see now? What do you see before you?'

"I could feel my breath within me, I could feel my heart beating in my chest, in that area, that was supposed to be my chest. I looked down, yet saw nothing. The blackness was still there, and it still enveloped me. The misty darkness. Where was I?

'Now, what do you see?'

"I saw myself.

"The darkness remained and I began to feel a heaviness lift from me. I knew something was odd, something was different. The visions did not come anymore.

"I then heard the clicking of a lock of some sort, and the blackness began to dissipate, and light began to filter into my world that I was in. And then I realized where I was.

"And when the lid of the coffin that I was in was fully opened, there he was. The man that I have seen and known for so many years, looking down at me in the dim, yellowish light: 'Wake up sleepyhead!'

PART TWO

DIRTY LITTLE SECRETS

I'm dirty dirty dirty –

Dirty I will be.

Dirty I will stay.

For I never need. I never want. I never stray.

I always leave.

You watch and wait and see.

Soon you'll be dirty too.

CHAPTER THIRTEEN

A long line of black stretch limousines followed a white hearse which led the procession down the Oak-lined street in the center of Medley. The brown casket could be seen through the rectangular rear windows of the hearse, visible through glass and framed by purple velvet curtains pulled back with gold cords. The next car in the procession was a long black Lincoln Limousine. Inside the rear window, sat a grey-haired Hispanic woman.

She occasionally would turn her head towards the window, staring at the small shops and immature trees that lined the cobblestone sidewalks, but her eyes were concealed by an oversized pair of dark sunglasses. At one point, she removed the sunglasses, and brought a white, wadded tissue up to her eyes, to wipe the mascara that had run down her cheek, and, shortly after, buried her face in her hands.

That was the scene as the motorcade passed the through the streets of the small town center of Medley; they passed through Danson Circle and went around three quarters of the circle; the line of cars passed some small antique shops with furniture on a sidewalk sale, and clothing stores whose doors opened to a brick sidewalk and a few small potted palm trees. As they near the church, a thick canopy kept the street in shade; like giant arms extending from massive trees that grew behind the small, single story buildings on either side of the street.

At the end of the avenue the white hearse made a right hand turn into Ascension Cemetery and stopped to wait for a tall, black iron gate to open. The canopy continued over the cemetery, and the trees that were scattered throughout the cemetery were also just as mature as the oaks that lined the streets - the only reminder of tropical Florida was the occasional palm. The gravestones were small and modest but there was a small stone monument that rose above the others here and there.

The feel of the town was more of a quiet, wooded oasis in the middle of bustling Miami. If one were to wander just a few mere blocks from the center of town the landscape would give way to interstates and urban sprawl, traffic and congestion.

"Here we lay to rest our brother, taken from this life suddenly and tragically." A priest dressed in white vestments and took place at the head of the gathering, standing at the head of the coffin. "Jean Carlo was taken at such a young age, in such a brutal way." He opened his bible and began reading scripture as the small group of mourners bowed their heads in respect.

Peering through the trees was Darius, dressed in a black suit and sunglasses, observing from afar the funeral of his victim. He had waited outside of the Cathedral of the Gardens church, smoking a steady stream of cigarettes, as the funeral mass drone on to almost two hours. He leaned against the hearse and exhaled a cloud of smoke. He thought about how much work it was in modern times to gather followers; and how easy it had been years ago, when he had made Antoine, to make a kill.

Certainly hundreds of years ago, there was not the forensic investigation as there was today. The encounter with the police just made matters worse. He was definitely taking some time getting used to a new society and culture – all made apparent when the flashlight shone in his face after he dropped the young man's body to the ground.

Shaking his head as the crowd began to disperse from the graveside service, he ventured away from the hearse and waited patiently in a network of trees until everyone had left. As he heard the purr of the last car engine fade into the distance, he emerged.

He stared straight ahead, looking at Jean Carlo's casket, lying in the middle of a sea of Astroturf and flowers lined by small, white folding chairs on either side. Any minute now the grounds keepers would be returning with their beat-up, rusted pickup to take away the chairs and bury the casket.

He had little time.

You're going to rise out of that casket soon, Jean Carlo. That's right my friend, it happens every time. It happens every time I make a kill. I do that, I do just that. I make a kill and then they come back. Why, you wouldn't believe how many of you there already are. Let's see…one or two a night, that equals to quite a lot.

I remember seeing you waiting. I remember seeing you sitting in the car, looking over at me looking at you, walking out and heading over to me.

But you didn't know what you were getting yourself into – you couldn't have possibly.

"Excuse me, sir?"

The voice broke the trance. His gaze had been fixed on the casket, waiting for the correct moment to open it and let Jean Carlo free.

A short, paunchy older man stood in front of him, grinning a toothless grin. Darius looked over towards the small path that cut through the center of the cemetery. He had been so absorbed in his thoughts, he hadn't even heard the truck pull up.

"Still paying your last respects?" the man asked as he started to fold the chairs. Darius moved closer to the grave. The grounds keeper continued: "Family's all gone. Everyone left about ten minutes ago. We just gotta get these here chairs in the truck and get this in the ground." He gestured back to the casket with the thumb as if he were a hitchhiker.

Darius sighed.

He certainly did not want them to bury the coffin yet. If they did, he would have to come back at night and dig it up. That most certainly was not appealing. He had to get rid of this old man.

The silver-haired man continued talking as he folded the chairs, one by one, carrying them over to the rusty grey truck. "Yeah…this is an old cemetery all right. Not rich either. Most people here don't have any money. No crypts, that's for sure."

Darius sat in one of the chairs. "What I am interested in is right here." He gestured to the casket.

The grounds keeper stopped. "Of course sir!" he said. "You are family? A friend? I saw you at the funeral. Over in the trees. Why didn't you come up here?"

"I suppose you could say that I am a friend."

"Do you want me to leave you alone for a bit?" The grounds keeper placed a folding chair against the side of the truck. Darius said nothing, but continued to stare at the casket.

"That's fine man…I will just go the other side of the truck for a bit and have me a Winston. You just take your time sayin' your goodbyes."

He retreated around the back of the truck and he was out of sight, and Darius didn't move until he detected the sweet smell of cigarette smoke wafting through the air.

He knelt next to the casket and felt the underside of the lid for the lock. As the old man would be coming back from his cigarette break in moments, he had to act fast.

He pulled the lock open with ease, yet the crack and splinter against the quiet afternoon alerted the old man.

"Everything ok over there?" the old man called over. Darius stopped what he was doing suddenly. He looked behind his shoulder; the man was standing in front of the hood, looking over expectantly.

"Just fine, thanks…" Darius croaked, clearing his throat.

"Oh, I see….I'm sorry sir, I will give you some more time," he said backing away.

Darius heard the click of the cigarette lighter as he slowly opened the lid to the casket. Gradually, the daylight seeped through the opening to the casket as the space between the lid and the base grew, revealing Jean Carlos' body.

There he was, lying in the satin as if he were asleep. His hair was slicked back with gel and he seemed to be nothing more than a lifeless corpse.

"What the fuck?" Darius heard the old man exclaim as his head turned around. The grounds keeper was standing a few feet behind him, cigarette in hand and mouth gaping open.

Darius stared the man down, his eyes beginning to transform to a pale pink, the color deepening to a dark red. He growled at the man.

The old man gasped, his mouth opened wide and his cigarette fell to the ground, in a shower of bright red sparks. He stepped back cautiously.

Darius stood in rage.

His fangs elongated from his mouth and his fingers lengthened; they became spiny and sharp pointed, like weapons. He grew in height and muscularity, shredding the dark suit that he wore in his human form. His skin changed from light and fleshy to a dark green.

He lunged forward, and the man turned to run, screaming for his life, tripping over the stones on the path lined by trees – just wide enough for a car to get through.

The man fell face first to the ground, terrified of what Darius had become. It did not matter that he was a simple old man who kept cemetery grounds for his simple living; Darius saw him as a threat regardless.

And for the thrill of the kill.

"You like what you see?" Darius asked.

The man rose from the gravel he lay briefly in a heaped mess upon, leaving a dark red stain on the stones below his face. His nose had broken when he fell, and blood poured down through his mouth.

"What – are you?!?" he cried, as droplets of blood shot away from his mouth like saliva.

"I am your last vision."

The man turned and tried to run again, but he could not escape the grip of Darius' muscular arm, which reached forward and grabbed the man's shirt.

Pleading for his life, Darius wrapped his demonic arms around the grounds keeper squeezing him tightly. He squeezed him so tight that the cracks of the bones in his arms resonated against the otherwise silent afternoon.

The man screamed. "Please!!" Darius did not listen. His arms continued to squeeze with an evil intensity causing the veins in his arms to engorge with blood, and the old man's eyes began to bulge out of his sockets. The man could no longer scream. His lungs were being crushed and the air was forced out of them.

His ribs crushed with a crack and the man lost consciousness, his head drooping to the side like that of a rag doll. Darius had almost made it through the limp body. Squeezing tighter, he ripped the body in two, as bright red blood poured onto the pavement. Shortly after came a shower of grayish colored intestines and digestive organs.

But Darius let the body drop to the ground. And then it became eerily quiet once again, as if nothing happened.

Staring at the ground, he saw what a bloody mess the man had become. The thrill now gone, Darius began to back away from the mess and decided to return to the grave. He immediately lost interest in the man once he was dead.

There was a loud crash from back towards the grave. Darius turned around, but the truck was behind him blocking his view.

What caught his attention was the noise coming from the direction of Jean Carlos' grave.

It hadn't sounded like a small twig snapping, or a car passing by. But it had been eerily quiet and the crash didn't sound like a branch falling to the ground – it sounded metallic like a casket falling off its runners.

Dressed again in his dark suit, he slowly walked around the truck, keeping cover.

Jean Carlo…I know you are over there. I heard you get up. I heard you rise from your coffin after I tore that old man to shreds. Don't think you can hide from me. I am here to bring you back to where you belong. I am sin and you are a sinner. And now, welcome to hell.

Darius checked himself the in the side mirror, slicking back his hair with his hand. Glancing to his right, he peered through the glass font cabin of the truck and confirmed his suspicion: the casket was lying on its side. The pillow was on the ground next to the coffin. And there was no sign of Jean Carlo.

He walked slowly over to the gravesite. He knew that Jean Carlo was alive and immortal. He stood and scanned the area. There were several thick trees that he could be hiding behind.

The afternoon sun was beginning to set, and the cemetery faced the west. So the shadows might soon reveal Jean Carlos' location. Perhaps.

If he really was hiding behind one of the trees.

Darius walked up towards the casket, straightening it back on its runners and placing the pillow back at the head. He walked back towards the mess of the old man, scooped up the remains with a shovel and dumped them into a wheelbarrow that he found not far from the pickup truck.

He dumped what was left of the old man into the casket, staining the white satin red and pink, and shut the lid.

Looking up towards the sky as his foot turned the switch to lower the casket in the grave, he wondered if Jean Carlo was watching everything. It did not matter. Jean Carlo did not matter. He was out there now, out as an immortal. And he would be out there unless someone turned him to ashes. Darius grabbed a shovel, ripped the blue tarp off of the nearby mound of dirt, and started to toss the dirt on the casket.

As he shoveled the last of the dirt into the grave, the old man was given a place of rest.

CHAPTER FOURTEEN

Asmodai stood above Antoine, looking down where he lay. Antoine was huddled on the ground under the collapsed tree, shielding his eyes from the wind and falling debris. Asmodai would not let him leave so easily. Antoine knew it was time to finish the ritual; and Asmodai knew it was time to collect a soul. But Antoine's soul was the burst of energy in question, and many times, Antoine doubted if he still had a soul left to give.

Antoine felt that when he had been born, when he grew into a boy, and when he started leaving the small house early each morning to work in the blistering sun in the coffee fields, that, then, he still had a soul. But he quickly fell down the path of corruption, and by the time he met Darius, it was questionable if his soul was even still there. Still, when he sank his teeth into the heart in the cemetery, his fate was sealed. The first moment that his shovel hoisted dirt from the ground, he sold his soul. And even if his soul was hiding somewhere faraway…it was in danger. Asmodai knew it and Antoine knew it without a word being spoken.

It was time to find a way to bring Darius back. Because now Antoine needed him.

Antoine knew, from reading *Les Livres Des Vampires* about the process of reanimation. There was no turning back. Besides, Antoine needed Darius to helm Sacrafice, there was no way that Antoine could do it alone.

When Antoine spit the blood out, it did nothing to lift the curse. Now it was time to pay.

Antoine slowly and carefully crawled through the foliage and into the cemetery clearing. The demons stood still, as if all pieces in an enormous game of chess waiting command for the next strategic move. Asmodai returned to his place near Darius' grave, trudging through a legion of loyal demons; for a moment he turned and stared intently at Antoine. It almost looked as if Asmodai smiled; Antoine could not determine for sure, but he thought he saw the edge of his mouth rise slightly. Asmodai knew he had won. But even when he stood above the grave, waiting to complete the ritual, his eyes never lost focus on Antoine's moves.

"Come," Asmodai called across the sea of gravestones, each monument raising a cement obituary in an ocean of grass. "Let us finish the ritual."

Antoine rose to his feet and proceeded slowly over to the grave where Asmodai was waiting.

Asmodai issued a command in his own dialect to the demon standing closest to him. The demon bent over and reached into the nearest grave, shoving a muscular arm into the dirt, and ripped buried casket from the ground. He took the coffin into both of his arms as dirt cascaded off of the sides, sending a shower onto the grass.

He dropped the casket on the ground with a thud, tore off the rotted lid, and with one arm, lifted out a severely decayed corpse. This body had to have been buried for much longer than the last one – the skin was completely dried and flaking, and almost entirely rotted away. It was heavily deteriorated, with many visible bones and rotted masses of old flesh that hung off the body like fabric.

Antoine reached into his pocket and felt the meaty warmth of Darius' heart when he reached the graveside. Taking it out, he handed it to Asmodai - slowly and carefully - as if it were the forbidden fruit.

Asmodai took the heart and raised it up to the sky.

The winds stopped for a moment, debris suspended in mid-air, and the clouds directly above them opened up and glowed a fire-like reddish orange in a circle that was like the eye of a giant hurricane.

Asmodai spoke in his own dialect, and then turned to Antoine.

"Remove your shirt."

Antoine obeyed, dropping his clothes to the ground. Upon reading the ritual, he lay down next to the rotted corpse without any instruction needed to do so.

The demon that unearthed the corpse bent over and ripped the dried and rotted heart out of the body, and threw it into the woods aside.

Asmodai then took Darius' heart and shoved it harshly into the chest of the corpse. "This body will come forth, it will rise as Darius, and it will be raised immortal once again, brought forth with the blood of his son."

Asmodai drew his sword from its sheath.

Antoine closed his eyes, and drew in his breath deeply as he felt his skin break. He exhaled and looked down, as the sword was carving a hole in the center of his chest. Asmodai dug through layers of skin, muscle, and pierced Antoine's ribcage. The blood that was beating in his heart started to flow out of his chest, spilling down the front of his body.

"Now get up," Asmodai commanded as he withdrew the sword. "Lower yourself onto the body and bring forth your maker!"

Antoine at first struggled to his feet and almost fell backwards, his energy drained. The wound to his chest was a piercing pain that throbbed and would not let go. He could feel the cool night air flowing through his body. Looking down, he saw his torn chest – crudely dug out with the demon sword, his skin, torn with hanging flesh and muscle; his heart, beating as had been for so many years inside of his chest. Antoine did as he was instructed. He mounted the corpse, one leg on either side of the torso, and brought his chest up towards the face. He raised his body; above the carcass so that the fresh, oozing wound in his chest was in alignment with the remains of the mouth, and aimed several bright red drops on the lips.

"Let it drink! The blood must be directly from your heart!"

Antoine squeezed his chest muscles together, milking the puncture in the center of his chest creating a flow of blood that dripped into the mouth of the cadaver. Slowly his blood drained, sending waves of pleasure throughout his body that he had not experienced before, and then, not before long, he felt a warm and livery tongue begin to lap at the hot flowing potion.

All of his veins were writhing in orgasmic bliss; the intensity of his pleasure was accentuated by the warm mouth forming beneath him. He shivered and he shook, as if reveling in the pleasures of his creating a new life. The blood flowed and flowed, and instinctively he squeezed his chest muscles harder together, causing the flow of the blood to increase.

"Feed him until you are near drained," Asmodai said. "You must give him all of your blood!"

Wincing and grimacing his face as if he were climaxing, the intensity of the pleasure was almost too much for Antoine to bear. The pleasure came in waves of altering intensity, however when a crest hit it became body-shakingly awesome. Several times Antoine felt as though he could not go on – that the pleasure was simply too intense and too much for his body to bear. But every time he turned his head up to Asmodai, he barked, "all of it!"

The corpse beneath him started to fill out – the flesh started to live and grow again; forming flesh, fresh blood, fresh skin. The feel of the mouth that suckled on the wound in his chest - which at first had felt dried out and papery, started to take a new, more lively form. The tongue would penetrate his body; the lips would caress his wounds. Each time the tongue entered his chest and massaged his beating heart, it became fleshier and felt more and more… alive.

Soon, the tongue felt animated and warm, like it was dripping with saliva. The rotted flesh began to ooze off the bones, collecting in a pile of oozing mess, amidst dusty, dried out body parts. The organs underneath revived and repaired themselves, creating veins and a flow of blood that started out slowly and became faster and faster as the skin began to generate.

Asmodai stood above and looked on in approval.

Antoine's blood started to fill the body, giving it life. Further and further, the blood drained out of Antoine and dripped into the mouth, permeating the corpse, fulfilling dark scripture.

As the skin regrew, and as the body filled out with newly grown organs and muscle, there seemed to be a hint of movement underneath Antoine. He had finally done his duty and given life back to Darius.

Squeezing the last drops of blood from between his chest muscles, Antoine flopped down on the ground next to the body, breathless and spent. Lost in a dreamlike state, he was barely aware of the demons retreating. He barely comprehended Asmodai's warning, and as the warning was spoken, the words sounded farther and farther away, as if he were speaking it as he was drifting out into a different dimension: "Take your maker and leave this place…you are mine now. And you will do as I will you! Don't ever make a move without me!"

Antoine felt blackness envelop him and did not wake until what felt like was much later.

And he woke up inside his coffin.

CHAPTER FIFTEEN

I hope that fucking monster doesn't see me!

One minute, I'm lying peacefully in my casket, listening to my family say their farewells – the next, here I am! Listening to the intestines of an anonymous grave keeper spill onto the pavement! Damn, damn, damn what the hell has happened to me?

Jean Carlo stood behind an Oak tree, feeling the warmth of the setting South Florida sun on his back, feeling the black suit jacket he was wearing absorbing the heat. That god-awful monster stood over next to his coffin, the lid still propped open.

He dared not move a muscle. He didn't even want to create a shadow.

This guy was bad news. First, he is a murdering psychopath, and second – wait a minute.

Jean Carlo returned his attention to his killer. A wheelbarrow was carrying the bloody remains of the guy who buried him…oh, Jesus. Oh sweet Jesus.

The coffin lid slammed and Jean Carlo heard the casket being lowered into the ground. The rudders clicked and pinged, and soon thereafter he heard the *fwummmp* of dirt being shoveled onto the coffin.

He peeked his head to the side of the tree. There was his assassin, standing over the grave shoveling the last of the dirt on the casket. It was almost full.

The killer gave the top of the grave a pat, and tossed the shovel aside.

What was his motivation? His mind raced as he backed away from the edge of the tree. *And how the hell did I get here instead of lying in my casket? Aren't I supposed to be dead?*

"Yes, you are."

Jean Carlo was so startled at the voice that crept up on him that he took a few steps backward almost losing his balance. When he regained control of his composure, there was the killer – looking at him straight in the eye.

Jean Carlo turned and broke into a run – he did not wait to find the answers to his many questions. He ran across the sea of gravestones, dodging to the left and to the right, running in a drunken, crisscross pattern – desperately seeking the entrance to the cemetery. He sought the sanctuary for a moment behind a large stone monument, catching his breath.

Peeking his head around the marker, he scanned the vast graveyard from left to right and back to the left again in an attempt to spot his assassin.

There he was. A tall figure, dressed in black – seen through an array of markers of all shapes and sizes - crosses, stone angels with assorted flowers and trees. And he hadn't moved. He remained standing next to the tree staring him down. Jean Carlo knew that, he knew that this evil entity was powerful and capable of much more that he was letting on.

"You're drunk, Jean Carlo," he said, suddenly next to him, as his assassin leaned against the same marker that Jean Carlo had been. "Drunk with death."

Jean Carlo caught his breath for a moment, startled by the killer's sudden and instantaneous appearance. He attempted to break into a run again, tripping over his feet and falling on the ground, wincing in pain as his head struck a small headstone that was partially concealed by overgrown weeds and grass.

The killer laughed as Jean Carlo held his bleeding forehead, crawling on his hands and knees to the cemetery wall.

"I killed you but you live!" The killer glared at Jean Carlo. "I drained you of your blood and still…you run! Don't you realize what I have done to you?" Jean Carlo did not bother to look back as he spilled through the rusted gate which squeaked when it opened. He did not bother to see Darius sprout black vascular wings from his back, tearing the suit that he had been wearing as the tattered bits of fabric dropped the ground like leaves. He didn't notice that Darius rose quickly and was flying; circling over the cemetery, ascending higher and higher above the treetops until he was a small, black speck against the bright blue sky.

He didn't see Darius above him, hiding high in the cotton ball clouds, watching his every move as he left the cemetery and ran down Chrome Avenue.

Darius, perched high in the clouds, had a commanding view of the landscape. He saw the man head out of the cemetery, turn on Chrome, and move quickly south – towards Coral Gables. He knew where he was going. He was going to where all go when experiencing something like what Jean Carlo had experienced.

The Astral.

It did not matter, Darius knew that. It would not be long before Jean Carlo would realize that he was no longer a mortal. He would soon learn that he would no longer exist in the same fashion that he had before, and that he would start to grow an insatiable lust to kill. And kill. And kill again.

Hovering above the city, his eyes continued to follow Jean Carlo. He decided to move again, and continued his journey towards the sun; he relished the warmth on his face, the wall of wind, and shortly thereafter his attention diverted away from Jean Carlo, and he turned East to head towards Lyon. It did not matter if Jean Carlo didn't want or accept his new darkness. He will be dark whether he wants to or not.

CHAPTER SIXTEEN

Paula could not believe what she saw. Antoine! Making out with Anthony!? She steamed at the idea. Everything she was ever taught about vampires, everything that she had ever learned, told her that vampires are not sexual.

Vampires do not have sex.

That would make Antoine a mortal, and all of this was a hoax. So then, Antoine was some schmuck who wanted some publicity, and make up some story saying he was hundreds of years old, blah blah, blah, and got The Astral involved to make a few bucks and become a local celebrity. How cheap!

Paula sat on the bench outside the Nagevesh residence. The night grew darker, and she looked up at the sky. There moon was gone, there were no more stars. It seemed as if the clouds were getting thicker – as if a storm were approaching. The wind started to pick up, and a slight chill developed in the air. She shivered, rubbing her arms. A gust of wind blew towards her face, and Paula felt the hairs stand on her arm, and when she ran her hand along her arm, she felt the goose bumps rise in her skin. She arose from the bench to make her way back to the car. She was going to stay and confront Anthony when he left the house, but the wind was picking up too much, and it was getting too cold for her to sit outside. The wind gusted so strong that the palm trees swayed violently, and debris began swirling around the street.

What is this? She thought. *This is quite a storm brewing.*

She walked down the sidewalk, down the street to where she had parked her car earlier, and dodged several palm branches that blew off the trees when she finally made it to her car. She dug into her left pocket to find her keys, and they weren't there. Then she checked her right pocket. Not there either. She patted herself down, closing her eyes in exasperation, now cursing herself, and wondering where she could have dropped her keys.

She turned her head and looked down the street towards Antoine's house, not wanting to go back. She wondered if she had dropped her keys when she turned away from the door to the living room. Had she been holding them when she crawled through Antoine's back kitchen door? She sat down on the ground, feeling defeated. Scanning the sidewalk, looking for a possibility – a *chance* that *maybe* she might catch the light glistening on her silver chain…but no luck.

She sat and sat, and then she sat some more and wondered how she was going to get these keys, especially if the two men were in the kitchen! They could be finished making out by now. She did not know what to expect.

Cursing herself for being so careless, Paula began to fight the winds and debris and made her way back down First Street, arriving at the imposing structure towering over her and looking down as if laughing at her – laughing at her in victory.

That's it girly girl! I'm going to swallow you up! I have had a psychosexual demonic owner who – guess what? Dined on the previous owner! That's right, he sucked the blood right out of him, tore his neck to shreds until the sheets on his bed were soaked – I mean soaked, dripping wet soaked – with his blood. And guess what else he did? Guess what else?!?

She heard a high-pitched laughter coming from the house. She shuddered. When she looked up she noticed something.

The house was completely and utterly dark.

That's odd, she thought. There were several lights on before.

A booming crash of thunder and bright flash caused her to jump. She looked up at the sky again. It was growing angrier, more intense.

The clouds swirled above, ready to break in a downpour at any moment. She did not have much time to get her keys and leave.

Another flash of lighting came – and this time it was blinding – the brightest strike of lightning she had ever seen in her life. She shielded her eyes, and as the flash passed - just as Paula was looking directly at the house, it revealed a very unkempt lawn. It looked like it hadn't been tended to in a very long time. The brush was overgrown, the lawn was tall and in need of maintenance.

That's pretty strange, she thought.

She did not remember a lawn looking like that when she crept through it a little earlier. There were weeds overgrown throughout the lawn, and the bushes were browned and crackly. There was an old soda can and a newspaper blowing around in the wind.

She stood directly in front of the house, and stared directly at it as the house stared back at her, staring her down.

What happened?

It looked like the house hadn't been tended to and hadn't been lived in for years. Certainly no lights were on. As it looked to Paula, a light hadn't been turned on in that house in *years.* Several windows were broken. The paint on the siding was fading, untended and peeling off. The brushes in the flowerbed in front of the house snaked up the side and crept up like fingers reaching for some unknown source. The two upstairs windows glared at her like eyes.

And then it happened.

There was a deafening boom and *crack!* and the rain came, and it came in buckets and torrents. Paula was soaked instantly. She stood there, now huddled and cold, staring at the house staring back at her. She stood completely still, dumbfounded.

Coming out of her trance, she ran up to the front porch, and noticed the door ajar. It swung open and banged against the side of the house in the violent winds. She went closer to the door, and debated going inside. She was totally confused, and not sure of what to expect. What was once a glorious estate, shimmering and elegant was now was before her in a state of wreck and disarray. As the wind picked up and the rain blew harder onto her arms, she made her decision, and opened the door.

The foyer was just as unkempt as the exterior. The house was still furnished, but obviously abandoned years ago. No one had lived here for a very long time, that was for sure. She tried the light switch next to her on the wall, not expecting it to work, and it didn't. There was another crash of thunder, and the lighting lit up the foyer as bright as daylight and it revealed a hallway to the back of a large, round table that was in the center. There was still a bouquet of flowers in an expensive looking vase on top of the table. The flowers were long since dry and dead.

She continued towards the hall, arms stretched outwards, using her hands as eyes as the foyer was quite dark save for when the lighting struck. She could feel years of dust piled on the woodwork and tables on either side of her. She carefully made her way to the entrance of the hallway, cautiously shuffling her feet along the floor. When the lightning and thunder struck again, the light reflected in a mirror at the end of a long hallway. She saw the hallway was clear of furniture and debris, so she decided to continue down with the hopes that there would be a room with a candle or some source of light. She continued further down the hallway, and it got darker as she approached the center of the house. With another flash of lightning, she saw that the mirror and the end of the hallway still seemed so desperately far.

Just as she was looking straight ahead of her, she glanced up as the thunder crashed once again, and the room filled another flash of lightning - bright as day - just for an instant, and revealed to her: she saw in the mirror, a reflection. Someone was behind her! In the foyer, someone was watching her!

Her breathing stopped, and her heart stopped in her throat. She closed her eyes.

Please, that was my mind playing tricks on me, she thought.

She did not move.

She heard a rustling behind her, from what sounded like it was coming from the foyer. *Just the wind*, she thought. There was another thunder crash and a strike of lightning, and she did not dare open her eyes. She was afraid of what she might see in the mirror. Somewhere behind her a door creaked. She decided to move ahead slowly. She was trapped. She had nowhere else to go but further into this house.

Then she jumped, startled, at a crash behind her. And it *definitely* came from the foyer. Sweat was pouring down her face, and she thought to herself that she may not get out of this house. She opened her eyes, just as lightning struck again, and she saw that the vase of flowers has been knocked off the table, and the vase shattered all over the floor.

Who did that? She wondered. She did not want to find out.

The mysterious reflection was not there this time. Was someone there? She could hear herself breathing. She did not want to find out where the reflection went, she did not want to find out what made the crash behind her, she just wanted to get out of this horrid house. Her breathing remained heavy, she could feel her heart beating in her chest, and she darted her eyes around – searching for some kind of a sanctuary. She now wished she had never followed Anthony in the first place. If she hadn't, she could have been out in Coconut Grove with the girls, or curled up at home with a good mystery novel.

Then she heard a floorboard creak again, just behind her!

She closed her eyes and froze.

But then her survival instincts took over. Her feet were no longer frozen to the floor. She broke out into a run, and ran into the nearest room to her - a door to the left. As soon as she got into the room, she slammed the door and locked it tight. Whatever it was must still be out in the hallway. She felt safe and alone in the room, and looked around for some source of light.

Her eyes adjusted somewhat in the darkness, and she saw that she was in what appeared to be a young man's room. A single bed was placed against the wall beside a massive stereo with towering speakers against the wall, a desktop computer, and posters. There was an open laptop on an unmade bed.

There was another crash, this time in the hallway. Much closer than before.

Paula stopped in her tracks. Something was out there…following her. Whatever it was – was still out there. Waiting for her.

And now she was trapped in this house.

CHAPTER SEVENTEEN

Sheldon rose from the same chair that had blocked Paula's view of Antoine and Anthony to refill his whiskey. His glass had been empty for some time now. Antoine got up himself and raised his hand in protest.

"Please, sit," he said. "I will get that for you."

"You are the most gracious host," Sheldon replied, as he returned to his chair; his voice was now with a slight slur in his speech. Antoine only smiled and poured the whiskey. Sheldon placed a new disc in the recorder and Antoine continued his story.

~~*

"I finally made it out of the coffin. It took all the effort I had. And then I finally got to glance around the room I had been laying in. It was an attic of some sort. Wooden floors, wooden beams. A sloping ceiling to a point at the crest, like I was at the top of a house. Candlesticks, old books. Cobwebs in the corner.

"I was wearing the same clothes that I had been before. But, I had no idea *when* it was. It felt like the next morning, yet it was dark as night.

"Or at least I thought it was.

"Now, I was immortal. But I did not know it yet. As far as I was concerned, the man who I had seen earlier and who I had a most astounding encounter with and who, I assume, placed me in this coffin at some point in the night was just a mysterious stranger. But, it did not occur to me that he could be a demon.

"However, I did have the notion that he was of something different. Not necessarily a ghost or goblin or spook but certainly not human. At least not human. Ah, those were different days. The days I was a mortal. The days I was human…

"But I was no longer human. I was seeing things through demon eyes; I was part of the quantum realm and I didn't even know it; I was part of the spirit world but I had no idea. I didn't know that I was no longer living; I didn't know that I was living in a different dimension while viewing the same reality that I had when I was human.

"I got up and started walking through the attic, and then Darius climbed up some stairs and appeared through a small square opening in the floor. I remembered him from the night before. But now, he seemed to jump out in front of me; he was so clear, so vivid and so sharp! Every color – the brilliance of his skin, his dark hair, and his piercing eyes jumped in front of me. He gestured for me to follow him. It was dark, but I did not need any additional light to show my way down the stairs, for I could see clearly every nook and cranny, every spider web in the corner of the floorboards and on the stairs stuck out in front of my face as if they were at eye level, right before my eyes; I could hear the scattering of paws to my left, and when I looked down and over the stairs to the floor I could see a small mouse scurrying across the floor, ducking under a newspaper that was lying on the floor, like in the shape of a makeshift roof, out the other end of the paper into a small hole in the wall across the room.

"And I thought to myself, what a loud mouse!

"Darius could see the look on my face, or perhaps he was reading my mind, because at the precise moment that I thought about the loudness of the rodent, he looked back at me and smiled a knowing smile. He then spoke to me: 'You will get used to your new senses, in time. You will start realizing that when you see things, and hear things, from where we are now, they are so much clearer to you. Everything.' And then turned around and continued down the stairs.

"We approached what appeared to be a parlor suite which had sloping sofas with dark wood trim, in front of large, bay windows that extended out further from the room over which hung heavy cranberry colored drapes which were shut tightly. The room seemed dusty, and had a very damp and musty feel to it. Whoever this mysterious man was, he was one of the elite. I was used to living in modest surroundings with my mother and sisters without much privacy. This, on the other hand, was quite elegant.

"Darius led me to an additional sofa in the center of the room, and ushered me to sit down in the center of it. I was still slightly disoriented, and stared quietly ahead; my eyes remained glassy and I did not speak. We sat for a while in silence. It was so quiet that I could hear the repetitive tick-tock of a clock somewhere in the room. Darius turned around to face me, his face contorted in a smirk, and he brushed his dark brown hair to the side. He sat in a chair across from the sofa, glanced around the room, and prepared himself to speak.

"'You are now of another realm,' he said. 'You have been chosen for immortality, but the price for that gift comes duty, homage, and penance. This is not the gift of a vampire. We are not vampires. Vampires live like animals and drink the blood of the living. If we do drink blood – and you may if you wish – we do it only for sport.'

"He was quiet after he said that. Darius examined his nails. I did not speak. I could not speak.

"There was a low rumble of thunder in the distance.

"'You will have to kill to survive, and I do not mean for food. You must kill to prove your loyalty to Tartarus' he continued, 'and you will always be denounced by God and banned to Hell upon your destruction for all of eternity.'

"I hear the thunder crack, closer, and I could hear the rain begin to fall, although none seemed to be hitting the windowpane.

"I looked up at Darius.

"I felt the knot rise in my stomach, cursing myself for my being so vain. If I hadn't been so easily swayed into sexual adventures and so easily drawn in by his masculine beauty, I most likely would not have gotten involved with him. My life was going to change drastically, I could tell. I did not ask for what was done to me, but I did not totally despise him for that either. When he sat and spoke to me about what I was, at first he seemed like he was very smug, like thinking 'that is what you get for being intimate with someone like me, serves you right' but then changed his tone as I became more interested in what I had become and where my new life would take me. As the hours passed and as he sat and spoke to me, like a father to a child or a teacher to a student, I became more accepting of my condition.

"My weakness and insatiable libido gave me this as a punishment, but I saw a ray of hope and a possibility that I could turn the situation around.

"'We are the Baal,' Darius explained. 'I created you, so I am on a higher level. I have deeper powers. We are immortal demons placed on this earth as outcasts from salvation.'

"Once Darius finished lecturing me on my do's and don'ts, he rose from his chair. He reached out his hand to help me up from the sofa, and said, 'Now it is time. I have told you what to do. Now you must go.'

"I couldn't understand what I was hearing 'Go?' I asked.

"'Yes, you must go…you need to leave this house, and create one of your own.'

"I was not ready to go out alone in this new state! I was like a child! 'Wait,' I said, insistently. But he ignored me, and made his was to the door. 'You must go, and you must go now!' he said, more firmly, his eyes turning yellow.

"The one who created me, who gave me this life, was now throwing me out and away like some discard, to fend for myself after only a brief tutorial session. The look in his eyes told me that I best not protest any more. His look was very stern and angry. I slowly began to make my way to the door, not breaking my stare into his eyes, giving him my most frightened, sad look, with the hopes that he would have some care in his soul and let me stay.

"But he did not.

"I got closer and closer to the door, and drew out the walk and much as I could. The night was cold and nasty, but there was no rain like I heard before. I gave one more glance in his direction, and stepped onto the porch before me. I turned around, saw him against the warm glow of the light coming from the front door, my eyes pleading one last time to stay, but he spoke before I could.

"'This is how it is meant to be,' he said and quickly shut the door."

~~*

Antoine stopped for a moment, let out a long sigh, and draped his arm over the side of the sofa. Gazing out the window, he saw flashes of lightning through the trees against a rainy, dreary night that was the rule. The sun no longer shined.

"I am a demon, Sheldon, through and through. I am straight from hell, and I am going to hell when I am destroyed. I am more than an immortal. I don't even exist in the same dimension that you do. I drink blood but I don't have to. I do it because I am forced to by the Greater

Powers. The most powerful demon is seeking me. And it's just a matter of time before he finds me."

"The most powerful demon?" Sheldon asked.

"Asmodai…" Antoine said, and shuddered.

"What does he want with you?"

"To collect payment."

So it has written, so it shall be. No turning back. Never, not ever.

CHAPTER EIGHTEEN

A sleek, voluptuous black Mercedes barrelled down the highway towards Anastasia Avenue. Hernan Perez was on his way home.

He had decided that he wanted to get home before the sun set, which was quite a rare thing for him. Today was not like any other day. He wanted to get home early and relax before heading back to the airport to fly back down to Caracas. He didn't know why he felt so tired, but being as busy as it was at the Venezuelan Bank and given the stress, he decided that some time home between trips is just what he needed.

And a stiff drink.

When he pulled through the gates and into the driveway at First Street, the garage door lifted and he saw that his son's BMW was not there. He let out an exasperated sigh, knowing the fact that he had a son that he could hardly control. He knew what Roberto was doing when he was out so late at night. Roberto even had the audacity sometimes to bring some of his tricks home, and that irked him to no end. When Roberto would have some respect for the house and the roof that he provided, maybe then would Hernan start to ease up on the beatings.

Many times, it saddened him to see his only son fall into a world of sex and drugs. He wanted to help him, but when the heat of the moment came, Hernan could not control his anger would become too confrontational. Roberto had a similar temper, and more often than not, Hernan would hit Roberto - calling him a faggot and a sissy who would not strike back.

Hernan parked the car and entered the house through the back kitchen door, rolling his eyes at a pop tarts wrapper and dirty glass that Roberto left on the counter for him as a welcome home present. He set his briefcase and jacket on the table, and proceeded to the sitting room to make himself a scotch and soda. He plopped down on the recliner, and flipped on the news.

Three scotch and sodas later, daylight now gone, Hernan awoke with a snort. He set his glass down on the table next to the recliner, then picked it back up, finished the remaining leftovers of melted ice and scotch remnants, and set it back on the table. He started wondering where Roberto could be. He let out an exasperated sigh. Up to that point, he had always respected Roberto's room. But for some reason, this day, he decided to go through it once and for all.

Maybe what he would find would give him some sort of clue as to why Roberto was always so disrespectful. Maybe it would give a clue as to why Roberto sank into his world of drugs and sex.

Hernan padded down the hallway, a fresh fourth scotch and soda in his hand, and proceeded to Roberto's door, which he found closed and locked. He heard something coming from the room- what sounded like some creaking noises, but he couldn't make out what it was. He leaned in towards the door, and held his breath. It sounded like the creaking stopped. As he stood next to the door in silence, the only thing that could be heard were the ice cubes knocking in the glass as he took a sip of his drink.

He then retreated from the hallway and went to the kitchen to retrieve the spare key. He hated how Roberto would always lock his door. When he returned to Roberto's door, he quietly unlocked the lock. The creaking had started again, and then it sounded like some sort of a deep, low moan was emanating from the room.

What is that? He thought. The door slowly opened, without a sound.

The covers to Roberto's bed billowed out, with movement underneath, like a giant air balloon. Something was happening under the covers – something was in the bed – something big. There was a rhythmic and methodical fashion to the movement – up and down – back and forth – side to side.

But again he heard a deep moan, like it was coming from a distance.

Father? Father, are you there?

He crept quietly into the room, and reached around the edge of the door frame to turn out the hallway light and stood for a moment in temporary darkness.

A pause in the thunder and rain lent to a blue glow of moonlight that flooded through the drapes and shears as Hernan's eyes gradually adjusted to the pale blue moonlit room.

There it was in the middle of the room, between the windows ; the bed, the same bed with a giant reaching pedestals, standing against the wall in dark contrast over the movement under the covers.

Dad? Dad are you out there? I am under here. Do you remember me, Dad? I am the same one who has always been here. You shot me into this world, and then you were there when I entered it physically. And then you weren't there. You weren't there when I needed you the most. The only one who was there for me was Eva.

Hernan could not move.

He knew, from the past – that Roberto periodically brought home someone, he knew what it looked like – and how the covers were moving so rhythmically it definitely looked questionable to him. But whatever was under the covers was so *big.* At least eight or nine feet tall, yet completely covered by the blankets.

I am under here but I know you won't save me. I know that you wouldn't save me if I were the last sick fuck on earth. Maybe I did things that earned me the sick fuck status – in fact, I think I have a ribbon somewhere in here that says "Sick Fuck #1" – but I guess now isn't the time to go looking for it, is it? Because you want to know what's going on beneath the covers…don't you?

All Hernan could do was listen to an occasional faint cry. And then Hernan saw the source of the strange noises.

Something was transforming. What was under the covers grew high and wide, like wings were opening and spreading. The cover ripped to shreds which fell to the floor, bit by bit, as the giant, spiny wings spread and spanned the entire room, opening and fleshing out, reaching towards the far walls.

Hernan took another sip of his drink. He nearly choked on the scotch when he saw what seemed to be a huge lizard, a giant head rising to the ceiling, taught with green muscles and scales tearing through its brown skin, a slithery tongue darted in an out of its pursed lips.

The monster muscular arms engorged as the demon revealed itself; the remaining small pieces of torn blanket dropped to the floor like leaves. Growing to maximum, the monster almost reached the ceiling, and turned and looked directly at Hernan with icy yellow eyes, a grin on its face, its tongue reaching out like a slithering snake.

Hernan dropped his drink to the floor. The glass shattered in pieces, and the remains of the scotch and soda spilled all over the wall and the floorboards, mixed with ice. He dared not move.

A giant winged monster was on Roberto's bed thrashing and crashing against the wall, showering plaster on the floor.

CHAPTER NINETEEN

Paula sat against the wall in the dark room. The wall felt cool…and real. It was the only thing that seemed real in this strange world. Illuminated only by the intermittent strikes of lightning, the flashes through the windows let her see the contents of the room - the bed, the stereo, now all covered in dust and unkempt and seemingly untouched for years. She placed her head in between her knees, closed her eyes and wished she wasn't there. And she wished that whatever was out in the hallway waiting for her, leaving her trapped in the house, was not there either.

But she knew something was out there…waiting for her.

Paula wasn't necessarily scared, but rather confused. Of course, when she first heard the noise in the foyer, the crash of the vase on the floor - dead flowers everywhere - she instinctively jumped. It was the normal human thing to do when surprised of a sound of that magnitude against a silent palette. And of course, when she saw the figure in the mirror – her first instinct had been to run.

But her feelings have changed somewhat now since some time had passed.

Paula was frustrated, because she was mad at herself for being trapped in this house with god-knows-what. And two, she was confused, she didn't understand who or what was outside the door, apparently standing guard, forcing her to stay inside this room.

The rainstorm appeared to be moving away, and it gradually got quieter. Paula continued to rest her head on her knees, as her state of consciousness drifted to the just-before-sleep stage - where one would be aware of sounds and happenings around them, but in a state of drifting off. And then her mind began to fill with thoughts of Antoine, and how they met.

~~*

She remembered the first time she looked up and saw Antoine's face. He was so tall, so beautiful, and like that of an angel. Paula was lying on the floor of the Cathedral of the Gardens, tears streaming down her face. She was huddled in the center of the pews, lying on the floor hugging her knees up towards her chest.

Her clothes were tattered and torn, she had a bleeding scrape on her face just below her left eye on her cheekbone, and there were bruises and black oil marks on her legs.

The physical pain she did not feel, but only the shredding of her emotional fabric, brought the tears – that flowed, cutting lines through the dirt on her face, creating small roadmap of despair on a face filled with regret and torment.

It was the lowest point of her life.

Through the night, she was inside the church, lying on the floor, crying, wondering why her child was killed, why it had to be her that would suffer with so much pain, so much earthly torture. But that was when she was feeling selfish. Her pain came in waves and pieced together like a tapestry…each type of pain she was feeling.

Whether it be for her child or for herself, each moment formed a piece of the tapestry, the dark tapestry of pain, that she was weaving so well that night.

It was earlier that night that Paula wanted to take her life, but she wound up taking her child's life instead. The baby, not yet two years old, was strapped in a car seat in the back of her small blue sedan. What Paula did not notice when she was strapping the child in was that she did not latch the belt over the car carrier, and she did not notice that because she had been drinking heavily. At the time she was doing this, Paula thought that nothing was out of the ordinary. In her mind, she was strapping the baby inside the seat, and she believed that she was on her way to her parents house to spend the night there, after ending things with Dominick.

Dominick, the baby's father but not Paula's husband, lived with her for a short time after the baby was born. He was a short, muscular Italian man with olive skin, a deep black goatee on his face, and a gold cross pendant hanging around his neck nestled in a chest full of dark hair; he always wore a tight white tank top shirt, which he wore almost always around the house with a pair of faded jeans.

Dominick was a mellow man; he was not violent towards Paula or the baby. He just simply did not pay them much attention. He was not employed most of the short time that he lived with Paula.

They stayed at her small, flat apartment in a building that looked like it had been converted from an old roadside motel near Calle Ocho. It was very small, very cramped and crowded. There was one bedroom in the back of the living room, with a double bed in the centre of the wall that she and Dominick shared - the same bed where the baby was conceived.

It was earlier that night, in that very bedroom that Dominick told her. They lay in the bed together, entangled in the sheets. Paula reached for a cigarette, and she could tell by the look in Dominick's eyes that he was about to drop a bomb.

"I don't love you, Paula, you know that," he said. "I can't stay with someone that I don't love."

Oh, the irony of it all. Of the whole situation. Just minutes after the torrid lovemaking had brought them both to bliss, Dominick so nonchalantly decides that he doesn't feel like their relationship is working for him.

Paula just stared blankly at the ceiling. "I know."

She knew this was coming.

Even though the two of them certainly were sexually compatible, she did not feel the love and compassion that she so much wanted and needed. As long as she had been with Dominick, and even more so after she carried and bore his child, she hoped, and clung to the thought that perhaps he would come around, perhaps he would become affectionate and love her the way that she desired to be loved.

"I don't understand this," she said softly, as her tears started to come. "I need you. I need you in my life…your baby needs you!"

"I stayed with you because I got you pregnant," he continued. "But I told you that I wasn't going to marry you. I'm not going to marry someone that I don't love."

Paula leaned against the wall, placing her hand in her hands, covered by her mussed blonde hair, and quietly wept.

Gradually, as they were lying there, as she finished her cigarette, stamped it out in the ashtray on the bedside table and flicked the light on so hard that the chain spun around the base of the light bulb. She sat up quickly, letting her pointy breasts hang free as the covers fell from her chest, and quietly wiped the tears from her eyes. She swung her legs to the floor and winced at the chilly tile against her toes.

She got up from the bed, and walked out into the small kitchen - which looked dingy and dirty with an antique looking gas stove, harsh florescent lights overhead, illuminating a small black and white checkerboard linoleum floor. Last night's dinner dishes – leftover spaghetti - were still in the sink caked with dried red sauce and strewn across the counter.

She got a small brown, slightly rusted teapot, filled it with water and placed it on the stove. She lit up another cigarette, and walked back to the bedroom.

"Then leave," she said. She glared over at Dominick and looked at him directly in his eyes. "Get out of my apartment, and do it now."

Dominick looked over at her, his eyes widened a little in surprise. He was not expecting that kind of answer from Paula. She was not that type of girl. She did not get forceful like this.

When they met at a small lounge in Kendall, it was Dominick, not Paula, who approached the other and spoke first. It was always Dominick who initiated sex. Generally, Paula would just "go along with" whatever the general consensus was, and take it. Even if she was not happy with the situation.

"Get out!" she said louder and more forcefully. She left the room. Dominick lifted the pendant on his neck and gave it a quick kiss.

He did not resist.

He pulled the covers away and rose from the bed. He bent over and pulled on bright white underwear, and then fished for his jeans. The pendant he wore, nestled in a forest of hair in the middle of his chest, caught the light and glinted in Paula's eye as he bent over. He put a small white tank top in a black leather gym bag that had been lying on the floor next to the bed, and walked over to the closet. He stopped for a moment, let out a short breath, and stood there for a moment.

There was little of his in that closet; most of his possessions were at his own apartment in Miami Beach, but there were a few collared shirts and ties, two pairs of jeans, some shirts and some underwear and socks, which Dominick had kept at Paula's apartment for those mornings after nights he spent with Paula - where Dominick would have to get ready for work or travel back home from Paula's place the next morning.

Dominick hastily stuffed the clothes into his gym bag, closed the zipper, and walked past Paula without even glancing into her eye for a moment. He charged through the small, newspaper-littered living room to a front door with a diamond shaped window three-quarters of the way up. With tears streaming down her cheeks, Paula followed.

Once he reached the door, Dominick turned the handle and finally looked back at her.

She returned the glance, her vision muddled by fresh tears, and almost thought she saw a hint of love and caring in his eyes; she thought she saw a tear, but perhaps that's really only what her mind wanted her to see. Someone who cared certainly would not be doing this, would not walk out so quickly on her and his child, but all he could say was, "You'll do just fine." And then he opened the door and left, not saying another word to her, and not glancing again in her direction.

After the door slammed she stood there, planted in the same spot on the floor as if she had grown roots, and cried softly. She leaned her head against the door frame and closed her eyes. Never before had she felt so alone.

So helpless. Deep down, she had wanted the love from Dominick, but he was not there to give it to her. All he gave her was his child. She turned her head in the direction of the sleeping baby's room – wondering how she was going to manage raising a child when she was all alone; her desperation in wondering how she would take care of it, in a cold, cruel and unforgiving world.

She held the wave of emotions back long enough; but the overflow of pain started to take over, and she dropped towards the wall with her back against the door, her arm slumped over her head, and cried hard, dropping to the floor. She let it all out.

Seconds later, the baby joined her.

And then the teapot screamed for attention, creating a chorus of wails heard through Paula's apartment after Dominick's exit.

CHAPTER TWENTY

Roberto fell asleep in Antoine's arms; the bed cover was damp with his tears.

But Antoine remained awake. He was feeling his hunger again. He loved being with Roberto, but he had to go out and kill. He felt the aching need to do it.

Being careful not to wake him, Antoine eased himself out from underneath Roberto's warm body, and slipped out from under the covers. He arose and stood in the center of room.

Slowly and quietly he dressed. Before he left, he tiptoed over to a small desk against the opposite wall, and found a small piece of paper and pen. He scribbled a note and dropped it on the covers so it could be read as soon as Roberto woke.

Antoine stood above the bed for a moment, looking at his sleeping creation. He was so beautiful, sleeping there in his mortal sleep. Roberto changed positions, and his right arm moved up and over his head.

Antoine gazed at his face one last time - the neat, shaved hair, the chiseled features, a thin goatee.

Eternal youth…you will always be young, my friend.

He gazed for a bit longer at Roberto, at the silently sleeping man in front of him, who he took from torment just a short while ago. He then fished the note out from under the covers, and he flattened out the wrinkles, and laid it on Roberto's chest.

~~*

Antoine glided as he moved and seemingly did not have footsteps – he made no sounds, and later, after silently closing the front door, he emerged in the very early morning – the hours when darkness still hugs the land and the night is at its strongest. He wiped some blood off of his chin that had dripped onto his clothing. Drawing a white handkerchief from his coat pocket, his wiped it but the red smudge still remained. His white shirt was now stained pink, so he buttoned up his coat to cover the stain.

Silently slipping out into the Miami night, the door to the Perez house closed behind him softly; Antoine glided down the front steps, down the path next to the artfully manicured bushes and a well-tended full, green lawn; his coattails trailed behind him. Through the iron gates, past the bench where Paula would eventually sit, and down the street to his parked Mercedes.

He got in, slammed the door, started the car and gunned the engine, and sped down the street down Anastasia Avenue.

He did not have much time. It was now past 5am.

He had to get back to the beach and retire. Not that Antoine was a mythical immortal who couldn't move about by day. But he liked to keep a pace and schedule to his life.

As the car sped back to South Beach, to the condominium on Ocean Drive, Antoine began to think about Roberto.

What a specimen, he thought. *He will be my creation.*

Antoine could not get the image of Roberto out of his mind. He did not know why the young man had made such an impression on him, but he did nonetheless.

Roberto was his.

It saddened him to know what Roberto went through on a daily basis. The head of the Perez household – Hernan - was a very violent, demanding man. He worked at the International Bank of Venezuela, located in the Brickell section of town. Roughly twenty minutes from Coral Gables, his autocratic attitude earned him top honors at work, which came along with top pay. It afforded the luxurious surroundings in Coral Gables but the attitude carried over into the home life. He traveled extensively, so that lent some relief to Roberto.

Eva Perez was a much different woman than her husband.

She was very loving towards her son Roberto, sometimes to the point of being overprotective. Roberto and Eva loved each other and spent a lot of time together. It sometimes created a solace from the wrath of Hernan.

Most of the time, at first, Hernan ignored Roberto. He knew his son was out "gallivanting" as he would put it, but he didn't do much to stop it. Roberto and his mother seemed happy, and most of the time Hernan was too busy working to care.

Because they were always ignored, Eva and Roberto became closer. From the point Roberto had been a child, Hernan's job became increasingly demanding, and then Eva and Roberto would travel together. They laughed and made dinner together; cried in front of movies together and went out to experience all the nightlife that Miami had to offer. It was Eva who was close by when Roberto began to enter manhood and sprout physically, eventually getting to the point where he was much taller than Eva; since she had him at a young age, they were frequently mistaken for a couple. It was always Eva who attended his wrestling matches and gymnastics competitions. She witnessed his childhood, and then, over time, she was witnessing his transformation into a man.

And perhaps that is why Roberto, in a sense, became the man in Eva's life.

Hernan was simply a figure, someone who provided for the two other family members but did not pay much attention to them. He was frequently either working extended hours or out of the country. He rarely paid attention to Eva or Roberto – when he came home, he would demand his dinner, and wait for it to be prepared while he downed his scotch and sodas while watching the news.

But there also were nights that he came home already drunk and would start questioning Eva about dinner – he would ask why it wasn't ready and waiting on the table – even if he came home from directly from a three martini lunch. Eva would always cower away from his anger, hurry over to the refrigerator, and nervously pull some chicken out to place in the oven. But no matter what she grabbed, it was always the wrong thing.

"I said I wanted a steak tonight you bitch!" And then Hernan would rip the package of chicken out of her hands and slam it on the floor. He then would grab Eva's shoulder and throw her against the counter. As her face typically was slammed against the side of the cabinet, she then usually huddled against the counter and wait for him to go into the sitting room to make his drink.

Most of the time he did. And almost always, after he left, she brought her hand up to her face, and more often than not pulled it away to see fresh bright red blood on her fingertips.

During these episodes, Roberto was typically either away or in his room. If he was in his room, he usually heard the crash across the house – which announced Hernan's arrival. On more than one occasion, he had tiptoed across the house, past a snoring Hernan in front of the tv, and into the kitchen where his mother was usually hurriedly preparing a meal, sniffling and blotting her forehead with a tissue. And on every occasion he saw her making dinner in that state, he would usher her over to the table, clean her wounds lovingly, and finish preparing dinner himself.

That's the way it usually went when Hernan came home from work already drunk.

Shortly after that period, Eva was diagnosed with terminal, late stage cancer. She quickly became very sick – she lost weight rapidly as she started to waste away; the cancer was eating her alive very quickly. During this time, Hernan became increasingly violent, taking out a lot of his anger on Roberto.

Perhaps he was upset about his ailing wife, and did not know of any other way to express his anger. Or perhaps he was upset with Roberto, who started a downward spiral of drugs and sex, leaving home – sometimes for days at a time with not so much as a phone call.

Several times Roberto would leave the house with a black eye, or bruises on his arms, and when his professors and friends would ask him what happened, he would just say that it happened during a wrestling match, sometimes he said it was during practice, or sometimes he said that he fell off the rings during a gymnastics meet. He started to get a reputation of being a horrible athlete, although it was quite the contrary.

Sometime later, Eva succumbed to the cancer, and passed away.

Hernan had been grief stricken, and became almost unbearable for Roberto. Roberto's downward spiral took a deeper turn, and that's when he got involved with the homosexual underworld. After Eva's death, he quickly became very promiscuous and started to sell his body for cash and drugs as well.

It got to the point that sometimes Roberto would have two or three different tricks in one night, and generally would never come home - except on rare occasion. He just wanted to stay away from Hernan and his violence.

Even though Roberto had the strength to put Hernan in the hospital, he still had some love and respect for the man and could not injure him in that way, despite the fact that Hernan saw no problem in beating Roberto on a regular basis.

So he did not fight back.

~~*

Antoine's Mercedes sped back north on Dixie Highway, which led onto I-95 northbound, and then up to the exit for MacArthur Causeway which led over to South Beach. And driving, thinking about Roberto, is when he decided he would come to save Roberto - save him from his misery. They could be together, side by side, demonic warriors; partners in the life that Antoine had come to know and make the best of so far.

Roberto had dealt with so much pain and suffering growing up in the Perez household; Antoine could tell that just from looking at his eyes when they were together. Given his twisted childhood, and the strange childhood that Antoine had when he was mortal, he saw a connection between himself and the young man, and thought that he would be a good partner to have.

When Roberto had been crying on Antoine's arms, Antoine felt like he needed to take away the boy's pain, to envelop him in the embrace he has come to give others in pain.

Roberto. Let me take away your pain. Let me be your guiding light. I will lead you through these treacherous waters, just take my hand and follow me.

That's right, you're gonna be my creation. My demon in the making.

I know that my visit exhausted you and you will sleep and sleep and sleep…but when you rise, the obsession will start.

And it will grow.

Your obsession will overtake you; it will gnaw at your every emotion, your every sense. Everything will be heightened, every sense, every passion. And all that you will want to do will be to find me.

But, my young accomplice, I will not be so easily found. Somehow, you will feel drawn to me, but I will be through miles of torment, of dark emotion, of wrath…that you will have to face and sift through before you see my face again.

And then, my demon, it might be too late.

You might not make it through. You might not be able to face your fears, your greatest sins – all of your hatred - in one giant netherworld of pain.

Welcome, my demon.

And when I enveloped you with my coldness you will transform into what you have always wanted to be.

I know that and you told me that. It's just a matter of time before you begin your transformation. You will see.

Wake up a mortal once again tomorrow. Follow the obsession. For when you find me, you will be Nesmaron.

Welcome my demon, and enjoy the ride into Tartarus.

CHAPTER TWENTY-ONE

Paula turned off the wailing teapot on the stove, but did not make a cup of tea. She settled the baby back down, then retreated back into the kitchen, and got a bottle of vodka out of the cabinet next to the refrigerator. She got a tall highball glass, a carton of orange juice, and padded into the living room and proceeded to make a very stiff screwdriver.

Taking the first sip and sighing as the alcohol warmed her insides, she lit another cigarette.

The power of alcohol.

Taking over one's mind, putting a veil over the eyes, shielding one from the horrors of the world. The form of escape so many have come to seek out, whether it be at home alone sitting on the couch, in front of the computer, or out at the bars, the shroud of alcohol takes one away from the harsh reality of life.

And that's exactly what Paula was doing, as she poured screwdriver after screwdriver, until she ran out of orange juice and got to the point of drunkenness that she did not hear the baby start to cry in the other room. She started pouring glasses of straight vodka and drinking them down, reaching a state of inebriation where she had no idea that the baby even needed attention.

She was getting herself deeper and deeper inside the portal of alcohol induced state of existence, in the fuzziness of the clouds, swimming in the clear marmalade, up towards the pastel stars of light that shone down towards her arms; where she pushed through the thick marmalade, swimming away from all the pain she felt.

But the power of alcohol is short-lived. She opened her eyes. The numbness, the feeling of warmth and comfort only lasts but a short time, and then reality comes back and sets in as one comes down. Paula sat back on the couch, her eyes glazed over. She stared blankly at the half-full bottle of vodka, sitting next to her glass on the coffee table. A cigarette burned in the ashtray, atop a slew of magazines, old candy wrappers, several remote controls and an empty condom wrapper. Then the glass seemed to be the only thing that existed to Paula. It stood out in front of her, above all else on the coffee table, it was the only thing that seemed to exist other than her in the room.

Then her eyes drifted slowly to the left, where she saw the bottle of vodka, and it hit her how much she had drank, in such a short time. She could not believe it. And she sat there and sobbed, a drunken sob, but there was no one there to comfort her, no shoulder for her to cry on.

Blinded by tears, she searched for the phone. Digging through clothes and newspapers on the couch, she finally found the cordless in between two of the cushions along with a copy of an entertainment magazine, and began to automatically dial the digits of her mother in Stuart.

Her mother picked up after two rings, and she heard the familiar, comforting voice.

"Mom…." she began, and that's all she could get out before she started crying again.

"Oh, dear, Paula, what's wrong?" her mom asked, automatically with a hint of concern in her voice.

Paula was so drunk and upset that she could hardly get the words out. "Dominick….." was all she said.

"What?" Her mother asked, urgently, "What has happened to Dominick? Paula, are you drunk? What happened?"

The line went dead, sending Paula's mother into a panic, she was calling out Paula's name, over and over, frantically wondering what happened to the line, but little did she know that Paula was lying there, on the couch, passed out from all the vodka she had drank.

CHAPTER TWENTY-TWO

The monstrous demon snapped his head in Hernan's direction.

The drink that shattered on the floor did not cause the activity to cease. The demon resumed sucking crimson red from Roberto's neck. The young man looked over at his father with glassy eyes as the demon took him further and the intensity increased yet again.

"What is this?!?" Hernan screamed. "What is this in my house?" He stormed into the room, and as Hernan moved the demon looked over and glared at him with a start, eyes bearing down on Hernan with an icy stare. The monster assaulted Roberto with such forcefulness and intensity that the headboard continued its own assault on the crumbling wall.

Hernan stopped in his tracks, motionless and speechless. Roberto stared lovingly at his father.

The monster held his stare with Hernan, holding him still, pinning him against the wall. The demon then grew larger and taller - to an immense size – spreading its wings, writhing and screaming.

Hernan was powerless to stop them and all he could do was stare. He barely registered the moment as he turned and fled.

Roberto developed a thin film of sweat as the demon screamed and the wings spread once again, and swelled in size, causing a river of blood to flow down the bed sheets. The demon held his icy stare, and Roberto did not snap out of his dreamy, lustful gaze. It was then that demon growled deep and chesty - very loud and grating - so loud that it hurt Hernan's ears and shook the walls.

And Roberto continued staring ahead, yet seeing nothing, as Antoine's breathing subsided. He transformed back to his immortal form, the monster gone back to Tartarus, the deed now done.

Regulating his breathing, Antoine rose and bent over Roberto who was now out of his trance.

"I told you that I would come to you," Antoine said. "But you came to me."

"Um hum," Roberto said.

"This will seal our pact. We are partners now. You will protect me, and I will protect you. Together, there will be nothing – and no one - that we cannot conquer."

~~*

Earlier that day, Roberto had been speeding north on US1 towards 95 north. He was headed to one place and one place only: South Beach. He knew that was where Antoine lived, and that was where he would look for him. He knew that, on the first night that Antoine had come to him, Antoine had said to wait to meet him until later that evening, but he could not wait to see the beautiful specimen who was so comforting once again.

The obsession had begun.

As he got on the freeway, heading north, he decided that he could stop at the market to buy some roses for Antoine.

He turned east onto the MacArthur Causeway, past the towering ocean liners, waiting to be filled with passengers and head out to the wide open sea, past the parrot jungles, Star Island, and then the fabulous towers of apartments and condos as he bore left to Alton Road.

After stopping at the market, the roses set on the passenger seat, he decided to park the little BMW at Flamingo Park. He wouldn't have to worry about feeding a parking meter there, and he could leave the car by the park and walk through the residential zones (where he couldn't park without a sticker) towards Washington Avenue, where *Sacrafice* was located, near 15th.

Antoine had mentioned *Sacrafice* briefly when they were together the night before, saying that it was a new club that was opening on Washington Avenue and that it would be unlike any other club that South Beach has seen.

Roberto didn't really know where to find Antoine, as Antoine had told Roberto to come to him, but Roberto figured that he might be able to ask someone he might run into at *Sacrafice.* Even though the club was not yet open, chances are there would be people around in the district near the club that might know about Antoine or his whereabouts.

Roberto walked briskly down 12th street, heading East towards Washington Avenue, with the red roses in his right hand.

The morning was hot, bright and sunny, and the trees of 12th street hung down, the branches reaching low down towards the hot pavement, like long fingers looking to scoop up an unsuspecting visitor.

Roberto began to sweat as he walked in the Florida humidity, and Washington Avenue seemed too far away, even though physically it was only three blocks. He passed the scores of parked cars that lined the streets, the art deco style, quaint little apartment buildings that looked to be out of a comic strip, towards the neon and glitz of Washington, now blandly white during the day in the bright sunlight.

All the buildings looked as if they were run-down and old, windows so blurred with age they looked like they were covered with wax paper; now not shielded by the darkness of night, Roberto could see that the buildings were old and dirty and dusty.

Still, colourful lines bordered the buildings, which, upon getting closer, Roberto recognized as the neon which had been turned off in the bright sunlight.

Roberto looked down as he was crossing Euclid and wiped the sweat from his brow that had gathered during his walk. The temperature was soaring, and he hoped that wherever he was going had air conditioning.

Roberto turned north on Washington and got a glimpse of *Sacrafice* from a distance, and then could see what Antoine was saying.

The architecture made the building stick out from all the pastel colours, light art deco style buildings of South Beach: it was very dark, and made of masonry stone to look like an old cathedral. Antoine was right, he thought, this is something that South Beach has never seen the likes of before.

As Roberto got closer to the club, he read a sign that said:

SACRAFICE

Prepare Yourself.

Coming Soon.

The sign stood out on Washington Avenue like stood against the backdrop like something of a different age; as if it didn't belong on this street full of kids and young adults who were incessantly wandering in and out of the doors of the petty merchants on the streets, bidding their doings well into the night.

The sign was just as oddly medieval as the club's building – which at a casual first glance one might mistake it for a church or towering cathedral. The structure looked strangely out of place for a place so trendy as South Beach; the dark stone, contrasting against the pale pastels and the light whites, still dark and ominous looking in the bright Florida sun.

Roberto swung the roses in his right arm, quietly humming "Fur Elise" to himself as he trotted down Washington, a song that he had played back in grade school in the concert band that for some reason popped into his head at that particular moment. And, as he skipped down the sidewalk, dodging passer-by, waiters serving cocktails at the outdoor cafes and young couples walking hand in hand, he approached what looked like a castle, a structure looming over the avenue like a giant, towering dark cathedral.

He looked up at the behemoth building, shaking his head at the size and monstrosity of it, decided to himself that Antoine had to be there. He could feel it, he could sense his dark lover of the night was somewhere within.

There was a sign near the entryway foyer, which read:

OPENING SOON.

Roberto ascended up the steps leading to the grand door, and placed his right foot on the first step, about to go up, when a voice stopped him:

"Where are you going, young sir?"

It was a man, with long hair, brown and straight, just past his shoulders, a white collared shirt on and a dark, black trench coat. Roberto thought the man looked to be Italian, but he seemed pale.

"Uh…" Roberto stammered, "I was going to find a friend of mine who lives in this area."

"I see…" the man said, carefully taking several steps closer to Roberto.

Roberto braced himself slightly, because he did not know the man nor did he know what this man's intentions were, and he took a step back, rising himself onto a higher level of the stairs. "I was just stopping by to say hello to him."

"And he lives here?" the man questioned, raising his eyebrows as he did so. "He lives at the site of this club?"

"I…I don't know." Roberto said. "I just had a feeling that he would be here."

"And why is that young sir?" The man took a few more steps towards Roberto, and, noticing that, Roberto darted his eyes around nervously, trying to find a way out of the situation.

The man seemed irritated, his face wrinkled up in a scowl. "Why did you think that your friend would be at this location? Do you know what kind of club this will be?"

Roberto looked down at his feet for a moment. "No, I don't."

"I see." The man said. "Well then, you do not know much about your friend. Antoine is what we call…a night owl." The man chuckled to himself slightly as he said this. The boy had no idea, apparently, what type of creature Antoine was. How the young man found Antoine so quickly, he did not know. Perhaps the two were drawn to each other by some outside force.

"Would you like me to take you to Antoine?" The man asked, extending his right hand to Roberto, as if to guide him down the steps and to the unknown like leading a child.

Roberto paused and thought for a moment. He looked down at the roses he had bought for his newfound friend, and decided to go with this man. He had to see Antoine again. He descended the steps towards the mysterious figure.

And then, the man took Roberto one more block down Washington, along the side of the gothic exterior, around the corner to 15th street, leading him to a door and a set of steps that ate their way down into the earth through the sidewalk.

It was only then that when the man was opening the heavy wooden door that Roberto noticed the small, smoked glass window leading into a black abyss. Roberto hesitated for a moment - realizing in a moment of clarity that he was going into the unknown with a total stranger, and that somehow this mysterious man knew he was looking for Antoine, without having to be told so.

CHAPTER TWENTY-THREE

The Astral's offices on Ponce de Leon were getting ready to close for the evening.

The sun had just gone down; the shoppers were straggling away from the Miracle Mile – just a handful of determined bargain hunters still remained. Many of the shops were closing their doors for the evening – one by one, the lights went out, and the grating sound of the silver chain gates pierced the quiet serenity of a street preparing for a nights slumber. Closed signs swung in front of doors, from shop to shop, and The Astral was no different. Anthony Peterson tiredly walked from his small, cramped office through the waiting room. He closed the blinds from the expansive windows overlooking the leather furniture, and straightened a pile of magazines on the coffee table. Making his way to the door, he drew the blind on the door and flipped the sign to say

CLOSED.

The Victorian style street lights were glowing a familiar reddish orange, lending a warm feel to the tropical street. Many benches were scattered over the brick and cobblestone sidewalks lined with tropical flowers – birds of paradise, orchids and ginger created a stunning colorful palette. The royal palms that rose out of the gardens cast long, thin shadows in the fading sunlight along the streets of Ponce De Leon.

Anthony snapped off half of the bright, overhead florescent lights, so any passer by outside would see that the business had closed for the evening. He straightened some magazines on the white laminate coffee table in the center of the stark, black and white linoleum tiled room behind the main lobby, and he went to the break room to make himself a cup of coffee.

It was going to be a long night.

He raised his hand to his neck, and touched the bandage. He had been with Antoine just several days ago, and his neck was still oozing bright red blood from time to time.

It was strange.

As he had been sitting in Antoine's living room, sipping a perfectly made vodka martini, Antoine had emerged from the basement.

"Sorry to keep you waiting," Antoine said as he had walked back into the living room, dusting himself off. Anthony had just taken a sip of the martini. Treasuring the warmth of the alcohol coursing down his throat, he closed his eyes for a brief moment.

And when he opened them again, Antoine's face was right in front of his.

Startled, Anthony started a fit of coughing, and Antoine reached around to pat him on his back. When he recovered and regained his composure, he spoke: "Antoine, I must ask you. You have that door in the kitchen. It leads to the basement, correct?"

"Yes," he responded, standing again, gliding over to the sofa. He sat down and crossed his legs, arms spread out on the back of the sofa.

His senses dulled by the alcohol, Anthony had to pause and think for a moment to gather his thoughts. He wasn't really sure where he was going with this line of questioning.

"What would like you to know, Anthony?" Antoine asked, this time leaning forward with his elbows on his knees, showing interest in what Anthony was asking about.

"Okay," he said, rising to his feet, slapping his thighs. "I am just going to come right out with it." He walked closer to where Antoine was sitting, across the room, and Antoine's eyes followed his every move. "What *are* you? I know that you're not a vampire…but…" He paused for a moment, as if searching for words.

"I am not a vampire," Antoine offered. "But I do have many similarities to them. I am associated with their kind. I do many things that vampires do. And I am immortal. Just like them, I am also damned from everything decent and good for eternity."

Some all too familiar thunder rumbled in the distance. The rain continued each night in Coral Gables, as it had night after night.

"Antoine, then what are you?"

Antoine stood. He walked over to the window, and gazed out into the rainy night. He stared through the window as he had so many nights before, and let out a deep, all too human feeling sigh.

CHAPTER TWENTY-FOUR

Paula gradually opened her eyes, and heard the annoying *beep! beep!* in her ear - the annoying noise that lets one know that the phone was left off the hook. What time was it? She did not know. Still in a stupor, she lazily looked around the room, wanting to know what time it was, but she could not see a clock. Her eyes felt heavy and puffy. And her head pounded. All she could think of was her mother. She had to get to her mother, and she would make everything okay.

She struggled to stand, and after one time of staggering back into the couch, she made it. She was still drunk, but since the short sleep, she felt she had her senses with her. She slowly made her way down the hall to her baby's room, rubbing her eyes. The baby was not awake, not making a sound, but it was evident she had been crying earlier as her cheeks had the puffy, slightly pinkish look of distress - the type when a baby cries and cries for long periods of time with no attention. But of course, Paula hadn't heard a thing.

Paula bent over, and staggered again. She braced herself on the side of the crib. She reached down and placed her hands gently around the baby, making to pick her up. She raised the baby to her chest, cradling the small child in her arms like a true mother only could.

Tears welled up in her eyes. She came to realize the fact that, even though her mother was supportive and always there, the only person she really had in her life was the baby. She held the child, cradled it in her arms, and suddenly decided to leave.

She had to see her mother.

She had to see someone in her life that she could speak with and relate to on an adult level. She put the baby back in the crib and pulled on an old, raggedy pair of faded jeans and a t-shirt. That's all she needed. Besides, given her current condition, she could care less about what she looked like or who she attracted.

Paula still stumbled around the house, lazily returning to the baby's room where the little girl had returned to a slumber. This time, while the baby was roused, the child began to cry, softly at first but then louder and louder as the small child was tossed around and jostled as if it were a rag doll, while Paula was packing a few items.

Starting out to the car, Paula stopped by the coffee table and took two swigs of vodka directly from the bottle. Staggering backwards, almost falling, and jolting the baby as well, she turned and headed out towards the car. She slammed the door and forgot to lock it. She swayed once more with a crying baby on her shoulder disappearing into the damp, moist, humid Miami night.

Paula's small car weaved through the lanes of South Dixie Highway, speeding towards Coral Gables. Tears streamed down her face as Sonny and Cher sang "I got you babe" on the radio. Of course that song had to come on. She and Dominick sang that song once at Bonnie's karaoke night.

Paula was still drunk, and was not sobering up no matter how many times she rolled the window down to the rainy night or how low of a temperature she set the air to. How did her life get to this point? Now she was alone, with a child to support by herself, no one to love her and no one to turn to.

The small car swerved dangerously to the side of the road, when Paula decided that was it. She could not go on any further. She cried, diverting her attention from the road.

The pain was too much. There was only one way to heal her pain, and she only saw one option out of her depression.

Turning a sharp left onto Andelusia Avenue, she gunned the engine, sending the small car into a shaking frenzy, as the engine desperately tried to get the car up to speed - the breakneck speed that Paula was coaxing it to go. She turned the car right into an alley so fast that the passenger side of the car lifted off the ground.

Regaining speed she headed closer and closer, closing in on the end facing a dark brick wall, not lifting her foot off the gas pedal even for a moment, the car gained momentum and speed.

She saw the wall looming ahead, growing larger and closer in the windshield, like a saving wall that would heal her pain. Closer and closer it moved, growing larger in the viewing pane of the windshield.

As the car came past the point of no return, she closed her eyes. The tears streamed down her cheeks through her closed eyes. She opened her eyes, and she took her foot off the accelerator and the whine of the engine lowered for just a moment. She tried to pump the brakes.

But it was too late.

All she said right before she hit the wall was "Mother…." through her tears, and she heard Sonny and Cher finishing their duet on the radio.

CRASH!

And the only other sound that could be heard were the desperate cries of her daughter, as she was thrown from the back seat like a football, crashing through the windshield and meeting her death on the brick wall before them.

CHAPTER TWENTY-FIVE

As the sunlight slowly crept across the room, warming and illuminating all that it touched, Roberto had slowly opened his eyes. He had gradually awakened from his sleep. It had only been a short while before that Antoine had been there, but once the sun touched his face, his eyes fluttered open.

He looked down and saw a small, slightly wrinkled piece of paper, and at the same time noticed he was alone. He assumed that the note must have been from his strange suitor. He had been glad to see the note, but at the same time he was disappointed that Antoine was not there in the morning to greet him.

The note from Antoine fell on the floor as he rose; he saw this and silently decided to read the note once he had showered and cleaned up and was more awake and alert.

Roberto, though, could not get thoughts of Antoine out of his head. He felt that it was some sort of destiny, or perhaps fate working, that brought him and Antoine together. He could tell that Antoine was different.

Roberto returned to his room with a blue towel wrapped around his waist. He walked over to his bed and sat down, picked up the note, and read it.

My Dearest Roberto,

I love you. And I want to make you my creation. Together, we will be in unison as one forever. I will come to you tonight,

A

The hand that was holding the note slowly lowered to his lap as he looked up, forward, but not seeing anything in the room. Even with his eyes open, he saw Antoine's face. He smiled to himself, revelling in the thought that Antoine felt the same way about him. It was too good to be true!

What did confuse him was why Antoine kept on addressing him as "his creation". Antoine did not appear like he was much older than twenty, but Roberto figured that he could be older and just gifted with excellent genetics. Nevertheless, Roberto felt great and thought that the two of them would be fantastic together.

Roberto got up from where he was sitting and let the note fall to the floor. He snapped off the towel and began his daily dressing ritual, in a happy and giddy mood like someone who was in love. He wore his typical attire – baggy jeans that hung below his hips, a tight white tank top accentuated by an oversized jersey, and once dressed exited his room and headed towards the kitchen to get some breakfast.

Fortunately, Hernan had left for work hours ago. Once having a small breakfast of two strawberry pop tarts and a large glass of orange juice, he ran out the garage door to his small BMW convertible. He had to find Antoine before tonight, he had to see him; he wanted to surprise his new friend by visiting him and bringing him some roses, to seal their pact of a commitment to one another.

The screech of the tires made a black mark on the pavement with a small puff of rubbery smoke as Roberto's small BMW peeled away.

Yes Antoine, you were right.

I am your demon. I am your demon and I am going to take over the world!

Thank you so much for creating me!

CHAPTER TWENTY-SIX

When Antoine and Roberto had still lay next to one another, after Hernan had run from the doorway where he dropped his drink, but before Roberto slept, they heard a bump from above; or a noise, the creaking of rafters here and there, letting them know that Hernan was still moving about in the house.

Roberto put his arms behind his head and sighed. "I hate him," he said, and closed his eyes as the noises continued in the background.

"Yes," Antoine replied. "I can feel your hatred."

Antoine rose from the bed, and searched for his coat. He looked up at Roberto and paused. "I have a question for you."

"What is that?" Roberto asked, sitting up in the bed expectantly.

"Well," Antoine continued, "Do you want him dead?"

Roberto paused.

He had not considered that before. His mother was already long gone, and it seemed that Hernan always succeeded in making his life miserable. But he had never before considered killing the man. Killing anyone before had never crossed his mind, actually.

"Or, rather, shall I ask, do you think you are capable of killing him?"

Antoine shuffled to the other end of the room and leaned against the doorframe, looking over towards Roberto. "Let me leave you with that," said Antoine, turning towards the door to leave the room.

With that, he quietly crept out of the room, silently as if he were a cat and shut the door behind him.

As Antoine left, Roberto's eyes got heavier. Sleep was creeping up on him. He wanted to fight it, to be awake when Antoine returned from going to the bathroom or wherever he was going, but it was proving to be too much of an effort. Gradually reality faded away, and darkness and dreams quickly overtook his state of being.

~~*

Antoine floated down the hall elegantly and with determination. Traveling further from Roberto's room he passed the bathroom door, and ascending the stairs he saw the door to the master bedroom at the end of the hall, slightly ajar letting some yellowish light into the dark hallway.

When Antoine reached the door, he stopped and listened. He heard the evening news, and Hernan snoring. Carefully opening the door, he entered the room. He saw the bedside lamp burning brightly, and Hernan sprawled across the bed, shirtless and snoring loudly, a giant midsection rising towards the ceiling with every breath like a small, pulsating mountain.

Antoine did not delay.

He immediately glided over to the bed, levitating above the sleeping man, and, looking down at him, saw in the man's face what might have once been an innocent boy. A young man who dated his first love from high school, who once was gentle, loving and caring.

What happened to you, Hernan?

There your son is, downstairs. Sleeping below. He has been waiting for your love for so many years, but you haven't had any love to give. He watched as you took your high school sweetheart down the path to hell…and he tried to save her from it by loving her. But now she is dead. It was too late.

Now she is dead.

So it's just you and him. So will you be able to do it? Will you be able to love your son and treat him like the man he so wants you to? Sure, I was down there, I was taking away his pain, but it was only to give him a gift. It was to give him a gift that you never could, Hernan. It was to give him the gift of love and eternal life.

So do I think that you can change? Do I think that you can love Roberto for who he is and save him from his sins?

No.

And he quietly sunk his teeth in to Hernan's neck.

At that instant, Hernan's eyes sprung open widely and he let out a horrid, deep throated scream. He started choking and coughing up blood. The scream did not do anything to stop Antoine. He drank and drank, as the colour in Hernan's face began to drain rapidly, and his flailing and kicking slowly subsided.

Once Hernan stopped moving altogether and his eyes closed, Antoine sat back up on the bed in a kneeling position and looked down at the pathetic mess sprawled out before him.

"Welcome," he said, with a bloody smile across his face, looking down at the corpse. "Welcome to my world, Hernan."

With those words, Antoine rose, pulled some tissues from the bedside table and cleaned his face, silently closed the door, and quickly returned to Roberto's room.

Roberto was sleeping soundly as if a baby.

He went over to the desk and found a small piece of paper and a pen, wrote a short note, and left it for Roberto to find in the morning. He quietly finished dressing and grabbed his keys, gliding silently down the stairs.

Then, Antoine slipped out undetected in the Miami night air.

CHAPTER TWENTY-SEVEN

The Cathedral of the Gardens was the largest, most beautiful and ornate Catholic place of worship in Coral Gables. Towering over the city like a glistening centerpiece, the cream-colored stucco walls, ivory statuettes of the twelve Apostles, and stained glass windows commanded attention and awe. The Spanish architecture blended with traditional European style construction gathered light from above; like rays from the heavens highlighted this majestic house of the Lord.

Surrounded by lush tropical gardens comprised mostly of purple and white azaleas, it is located near the Venetian Pool and surrounded by weeping willow trees, palms, mango trees and orange bushes. The brilliant green grass framed the stone path leading up to the magnificent entryway, which was lined with more bright and vibrant tropical foliage. All of the gardens were meticulously manicured at all times.

It was truly the church of the wealthy and the wealthiest church; not only did the congregation donate thousands upon thousands of dollars to the coffers but also paid for quite extravagant living quarters for its clergy – despite their vows of poverty they had taken when ordained; but it did not matter.

This was Coral Gables.

It was the "Beverly Hills of Miami", and things "just ran differently here." The church reflected the status of the towns' citizens. Nonetheless, it was still so beautiful with towering stained glass windows, overlooking multiple statues rising from ornate and sculpted gardens it looked to be a work of art.

Antoine Nagevesh strolled quietly down the sidewalk that bordered the Cathedral, and although he did not usually venture inside, he knew he needed to tonight.

It was not often that Antoine would venture into the house of God. He rarely did during his mortal life, and now it was even a more rare occasion. He knew, though, that he was being called. He was being called to come. And when he was being called, he did not listen to the orders from God to stay out of his territory. But then, he sometimes wondered who the orders were actually coming from.

Turning up the path, he ascended the stairs, passing giant mortar columns and marble flooring, into the grand entryway, past the rounded doors of mahogany, into the foyer and through a second set of stained glass doors. The worshipping area was lined with giant pews, marble floors, with the Stations of the Cross carved in stone bordering the top of the walls, against the ceiling.

And looking down the aisle, he saw a woman, lying on the floor in front of the steps to the Altar, lying in a heaping mess on the floor. He strode towards the woman, seeing her face buried in her hands, crying quietly and sniffling.

"Why do you weep, dear Paula?" he asked softly.

She did not answer. He knelt down next to her, placed his hand on her head.

"That is okay. You do not have to answer. I know why you cry so much."

"I did not realize what I was doing…" She turned her head towards Antoine, and from her viewpoint, looking up on him, she saw the light behind him, making him glow – to her he truly looked like a saving angel.

"I killed my child," she said, beginning to sob again, burying her face in her arms. "*I killed my child!*"

Antoine bent down, and gently picked her up in his strong arms. He drew her close to his body, and placed her head on his chest, wrapping his arms around her small, shivering body. He then ran his fingers through her hair, comforting her and placing a kiss on her forehead.

"You did not know," he said. "You were influenced by a force greater than you will know. This was willed to happen."

He placed her on the floor, on her back, and she gazed up at his seductive eyes. He took her hand and led her out from the Cathedral.

"Let me be with you, Paula. I will take away your pain."

He brought her into a clearing of bushes, and he started to unbutton his shirt, one by one, slowly, as he spoke to Paula: "You have dealt with this pain all of your life. Only you can let me in. You need me to take it away from you and show you the pleasures that you need right now."

He let his shirt fall off of his shoulders, and the shirt dropped to the ground; Paula's eyes followed the shirt as it floated slowly downwards.

And then she looked into his eyes.

Antoine held his gaze for a moment, their gaze locked.

"It is only you who can accept this offer of passion, but I will show you passion that you have never seen before, take you to other worlds and realms sending you over the edge of exquisiteness."

As she lay back on the cool grass, she propped herself up on her elbows.

She could not take her eyes off of Antoine. She continued to stare in his eyes, and thought for a moment that his pupils were moving. For a moment, for just a fleeting moment, she felt a creep of doubt. She thought for that moment that maybe Antoine was not a fraud; maybe he was in fact the dark creature that people claimed him to be.

Now he was crouched before her. He was the most beautiful creature that she had ever laid eyes on.

And what about his eyes? It did not matter.

Antoine took control of the situation; laying her out and caressing her breasts, he fluttered his hand along her thigh. He lightly kissed her neck. "Take me, you will not regret it. Let me heal you."

As he kissed her neck, he began to slowly run his free hand under her shirt, caressing the mounds of her breasts, as he discreetly kicked off his boots. For a moment, he stopped and looked her in the eyes.

"Now, it is time, dear one. It is time for your pain to leave you forever."

He got up on his knees, and towered over her.

She looked in his eyes one more time, looking straight up the chest of this dark mysterious creature.

Paula then sat up and took her hands to Antoine's belt. Antoine no longer said a word. He no longer needed to. And that was when Antoine took away her pain.

He lowered himself and began to kiss and undress her, pulling her t shirt over her head, revealing her supple breasts, her soft pale skin, taking his tongue between the cleavage, and trailing it down to her waistline, gently undoing her jeans, as she squirmed with the feeling and joy of being with Antoine.

And when he entered her, she was overtaken. She had never experienced anything like it; no other lover had ever amounted to Antoine.

Antoine's long and livery tongue lapped at the crevice of her chest, his cold saliva burning her skin, mixing with her hot sweat. The faster and more determined he moved; the deeper, the more he physically transformed above her; his skin changing to a scaly green and brown.

Giant wings sprouted above them spanning the length of the clearing, and the couple began to levitate. The monster above her carried her into the sky, and as Antoine looked up from his prey momentarily, he was staring in the face of a statue of Christ.

He stopped for a moment. Paula froze.

The statue stared at him in suspended animation, holding a grip on him. Grimacing and struggling to get free, the two continued to ascend.

Floating away and upwards they gathered speed and Antoine continued as they floated over Andelusia, up and into and through the clouds hovering over the city of Miami.

Her pain was healed.

All the pain that Dominick caused; the pain of the death of her child, her drinking, growing up with an abusive father; all that was washed away as she flew with Antoine above the vibrant, glowing metropolis. It all seemed so beautiful from that height, the glistening lights of the skyscrapers, the beauty of the glistening water, dancing in the moonlight. The lights of the cars, moving about the city streets and highways all off to some unknown destination.

What a way to spend an evening, what a way to enjoy and revel in the love and pleasure that someone like him can bring a woman!

Oh, Antoine!

CHAPTER TWENTY-EIGHT

Roberto stood in total darkness.

The mysterious man disappeared into the enveloping blackness of the small hallway before him. Roberto did not know nor could he fathom what type of building this actually was. This looked like no club he had ever seen before. Although they went in through a side entrance, it felt like the space had changed around him. He didn't feel like the hallway was the same as when he entered. That much he felt deeply. And the whole feeling of the building conveyed a feeling of death.

He fished through his jeans pockets, and found a lighter.

Along the hallway on both sides were doors, doors leading to the unknown, doors leading to places or rooms that Roberto had no idea where they had gone. He struggled in the darkness to see the man, but he could barely make out a shadow. He felt all alone. And all he could do was walk forward, for the door he had entered through was no longer there.

Shuffling forward on his feet slowly, he could not determine what direction he was going. He did not feel that he made any turns in the hallway, but again, he could not tell if the hallway itself was turning as he moved. Roberto had no idea how far ahead the man had gone, and he had no idea which direction he was headed. He winced at the searing hot pain on his thumb as the lighter heated up; he cursed and let it cool.

"You up there?" he called ahead. "You still there man?"

No answer. Only silence, save the crinkle-crinkle of the plastic wrapped around the roses. It would scrape up along the wall next to him with each step he took, and the sounds pierced the silence quite easily.

Roberto stopped and tried to look ahead. He flicked his lighter again, and it sparked, but no flame. He shook it and smacked it a few times. After a second attempt, the flame ignited. "Man...you there?" Roberto stopped. If he truly was all alone, he did not want to go on any further into the black abyss.

Nothing.

Roberto heard a faint *click* far ahead – a shrill snap against the silence, like someone turning on a lamp in another room. A faint light emitted from a great distance down a dark, black passageway, but it was not enough light to lead his way, and it was quite far ahead. Still, the light was enough to allow Roberto to put his lighter away and look around. He saw something around him that seemed like wooden slats, pressed up against an earthen wall. He looked down, and caught a shiny, square object inserted in the wood, recessed into the slat. But then he craned his neck and saw the wood follow a path across the ceiling, and around and down the other wall.

A door.

And then it slammed behind him.

How long was this hallway? he thought. He tried the door. It was heavy, a strong and impenetrable dark wood. The handle would not budge.

He was forced to move further inside.

He decided to make his way up towards the faint, yellowish light and he got towards the wall to his right and used his hands to help him along the wall. The light was very dim, but it was a welcome respite to the blackness that he felt when the door slammed and his eyes were adjusting.

Had he been trapped? And who trapped him?

Several feet down, he came across another door. It was not unlike any household door, however, right in front of the door the floor was much darker than the rest. It stood out like a giant square panel. On the door, there was no doorknob. That he could tell, but it was harder to tell exactly what type of flooring was in front of the door, and he was unsure if that section of the floor was some sort of panel or button. It was too oddly square…and stood out much. And it extended across to the other wall. The darkened section of floor, the panel, definitely seemed too large to jump across.

He stopped.

Bending down closer to the floor, he saw clean lines against the earthen floor, like giant black tiles. Like a gigantic button.

Roberto paced back and forth for a minute, his eyes shifting from the door, to the panel on the floor, and back. There was no way around this, if Roberto wanted to continue, he would have to step on this section of the floor. And he didn't know what would happen once he stepped on the panel.

His eyes were much better adjusted to the light now.

Looking up, he saw a small ledge about six inches from the ceiling. He figured that he could always grab onto the ledge and carry himself over this large panel in the floor.

"What the hell," he said, and jumped up and grabbed the ledge with one hand on the first try, hanging in the air and swinging slightly. He had caught the ledge with his left hand, and held the roses with his right hand. He took the roses and shoved them down his pants to where just the flowered tips were peeking out about his waistline. He swung his right arm up to the panel and steadied his grip. He found it to be cool, but dusty.

No problem. It was only about 10 feet for so.

Before he would know it, he would be on the other side and continuing towards the dim, dusty light at the end of the hallway. Or at least what he assumed was the end of the hallway. Either way, it was still the unknown.

He slid his hands to his right, unsettling what seemed like years of dust. His eyes started to water, clouding his vision. And then….*achoo!!*

Achoo!

The sneeze echoed down the hallway. He snuffled, balancing himself on the ledge, hanging in the mysterious hall made of dirt.

The sneeze almost caused him to lose his grip on the ledge. He was still about a foot or so from the beginning of the panel. Directly above the panel he had to be more careful.

He kept his head turned down to avoid the billowing dust disturbed by his gripping hands, and he began sliding down the ledge again. His legs swung back and forth as he slid, and before long his legs were swinging over into the airspace above the panel. And then he noticed something that he did not notice before: the wall next to the panel in the floor was the same material (or at least appeared to be the same material) as the panel.

He stopped. What now?

He didn't remember the wall looking like black tile before. He distinctly remembered the panel being only on the floor.

But now it had built its way up the wall, getting closer and closer to his swinging legs.

Roberto decided that he was going to try to swing his legs and try to swing his way over the panel to the other side. Hopefully the years of sports will have paid off.

He gained momentum, holding his legs outward to avoid the wall panel, and used his arm muscles to steady himself on the ledge and leaped. He was flying through the air for what seemed like an eternity, and then, hit bottom.

He hit the floor hard, causing the wind to get knocked out of him for a moment. He lay on the dirt floor waiting to breathe. Luckily, he did not hit his head. The floor appeared so hard as if it were marble, yet made of earth. Definitely it was of the hardest earth that he had ever felt in his life.

He could not place what type of material or stone the floor was. He looked down, and saw he was lying on his back on the floor, and he had made it! His head was past the panel, and he was lying on what appeared to be a stone floor, on the other side of the panel. Had he truly made it?

He turned his head to the right and let out a breath. The door was open. His right hand was on the floor, and he hadn't realized it had touched the panel.

And that was all it took. The door was open, against the wall, letting very faint light in, not much, but just enough to see a pedestal table with a vase of roses lying dead on the floor in a mountain of broken glass and watery mess.

~~*

Roberto let his head fall back to the floor, sighed and closed his eyes. Exasperated, he did not know what to do. Every horror movie he had ever seen told him not to go through that door. All that was there was blackness. This building was a strange place, through that door was the unknown, and his instincts told him to just turn around. Turn around and leave, leave and wait for Antoine to come to him that night like he originally said that he was going to do.

But on the other hand, Roberto was curious to see what was beyond the door.

While the building was strange, and given the fact that the hallway he was in seemed incredibly long – apparently far longer than the one block on Washington Avenue that the structure encompassed outside. Roberto still felt oddly drawn to its darkness, just as he was drawn to Antoine the first time they saw each other.

All in all, he decided at the very least he should get up. Rising to his feet, he brushed himself off, took the roses out of his pants, which were only slightly crushed, and turned around to face another wall.

Roberto stopped and stared at the wall.

What the fuck? Where did that wall come from?

The floor was no longer a panel, now the area in front of the door blended in with the rest of the floor. Given that the door was open, Roberto now got a better feel of what the hallway looked like. The building had a whole medieval feel about it, almost like a castle, and the walls and floor were a uniform dark stone masonry.

The door, with squared off corners and heavy wood, stood open against the wall beckoning Roberto to enter.

He now only had two choices.

He didn't know if he was getting delusional, but now all he could do was go into this strange structure further or go through the door. But the darkness did not continue to hold his attention.

His head looked forward down the hallway, where the light had come from earlier; now only a few feet beyond the faint light that he stood in the darkness took back over and swallowed up the hallway; but what caught Roberto's attention was not the overpowering blackness.

The light at the end of the hallway – very faint and far, far down and further away now it seemed than before, was now accompanied by a slight methodic rap, like a metronome, like something hitting the wall, over and over again…*rap*…*rap*…*rap*…

The noise was light but methodical and determined, and coming from the direction of the light.

And that is when Roberto realized he was no longer alone. He heard a voice.

"Hello young man."

Roberto stopped in his tracks. He saw no one. Who was that? Roberto did not know what to make of the noise or the light, so he decided to enter the door that beckoned.

It became pitch black as he crossed through the door; the roses and table were indiscernible through the darkness that spread as he walked over the threshold. Even the dim light that was now in the hallway did not penetrate. Roberto stopped for a moment before he entered, pausing for one final minute. He squinted and peered inside, in a desperate attempt to see something, but all he saw was blackness.

Was this the right decision? He was soon to find out.

CHAPTER TWENTY-NINE

Darkness.

Into the black abyss.

Roberto immediately regretted his decision to continue into the room, as the door slammed behind him, enveloping him in total blackness. He turned around to try and see if he could push the door open, but all he could feel was the stone masonry of the wall.

The door was gone.

Where was he? He checked his pockets for the lighter, brought it out, and started clicking it. It was low on butane. Not great, but at least he will be able to find out where he is and maybe if there is a way out.

Click! went the lighter and the small, dim glow of the light revealed a silver coffin resting on a stone slab. It was too dark to see beyond the coffin; it was unknown if there were any additional doors in the room, or even where the room ended and the walls began. Or if there were even any walls to begin with.

Or if there was anyone else in the room with him.

The mysterious man that Roberto had encountered on the steps had disappeared shortly after ushering him inside this strange and macabre building; now he couldn't determine if he was alone in the room or who might be in the casket.

Or what might be in the casket.

Roberto moved forward slowly and stopped above the elegant looking silver coffin. He looked down and revisited his mother's funeral. He remembered watching the morticians lower her tiny body deeper into the white satin interior, and then shut the lid, closing her into darkness for all of eternity. The casket looked very familiar. It was the same silver color. It was very shiny in the dim flicker of the lighter's flame, and he could see on the closed lid the flickering firefly reflection.

And then the lighter ran out of butane and went out.

Total blackness once again.

Roberto stood still, and did not move his feet for he did not know what would come next. The room was so utterly silent it was eating him alive. He now regretted his decision of even coming to this building, he didn't understand why he felt he needed to see Antoine today.

But it was too late. Now he was trapped.

He didn't even dare move, for he knew just a few feet in front of him was the casket. And he dared not attempt to feel his way through a pitch black room for fear of toppling the coffin off of its slab – and maybe – just maybe, waking up what might be inside.

That was when the bottom of the wall, where the wall met the stone floor, began to take on a glow of an orange essence. The glow was as if there was a recessed floor around the perimeter of the room and it filled the dim light. It was as if there were a bright fire or furnace underneath, and it lit the room in a dark orange eerie glow that once again reflected on the silver casket.

It felt like there was a fire in the room, lighting up as if there were a blazing fire in the fireplace, yet there was no fireplace in the room.

It was an empty, stark stone room – with just a silver coffin on a stone slab, in the middle of a stone floor, with a warm, orange light that reached up the walls like fire along on the edges under the floor.

There was an audible *click* that reverberated through the silent room which brought Roberto's attention to the coffin.

Roberto could tell one thing. The sound came from inside the casket.

Was something was moving inside? Was something was trying to get out? The click let Roberto know if that whatever or whomever was inside wanted out, they knew the way out.

Roberto dropped the roses, and his eyes darted around the room, scanning the walls.

He wanted to run, but there was nowhere to run to. Behind him, there was now just a wall. There was no longer a door, or even the imprint of the door.

Just a wall.

How had the room changed around him again? The walls seemed to be closer to him now, as if they moved inwards, but in the blink of an eye. They trapped him in what felt like a small closet – he felt like he was almost on top of the casket, yet he was not, and as the walls kept closing in on him the flames began to take shape and finger out from the walls.

There was nowhere to hide. Nowhere to go.

The heat from the fire increased, and grew more intense as they shot out of the floor – and the flames now felt their way through cracks in the wall. The room was much brighter now, filling quickly with flames, and Roberto's attention diverted back to the casket.

There was a banging on the casket lid. Hard, and deep.

The casket was moving – rocking back and forth on the slab, knocking and banging, coming close to falling.

Where the fuck am I?

Roberto ducked quickly on the ground as a thin arm of flames darted past his head – so close that he could feel the heat from the fire and it felt as if it singed his hair. The flames soared over his head and grew larger, reaching for the casket.

The flames enveloped the casket and danced on the lid and Roberto now realized that the room had shrunk even more. He was struggling to stay away from the fire, and was so close to the coffin that it was almost touching him.

There was a small, round light that appeared above the casket in front of him. When he looked closer, he thought he saw people on the other side of the round light. Like he was looking through a tiny window.

And then he started putting the pieces together.

His mother had been cremated. He knew where he was.

"Roberto….." It was a woman's voice and was coming from his right. He closed his eyes.

The coffin lid started to slowly open through the flames.

"Roberto come this way and follow me….." the voice continued

He struggled in his mind, arguing with his sane and rational side, that these events could not be happening and were just in his mind. He did not know nor did he want to know what woman was calling him. But he chose to open his eyes.

It was Eva.

She stood in front of what appeared to be another hallway, long but leading quickly into blackness, reaching towards some other unknown destination. She had the same long brown hair she did in life, the same beauty and the same eyes. Like she was still alive, beautiful and healthy, before the cancer, before the beatings. She was wearing the same white, flowing nightgown she had during life. "Come follow me Roberto…"

The apparition did not wait for an answer, but rather turned without further words and disappeared down the hallway, quickly being engulfed by the black abyss. "Come follow your mother, Roberto…" Her words trailed off as she got further away.

He followed her. The oven had gotten so small that he only had room to crouch next to the casket, which was now engulfed in flames.

He turned his head away from the hallway for a moment to find the casket lid still open.

He could not see what or who was inside, only darkness. But something looked like movement, like something was reaching towards him through bright, hot fire.

That was when he ran. He sprinted into the hallway, away from the flames; away from the burning casket. Away from the intense heat of the oven.

The mysterious figure was far ahead, and she was illuminated in bright white, but all he could see was her, and the light surrounding her. Had he died? Was he in heaven now? Or was this hell? But the question that posed Roberto's mind was, where did this dark tunnel lead to? And where was his mother leading him?

And, the question that replayed in his mind over and over: was that really his mother ahead?

Roberto stood at the entrance of the passage. He turned behind him, and saw the casket. The lid was still open. And there was definitely someone inside the casket, he was certain now. Roberto attempted to look more closely at the coffin, but could not tell from the distance that he was at who or what was inside. There was a body lying inside as if dead and immobile, clad in black, appeared to be male, but from the rustling earlier, Roberto doubted that the body was dead. It certainly had to have been dead now in the flames of the oven.

"Roberto…." Eva turned back to face him. "Come away from that room. Follow me this way…" The sound her words reverberated against the dark stone earthy walls of the passage, beckoning him to come.

Roberto was in a quandary. If he followed his mother, or whatever that was that looked like his mother, he was venturing more beyond into the unknown, and further into this strange entity. But who was in the casket?

Curiosity overtaking him, Roberto turned once again towards the casket. The body lay there, still, as if on display in a viewing room – the body was apparently untouched by the flames. The body looked dressed and ready for mourners to pass by, and kneel in front of the casket to say a final prayer and to pay respects.

But there were no mourners here.

He turned back towards the passage, resigned to the fact that he was be sucked in, farther into this netherworld and he had no choice in the matter.

Then there was a rustling coming from behind him. Like the casket moved. Then a scraping, like a wooden box being slowly dragged across concrete.

Roberto couldn't get it out of his mind. He dared not turn around, for fear of what could be happening with the casket. Instead, he stared forward to where his mother had been, as she disappeared into the dark, black abyss of the mysterious tunnel. She turned a corner far off into the distance, disappearing into blackness.

Now it was time, it was time to face his fear. Roberto wanted to turn around, but his feet would not let him. And then a commanding, male voice called to him.

"Roberto!"

He closed his eyes shut tight. Oh, shit, oh, shit, oh, shit.

He did not want to think about what was happening behind him. Whoever that was lying in the casket was dead. Dead and in flames. They were dead.

Roberto let out a breath, and gathered his senses. As he turned to his left, the casket started to come into view.

But there were no more flames.

The room was no longer like that of an oven. The casket remained, lying on a stone slab in the center of the cold, grey room.

He dared not turn around farther. Whatever was going on in here was fucking with his mind. He already had his answer as to who was lying in the casket.

The flames, now receded, the room was once again like it was and the orange glow around the perimeter gave just enough light to see the contents of the open casket. Through slightly closed eyes, and uttering a long breath out of his lungs, he came to the revelation that the voice belonged to one being and one being only.

The voice that called him earlier in the commotion of the fire, a voice that was male.

His father.

And what was Hernan doing here, lying in the casket? That Roberto did not know. His mother had been dead, but Hernan was very much alive.

But this building.

Somehow this building was reading his mind, and dredging all of his thoughts and laying them out before him.

Roberto saw his father standing in front, towering over him and the casket, staring down at Roberto through slanted, angry eyes. He was wearing a dark blue suit.

"*You slimy little faggot child*!" he hissed. "You killed me! Just like you killed your mother!" He took a step closer to Roberto and lunged forward. Roberto braced himself to run, but he did not move yet. He was too stunned and shocked and none of the events were making any sense to him.

"Don't think I didn't know what you were doing behind my back! You sick disgusting *fucking DEMON*!" He screamed at the top of his lungs and reached his arms out for Roberto, knocking the casket onto the floor, spilling its contents of satin liners and sheets and an American Flag. Roberto broke into a run, leaping down the dark corridor where his mother had disappeared, tripping on rocks that jutted out from a watery floor, and coughing at the mustiness.

He had a distinct advantage over Hernan.

But there was only so far that he could go. The passage was dark and damp, the earthy floor was covered in water, and Hernan was closing in on him. The only problem now was Roberto had no idea where to go. Getting further from the strange room, the passage got darker and darker, and Roberto had no source of light. He had to get out this, and had to find a way to get away from Hernan.

Or whatever it was that looked like Hernan.

And then it happened.

Somehow, someway, a door appeared before him down the hallway. He could barely make out the form in the darkness, and it was made of the earth, but he could tell for sure that it was a door. There was a small, single solitary overhead light with no apparent source, shining down on the door. Hernan was closing in on him.

"*Fucking little faggot!*" Hernan screamed, charging towards him, splashing through the water. "You're going to hell!"

Roberto had to make it to the door, and the hopes of safety beyond on the other side. Running through small puddles of liquid that smelled like rotten eggs and sulfur, and feeling rats crawl over his feet, Roberto made it to the door and stopped suddenly, bracing himself against the massive frame. Where the door led, Roberto did not know. But when he looked closer, he could see the word carved into the wooden doorframe: MEMORY.

But Roberto then got the sense that Hernan was no longer chasing him. Due to his youthful vibrancy and energy, Roberto had always been far ahead of Hernan and was unable to look back and see him, however now, standing at the door catching his breath, he could not only not see Hernan and but also sensed that Hernan gave up.

Or did he?

Where was Hernan? *What* was Hernan?

Roberto was in another quandary.

He could return to the way he came, and face him. Face his fears. The casket in the room. What came out of the casket. Or, he could open the door to MEMORY.

A large and inviting round handle stood out against the door, like a giant, silver plate.

Roberto backed away from the door timidly and carefully, not exactly sure what was waiting on the other side. As his sneakers splashed muddy water from the earthy floor below, Roberto turned quickly and headed back to face Hernan.

Or perhaps to escape the unknown.

Wherever that door led to, Roberto suspected that it led further into this strange building. And further from a way out. Turning the corner, Roberto started heading closer to the dim, orange light that emanated from the stone room at the end of the passage, leading way to the spilled casket and the dank, stark room.

When he arrived, nobody was there.

Roberto entered the room, and all he saw was the casket. The casket was laying on its side, the contents spilled out on the floor; satin pillows and blankets, a silver crucifix, and a folded American flag.

But Hernan was nowhere to be found. And there were no doors that marked where he could have gone.

There was one thing that Roberto knew. Or, at least he thought he knew. Hernan was in the casket. Or at least something that looked like him. Was this a premonition of the future? Or was Hernan really dead? Or was Hernan hiding in the casket to attack Roberto? How did Hernan know that he was coming here today? There were too many unanswered questions.

The longer that Roberto stayed in this building, the more he felt like he was sinking closer to madness; the more he felt that the building knew his thoughts and secrets, and he was have an increasingly difficult time distinguishing what was reality and what was not.

When Roberto looked up from the casket, he saw across the dim light of the room that there was another door on the far wall in front of him.

That door was not there before, he thought.

Roberto decided that if he was going to get out of this building, he was going to have to find a way out – and he may just have to go further in.

He looked to the left.

As there was before, from where he initially entered this room, there was just a wall before him. No hallway, no panel in the floor, nothing. Just a wall. He turned around, towards the dark, earthen path that led to MEMORY.

Another wall!

What was once there, now no longer is. Roberto had no choice but to go through the newly formed door.

Another mystery of where it would lead.

It could be a way out, or it could draw him even deeper into this structure. MEMORY was no longer an option.

Once again, the rules have changed.

~~*

SECOND PROLOGUE

SOUTH OF CAIRO

Many years ago –

The night sky in Luxor revealed a vast array of tiny white stars, etched in the sprawling dark blue pallet. Antoine stood in a small clearing of sand in the middle of the desert, his arms crossed before his tall, dark stature - staring up at the stars, running through his mind, over and over, his plans for the future.

The cup was his.

Standing before the large sandy brown mountain, in front of the stone slab door covered in worn and painted hieroglyphics which informed the contents of the tomb:

Tutankhamen.

Antoine stood over the excavation like a learned professor, wearing his signature long black coat. Suddenly, he broke his gaze to the stars. Shaking off his temporary distraction, he entered the dark abyss of the tomb.

"The Cup of Christ," he commanded to another immortal that had been digging at the cave floor dirt with his hands. The follower looked up and snapped his head in the direction of Antoine's deep, booming voice of authority: "It's in the tomb with him. In the coffin."

Antoine pointed further into the compound, signaling with his hand that the place to dig was not out in the foyer but inside – in the inner chambers. The immortal immediately heeded the command and dropped the dirt he was holding, following Antoine like an obedient canine, crawling on the ground like an animal.

Antoine continued further inside the tomb, through falling rock and sand, deeper until he was no longer able to walk. Swinging from hanging rocks into an even smaller cave, he was forced to drop to his knees and crawl. He winced in pain. The cave floor was covered in rocks and small stones, and he felt their small, indomitable solidity dig at his knees. But that did not dissuade his determined pace.

Amidst the darkness, the decline leveled and then gave way to an incline, and he climbed up a small mountain of rocks and boulders as the cave opened up once again, revealing the first of the four rooms of Tutankhamen's final resting place. It was a seemingly insignificant room with walls of clay and rock, an overtly soaring stone ceiling and a small, square window towards the crest of the top – signifying the possibility that this tomb once saw daylight before it was swallowed by the earth.

But what drew Antoine's attention was not the clay walls – it was not the oddity of the small window – not even the gleaming, dusty treasure which created a stark contrast to the dullness of the room – it was the four luminous gold coffins in the center of the treasure, standing guard as if they were elemental patriarchs.

Standing next to the coffin was another man holding a flaming torch, dressed similarly to Antoine, with the same long, dark and flowing hair and black coat – but this man had much lighter skin, perhaps like that of a European - with pronounced facial features and a slight lankiness about him. He was standing in the center of the room, staring up at the high ceiling, amidst a sea of golden treasure and coffins.

"Darius!" Antoine called shortly, descending a flight of stairs that was below the small opening towards the top of the room that he had to crawl through. "All I want is the Chalice. None of this is important."

"It's unbelievable," Darius said, shaking his head and staring at the coffin. The casket cast an aural yellowish glow in his face.

"What did you say?" Antoine called from atop the stone stairs.

Darius turned to face Antoine. "I was just saying it's amazing how the Cup of Christ got in there. Look at this!" Darius gestured his arm around the room. "All this treasure….it's so…old."

"Tutankhamen lived several thousand years before Christ," Antoine explained. "But time means nothing to her."

Darius lit another torch for Antoine. The treasures glistened in the light from the fire, sending a warm glow throughout the chamber. Darius turned to face Antoine, who had reached the floor, dusting the dirt of off his pants and jacket.

"Come now, Antoine," Darius said. "Do you think I have forgotten why we are here?" He turned to the nearest coffin, smirking, and walked to the center of the room, to the four gold painted coffins that were framed by the mountains of gold and jewels. "There it is." Darius waved his torch over the top of the coffin. "Tutankhamen. It is in there."

Antoine walked over to the coffin, quietly and reverently. "We need to open it. Night will be fading soon."

"Azra!" Antoine commanded, turning his head to summon the immortal. He came expeditiously, carrying with him a small brown leather bag, handing it to Antoine. Darius came over from his place at the coffin and took Antoine's torch.

Setting the bag on the floor, Antoine unzipped it and pulled out a long, dull tipped stake, and dug in the bag deeper for a small hammer.

He lined up the rounded point of the stake with the crease on the edge of the coffin – where the lid met the bowl – and Antoine gave the hammer a loud *bang*! A small shower of sparks poured down from the coffin.

The lid did not budge.

Antoine continued and continued, causing some but not very noticeable damage to the artifact, sending loud booming echoes of the noise cascading to the top of the chamber.

After what seemed like several minutes of pounding and hammering, the top loosened somewhat; just enough for Antoine and Darius to bend over and take the lid with their hands try to lift it with all their immortal strength.

Thousands and thousands of years of dust billowed from the coffin like a giant cloud, and the lid that was sealed before Christ walked the earth was about to be opened.

The two immortals held the lid in their hands and stood above the coffin. As the air cleared they saw their prize: Tutankhamen. Holding the cup of Christ in his hand. When the lid was dropped to the floor with a crash and a large cloud of dust, Azra explained to them how the Cup of Christ managed to find its way into Tutankhamen's coffin. "Claret did it," he said.

"What I want to know," Antoine said, wiping the dust off of his hands, "is how Claret got that Cup in this coffin. I know she was infatuated with Christ, and I know that she killed Tutankhamen…but how did she do it? The two lived thousands of years apart. This Chalice would have been right here when Christ was supposed to have been drinking from it at the Last Supper."

"Claret," Darius said, musing. "What an evil bitch…"

Antoine broke his gaze from the chalice and looked at Darius, expectantly.

"I haven't heard that name in quite some time," Darius admitted, speaking to Antoine. "She lived during the times of Jesus Christ. She had an obsession with Him. But how did it get here?"

Antoine reached in the coffin, carefully and respectfully amidst the remains of the boy-king, past the golden burial mask, and placed his fingers around the jeweled stem of the chalice. It stood out abruptly in this chamber of gold and jewels – it was a plain and simple chalice made of stone.

He held it up to the light of the torch. "This is the cup that will bring me eternal salvation," he said. "With this cup, we will no longer be damned. It is the key to our immortality."

Azra broke the silence that had permeated the chamber after Antoine had finished speaking. "They say that Claret still walks the valley. They say that she is still alive and walking the sands!" His eyes remained wide as saliva dripped from an extended canine. He tugged on his beard.

Antoine eyes darted over to Azra for a moment, as if analyzing his comment. Saying nothing, he grabbed the brown bag from the floor and gingerly placed the goblet inside.

"This is all we came for," Antoine said. "We should leave now."

Azra looked down at the bag and his mouth dropped open.

"You took his precious gift!" he screamed in horror.

Azra turned and ran, tripped up the stairs, and fell flat on his face. He immediately rose and frantically clawed his way back through the opening to the cave.

Antoine and Darius stared at each other, without an answer for what just had happened. Antoine raised his eyebrows and shook his head.

As they lifted the coffin lid and placed it on the bowl, the ground began to shake. A massive earthquake shook the coffins off of the stone slabs that they had been resting on and the treasures surrounding the tomb fell and shook and dropped to the ground.

The ceiling showered dirt and rock on the two immortals, threatening to collapse. From the corner of the ceiling, a waterfall of earth and sand fell down below, quickly covering up the contents of the tomb.

"Quickly!" Antoine said. "Over to the stairs!"

Amidst giant boulders now falling from the top of tomb the two dashed to the foot of the stairs as the ground opened from beneath them, as the floor split in two – and flames shot out of the giant fissure. Climbing up to the entrance to the cave, Antoine turned and looked back at the room of Tutankhamen, staring at it one last time, in danger of being swallowed up into the bowels of the earth.

Fixated on the scene before him, he saw that the earth was furious, the room shook and the walls crumbled but the treasures and coffins did not die; they did not fall down into the fiery red abyss; they sat in place, as if standing command and protecting what was to be discovered.

But the angry flames died down just as quickly as they enraged. The giant cracks in the earth slowly filled in as the earth rose to correct itself; to close up as the coffins and treasure stood its ground.

The room was as they had come to it.

There were no more flames. The coffins were placed on their stone slabs as they had found them. Antoine snapped out of his stare at the whole scene. "What?" he asked himself, confused at the situation.

"What did you say?" Darius called back up from the bottom of the hill, as he continued to the entrance.

"The tomb! It's like we never touched it!" Antoine slid down the hill, kicking up sand and rocks. When he got to the bottom, he stood up, dusted himself off, and joined Darius at the opening. The sky was still dark and filled with stars.

"When I looked back inside, the crack filled back in. The fire put itself out. It was like we were never there!"

Darius clapped the dust from his palms, and mounted his camel.

The earth shook again.

This time it was much more intense; Antoine lost his balance, falling to the ground, and the camels panicked. Darius was thrown to the ground, his face hitting a large stone that rose from the sand at full force. The rocks around them began to loosen – the entrance started caving in and covered their steps with giant boulders, rock and dirt.

And then the shaking stopped just as quickly as it had started.

Lying on his back for a moment, Antoine thought that maybe this was all a dream. He turned his head and looked over his shoulder, and saw what looked like no more than a mountain behind him. There was no cave opening; no hieroglyphics. It just looked like a brown, sandy mountain in the middle of the desert.

Darius shook his head, showering sand on the ground. He rose to his feet unscathed despite his fall against the stone. Antoine also stood, dusted himself off, and grabbed the bag. He looked inside, and checked the cup. There it was. The Cup of Christ, he thought. It wasn't a dream.

He really did have it. And Claret must be upset.

"We will see," Antoine said, as he and Darius walked from the cave, leaving what would become the archeological find of the century buried under rock and silt.

There it was behind them, as the two immortals glided away into the night, the entrance to Egyptian mystery and mythology swallowed by the earth, hidden from day and sun and light, preserving the mystery that wouldn't be discovered by mortals for over another century.

~~*

PART THREE

THE COMING OF THE GREEN MIST

Not before long, the mist will come.

The mist will come and do its task.

It will clean you up. Scrub you down.

Rid you of your misdeeds.

The monsters will come and swallow you up.

All before dawn…

CHAPTER THIRTY

There was one day that a terrible dark green mist overtook the city of Miami.

It did not just happen in the alternate dimension that Paula had lost herself in; it came to normal everyday society as well. The city began to slump farther and farther down into a cesspool of evil – yet on the forefront, it appeared as if the city were hot and thriving.

Antoine was definitely in his prime.

He was not only the focus of the intricate and detailed investigation of The Astral – which brought him not only some interesting companionship but also some substantial income, but he also managed to rise to the top of culture, becoming known as a spiritual healer on television and also being regarded as a prophet. From the shows that he conducted on stage he was able to raise millions. And with that money he not only financed his opulent lifestyle but also stockpiled large amounts of cash – mainly underground underneath the bowels of *Sacrafice*.

He did not venture to banks.

Beyond the dance floor, just behind the stage – where the walls were painted black and covered by heavy, hanging black drapes that reached down towards the floor from a soaring ceiling – there was a door. It was a door painted black and flush with the wall, that was unmarked and untouched, and there was a small padlock securing the handle.

None of the club staff that had been hurriedly preparing for the upcoming grand opening even knew of the doors existence; most of the time the drapes were closed and covered it. And even if they had known the door was there, no one held the key.

Except Antoine.

And Antoine was rarely seen at *Sacrafice*; he wasn't even known as the owner and operator of the nightclub. It did not matter. He didn't care for that, he had bigger and better things to plan.

It was the same evening before that Antoine had stared and stopped, as he stood in front of the impatient traffic that was congesting Washington Avenue, and listened to the horns honking and engines purring in the heat and exhaust.

It was just after Claret had closed the door, as Antoine stood, waiting and wondering.

It *had* to have been her. He knew those eyes. It did not matter what body she possessed; it did not matter what form she took.

The eyes told him.

And as he stood cherishing the cool wind in his face, feeling the refreshing air that was a relief to the stifling heat, he dug his hand into his right pocket, and fished around until he felt the smooth silver.

The key.

And when he was climbing the grey stone steps to the cathedral, and as he opened the large, imposing wooden door which grated against the concrete, he drew the key from his pocket as it gleamed in the fading sunlight.

He entered and stepped into blackness.

The door closed behind him with a deep thud, and he felt the air push against his back. As the darkness enveloped him, he scanned his surroundings.

The foyer of the club had purple velvet carpets and real, flaming torches on the wall. But Antoine did not care about that. He did not even notice that the torches flamed as he walked passed them or that the door locked itself; he did not notice the crash and bang of the security bar reverberating against the deafening silence.

He was heading to the door behind the heavy curtains.

He crossed the dance floor and climbed the stairs to the stage. He drew the curtains back with a pull cord, which exposed the back wall. He again withdrew the key from his pocket.

The click of the lock releasing pierced the silence and the door slowly creaked open.

Antoine could make out the stairs, but they quickly led to total darkness.

There was a small light bulb hanging from the ceiling just inside the door, with a string pull cord. Antoine pulled the string on the side, and the chain snapped, but the light turned on. There was a dim glow against the blackness.

The walls were earthen and brown, and the light revealed a landing just below the threshold of the door, which winded down to stairs that led downwards to total darkness. Antoine stepped down onto the landing and quietly closed the door behind him.

The light seemed to fade, from a musty yellow to pale brown.

But Antoine did not pay it any mind. All he wanted to do was get below. He wanted to get down to the depository.

He slowly eased himself down the stairs. He kept his back against the wall, and felt his way down each step. He was merely a shadowy figure in the increasing darkness.

But he was not alone.

Many times before, Antoine had ventured down these very same stairs with the very same objective. Many times before he had closed the door and turned off the light and walked down the stairs without any problem, without any event.

But today had been different.

Today, there was someone else down here with him - that he could sense. He felt the presence of another, but he couldn't quite put a handle on who it could be.

Then he heard a splash of water below, like someone had stepped in a puddle.

He stopped for a moment, and held his breath. He was vulnerable; he was not prepared for battle. He replayed the day's events through his mind, and wondered who was making the distant noise; he wondered what footsteps were down there.

Could it be?

It could not be Claret. She did not know he was watching her…could she have?

There was no one else except Darius that knew of the existence of these underground catacombs, and Darius would not be here.

What mattered were the splashing sounds that came from the darkness below; the scraping against the walls, the sounds that were making Antoine feel like he was a scared mortal again. It sounded like someone was walking around down there.

But he continued down the stairs, more cautiously this time as he was unsure who was down there. And then he thought of a name.

Asmodai.

It was Asmodai that has pursued him since he dug up Darius in Lyon. It was Asmodai that pledged in the Cave of Crystals that he would continue to pursue Antoine; that the prophecy had not been fulfilled; that payment must be rendered.

There was no way.

There was no way that Asmodai was down here. He always made a grand entrance, with storms and fires and earthquakes.

Didn't he?

Continuing down the stairs, he reached the puddles of water himself, slightly startling himself when he splashed in the water, feeling the wetness permeate his boots.

The two things that Antoine feared, the only two things in all of earth and all of time, kept invading his mind. No one else, no other spirit, only the two that he was running from, only the two that he feared were all he could think of now.

And Claret would not make an entrance like Asmodai. Hers would be much more discreet.

He felt his way along the wall. Cool moss carpeted the walls for most of the way. He remembered that specifically. Antoine carefully tiptoed through the murky waters. Each splash reverberated against the quiet. Shortly he would be coming to the cremation chamber. There he would be able to store his cash and leave.

Looking ahead, he thought he saw a figure in the darkness that looked like a translucent floating head, floating several feet above the floor.

He stopped.

He knew that what was created in here was a force to control the mind. The walls would move. Things would appear that may or may not actually be there.

Doors would mysteriously appear and move. But it was all something that he created. It was an entity that he always believed that he had control over.

Unless something else was inside controlling it for him.

He peered forward and tried to see of what or who the apparition was; he knew that he must remain in his mortal form, he could not transform. He could not risk the act of aggression.

He must remain as is.

He did not want to risk angering whatever was there. And he had a feeling he knew who was there.

The apparition was too blurry to decipher what it was; it remained a glowing blurb cutting through the darkness and floating in the passage perhaps ten or twenty feet in front of him. It pulsated and glowed, but did not move closer to him. And it was blocking the door to the Chamber where he needed to go.

Antoine did not even bother to duck behind a rock or a wall; it was too late now. He was right in the sight path of whatever this glowing blurb was.

It grew in size tremendously, like a giant cloud of gas. It expanded, bouncing against the walls and moving closer and closer to him.

He thought that he should run, but then decided against it.

This was his creation. This was his house and his realm. He mentally willed it to cease.

But it continued to pulsate and grow.

Soon, it would be engulfing him as well. He again considered turning and running, but doing that would be relinquishing his power and control.

But it was too late.

All of a sudden, he felt a cold like no other. It chilled him to the bone; it was a frozen, death cold…like the chill of a coffin in the dead of winter.

The apparition began to engulf him, the brightness surrounded him and blinded him. He felt as though he were being catapulted into some sort of portal, into another dimension.

He felt a suction of gravity, as he was pulled deeper into the white deep dark, he relented to the brightness and the forces that surrounded him.

It was useless to resist.

As he was dragged further and further in, he felt a wetness – a soft and spongy substance coating his arms and hands and legs.

He closed his eyes, and his heart beat faster. His mind was racing. He opened his eyes, trying desperately to get his bearings. The brightness calmed, his eyes adjusting, and he saw that he appeared to be in some sort of a giant, translucent egg.

And the egg was filling with a clear, thick fluid very rapidly.

He tapped the ceiling of the egg. It wobbled. And though he desperately tried, he could not punch through it. He tried again and again, as the mysterious freezing cold fluid crept closer and closer, first covering his knees and then reaching his thighs; he continued scratching, tearing and punching at the walls; he could now see outside of the translucent material and saw the passage before him – the puddles of water below now boiling, as steam billowed around the outside of the egg.

The fluid reached his chest and finally his neck and Antoine shivered. It was a deep cold like no other. It reached his chin and caused him to submerge; his movement was greatly restricted as the viscosity of the liquid was that of a sludge or slime.

Antoine closed his eyes and relented. There was no use of fighting anymore. Nothing could save him now; he could not transform, he could not win.

His powers were useless. He flopped down, settling in the liquid, now completely submerged.

Considering for a moment his fate, Antoine wondered how the spiritual intrusion of this magnitude could be allowed in a place that he thought he had total control over.

Something, or someone, has broken through the barrier.

Now held captive, Antoine did not dare to think what lie ahead. All he knew and all he trusted was now in question. Somewhere his plan went wrong, somehow. Wondering whether it could be the powers of Claret or Asmodai – both with scores to settle – he relented and wished Roberto was with him. He called on Darius to no avail.

What Antoine knew was that he was delving into dangerous territory from the moment he dug up Darius; he knew that revenge would be sought the moment he took the cup out of Tutankhamen's hands; but what he didn't know was that the one who betrayed him was the one he would least expect to.

CHAPTER THIRTY-ONE

A silver plate covered with a giant slab of beef was set down in front of Jean Carlo with a bang. He stared at it for a moment, not expecting to be eating a giant meal down here.

"Eat! You will need your strength!" An old, chubby grey haired woman smiled at him as she piled potatoes and brightly colored vegetables on the plate. The woman turned and went about her way, but turned around and looked back one last time. "Eat!"

Jean Carlo raised his eyes towards Anthony.

"Go ahead and eat," he said, cutting into a piece of meat himself. "We are welcome here."

Jean Carlo started to slowly pick at his food, and as he swallowed his first few bites, he began to feel somewhat better. Anthony continued speaking while they were eating.

"There is a lot going on right now. A lot of evil things. The man you saw in the cemetery is named Darius. He is inherently evil. You saw yourself what he could do. And when you woke up inside your casket, you saw what he did to you. I know what happened to you, Jean Carlo. I know that right now you are somewhat confused, but things will clear up for you. As Darius had been chosen for the destiny that lies before him, you have been chosen as well, but I have intervened and called you here for a different mission."

"What sort of mission is that?" Jean Carlo noticed he was feeling amazingly better. He perked up considerably, and was looking and feeling much less like the corpse he had been just moments earlier.

"You are looking much better," Anthony said. "These foods and the wine that you drink are healing you. This is not the world that you have known. You will never know that world again, I'm afraid."

Jean Carlo set down his fork and his wine. Turning towards Anthony, he pressed for an answer. "What has happened to me, Anthony?"

"You have died," Anthony explained. "But when you woke up, and found yourself in your casket, and when you got out of it and hid from Darius, you have begun to transform."

"Into what?"

"Darius chose you because he had wanted another child. He has one who has risen to power, his name is Antoine. I will tell you more about Antoine later – he is at the center of this."

"And since he chose me, I have risen from the dead?" Jean Carlo's face twisted in question. "Where am I now?" His eyes scanned the room. It was boisterous and noisy, full of people, buzzing with activity, like a giant restaurant in an underground cave, with dim lighting, surrounded by walls of stone.

The acoustic veil of myriad conversations taking place at the same time permeated the room.

"You see all these people?" Anthony asked. "Each one of them has passed into this new dimension. You have passed through to this dimension as well. Others have passed into other dimensions – mainly brought forth by demons and immortals. This place here is a place of warmth and safety. You will want to stay here for the time being. If you go back outside, the world may look the same to you, but it won't be. No one noticed you as you came down here, did they?"

Jean Carlo shook his head.

"Of course they wouldn't. You are in the astral plane. The problem is, here…this dimension changes drastically when the sun goes down. It is *not* safe to go outside at night when you are here. The darkness is real, and it *will* get you. You don't know what you will find, and when you do find something, you may wish that you hadn't found it."

A short, paunchy grey haired man in the center of the table then stood and tapped his fork on his glass, drawing the attention of all who were seated at the grand table in the center of the room. Conversations gradually ceased, and attention was drawn to the speaker. Jean Carlo slowly turned his head to the center table as well.

"Good evening," the man said. "I hope those of who are new and just arrived know the ground rules. No venturing out and up the stairs. You are here for a reason, a good reason, and we expect you to stay. Secondly, no transformations here. They waste your energy and are forbidden. There is no room for extended auras in these catacombs. You may seriously injure those around you. And also, for those of you that are new, I will reiterate the purpose of holding you here."

"That is the director of the Astral," Anthony whispered to Jean Carlo. "He formed this society after years of research and investigation of prominent immortals. He is finding out their true purpose."

Once Anthony finished explaining who the man was, Jean Carlo returned his attention to the speaker: "– up above will waste your powers and cause you to engage in battles you otherwise should not be engaging in. Here, you are to rest, save your energy, and we will call upon you when needed. Soon, soon, we will."

The paunchy man stopped talking as the conversations gradually started once again. He looked over towards where Anthony and Jean Carlo were sitting, and made eye contact with Anthony. Jean Carlo looked first at Anthony and then glanced over at the paunchy man. The paunchy man then looked Jean Carlo in the eyes and smiled slightly. Jean Carlo saw the paunchy man back from where he was standing, and disappear behind the animated diners.

Moments later, as Anthony and Jean Carlo continued eating, Anthony felt a small tap on his shoulder. He turned around and saw the tired face and stringy hair of the paunchy man. The paunchy man drew his finger up towards Anthony's ear, and flicked it, signaling to Anthony that he wanted him to come and speak to him. Anthony excused himself, and lay his napkin and fork on the table, as Jean Carlo looked on.

The two men stopped and faced each other several feet away, out of earshot distance. "Is that him?" the paunchy man asked, glancing back over at Jean Carlo. He had stopped eating, but was still hunched over his plate, holding his wine goblet from the stem; he was casually glancing over at the two men talking, looking down again, and back at the two men, who had since retreated to a corner.

"Yes, that's him," Anthony responded, gently grabbing the man's arm, pulling him closer into the corner.

The two men again looked over at Jean Carlo, and saw that Jean Carlo had to have been looking over back at them, because his head had snapped back down, and stared down and studied the food.

"So that's the man of some great importance," the paunchy man mused, not breaking his gaze. "My, won't Darius be surprised to discover that he is here."

"That's why I want to be sure that he does not leave this sanctuary," Anthony said. "If he goes outside, he will be hunted. You know that. We can't bear to risk him. He is too important."

"Yes, I agree. We need him. I can feel from the way Antoine speaks to me, that he doesn't want this to happen. Sometimes I can look inside him, as he speaks to me, and see sadness and regret for what he has done. But it doesn't matter now."

"Antoine walks and acts like he is controlled," Anthony said.

"Oh, I agree," the paunchy man said. "Sometimes he misses his mortal life, but it was the sins of his immortal life that has landed him in the situation he is in now." The paunchy man gestured over to Jean Carlo. "Now he…" he said, "…he is the one that Darius made. He is

Antoine's sibling. Antoine can't be stopped because Antoine is trapped. Jean Carlo is the only one that can stop him."

"And what about Nesmaron?"

The paunchy man stopped.

He hadn't thought about the young man that Antoine had borne. That was a different story, and there was a different motivation. "Don't mention that name, Anthony. Because Nesmaron…the demon that will come…is the one that Jean Carlo must face."

Jean Carlo again looked up at the men. They returned to the table. The paunchy man approached the table and extended his hand to Jean Carlo. "Jean Carlo," he said. "You are a very important addition to this Society. I wanted to make sure that you will be well taken care of. Much more will be explained to you in the days that you are here. But please remember...do not go topside. Please don't. And if you need anything, anything at all, please ask for Sheldon."

~~*

CHAPTER THIRTY-TWO

Darius Sauvage. Demon god!

It was long before that Darius and Antoine had the encounter under the moon and stars that Darius had transformed.

Many hundreds of years earlier, in fact.

But the genesis of Darius' story will have to wait. Because in his new life, Darius led Roberto into *Sacrafice*...an unexpecting, innocent young man.

Did Darius want to transform Roberto into a dark demon? Was Darius still building his legions and his minions? Perhaps not.

But why did Darius care about Roberto? The Demon Darius had so much of his own web to weave; he loved his immortality and had shared it with Antoine.

But Antoine was not so accepting of the new fate that had been bestowed upon him.

That is right.

The genesis of Darius' story will indeed have to wait.

The beginning of this story will start, rather, when Darius and Antoine first encountered each other, back when Antoine was still a mortal. When Antoine was bedazzled with women who he later took away in ecstasy when Darius was discreetly watching, and waiting for the right moment to take him.

It was a night like any other; it was then that their eyes met for the first time.

It was if Darius had beckoned Antoine to look and lay his eyes on the strange brooding specimen. It was like the moment in a movie when the music stops and the hero and villain see each other for the first time.

And of course after that, when Darius figured in a much greater part in Antoine's immortality, the events came forth that led up to Antoine's placing Darius in an earthy grave. And it was the first time of many times that Antoine would attempt to destroy Darius and place him in the ground.

~~*

"Wake up, sleepyhead!"

Antoine opened the coffin lid, and sat up, quite perplexed as to how he got there. The last he remembered, he had drained himself of almost all of his blood, and collapsed in the cemetery.

The coffin lid opened slowly, and a faint dim candle light crept in, slowly swallowing the darkness, exposing Antoine to his first new night. There was his face before him…Darius.

Just as he remembered him from the forest the night before.

Darius.

His long, flowing brown hair. The smile on his face like that of a Cheshire cat.

The youthful beauty.

Wake up, sleepyhead.

Those words reverberated through his mind like a metronome. He heard them played in his mind, again and again, throughout the years of his immortality. But here he was, as the coffin lid opening above him, acting as if hearing those words for the first time.

~~*

The tutoring started out plain and simple.

Antoine, getting acclimated with staying up during the night and sleeping during the day, avoiding sunlight and becoming an unseen shadow in crowds of people, blending in as if to become invisible, and drinking the blood of an unsuspecting unfortunate soul who came across his path, did not at first hold any animosity towards Darius.

Darius taught Antoine in the ways of vampires, all while Darius learned the ways of demons from his Maker. The line continued, deeper and deeper into the past, deeper and further down the ancestral line of demons, back into the past when the first earthly demon existed.

The ways did not change, and, Antoine learned, many of the myths of the vampires were true, and, in turn, they were to live by those principles for a time.

Taught by Darius from day one, Antoine learned never to venture out into the sunlight. Not that it "killed" or "destroyed" him, but rather weakened his powers greatly, and that he was much closer to a mortal – at least in terms of vulnerability - while out in the daylight.

"Keep away from the sun, at least for now" Darius frequently explained. "It will not hurt, nor will it kill you alone. But be wary. You can easily be killed by other forces when moving about by day. You will grow and evolve in time."

"What other forces?" Antoine asked.

Darius did not look Antoine in the eye when he asked that question.

Darius stared down at his desk in the quaint, dimly lit library that the two had been conversing in. He slowly rose from his chair, stepping towards the left over to the fire that popped and crackled, and added another log to the flames and closed the screen. "There are many forces which could hurt you when you move about by day. I speak to you now, not because I want to dwell on this subject, but to protect you."

"Protect me from what? The forces?"

"Let me finish," Darius pleaded, returning to the desk. "When you move about during the day, you must use extreme caution. You are not really demoniac during those hours."

"So what am I then?"

Darius paused for a moment, as if searching for an answer. "Right now, you are in your infantile stage, Antoine. I am culturing you in the ways of the vampire, because, at this early stage, that is basically what you are. Vampires are a small night creature with little of the power that you are destined to have. You need to build up your strength. You have been chosen."

Darius stoked the fire as he spoke.

Turning back around to face Antoine, he continued: "I am much more than you. I have already gone through my stages of what could be compared to a vampire, and now I am much more powerful than a simple, silly vampire. I am of the Baal. You right now are basically the walking dead."

Those words resounded in Antoine's head over and over again.

The walking dead.

Wake up, sleepyhead!

"I am dead," said Antoine, pensively, staring at the fire as is hypnotized.

"You are dead."

Antoine rose from his chair. He slowly walked over to the fire, his gaze never left the blaze, which grew more and more intense as Darius stoked it.

"Right now you are in gestation," Darius explained, turning from the fire to face Antoine. "Eventually, you will become of the Baal. Right now you need to start with the ways of the vampire, and when you are ready to elevate to Baal you will…you will become closer to Tartarus and…"

"What can kill us?" he asked, still staring at the fire.

"It's different for both of us, since we are on different levels. Like I said, I am a full demon of the Baal. You need to follow the ways of the vampire, however simple they may seem, to survive. Once you are Baal, you will have much greater power and it will be much more difficult to kill you."

"What then, will kill a vampire?" Antoine asked.

With those words, Darius' head turned over to Antoine. He had previously been staring at *Les Livre Des Vampires.*

"Kill a vampire?" he asked.

"Yes."

Antoine turned from the fire, finally breaking his gaze. His long jacket swung with his body, barely missing the flames. "How do I kill a vampire?"

Darius rose from his chair.

He was not expecting such a question. As he rose and walked in the direction towards Antoine, he began to speak.

"That," he said, pointing to the book on the desk, "Is '*Le Livre Des Vampires*'." He returned to the desk, picking up the book and bringing it over to Antoine. "It is a textbook," he continued, "giving the reader insight as to what a vampire actually is. Why do we exist? *How* do we exist? And, as you asked, it tells what can bring our existence to an end."

"And you have read to that point in the book?"

"Yes, I have, and beyond. It will also answer some of your questions about the gestation to Baal." Darius opened his hand and gestured towards Antoine – who stood very close to the fire.

"Come back to the desk with me," Darius said. "I will show more to you. And you will see that you do not want to be standing as close to that fire as you actually are."

CHAPTER THIRTY-THREE

Once Antoine got acclimated to his new life as an immortal, and learning the ways of vampires and preparing himself for his gestation, he began to distance himself from Darius. As the days, and the months, and the years progressed, Antoine began to feel a deeper hate for Darius. But, it was shortly after that encounter they had in the library on that cold winter night that the pair were separated. And it was not fate that brought their union to an end. Or, perhaps, it could have been fate.

A fate controlled by Antoine.

Antoine killed Darius for the first time just a mere six months after Darius made Antoine. And several times over the years, Antoine would kill Darius again, and again, and again. It wasn't only that Antoine was capable of killing – being immortal he was expected to kill every day. The killing of course became a source of survival, but it wasn't necessarily the reason for it.

Darius killed primarily for fun and sport. Antoine had his reasons for killing, and he kept rationalizing with himself that it was for survival, since Darius had initially taught him the ways of the vampire and had explained to him that the reasons for the vampire tutelage was for preparation for gestation to Baal.

Killing one of his own kind - his maker - was different than Antoine's usual killing. The rebelliousness of it all made it more like a human taking the life of another human. For Antoine to kill Darius, it took the same hate and energy he had when he killed the unsuspecting suitor at the café so many years ago in his mortal life.

"Fire," said Darius. "That is an element which can end us."

Darius turned to a page near the end of *Les Livre Des Vampires.* The opened page showed a picture of what Antoine assumed was an immortal or vampire or some other entity being burned alive. The crude drawing was an artist's rendition, and it was somewhat hard to discern exactly what was going on in the drawing other than the obvious fact that someone in an apparent human form was being burned and charred to ashes.

Darius turned the page, and another drawing appeared. The stake still stood in the drawing, however there only appeared to be a pile of ashes at the foot of the stake, and there were several people standing around, as if they were observers to the killing.

Darius continued, focused on the picture, staring at the scene as he spoke. "Driving the blade through the heart of the immortal is what held him in place as he burned to ashes. See the blade sticking out from the stake? That is what held him there."

Antoine looked closer at the picture.

"And what is that?" Antoine asked, pointing at the drawing to a blurry object held to the stake by the blade. "What is that there?"

"That is the heart."

Antoine looked closer. He could not tell it was a heart simply by looking at it. "It appears unscathed," he mused. Antoine looked further down the page, and saw a footnote near the bottom of the page that explained that the mysterious object was the heart.

"The heart," Darius said, "is the center of an immortal. The human, the center is the brain. You can take away an immortals brain. You can take away our lungs. But our heart…that cannot be killed. Look in that picture, Antoine. This immortal…he has been crippled.

That is all. His heart is affixed to that stake. But if one were to raise him, he would walk again as an immortal as if he had never died."

An immortal dies, but then never really dies. The humanlike form is gone, destroyed, but the soul lives on. Lives on and waits, waits for someone to raise it. Waits in the darkness and solitude of a casket, feeling the dank cold surrounding it, feeling the coldness of the earth burying it, sealing it from day and night and air.

The dead await in the coffin as if buried alive, but then the immortal never really dies, and exists in the claustrophobic satin box in total blackness and isolation; waiting in agony and torment of its own personal hell for an undetermined amount of time leading up to eternity.

~~*

Darius closed the book.

The fire crackled, and let out a small pop, sending a spark onto the carpet in front of Antoine. He stepped forward onto the small, burning ember and stubbed it out. "To snub out an immortal..." he said, under his breath. "That is the only way?"

Darius pretended he did not hear. "Ashes, Antoine. Ashes. You will see. The heart will always remain. You could burn an immortal to ashes, to where there is nothing left. But the heart will remain, and it will remain until it is claimed by the protector."

"Who is that?"

"The protector of everything evil. He collects souls for favors."

"What kind of favors are those?"

"You will never know until you need him. And he comes when you least expect it. If you encounter him, he will not stop until he has your soul."

Antoine shuddered as Darius got up to place the book back on the shelf.

Over the next six months, Antoine grew much more distaste for Darius. But the two remained together during that time, side by side, killing, drinking and enamoring the people of Lyon. The two became inseparable, despite Antoine's growing hatred. The hatred came each evening as the coffin lid opened and he saw Darius' grinning, chiseled face and long, dark locks – a dark silhouette against the dim candle light. It appeared as if Darius could not be trusted. Or could he? Antoine could not reach inside Darius' mind.

That was no surprise.

Never could an immortal look into his makers mind. It was a spiritual impossibility, no matter how hard the protégé tried.

Antoine did not trust Darius because of any disloyalty - that was not the case. The two fought and hunted together like brothers; they attended plays and visited fine art galleries in Paris like lovers; it was the look in his eyes that Antoine came to distrust. There was just *something* about Darius that Antoine could not figure out.

Darius chose Antoine to be an immortal due to Antoine's blasphemies against God in his life. The sexual adventures.

His capability to kill.

Antoine understood that.

What Antoine could not understand was the secretiveness, like Darius was holding something back. Like there was a deeper, more destructive force behind their existence that Antoine would coil in terror from if he even knew his part in the grand scheme of living in immortality.

Yes, Darius was not telling the whole truth about the powers behind their existence. And Antoine knew, deep down, that their existence was inherently evil. And this upset him. While he was essentially a sinner during his short life, he did not want to live damned to evil.

But he kept these feelings from Darius.

The two had made the journey back to Lyon numerous times, in a horse drawn carriage, as Darius leaned his head on Antoine's shoulder, resting his eyes. And it was later on, after returning home, that Antoine decided that he could not stay. But there was no way that Darius would let his dear protégé go.

"Darius, I cannot stay here anymore," Antoine said, as he was standing before the fire. He turned to Darius, and looked him directly in the eyes. Darius was still seated behind the table in the center of the library, with *Les Livre Des Vampires* open in front of him. Darius said nothing. And when Antoine glided out of the room, he did nothing, save to turn and watch Antoine go.

Antoine barreled out of the front door, the door banging against the wall as he threw it open, the nearby windowpane shaking in its frame. And Antoine disappeared into the night.

CHAPTER THIRTY-FOUR

Crack!

Sparks flew as Antoine's pickaxe clanked against Darius' coffin liner. While it was not customary in the times that Antoine killed Darius to line graves with cement, Antoine chose to seal Darius' coffin in concrete for an added extra measure of protection.

It was still the wee hours of the morning.

There were no hints yet of daylight in the sky. The blackness was still enveloping, a deep dark sky that cascaded down to the grass, to the swirling white mist that made the gravestones seem as though they were sitting in newly fallen snow.

Antoine did not mind the loud clank that pierced the night silence as his pickaxe tore away at the lock on the grave liner. Despite being several hundred years old, Antoine mused at the fact that the lock was in excellent condition with very little rust. It has cost quite a bit, but again, he wanted an extra added measure of security, so Antoine bought the best lock he could find for the liner. Don't want your maker rising from the grave and getting revenge on you for killing him, do you?

Antoine still grimaced somewhat at what the chore that breaking the liner open had become. But with several more cracks that reverberated against the other crypts and stones and the mausoleum on the side of the cemetery, the liner could take no more and with a loud crack it split in two.

Antoine looked around. The crash had been so loud and grating that he could feel it rumble the ground beneath him.

Staring into the woods before him, he stopped for a moment, temporarily forgetting the freshly dug up grave before him, and stared more intensely into the thick, dark forest.

There was something out there. He could feel the presence.

Yes. And he had read about this before. Raising an immortal was a risky undertaking. It opens up the doors to different dimensions.

Antoine returned his attention to the grave. He bent down into the grave and began to hoist each piece of the broken liner to the surface of the ground, throwing them aside.

A tree snapped in the forest on the edge of the cemetery as Antoine snapped his head in the direction of the woods.

It definitely was coming from the forest. Something was rustling in the woods, but he could not make anything out, as the darkness was still to enveloping. He stood on the coffin, ducking beneath the edge of the grave, as if hiding from an undetermined potential...killer? Or was it just an animal?

More rustling came...and through the darkness, as Antoine peered above the grave, he saw some bushes moving. Yes. Something was indeed out in the woods.

Now his fears were confirmed – the thunderous boom, which shook the ground, and resulting limbs snapping confirmed that an entire tree just fell. His breathing quickened. He ducked down further into the grave.

The leaves rustled. Closer this time.

Whatever it was, it was moving towards the graveyard. Another tree snapped and fell. Antoine crouched further down into the grave until he was down as far as he could go.

He felt the ground shake with what sounded like heavy footsteps.

"Darius…." A soft voice emanated from the casket.

"Darius? Are you going to raise me from the dead?"

Antoine snapped his head down in the direction of the casket, just barely visible through the broken liner.

"Darius."

Who was in that coffin?

Antoine's heart was beating fast, and sweat was pouring down his face. He reached his arm topside to grab the axe.

Antoine seemed puzzled. Something wasn't making sense.

He had to break open the casket fast. Something inside was calling Darius' name. Hoisting the axe above him, it came down hard on the lid and broke it into pieces. Tossing it aside, he frantically tore at the remaining splintered shards of wood, and gasped.

There he was. There *he* was. Lying in the casket. Dead as a pile of bones and ash.

But it was himself, no doubt. His heart raced, his skin slimy with the sweat and dirt.

Glancing at his arms he saw he was no longer wearing the black coat that he was when he entered the graveyard.

These are not my clothes!

He reached into the brown tarp bag, searching for something, perhaps a knife, so he could look at his reflection. Eventually finding one, he brought it up in front of his face sideways to serve as a mirror.

When he saw, he dropped it to the ground.

Waking up, covered in sweat, Antoine shook his head. Was it a dream? How was he back in the graveyard – again?

He opened the coffin lid, and it creaked as he did so. Sitting up and draping his arm over the side of the casket, he replayed the dream in his mind, over and over. Was the dream a replay of his encounter with Asmodai?

Or was it a premonition of events to come?

CHAPTER THIRTY-FIVE

The Castillo family had moved to Miami shortly after the birth of their first and only son, Jean Carlo. The year was 1976, and Jean Carlo was still just a baby. His parents, Hector and Elsa, did their very best to give their son what he needed – or at least as much as they could afford. In the beginning, Hector would work driving trucks during the day delivering produce through the region before crashing for a few hours after dinner. Then, later at night he would hop on the train to downtown and clean office buildings in the towering skyscrapers, until the sun would peek across the sky.

And then the process would start all over again.

Jean Carlo lost his father when he was only ten.

After ten years of working two jobs and losing sleep night after night, he could not take it anymore. He loved his wife, and he loved his son. But he could not take the long days anymore. So one night, shortly after Elsa had turned in and had kissed him goodnight, after he had hugged his son and told him goodbye, Hector walked out the door, and he never returned again.

Once the door closed, he walked right past the rusted car sitting in the driveway, and continued walking down the street. He walked further and further down the dark, wet streets of Miami, splashing through the water and puddles on the streets that reflected the moonlight.

It was eerily quiet; there wasn't any activity - which seemed rare for this city – but Hector did not pay it any mind. The destination that he had in mind was not far, and he knew the way anyway. What he hadn't noticed was that he had walked all the way to Miami Beach, and was actually several miles away from where he had started.

Reaching a street corner, he looked up.

There were no clouds in the sky and the moon shined brightly, guarding over the sea of stars. A light and cooling wind blew. He crossed the street, and spotted a lonely grey door – his destination was nestled next to a large dumpster against a brick wall. He stood for a few minutes in front of the door and closed his eyes, exhaling. He glanced to the right and then to the left one last time.

There still was no one there.

He knocked on the door three times, and stood waiting for an answer. A few minutes later, the door opened to complete darkness.

He stepped in.

"Don't say a word," a mysterious female voice commanded.

The door slammed, swallowing Hector in the darkness. He never once for a moment doubted that he had done the right thing. He knew that he would no longer see his wife, he knew that he would not witness the rest of Jean Carlo's childhood.

But he chose this path.

He heard a pop – a snapping sound and after the resulting, smoky smell of sulfur in the air. He saw a hand holding a burning match in a small circle of yellowish light surrounded by darkness. The flame reached into the blackness and cast a faint glow, as a hand brought it to a candle, igniting the flame.

He saw a woman with red hair. She drew her finger to pursed lips. "Come with me," she whispered.

She led him deeper into the building, and their footsteps clanked down a set of steel stairs. Hector had to dodge old Styrofoam cups, crumpled papers and other trash carefully to keep from tripping. She held the candle, and although she stood next to him, he could barely see the stairs before him.

And that was for the best.

What he did not see was coming around the corner was a room prepared just for him. He could feel the stone walls, but most striking were the people in the room. They were dressed in black; giant flowing robes that covered their faces and reached to the floor, covering them to stand like chess pieces rising from the floor; each one indistinguishable from the next.

In the center of the room was a square stone slab, a solid structure rising from the floor. Four black metal hooks rose from each corner on the top surface.

"I have prepared this place for you, as you had requested," the woman said, glancing in his direction and smiling as they stood in the large, sloped doorway to the room.

Hector looked up.

An iron cage hung from the ceiling, and there was a giant fire burning inside. The flames moved steadily in a circle inside the cage, and were completely contained, as if it were being manipulated by an unseen force. He lowered his gaze and looked ahead and around the room, he saw that the black hooded ones were gathered in a semicircle around the slab.

And he knew what that slab was.

He already knew of the dark forces at work here. And he knew why he must sacrifice himself tonight.

Several years earlier, he had noticed a change in his son.

Jean Carlo became increasingly quiet and distant, not really spending much time outside him room other than going to school. It got to a point where Jean Carlo would come home, slam the door behind him, stomp up the stairs and lock himself in his room. He generally would not come down until the next morning. He was not eating, and had lost weight. He didn't really ever look his father in the face, even when being asked a direct question. And when he did look at his father, Jean Carlo looked like a skeleton. The skin hugged his skull; each ridge of bone was pronounced, and his eyes stared straight and wide.

And it was those changes that prompted Hector to look through his room one day when he had called in sick to work. As he dabbed the tip of his nose with a wadded tissue, he sniffled as he rifled through drawers of socks and shirts and found something that no ten year old should have in his dresser drawer.

He dug down into the clothes, and felt the stiff, cool edge of a hardback book. He fished out several books, each hidden vigilantly between bright red and blue t-shirts and brilliant white tube socks; each book large and thick bound. As he pulled each book out, he dropped them to the floor and shook his head

He ran to the other room for his phone and quickly called Elsa.

"He found my books!" he screamed into the phone, his voice still very nasal from his cold. "How could he have found them? I had them locked away!"

"He asked for them, Hector," Elsa replied. "I gave them to him."

"What? When?"

"He has shown a great interest in religion. He even said he might be interested in becoming a priest. It's not like it isn't out there. With every good, there is evil. You know that."

"I had hoped to have put that behind me."

"Then why do you still have the books?"

Hector squeezed the phone until his hand turned red and the veins were showing through his skin. He did not like it when his wife demanded such answers; she knew that he had gotten involved, in his younger days, with parapsychology and demonic research. He had almost lost his life during a sacrificial ritual where he had been forced to slit his cheeks down from the ear to the jawbone and have his face covered with a plastic bag as it filled with blood.

Touching one of the scars on his face, he considered the question. "You know why I have the books, Elsa. I have them because I cannot get rid of them. They are not something I can just throw away. They will haunt me for the rest of my life. I have tried trashing them, and they would always show up again. As if someone came and put them back on the shelf. That's why I locked them up downstairs. And now here I am finding them in our ten year old son's room!"

"It's part of religion, hon, and he has an interest in this."

Hector stooped down on the floor, examining the books. He pulled out a book, *Les Livre Des Vampires.* He closed his eyes and sighed. A book filled with evil, lust and demons. "It's unhealthy for him to have this interest, even if it's for an interest in priesthood. He is far too young. I am taking these books and burning them."

But he never did burn the books.

As he stood before the hooded brethren and prepared to accept his fate, two of the members walked up to him and grabbed him roughly, snapping his arms behind him as if he were a criminal and shackled him in chains.

The woman removed her hood.

He red hair framed her face, with was youthful and beautiful. Her bright red lips smiled to reveal gleaming white teeth. But they didn't stay white for long. Hector looked more closely at her teeth, which were beginning to elongate and spike.

The teeth grew sharp like the tips of swords, and turned black and putrid and dripping acid to the floor which vanished into tiny puffs of smoke. Her tongue slithered out of a proboscis turned black and acrid; the sliver tip darted in and out between her fangs like a giant serpent. The skin of her face transformed slowly as the black skin fingered its way across her cheeks.

Hector was guided over to the slab by the two followers, and he looked up. He did not resist, but rather scanned the room once more, noticing the hooded brethren. They pulled their hoods back, and Hector saw that he was the only mortal in the room.

Something was out of place.

Each face was a serpent. All of the faces were moving and changing; often the eyes would replace a slithering tongue, and the cheeks would sink in and hug the bone; or the ears would move to the center of the face, as the eyes moved down towards the neck. But one thing was for sure – one thing that Hector had been certain of. Was that the faces always were moving; and they always were laughing and slithering.

Slithering.

And then she came to him. She grabbed his arm. "*You stupid fuck*!" she hissed. "You shouldn't have done that! You shouldn't have! I know what you were thinking when you were rooting through that drawer! You wanted a pair, didn't you?"

And then, he felt a twinge of regret.

He did not want to die this way.

He did not want to live out the rituals that he so often read about, night after night, feeding a hobby that became an obsession. For the first time since he had entered the door, he started to struggle.

"You fucking *fuck*!" She slithered her tongue along the side of his cheek. He felt a cold hot flesh pierce his skin. "They looked enticing, didn't they? A nice pair of tighty whiteys right next to your books."

He grunted as the chains clanked against the quiet dull roar of the fire. He tried to speak, although he tried many times and with great effort to shout and scream; but it would not matter. He was too far down. Deep down the flights of stairs that he was led, further down into the recesses of the catacombs – no one could hear a scream anyway.

The fire surged and fingered its way down towards the altar; as if commanded. The fire swelled, and brightened the room. Hector felt the sweat bead on his forehead. The Lead Serpent slithered up his side, wrapped itself around his arm, tightening its grip tighter and tighter until his arm started to turn purple. He cried out.

The two serpents that held his shackles were still a sickening cross between mortal males and snakes, their greenish muscular limbs pulling the chains tighter until he cried out.

There was no use in resisting – but he tried nonetheless.

His muscles swelled as he felt them filling up with blood, and he lunged forward onto the altar. The female serpent hissed and spit, wrapping itself around his arm even tighter, and as he lay on his back on the altar, he tried pulling at the snake to get it off of his arm.

"Do not resist me!" the snake hissed at she bit his cheek, piercing his skin sending a shower of blood in a river on the floor. Her eyes stared straight into Hector's. "You dreamt this!" She said. "You wanted this! You asked for this! And now the fate is yours – you will die on this altar as so many have died on this altar before. It is too late now for forgiveness, it's too late to reverse this passion!"

He jumped up but was immediately stopped by the serpents that had held his shackles. He stood before the group, his eyes locked with theirs, their places held. The group was closing in on him. There would be no mercy here. A sacrifice must be made before dawn. And Hector was the perfect candidate; his dark side lured him in, curiosity overtaking him.

"This is what happens to miserable fucks like you!" she said, drawing her arm up in command.

They closed in on him – the two serpents completely transformed and wrapped around his waist, squeezing him until he collapsed down onto the altar.

He tried to scream but couldn't.

He was picked up and thrown back down on the altar, so hard that blood oozed out from under his head, causing a small pool to form and drip down the side of the stone slab.

Several of the watching serpents slithered over to the dripping blood and began to lap and drink it. Three man-serpents held Hector down as the snakes that had wrapped themselves around his torso loosened and dissolved into chains, linking themselves onto the hooks on the slab, tightening over his body to a death grip.

The female serpent transformed back into a cross between a snake-demon, and stood over Hector, now unable to move in the chains confining him on the altar.

"This is the moment you have lived your life for," she said, looking down upon him. She drew a sword. "Azra!" she commanded.

The sword burst into flames.

She swung the sword back and forth slowly over where Hector lay. "On the dawn of the new century, the demons will descend upon the earth, and one will rise. One will rise from the ashes below; in the bowels of the earth he will stay and wait and eventually resist. But before his resistance, the cities will fall. The cities will fall and be swallowed by the gods!"

She swung her sword down, and a loud clank and sparks came from the hook that she pierced. Hector winced, knowing that she did not miss her target. He felt one of the chains had loosened.

The sword came down again, and she spoke: "One man shall rise from the grave and resist me! And you! You will be the bearer of the son of the resistance!" Another shower of sparks fell to the floor, and another chain loosened. He felt the blood rushing back to his limbs, although the pain from the chains had cut through his skin, and he was bleeding through his clothes.

"Go!" she screamed "Leave this place now!"

The room of serpents rushed upon the altar, covering him as he struggled to get up, now weakened from the blow to his head and the grip of the chains. But her sword cut through, showering blood throughout the room, spurting it's red rain upon him; creating a parting path that led to the stairs to the world above.

He crawled as fast as he could across the floor as the female serpent crushed and held back the rushing serpents battling her own followers. She showed no mercy except to Hector. She knew he could not be killed, although she had wanted to. Although the room of serpents wanted to, she had no choice but to let him live. For no matter what evil he may have had running through his veins, no matter what evil he was capable of, he was destined to raise the one who would find the shining beacon of hope rising through the darkness and agony.

So it was written, so must it be done.

CHAPTER THIRTY-SIX

Thunder rumbled in the distance and rain pelted on the windowpane in Roberto's old room and awoke Paula from her semi-asleep state. Gradually opening her eyes, she looked across the room in a dazed condition. She realized where she was after a minute of "clearing out the head" and that she was trapped. After a moment, she remembered her predicament. She was trapped in the house on Anastasia Avenue, and whatever was outside the door she felt was still there.

Darkness and pain.

That's what it was. Something mysterious outside the door, waiting for her. For some reason not yet to be determined.

But it was there.

She heard it breathing.

With each breath it took the door shook, in and out, in and out, deeply and raspy and grating – in unison with the rattling of the door in the wooden frame.

Paula tried to tune out the breathing and listened for other faint sounds – anything that indicated life other than what was on the other side of the door as the thunderstorm passed and quieted.

Nothing.

But all she did hear something as if there were a scraping, but it wasn't really a scraping. Like something was pacing back in forth in front of the bedroom door.

Keeping guard.

And it also sounded more like a muffled, strained breathing.

So it was there. Waiting for her.

Looking towards the door, Paula could barely see ahead the ten feet splayed in front of her; she saw a smattering of music discs, some clothes, and every so often when the lightning would strike (even though it got fainter and more infrequent as the storm moved farther away) she would see the pale blue walls and posters of muscular athletes and thin supermodels.

Paula seemed amazed that she was in this room. This room was where it all began.

She reached into her pocket and grabbed her cell phone. She woke it up and used it for a light. She found the door - a faint luminescent glow on the eggshell white - and just then the doorknob rattled.

It was trying to get in.

Paula opted against going to the door and taking her chances with whatever was in the hallway standing guard. There had to be another way out, besides the door before her.

As she scanned the room with the light on her phone, she saw there were no other doors, just a closet. And even as she rose to quietly tiptoe over to the closet and inspect the tiny enclave, she found nothing but pale white walls and clothes, books, boxes and magazines. Nothing that seemed of any interest and nothing that would be of any help to her.

Looking at the ceiling in the closet, she did see a small door painted white to blend in with the walls. Most likely the entrance to an attic or some other storage room. But this was no time to explore. This was no time to venture deeper into this strange house; it was time to get out.

For the moment, the rattling stopped. It appeared as if the monster were waiting for her to do something.

But she didn't have to.

She didn't have to break through the door and sacrifice her life, she didn't have to make any rash decisions at that moment. She fell against the hanging clothes in the closet she had been rummaging through as a giant sphere of light appeared in the room, giving off a pale blue and white light, illuminating the entire room. Once the light swelled, it faded, revealing the silhouette of something that looked like a man.

But it couldn't have been a man, considering the outline. The head was too elongated and it appeared to have pointed spikes jutting from the head.

"Come out and see me, Paula," the figure said. She hovered in the closet, covering herself with clothes, as if they would provide protection had the figure become hostile. For some time, it didn't.

"Paula, I have answers to the many questions that you now have," the voice continued softly.

The voice sounded male, but she could not tell for sure. It could have been a woman, but the voice was very deep - Paula had been sure of that now that it spoke again. The voice almost sounded like that of a child.

It took a step closer to her, and she cowered just a bit.

"Come forward, Paula, do not be afraid. I will not hurt you." The figure spoke with warmth in its voice, and that warmth made Paula feel that maybe the figure could be trusted. Even so, at the point she was at, she didn't see how anything could be worse than the thought of what was on the other side of the door.

"I have calmed the demon on the other side of that door. He is frozen and will not harm you while I am here."

Now Paula could hear more clearly, she could tell that the voice was female. The more she heard it, the more it sounded loving and reassuring. At the moment, it seemed to her the only thing that possibly made any sense in the madness that the world had been her voice. Whatever she said, no matter what, seemed like a ray of hope.

Paula slowly and carefully exited the closet. The clothes she had been sitting in dropped to the floor. The figure started to glow, and transformed into a beautiful woman with straight auburn hair with pale skin. She was elongated and thin, as if she could be a model.

But she continued to glow in transparency, with an aura that reached out into the darkness. She seemed so out of place in the dull, dark world.

"Certainly you have questions?" she asked, as she sat down on the bed like she was weightless.

Paula kneeled in front of the woman, sat back on her shoes and gathered her thoughts for a moment. "I…" she stammered. "I don't even know where to begin…" She shook her head with a worried look plastered on her face, wondering what could possibly have happened. "Where am I?"

During her tenure at The Astral, she had always had an interest in the macabre and the paranormal but never had an experience that could be considered of that nature. She was a staff member simply for her interest and appreciation, not for her experience.

"I have been certain you were wondering where you are," the woman said, looking about the room. Paula shook her head slowly.

"You crossed over to this side of reality. It's an alternate dimension which exists right along side of the reality that you have come to know and experience throughout your life. The difference is, it is reality to us. It is not to you. It is reality to demons, to the creatures of the Netherworld. Warlocks, immortals, those creatures – and many others - cross over to this dimension quite often."

"How did *I* get here?" Paula finally asked.

"Let me explain," the woman said. "You did not fall into this dimension by chance, although many people do. Many are pulled into this dimension at the moment of a sudden violent event – like a car accident or a shooting – just before their body dies. Others fall completely by chance. Depending on their beliefs, they might collapse into the reflection of a puddle and wind up here."

"So you are saying that this is where people go when they die?"

"Not exactly. In some cases that could be true. But this is another dimension. This is not heaven nor is it hell. But as you can see, the spirits run free. And it is not a safe place for a mortal like you."

"How did I get here?" Paula asked again.

The woman smiled warmly.

"You did not get here by accident. You were chosen."

Paula sat down for a moment, and collapsed in a pile of old clothes. She didn't know what to make of being chosen. Whatever she was chosen for, she didn't want to accept. Wiping her face with her hands, she looked back up at the woman, who now stood.

"You don't have much of a choice, I'm afraid," she continued. "You are here, in the land of the immortals, and you will run continuously from demons as long as you are here. The only way that you have a hope of returning to your reality is if you submerge yourself deeper into *this* reality."

"How do I do that?"

"You will fulfill what is written," she said, as she slowly walked around the room. She stopped at the window and pulled the drapes to the side. The window revealed nothing – it did not reveal landscaping or a moonlit night. But just…nothing. "Your affiliation with Antoine Nagevesh is what initially drew our attention to you."

She sat up and crossed her arms. "I don't have an affiliation with him."

The woman released the curtain, and it fell back into place. Her head snapped over to look at Paula. "Oh, but you do," she answered. "Antoine has been an obsession of yours now for several years. I know everything, Paula. I see everything. I know about your encounters with him, I know about your baby. You see, your affiliation with him is why I chose you."

"For what?" Paula replied back, fighting back tears of exhaustion and defeat. "What am I supposed to do?"

"Antoine has two very powerful beings pursuing him. The two most powerful spirits in all of existence. He has betrayed one, stealing a precious gift. And the other…" her voice trailed off as distant thunder rumbled again.

The storm was returning.

"The other is looking to collect his soul."

Paula thought about what she had just heard. What spirit would want to collect Antoine's soul? Certainly there was more to Antoine that would meet the eye. But that still didn't matter to her, and the thought did not stay in her head for long.

"You will be needed to birth what will become his nemesis," the woman instructed. "You will be with child again, impregnated in this world, in this dimension. That is why I chose you."

She came over to Paula and extended out her hand, offering assistance. She smiled and looked down at Paula. "Stand up," she said. "I know what you are thinking. But I'm afraid this is what is willed to happen. Your thoughts are open to me, they are open to any of these demons. Here, there is no hiding. There is no hiding from the monsters that roam these streets."

"And what if I don't do this?" Paula asked as she rose to her feet. "What if I avoid this?"

"You can't. You can try all you like, but it will happen. It *will* happen."

And with a quick flash of light, she disappeared, and Paula was once again left alone in the room, now with more questions than ever.

CHAPTER THIRTY-SEVEN

Dinner had ended and he was shown to his quarters.

The bed that Jean Carlo lay in was very plain and simple; it was a simple stone slab that jutted out perpendicular from the wall, which was on the side of a small, stone room with a single wooden door. It seemed more like a prison cell. But it was really only a holding room. As he woke and rubbed the sleep out of his eyes, he wondered what time it was. And he wondered how long he had been sleeping, and he wondered how long he had been in this small room.

He vaguely remembered meeting the Astral Director at dinner – but for some reason he felt like that was very long time ago. Maybe even years ago.

The watch on his wrist was not working and had a crack in the glass; and there were no clocks.

His mind continued reeling from all of the information that Sheldon and Anthony had fed to him. While he was still in a state of shock and disbelief that he had passed from his mortal life, he remembered that he now existed in an alternate world, and he still believed that the whole magnitude of the situation had not set in.

A knock on the door interrupted his thoughts.

He got up and slowly padded over to the door, and cautiously opened it a few inches.

A tall, grey-haired man stood outside smiling a toothless grin. His receding hairline accentuated a large forehead – yet his silver hair extended far below his shoulders.

"Good evening," he said shortly, and pushed the door open, startling Jean Carlo for a moment. He entered the room so quickly that Jean Carlo had to step back. "I have your obituary," he said. "I thought you might want to read this, since you seemed so distant when we were speaking earlier."

The visitor extended his hand with a small newspaper clipping. Jean Carlo took the clipping from him and read it. After a short period of silence, he spoke.

"This…" He closed his eyes. "This doesn't make any sense. What are you saying here? Something that I have been told over and over since I have been down here?"

"You have passed to a different dimension, yes. You were killed by Darius for a different purpose, but we intervened. We called you, and you came. It's interesting…Antoine had since made himself a child since he had been in Miami. And Antoine is Darius' child."

"Right, you were all telling me this over dinner."

"Yes, but Darius was never satisfied with one child. He wanted many – and he would always transform them into his minions – his followers, if you will – because what is going on out there is a lot deeper and more serious than you might understand."

"What is going on out there?" he asked, suddenly more interested in the conversation.

"Antoine is in debt to Asmodai. He reanimated Darius, and for that, Antoine owes Asmodai his soul. But Asmodai is coming. He will be searching for Antoine, and Antoine knows this. That's why Antoine hardly ever crosses over anymore – he feels safer, I suppose, on the other side. But those on this side will pay."

"You mean to say that…"

"...that is why we are not safe here. We are hunted." He gestured up to the ceiling. "Out there...up above. Those who are up there are not safe. He is coming. And he will stop at nothing to get to Antoine."

Jean Carlo stood and took in what he had just heard, sighed shortly and gave his mind some time to digest all of the information. The visitor kept saying that this was all told to him by Sheldon, that everything was discussed over dinner, but Jean Carlo's memory was very blurry. It was like watching a picture that was out of focus, and he couldn't sharpen it. It was as if he were hearing it again for the first time.

"You are hunted, we are all hunted, and there are even those who are trapped above and they have no way to get back to their reality without going deeper inside the realm."

"What do you mean?"

The old man brushed some of his hair that had gotten in his face and hooked it behind his ear, and moistened his lips with his tongue. He stopped and raised his hands. "Okay. You came here after death. You rose from your coffin. That was the plan, and the moment you exited your coffin, you had passed over. To here. To *this* side. It's the natural progression. There are some others who came here by chance...but you...you were always meant wind up here..."

And for a moment, the man's soft voice was drowned out. Jean Carlo was back in total blackness.

He opened his eyes and fumbled around, but couldn't move. Something was restricting him. He couldn't see and checked his pockets for matches or a lighter, but found nothing.

Totally empty.

He squirmed, tried to move, but couldn't. Something was constraining him.

The only sound his could hear was his shallow breathing. He thought that this must be some sort of dream, that soon he would wake up, and he would be in his bed at home, warm and safe. Because where he was now, it was cold. It was the coldest cold that he had ever experienced in his life *ever.* It was the type of cold that you felt deep inside your body; the kind that chilled your bones until they hurt.

And then he thought he heard something. Was it a voice? Something muffled. It sounded like it could be someone speaking, but he couldn't make out what was being said. And then he heard a different noise – a sound that still seemed to be a voice, but not quite so deep.

They chorused together like a hushed conversation. Yes, that was it. He could tell that now. Two people had to have been speaking. But why couldn't he hear them? What was he in?

He ran his hands along the sides and felt a soft and velvety pillow. Was he in bed? No. It couldn't be. At least not in *his* bed.

He played the events of the last night that he could remember in his mind. He remembered driving north on Alton Road, heading towards Flamingo Park. He remembered what he was going to the park for, too. And it wouldn't have been the first time that he had awoken in a strange bed after a night of heavy drinking and sex.

But this seemed different.

*Whatever sick fuck did this to me…*he thought, and stopped.

There was a man.

He remembered now.

He remembered sitting in his car, the engine and lights cut off, the windshield just beginning to show signs of steaming up from the deep humid air. He recalled looking through that windshield and seeing a tall, quite attractive man standing down the sidewalk against the park hedges. He had long brown hair. He remembered.

It was slowly coming back to him, like a drunk's memory returning after a night of heavy drinking. Yes, the man was tall. He was wearing heavy clothes that seemed rather out of place for the warmth and humidity of Miami Beach in the summertime.

But he was drawn to man's eyes.

His aura. His attraction.

Yes, he remembered that much.

This mysterious man had given him a wane smile, made eye contact, and then Jean Carlo's mind drew a blank. He just plain and simply could not remember what happened after his car door opened.

And here he was.

Was that the sick fuck who locked him up in some sort of chest inside his house? Deep in the basement?

But then Jean Carlo was startled as the entire box he was in shook and there was a crash to his right, like someone took an axe to it. A small slit of light crept in, and he saw just a bit of the ivory interior.

Wait a minute.

What the fuck did this sick fuck put me in?

And for a moment, he was blinded. The darkness was chased away by the bright afternoon sunlight, reaching in with a vengeance, and as his eyes adjusted to the new light, he saw standing above him the silhouette of a long-haired man who did not speak…

~~*

Jean Carlo had forgotten where he was. And as he came to, he remembered. Looking around the small stone room, he saw the visitor, still speaking, seemingly unaware of his mental exit.

"…You sounded so distant before that I thought it would be prudent to bring this to you, Uriel." He gestured to the obituary, which Jean Carlo had set down on a table across from the bed.

Jean Carlo stopped for a moment, shaken out of his dream. "What did you say? Uriel? Is that your name?" he asked.

"No, I called you Uriel. My name is Jonas Mayer."

"Why did you call me that?"

The visitor entered and sat down on the bed, in the middle of a pile of bedclothes. After a few minutes had passed, he looked up at Jean Carlo and spoke softly, so softly that Jean Carlo had to strain to hear him.

"That is *your* name, dear sir."

CHAPTER THIRTY-EIGHT

As Sheldon's small, four-cylinder Escort puttered down Andelusia Avenue, he was too engrossed in Antoine's file to notice Anthony's car – which was parked just merely across the street from Antoine's house, or Paula's car, which was parked a block away. He was driving, but his head was moving back and forth, alternating between looking through the windshield at the road and thumbing through Antoine's file, which currently was a mess of papers bound by a manila file on the passenger seat.

Sheldon was excited about all of the information he had gotten about Antoine's history, his mortal life, his transformation, and his life as an immortal. He had to rush back to the office and enter all of the information into the database!

Speeding down Andelusia, he finally came to US1, just making the light and squealing the tires, headed north to Coral Way to the office. It did not take long to get there. He darted into the garage, zipping into his parking space so fast that he parked his car on a slant straddling two spaces. He did not care. It was late. He heaved his plump, round body out of the small car, grabbing the file and all its contents as he did so.

He rushed into the office, slamming the door behind him. He sat at his mammoth desk, he dumped the entire contents of the file out on the surface. Immediately reaching for the discs, he put one in the player:

"So why are you here? You want to know how I got to be in this position? Oh, what time is it? Yes…I suppose I could tell you a little of how I came to be, how I came to exist. But, first I have a question for you. Yes, take a sip of the brandy."

That was nonsense. He pushed fast forward, and the usual squeaks and chipmunk-style voices emanated from the recorder. Antoine was very hospitable, but he didn't really care about pleasantries. He needed to find Darius. There was something about Darius! The recording continued.

"I opened my eyes, and looked down. The tree tops were below me, and I could see the bridge and the brook where he came upon me, I saw the path where I saw the red eyes, where I was running from the sounds and the eyes which I could not determine where they were. And then I could see the roof of the café, and it got smaller and smaller and began to look miniscule."

There was a piece of it. The Day of Transformation.

Darius.

And Darius was the one who Antoine had unearthed. And, according to Antoine, he unearthed him just recently. Why would he unearth the immortal he killed so many years ago?

There was a knock on the door.

The door opened by itself before Sheldon had a chance to answer it. Standing in the doorway was the silhouette of a man; light emanated from the background, as if some strange glowing entity were behind him. Sheldon sat frozen at his desk, his right index finger holding the pause button.

He held his gaze towards the door. "Anthony?" he asked, inquisitively. "What are you doing here so late?"

But the dark figure did not respond.

It moved closer.

Sheldon sat in disbelief as he watched the shadowy figure glide into his office, but did not move. He couldn't. He was like petrified wood. And he felt beads of sweat starting to form on his forehead. Even all the whiskey did nothing to calm him.

Something told him that the figure was not Anthony.

Still in the shadows, the figure was now much closer, hovering over the desk. Sheldon debated on whether to reach to his brass lamp on the edge of the desk – which would put an end to the mystery – or sit back in his chair.

Sheldon finally mustered enough courage to speak. "Who…who are you?"

The figure came closer, and Sheldon could finally make out a face. Long, brown hair, framing a pale white face. Could it be?

"Darius?"

"Yes," he finally spoke. "I am Darius."

Sheldon sat back in his chair, smiled and chuckled softly. "Wow, it's so great to finally meet you!" For the moment, his curiosity was peaked. Questions started running through his mind – why did Darius come here? What would he want with me? How did he even *know* about me? And then Sheldon stopped for a moment.

Antoine.

That's the only way that Darius could know about me, Sheldon thought to himself. But his curiosity took the best of him. His obsession started to take center stage, leaving regards to his safety to the wind.

"Do you mind?" Sheldon leaned forward in his chair and opened his drawer. He fumbled with un-wrapping a couple of new audio discs. "Do you mind if I ask you a few questions?"

Darius lunged forward until he was at the edge of the desk, and he slammed his fist down on the desk. "I am not Antoine!" he insisted. "I am not here to tell a story!"

Sheldon froze, his mouth hanging wide open.

Thoughts entered his mind about his safety. He looked Darius in the eyes. They were yellow and intense. Sheldon gingerly placed the discs back and closed the drawer slowly so it wouldn't make a noise.

"I know what you are running," Darius said with a harsh tone in his voice. "I know what you are *forming*."

"What are you talking about?" Sheldon asked.

He lunged forward again, jumping onto the desk and grabbing Sheldon by his collar and pulling him forward until Sheldon could feel Darius's hot breath.

"Don't even try it!" Darius exclaimed, with laughter. "I am keeping my cool here. I am letting you live. But I know what this 'society' is all about…" He gestured wildly around the room with his free arm to accentuate what he was saying. He pulled Sheldon closer to his face until Sheldon was lifted up from the chair. "*You have something of mine.*"

And then he dropped Sheldon back in the chair, and the chair leaned back so far that it fell over backwards, and Sheldon crashed on the floor.

Darius laughed, throwing his head back at the sight, and jumped down from the desk and instinctively brushed his legs off. "You are such a fat fucking drunk slob," he said, shaking his head at the comment. "Imagine…a fuck up like you! Organizing the fucking resistance!"

Darius started pacing. Sheldon got up, corrected the chair, and stood behind his desk, saying nothing.

"I'm sure you would like to go home, wouldn't you?" Darius asked, stopping his pacing and glaring right at Sheldon.

He did not respond.

"…yes, home in your bed, sleep off the booze, maybe jack off to some internet porn and pass out until noon tomorrow…that's what you would like to do, I'm sure. But no." Darius came close to Sheldon again, but did not touch him.

"You're not going home yet," Darius said. He calmed and softened his voice. "You don't want to see me angry, dear sir. But I came here because you have something of mine. Antoine may tell the world about his story – but I am different. So I doubt you may have heard. Antoine and I are two very different creatures. But I might as well tell you. I have created a son. One who I want to mold into my successor. But he has given me trouble. I don't hold him accountable for it – yet. But I hold *you* accountable for it, dear sir."

Darius put his arm around Sheldon and ushered him towards the door.

"So now, you need to come and take me to him. I know he came here. And I know you are holding him. I see a lot, dear sir. I know a lot as well. I have the power of knowledge. That is my weapon. But don't mistake." Darius squeezed Sheldon closer. "I will rip your fucking heart out and eat it in front of your fucking face if you don't take me to him."

Sheldon stopped breathing for a moment. He held the air in, desperately running methods of escape through his mind, and stopped. This was silly. He was supposed to be leading a spiritual *revolution* and here he was…standing before the enemy acting like a fool. A schoolboy. A coward.

So he cleared his throat, preparing to speak.

"Darius," he began, "There is nothing here. You are mistaken. We are a simple group of people that investigates demons, the paranormal…vampires. We call ourselves The Astral. We truly mean no harm to you. We want to *help* you. That is our goal!"

"Simple fool!" Darius screamed as he lunged forward and grabbed Sheldon's shoulders. He slammed him against the wall so hard that plaster fell. "Do not lie to me! If you don't reveal where he is I will kill you! I will take you and bury you in my grave!"

Sheldon nodded and raised his hand to his lip as his mouth started oozing bright red blood. He ran his hands through his wisps of hair, pulling bits of plaster and dust out. He did not know what to say to Darius. Darius knew that he was lying, he knew that Jean Carlo had come here, but he didn't seem to know about the Catacombs.

Good.

Darius' emotions were running too high to be lying himself. Given the display, Sheldon could tell that Darius was truly frustrated.

"This is a waste of my time," he finally said. He stepped closer to where Sheldon was laying on the floor, in the pile of broken plaster. "Stupid, silly old man. You think that I won't find your secret little society. I will. And I *did.* Trust me. I have more power on my side than you can imagine. You will see. Asmodai will come, and he will find all he needs to find. It's not much longer now. Just wait and see. *Consider it a warning.*"

With those words, he exited the room so fast, with a giant burst of wind and bright light like an explosion. And when the air cleared, Sheldon saw a gaping hole where the door to his office used to be.

CHAPTER THIRTY-NINE

"Thank you Sir," Antoine said, looking Frank Magellan in the eye seductively, as he gently took the ball-point pen from the business magnate's white liver spotted hand. "You have invested in what will be the new wave of a lifetime," he continued. He placed down the contract on a pile of contracts at the head of the conference table. Darius brought another pile of contracts and handed them to Antoine, who in turn placed them in the pile as well.

A few investors cleared their throats, while others took a sip at their water. Antoine and Darius made eye contact and smiled discreetly and knowingly. Everyone was on board.

"Your return on your investment will be substantial and immediate," Antoine stated. He stood proudly at the head of the conference table. "I promise all of you, you will all be very wealthy. Investing in a…a *project* of this nature will ensure your financial security."

He placed his hands down on the table and looked everyone in the eyes directly. "You will all be my closest advisors. I will do nothing without you."

Once the meeting adjourned, the members rose from the conference table and began to herd towards the doors. There were twelve investors – and Antoine hand selected them. All of them were wealthy, powerful business moguls and all have the capital to expand *Sacrafice* to worldwide levels.

The investors saw a business proposal that was well crafted, exquisitely written and expertly presented. Antoine and Darius each possessed the gift of persuasion that was needed to capture the commitment of each investor.

And each investor signed with minimal resistance.

Once the presentation concluded, Antoine and Darius walked around the table to each investor and answered specific questions – but of course giving answers that seemed, at first, as specific and detailed, however when re-examined were actually quite broad and overly general.

But that was the gift of persuasion that each immortal possessed. It did not take much effort at all to convince the twelve fiscal geniuses to agree to support Asmodai as a demonic legion and sell their souls, damning themselves to Hell, while pouring out mountains of financial support.

"Imagine a corporation that requires a substantial initial investment," Darius had offered during the presentation. "But the return would be…astronomical. Limitless." He stood at the head of the table, and spoke directly to the investors, making direct eye contact. "Of course there are elements of risk involved. But then there is with just about every business deal, isn't there?"

Some of the investors nodded in agreement.

"What I can guarantee you," Darius continued, "is that your return will be substantial. VERY substantial. And you will be taken care of for the rest of your lives."

Darius walked to the door and stood before it, and quickly turned back around to face the investors. Some had swiveled in their chairs to face Darius.

"This will be the last business deal that you ever need to make," Darius said as he swiftly disappeared through the double doors.

~~*

Roberto was listening in on the meeting of the investors through the doors. He was startled somewhat when Darius passed through the doors.

"Come with me, Roberto," Darius commanded, forcefully grabbing his forearm, pulling Roberto behind while he drifted down the hallway. Darius seemed frustrated, and was moving quickly across the wooden floor, past photos of various famous figures.

Roberto had to break into a run to keep from falling down as Darius dragged him with a vice-like grip. The hallway full of pictures seemed to stretch endlessly, and it was by far much longer than Roberto had ever remembered it.

Looking before him, he saw the back of Darius' coat, flapping in the wind that seemed to appear out of nowhere as if the two were traveling through a wind tunnel set at a high velocity.

Darius called back to Roberto over the roar of the wind. "I know you have this infatuation with Antoine. But you have no business eavesdropping. These matters do not concern you."

Roberto did not understand why Darius would be upset at Roberto overhearing what seemed to be essentially a typical investors meeting. Nothing seemed out of the ordinary to Roberto about that. But his afternoon in the bowels of *Sacrafice* definitely resided in the back of his mind. He certainly did not forget that.

Still running in the seemingly endless hallway, Roberto started to resist. He started to pull his arm back towards his chest, trying to stop

Darius, but there was no use. Each time he pulled his arm, Darius tightened his grip.

The hallway began to change around them as they ventured further and further away from the conference room. To Roberto, it seemed that they were miles away from the doors to the conference room, it seemed that they must have gone underground at some point, for it felt that they must be on the other side of the city.

But when Roberto looked back, they seemed to be just a few yards from the conference door. But they continued moving, and the hallway started to darken. The white, plaster walls gradually crumbled away to reveal darkness and green – like the earthy, mossy walls that Roberto remembered before. The floor was no longer wooden and hard – it gradually softened under their running feet.

And the conference room doors were still visible as Roberto looked back again, but now much smaller and farther away. But this time, when he looked back, he felt as if he was peering through a window, like he was looking at the wood and plaster hallway from the outside looking in. Or as if he were watching the hallway on television.

And then Darius stopped.

They stopped and the hallway suddenly grew pitch black. It was so dark that Roberto could not even see Darius in front of him. A torch ignited on the wall next to them, as if on cue.

As his eyes adjusted to the dim glow of the flame, Roberto scanned his surroundings. They were definitely in what seemed like a mossy cave. The walls and floor were made of dirt and earth, and there were roots hanging from the ceiling and jutting out of the walls.

But when Roberto turned around to look behind him, he saw what made the pit of his stomach knot up like he just got punched in the gut.

There was just a wall behind them. Moss, dirt and roots.

No conference room here.

Darius turned around. But it was not Darius…the face was ghastly green, with a snout like a canine; acrid smoke rose out of the nose and mouth; acidic saliva dripped to the floor, as little puffs of smoke rose from the mossy floor.

The figure grew, sprouting muscles and lengthy limbs, the fingers growing spiny with razor sharp nails, jutting out of the muscular hands attached to roping muscular arms.

The monster reached towards an unseen ceiling as the muscles stretched at the fabric and ripped the clothes off its body, revealing a greenish muscular chest with spots of brown.

The tattered fragments of the clothes dropped to the floor in pieces.

Roberto tried to turn and run, quickly forgetting the wall that had formed behind them.

He quickly ducked and was able to swiftly ease between the legs of the towering, lumbering demon.

Looking ahead, all he saw was blackness. The ground beneath him was soft and mossy, wet and muddy. But he continued to crawl deeper into the unknown. He was not going to let this demon take him. He could not.

Crawling further, he reached into his pocket and fumbled again for his lighter. There it was, but it was wet from the watery floor. It did not matter. He pressed on into the blackness.

The moss and dirt fell from the walls as the booming, thunderous steps started behind him. If Asmodai wanted to impregnate humans to create a spiritual army, he was not going to be one of those minions.

Whatever this beast was, it was slow. Its gargantuan muscles were slowing it down. And Roberto's athletic ability was working well for him, as he crawled like a spider quickly along the watery path, deeper and deeper into *Sacrafice*.

~~*

Sheldon sat at his desk in The Astral studying Antoine's file, listening to the audio discs, pausing every few moments to take notes.

The more he listened and the more he read, the more uneasy he became about the whole situation. Antoine was viewed in Miami as a leader, a healer, and a spiritual guide.

He took away pain.

But Sheldon knew there was something darker, something more sinister going on beneath the spiritual front that was yet to be revealed.

Sheldon knew that Antoine was an immortal. Sheldon believed, and took Antoine's stories as fact, not fiction. Which is what Sheldon was afraid of.

There was a knock at the door.

"Come in," Sheldon said, his eyes never leaving the file.

Anthony stood in the doorframe.

"I am going to see Antoine," he stated. "Antoine said that he has an invitation to extend to me."

"I am scheduled to see him one last time tonight," Sheldon replied. "Why don't you see him tomorrow?"

"Fine," Anthony replied, turning away, about to leave. "Oh, one more thing,"

Sheldon looked up from his paperwork, expectantly.

"No one can find Paula. Rumor has it that she snuck out to see Antoine last night, but I don't know for sure."

"Well, if she shows up there, she will certainly have some explaining to do. If I see her, I will talk to her. As for you, wait until tomorrow. That's an order. I will be seeing Antoine alone tonight."

Sheldon arose from his chair, stretched, and gathered up the file, which was strewn across the desk creating a sea of papers.

"As for me," Sheldon said, "I am looking forward to another glass of that great whiskey he has!"

Anthony smiled wanly and left.

As he left the Directors office, he knew he would have to come up with a plan to see Antoine tonight. Since Sheldon was scheduled to see him, he would have to follow and wait and talk to Antoine after Sheldon left.

But Paula could mess up the entire plan. Antoine was very, very specific about wanting to see Anthony – tonight. Antoine made it sound as if the time was critical, and the time was an issue, and that if he didn't see him tonight that Anthony would miss out on an opportunity.

He hoped not to see Paula. She was talking earlier in the day about going out to Coconut Grove tonight, but that could have been a lie. Anthony knew she had an obsession with Antoine.

Nevertheless, Anthony waited for Sheldon to leave the office, which seemed to take hours, and then he took it as his cue – he quietly slipped to his car, avoiding as many public areas in the office as possible, so co-workers would not notice him leaving, and there would be no questions to answer, or no obligatory goodbyes.

He slipped into his car, watching Sheldon drive away. He waited about five minutes, and slowly pulled out, leaving the headlights off.

Driving slowly the entire time, he kept his distance from Sheldon, but keeping Sheldon's Escort in his sight the entire time, as he turned from US1 to Anastasia and finally to Andelusia. Sheldon parked in front of the Nagevesh residence, and Anthony hung back about a block away, cutting the engine and waiting with Antoine's estate in his direct front view.

What he did not notice was Paula's car, parked a block away.

And he did not notice Paula following him, from the moment he left the garage, just as he was following Sheldon in a game of cat and mouse completely unbeknownst to the players. Paula had the upper hand. Patiently waiting for three hours in the hot garage in her car, she managed to convince the office workers that she was planning a night out in Coconut Grove. The long, hot wait paid off. She mopped some sweat off her forehead. She knew that Sheldon was seeing Antoine tonight, and she knew that Anthony was planning to as well. What she wanted was in on this case to satisfy her curiosity and obsession with Antoine.

She also knew that if Sheldon saw her, deliberately trying to horn in on a case that was clearly not assigned to her, that she would definitely be in hot water back at the office. But that was fine. She had no plans to see Sheldon that night.

Anthony was another story.

He was always a friend, always an ally. What she definitely wanted to find out was why he was following Sheldon, and why Anthony wanted to see Antoine that evening. What was so important? What could not wait?

So Paula had the best parking spot – nestled between some trees on the corner, with a sight of Antoine's estate and Sheldon's Escort to her left, and directly in front of her, about twenty five yards away, was Anthony's Jeep.

Of the three destined to see Antoine, she most clearly had the advantage.

CHAPTER FOURTY

Andelusia Avenue.

What a desolate trash-laden barren wasteland it had become. Looking at the behemoth houses imposing their shadows across the tree-lined street, one could see that each house suffered the same fate as Antoine's – it seemed as though none of the houses had been lived in or entered for years. Cracked windows were everywhere, a rat scurried across the pavement dashing towards a sewer amidst crumbled papers, cigarette butts, broken glass and ripped wood littered the street that appeared as if torn off of a house.

Then, of course, were the wrought-iron benches that lined the sidewalks on Andelusia, where various shoppers would have waited for the Coral Gables trolley to scurry them across town to Ponce De Leon, or perhaps the shops lining Coral Way. No longer were the benches there, for the few that remained and weren't ripped off the pavement or bent and torn askew, were deeply rusted or severely mangled.

Paula sat, huddled in a small bush near a crop of twisted palm trees, shivering, scared, not knowing what had happened and where everyone went. And she didn't know what to do next. She quieted herself, breathing shallow with the fear of disturbing the demon that had pursued her outside of the Nagevesh house further down First Street.

Once her visitor had left, the demon had crashed through the door, splintering wood and sending plaster cascading in a shower to the floor. She had fallen backwards, startled by the blow. Her survival instincts took over, and she jumped over to the window. Unlocking it and throwing it open, she jumped outside the window face first into the bushes below.

Crawling through the front lawn, she heard the demon inside the bedroom, screaming and thrashing, sending walls crashing down.

Another crash behind her.

She had turned her head, and saw the monstrous demon hurtling through the side of the house with little effort as plaster and cinder blocks fell to the ground. Nothing was stopping this monster.

She had made it several blocks away, closer to US 1, when she felt that she had outrun the demon and managed to gain some sort of a sanctuary.

She lay near some bushes and leaned her head back on a tree stump and savored the quiet, tears beginning to stream down her face, carving small paths on the dirt on her face, making it look like a blackened roadmap.

What is going on? She shook her head. *Where has everyone GONE?*

Perhaps she fell asleep.

Or maybe she passed out, or fell unconscious for a few moments. But, when Paula opened her eyes, she saw a face in front of her. Not directly in front of her but a few feet away. Not an actual face, but rather a disembodied head, hovering over the sidewalk.

She blinked her eyes sleepily. *I must be asleep.*

She strained to look through the bushes, unaware if the face was looking at her or not. But deep down, she knew it was. The face was staring right at her, and the face knew she was there.

But where is the body?

She did not move. She did not dare make a sound, or a whisper, or even breathe. She sat there, frozen with fear and frozen in time, staring down the face before her that seemed to have misplaced its body.

Who is that?

The face, as she squinted and looked more closely at it, seemed to be that of a man. A young man, for sure. It did not look as if the face were more than thirty years old. Long flowing brown hair that waved in each direction framed the light complexion, deep blue eyes and supple lips. But that is where it stopped.

If the head were to come closer, Paula might be able to determine more closely who or what was staring at her. But she knew, and closing her eyes she knew, that she did not want that face to come any closer to her. She wanted that face to go away, she wanted to look through the bushes ahead of her and just see Andelusia, not some bodiless head before her.

And then the head began to float. Closer and closer it moved towards Paula, slowly and silently.

Paula huddled in the bushes, staring with intensity and fear. She shook, and took in a breath.

As the head levitated closer to her, a body started to fill in beneath it. She strained to look at it, as the body that was forming was partially covered by a swirling white mist. As the strange form glided off of the street and onto the sidewalk, now in spitting distance from Paula, she started to make out a man's clothes.

The clothes that the man was wearing was a light t-shirt and a faded pair of jeans, but the t-shirt and jeans were marred with dirt and stained with blood. There was a tear at the top of the t-shirt near the collar, and another tear in the jeans by the knee.

And then the neck, now more prominent below the head, which was covered in dirt and blood, the wounds on the neck still fresh and oozing blood and pus, spilling out over the shirt staining the formerly white fabric.

The eyes were the most prominent; and as the figure moved even closer to Paula, the eyes began to stare at her with such intensity that she cringed.

She knew those eyes, and she had seen them before.

The intensity of the stare subsided. There was no more feeling of anger; now anguish. It seemed as if the eyes were crying out to her, in fear and in pain and in a begging need for help.

It stopped at the end of the sidewalk, where the cement started to meet the earth. The eyes continued to stare and beckon, as if she were silently being requested to come forth.

Come forth.

Come forth, and see me in all my glory.

But the man was not glorious.

He was unkempt and covered in blood, and he looked like he was dinner for a group of vampires or demons.

Paula did not move.

She remained stone cold and still. This figure appeared so rapidly and without warning. If she were to turn, could it instantaneously relocate right in front of her escape path? Given her encounters with the demon back at the Nagevesh residence, she did not want to even try to interact with this being.

And, then, she was torn.

But Paula knew that she did not have much time to react. She had to make a decision, and she had to make it fast. The man was drifting closer through the mist on the sidewalk, and closer, closer to her hiding in the bushes.

And she stopped breathing as the mist started to clear and revealed the mauled and mangled body standing before her.

CHAPTER FOURTY-ONE

Opening night.

Saturday, one in the morning. The techno beats thumped loudly just past the grand entrance doors to *Sacrafice*, and there was a line down the block on the sidewalk next to Washington Avenue, kept in order by a procession of red velvet stanchions separated by brass stands, containing the dapperly dressed Miami elite standing in queue on a lengthy red carpet; even some of the upper echelon of New York and Los Angeles came to South Beach to attend the opening of the much-hyped grand opening celebration of *Club Sacrafice.*

There were two very large doormen in front - both gigantic bodybuilders dressed in black that no one had seen before in the city. Perhaps flew in from New York. The crowd attending the grand opening was a mix of ethnicities and backgrounds; pretty much anyone who could afford the entrance fee could come in and party however they wanted to on opening night.

The doormen simply kept reporters and riff-raff away from the grand church-like entrance to the venue. Every time a young party going fellow with his young date tried to make it past the long, snaking line to say that "We are on the list" a gigantic, trunk of an arm extended forward and pushed the would-be partier back into the crowd without a word uttered.

A tall brunette woman in a short, tight-fitting bright red dress appeared in the doorway to the club and slinked down the stairs towards the guards. She was holding a clipboard in her right hand, clicking against the sidewalk in matching red stiletto pumps, smiling with fire-engine red lipstick, and magically produced a sleek wireless microphone from her left hand.

"Good evening!" She exclaimed. The crowd cheered. "This is the night you have all been waiting for!" she continued and gestured back to the grand doors at the top of the steps. "This, I promise to you, will be a nightclub experience like you have never experienced before!" The cheers swelled.

The thumping techno music hit a crescendo as she finished her words, and she climbed the stairs towards the door. She turned around as she reached the foot of the stairs just outside the main entrance. "I hereby open the doors to Club *Sacrafice*!" She opened the grating iron doors outward, and thumping music of a different kind wafted out the doors along with smoke and mist, red and blue lights, and drowned out the music that had been playing outside. The woman seemed to vanish into the mist as she walked through the door.

The crowd was growing impatient, but still held in check by the massive guards. One man dressed in black ducked under one of the ropes about ten feet back in the line, and tried to run up to the doors, but one of the guards effortlessly grabbed him by the neck just as he was making his way up the first of the steps, and threw him into the bushes on the side.

"No cutting in line or you *will* be ejected!" he barked in a monstrous deep voice. The guard scowled at the crowd with fiery red eyes. A stunned woman also dressed in black slowly stepped backwards. She exited the line, and as she turned back to look at the guard, she stared with eyes as large as plates, her face suddenly contorted; she cautiously headed to the bushes and kneeled down in front of the man.

A mysterious thundering voice overtook the music "Welcome brethren! Come forward now!" The guards removed the roping that had been blocking the crowd and the crowd slowly filed forward, climbing up the stairs and to the doors – all staring forward, all gazing upon the doors and the smoke. The music continued, louder than ever.

As the first followers entered the main doors, the mist became so thick the one was not able to see in front. It was a walk of faith under a shroud of uncertainty as each person disappeared, one after another.

The mist lifted somewhat to reveal a long hallway leading towards a large room with soaring ceilings. Most of them were impressed by the earthen walls, and the stone floor, feeling it added to the gothic feel of the venue. Many snapped out of their trance as they entered the main rooms, and looked upwards at the soaring ceilings; many darted their eyes towards the lights, the bars, the sounds and the smoke, taking it all in.

In the great room, it appeared like any other nightclub on South Beach. The ceilings reached upwards to an impressive laser light show, an extensive bar on every wall, and gigantic marble statues of Greek gods on every corner. Truly this was a nightclub that South Beach had never seen before. Marble floors. Premium liquor at every bar. Floor to ceiling mirrors. All was put there by Antoine to impress and lure them.

Above the sprawling dance floor was a mezzanine, where clubbers could sit in expansive lounge-style black leather furniture, where the stone walls continued dotted with real burning torches. Between each set of torches was a wooden door which, to many of the guests discovery, each was locked.

The clubbers danced and partied at the massive club, sat on the mezzanine guzzling martinis, reveling in the gothic feel. Some passers by could overhear conversations about the nightclub mysterious owners - no one knew who they were, where they lived or where they came from, but all agreed that the nightclub was a hit. It would draw thousands from around the world.

Except for Gizelle, who could be spotted easily in the darkness with her bright red dress working the crowd, there was no indication of any staff. Even the bars were self-service. And the owners still have not made an appearance.

~~*

Despite the gothic feel of the exterior and the public areas, *Sacrafice* had a very businesslike, very professional and very impressive looking executive boardroom. It was a soaring room above the main dance floors of the club, with a giant, mahogany table in the center, which looked roughly the size of North Dakota when viewing it from the main brass-handled double doors.

The table was lined with very puffy and very comfortable looking tall-backed black leather chairs, and beyond the vast table there was giant windowpane that overlooked the main atrium to the nightclub.

This was the room where all of the decisions were made.

And Antoine and Darius spared no expense here. The table was always set with still and sparkling water, a choice of lemons or limes, legal pads, ball point pens (the kind that felt really heavy when you picked them up) and black blotters that had the insignia of the lion on the top center.

The table was covered with reflective glass, had a phone built into the head chair, and with a video surveillance system in front of the head chair built into the table, with which the user could use a single plasma monitor (also built in to the table) and switch between 25 cameras throughout the venue.

~~*

Hernan Perez slowly opened his eyes.

They felt gritty, like he had been sleeping for too long, and his head was pounding. He assumed that the pain was brought on by the scotch and sodas he had earlier.

Coming to his senses gradually, he suddenly winced at the pain in his neck, instinctively drawing his hand up to the source, and let out a gasp when he touched the tender region.

As any curious mortal would do, he opted to get up, look in the bathroom mirror and inspect the injury. But when he rose from the bed, he looked down. "What the fuck?"

The sheets were red. Covered in blood. He raised his arms. He looked at his torso, lifted his legs.

He checked himself thoroughly, giving his body a pat down. Other than the pain on his neck, there appeared to be no additional injuries. He decided that the blood either came from his neck where the pain was centralized, or someone else.

Roberto!

He ran down the hall to Roberto's room, and tried the door. It opened with ease. For once, he didn't lock the door. The bed was unmade and clothes were scattered about, but nothing seemed to be amiss. Roberto was already gone.

Hernan brought his hand again up to his neck, remembering his pain. He backed out of Roberto's room and turned down the hallway to the bathroom that was next to Roberto's room. Entering and flicking on the light, he stared wide-eyed at the mirror, aghast. He could not seem to take his hand away from the wound.

"What the fuck?!" he screamed, but no one heard him.

CHAPTER FOURTY-TWO

"Paula, I need you to come out of the bushes," the figure extended his good arm. He stopped down to her level, and looked at her through the foliage. "Come with me." He gestured with his hand.

Paula's foot was still in pain; it even throbbed a little. As she moved her head closer to the wall of leaves in front of her, she squinted and concentrated more on the figure in front of her. The man seemed oddly familiar.

It was Anthony. She just knew it.

She barely recognized him. But it was Anthony, her fellow researcher, kneeling before the brush. He was severely mangled and covered in blood, but she was sure that it was him.

"Anthony!" she exclaimed. "What happened to you?"

She began to crawl slowly out of the bushes, closer to him. She cleared the brush and struggled to get up to her feet. "How did you get here?" She scanned the area. She saw the mess on Andelusia once again, noticing the abandoned houses with the cracked masonry, the trash laded streets all before her, she sighed. "How did *I* get here?"

"There is no time to explain," Anthony replied. "We need to get you to a safe place. It may already be too late for me, but you can be saved."

"Where are we, Anthony?" Paula asked, balancing some of her weight on Anthony's good shoulder. With some effort, he managed to keep her up, but it was difficult for him with only one arm. Paula noticed this, and removed her hand from his shoulder. Wincing at the pained that followed touching her tender foot to the ground, she began to follow Anthony, who was already making to leave.

"The last thing I remember, I was in front of Antoine's house," Paula said. "And then, this." As Paula looked down the street, she noticed a mist coming from the other side of the street, billowing from the other side, reaching towards them.

"Look at that!" Paula said, pointing to the other side of the street.

The houses on the other side of the street were becoming completely swallowed by the greenish mist. It was as if a giant cumulus cloud was moving slowly towards them, swallowing everything and devouring anything in its path.

Anthony held onto Paula with his good arm, pulling her towards him. "That is why we need to go. I will explain when we get there!" He started to limp down the street. But he was outrunning Paula. She looked across the street again at the mist.

The mist was dense.

It was getting worse – and it was so thick that they could no longer see the houses on the other side of the street at all. It was just a cloud of swirling green vapor. Paula looked over as they were running and tried to make out anything – a roof, windows, or a treetop, but she could see nothing.

"You don't want to know what is in that mist, Paula."

It was creeping closer. The entire sidewalk on the other side was gone, and now a thin layer was reaching towards their feet. It swirled around them in thin, smoky fingers as they hobbled, closer to the end of the street.

Paula did not know where Anthony was leading her. She was only following him and placing her life in his hands as he was the only familiar face in this strange world.

"I know where we can go to get some rest and sort this all out," he explained, looking behind his shoulder every few minutes to make sure she was still there and not collapsed in a mess on the sidewalk. "We will go to the Cathedral," he continued, pointing through a thick of palm trees. Through the trees Paula could see the cross rising from top of the Steeple against the ashy night sky. A possible sanctuary.

But the mist was quickly getting closer.

And turning darker. Paula snapped her head towards the swirling cloud, now halfway across Andelusia. "What was that? I just heard something!"

"Come on Paula! That mist is pure evil! You don't know where you are right now! The mist is swallowing up the city!"

Paula struggled to keep up. But as they struggled down the street together, Paula could not help but look back to see what they were trying to outrun. And when she looked, all she saw was a dark green cloud, growing in size, but what she heard was much different.

Much more unsettling.

Despite his injuries, Anthony's athletic ability kept him considerably farther ahead than Paula.

"Look at it, Paula," he said as he pointed. For a moment, it seemed as if the mist stood still, facing them off. The swirling of the mist took on faces and figures, and began to proceed once again. Looking up and down the street, mist spanned the city. The entire northern half of the city was swallowed up.

The only way to go was south.

Towards the Cathedral.

CHAPTER FOURTY-THREE

Jonas darted through stone hallways filled with people scurrying about.

It seemed like everyone was running around with something important to do. Jean Carlo followed, but struggled to keep Jonas in his sight as everyone was wearing the same colored white robes, and Jean Carlo noticed another thing when they were navigating the maze-like hallways: all the men had white hair like Jonas. The whole place and all of the people he was now surrounded with were perplexing to Jean Carlo.

Maintaining a distance of about ten feet or so behind Jonas, Jean Carlo called forward over the buzz of activity in the hallway for Jonas to slow down. But Jonas did not.

"Where are we going?" Jean Carlo finally shouted up to him. Jonas stopped and turned to face Jean Carlo. Soon, the two men were standing right next to each other in the middle of the hallway. People continued around them to various unknown destinations. "What is everyone running around for?"

Jonas looked Jean Carlo straight in the eye. "There is going to be a Great War. It will be unlike any other war you have ever seen in your mortal life."

Jean Carlo stopped for a moment. "What are you talking about?"

"There is no time to explain right now," Jonas said. "I will explain to you when we get topside."

"Topside? I thought you said that we shouldn't go up there? *Especially* at night!"

"There are stranded souls."

"Aren't they up there anyway? You yourself said that this 'dimension' that I have found myself in is full of lost souls, demons…" Jean Carlo's voice trailed off as his attention was diverted to several large muscular figures with grey skin that looked like armor that passed the two men were they stood talking in the busy hallway.

"What are they?" he asked after the figures had passed.

"They are the Metatron. They are going topside to fight the battle with Asmodai who is leading the demons."

"Metatron?"

"Yes…" Jonas said, his voice trailing off as he turned around and began to follow the three Metatron. "Come on! Let's go!"

Jonas started running to keep up with the Metatron. Jean Carlo had no choice but to follow. Too many questions were unanswered, and after all of the warnings, he was somewhat uneasy about going topside.

~~*

The small room that the Metatron had entered seemed to look like a War Room, and everything was grey and blended together, except for the sea of papers on the grey conference table that took up almost the entire room. There was a giant screen at the far wall opposite of the door, and the expansive grey table was lined with equally grey chairs. In each chair, there was a large, grey muscular Metatron.

The Metatron were a group of supernatural beings with a specific objective: to eliminate the demons of all levels, but they were powerless against the fury of Asmodai. Each of these beings had a purpose and a specific demon to target.

Jean Carlo stopped at the door once he arrived to the War Room and watched Jonas slide past the Metatron, ducking behind chairs and sliding up to the front of the room. There was one standing up front, appearing like a General and Commander to the remaining group that waited patiently at the table. Jean Carlo observed Jonas speaking to the being at the front of the room, but no matter how much he strained, he could not hear what they were saying, despite the fact that the Metatron that were sitting around the table were silent and still.

Jean Carlo returned, squeezing behind the chairs once again, and rejoined Jean Carlo.

"All these," he said pointing back to the table, "are Metatron. Their specific purpose is to annihilate the demons. Each one of them sitting around the table has a specific sin to target – and as you may know, there are seven Cardinal sins."

Jean Carlo nodded in agreement, but still did not understand what his own purpose was in this spiritual army.

"Pride, Envy, Lust…" Jonas started, grabbing Jean Carlo's hand, leading him to the opposite corner of the room where there happened to be two small folding chairs which the two men sat in promptly.

"Let's see…what else?" Jonas whispered to Jean Carlo as the General began talking in a language that the two men could not understand. "Ah yes…Sloth, Gluttony, Greed and Wrath. Each of these angels specifically combat each demon that is behind each sin. So, now you see their purpose. They meet in this very room each evening for a briefing before they go out topside and hunt."

"What is my purpose in all of this?"

"Shh! I am getting to that, Uriel. Just listen!"

There he did it again.

The old man called him that name, and he didn't understand where it came from, or what purpose that it had. But Jean Carlo was beginning to think that there was some deeper purpose for his presence here; Darius had killed him, but he did not die. He lay in his coffin waiting to rise, he waited for Darius to come back and open the lid and stare at his child that ran away, the child that ran away and now is in hiding underground.

Where did Darius go?

Oh I am here young one.

You don't think that I am here watching your every move? You don't think that I don't know where you are right now? You exist there because I allow you to exist there. You sit there and wait and listen and wonder when you are going to see me again. But you don't decide that young one. Because you know what?

I am around every corner.

Especially here.

You think you are at home? You think you are safe all snug in your bed with the covers pulled up tight? Nope sir! I am here and I am everywhere.

I made you!

And I will reclaim you, just wait and see. I watch and I wait. When you left the cemetery, I allowed you to go. Do you honestly think that I didn't have the power to stop you, when you were walking down the street like an old, poor reflection of a mortal?

And now I know exactly where you are. You are right below ground, right beneath the offices where Antoine loves to spend his time, hogging the spotlight like he always has.

Antoine dug me up and maybe he shouldn't have. He pulled my coffin out of the ground and shoved my heart into a rotted corpse and –

"- Uriel? Are you listening to me?"

Jean Carlo snapped to, and looked around the room. None of the Metatron were there anymore. The meeting must have concluded. The room was empty except for him and Jonas. There was still a sea of papers on the conference table, and all of the chairs were in a state of disarray as the occupants had apparently neglected to push the chairs back in when they left. It looked like they left in a hurry.

"And where have you been?" Jonas asked.

"What do you mean?" Jean Carlo asked, blinking his eyes and rubbing them as if he were asleep.

"What I mean is that you were sitting next to me the entire time, but when I spoke to you several times, I looked over, and saw that your eyes were white. I mean totally white. Like you had no pupils! There was nothing there! I could tell that you had left."

Jean Carlo stopped for a moment to think about what Jonas had said. He had left this body? He touched his arm for a moment, and it felt normal. He didn't feel any different than he did for as long as he could remember, and his memory was long. He remembered when his mother washed him as a young boy, he could still feel the soapy sponge gently rubbing on his forearm, and he remembered the warmth of the bath water.

But this entire time he had been sitting right in the same, cold folding chair. He remembered that much. He didn't see anything, and he didn't remember anything about the briefing. All he remembered was Darius speaking to him.

Jean Carlo shuddered.

"You were gone, Uriel, you weren't here. Your body was here next to mine, but I could tell, your spirit was somewhere else. Your eyes were white, they were glazed over, and you were speaking to yourself. But I didn't stop you. There would have been no sense. I would not have been able to wake you."

"So what did I miss?"

Jonas rose from his chair. "Come on," he said. "I will have to fill you in along the way. I am not stupid. I know that Darius was speaking to you. I know he is the one who made you, and he is going to be coming for you. I will be honest with you, there will be no hiding from him. You must face him. That is the only way to be free from him, especially in this world. You must face him."

"And what if I don't?"

"Then you are destined to live down here for eternity and you will be in this realm forever. You won't ever progress to the more enlightened state of being that we all strive for. You are dead, Jean Carlos. It is time to recognize your self here, it is time to embrace the genesis of Uriel. That's who you are in this world. This world may seem to you like the world you once lived in, but once you go topside, you will see that it is *quite* different."

"Different? How?"

Jonas seemed exasperated as he flung his arms in the air and slapped them on his thigh. "Haven't you been listening to anything I have been telling you since you arrived at dinner?!"

Jean Carlo didn't understand. He had been listening intently since he was served a slab of beef on a plate before him.

"You may have been hearing what I was saying, but you certainly haven't been listening. The streets above are being submerged in a dark green mist. This mist is pure evil. Asmodai is coming, and he is coming for more than just Antoine. You see, Antoine thinks that he is safe. He isn't in this dimension. He found a way out. But he is wrong. Asmodai is after him, and Asmodai moves through different realms with ease. If he is called, Asmodai can cross over, and he can do it will until his target is destroyed. Antoine is his target. And as long as Antoine exists, Asmodai can cross over. Freely."

While Jonas had been speaking the two men had navigated the same hallways they had when coming to the War Room, but this time, the hallways were empty. They were brightly lit but deserted. There was not a soul, and when Jonas had been speaking, there was an echo.

This time, Jean Carlo was listening. And he didn't even notice the destination, because he was following so closely and listening so intently to what Jonas had been saying. Yes, this Antoine seemed to be responsible for this entire war. He called the worst demon that could have been summoned.

Asmodai.

Lost in his thoughts but managing to keep close behind Jonas and take in everything he was saying, Jean Carlo did not notice the grey, barren, starkly lit hallways. He did not notice the emptiness and the fact that, when just a little while previously the hallways had been crowded and busy they were now devoid of any presence but these two men; he didn't notice that Jonas was undressing and shedding his clothes, and he certainly didn't notice that they were now at the base of steps which looked like the same set of stairs that led above to the offices of The Astral; the same stairs that would led up to impending death and the terrible green mist that Jonas had said was overtaking the city and devouring it, letting the demons run free.

Yes, Jonas stopped and did a double take when he realized that he was ascending a set of stairs that seemed all too familiar.

"What is it?" Jonas said, realizing that his partner had stopped mid track.

"I thought you said that going up there was forbidden?"

"Oh it is," he explained. "But not for you. You see, what you didn't hear in the briefing was that you and I were set to go out there tonight. The mist is coming – in fact, it's probably already here by now – which means Asmodai and his army have already spread out and begun their assault. But we have to get the lost souls who are still out there. There are several. And you have a specific duty. It's the whole reason why you are here in the first place, from the moment that you awoke in your coffin."

"And what is that?" Jean Carlo asked.

"You haven't figured it out?" Jonas asked. "You are destined to destroy Asmodai. You will face him tonight."

CHAPTER FOURTY-FOUR

The Green Mist.

It swirled its ugly dark demonic faces, devouring each building; one by one it claimed each one – as it waited across the street, snickering and laughing at Paula and Anthony. As the two looked across the street, through the sea of strewn papers and crumbled aluminum cans, past the wrought iron benches that were skewed and twisted; they saw the darkness, they saw the green and they saw the mist, waiting for them.

Waiting to proceed across the street and devour them.

There wasn't much farther to go to the Cathedral of the Gardens. They were getting closer, Paula could tell. Looking up towards the sky, she again saw the beacon of hope, the steeple which stood out against the dark sky.

"Come on, Paula, we have to hurry," Anthony said as he walked over to where Paula had briefly stopped to stare at the sky. She closed her eyes for a moment, and drew her breath in.

They reached the end of the street and entered a small wooded patch, taking a path to the south in the direction of the steeple. When they emerged on the other side of the trees, the Cathedral was in sight.

Paula remembered her night with Antoine as she entered the main doors of the Cathedral. As were the other buildings in the city, the

Cathedral was also in a state of destruction. The main doors didn't even exist anymore. Both were hanging to the sides, off of the hinges, leading into the darkness of the church inside.

"How is this going to keep us safe?" Paula asked, as Anthony padded down the center aisle of pews closer to the altar.

"Oh, demonic forces will not enter the House of God. We will be safe here."

The interior of the Cathedral was a stark contrast to the chaos and destruction outside. Even though the front doors were hanging to the sides, the interior of the church was relatively untouched. Each row of pews was neatly polished and all of the liturgy and song books were tightly tucked into the cubbies on the back of each row.

Approaching the altar, Paula looked up, and noticed the expansive ceiling, adorned with giant hanging light fixtures – but they were not like the elegant crystal chandeliers she saw at the hotels in Miami Beach, but much simpler and almost rustic looking.

The interior of the church was dark wood; the pews blended in with the floor and the walls, and sculptures of the passion lined the walls up towards the ceiling with small stone carved caricatures depicting the crucifixion of Christ.

Anthony entered a small door to the left of the altar, which must have been, Paula assumed, the vestment room. "Come on, Paula. I will explain when we get to safety. We need to get away from that mist."

Paula looked behind her shoulder, towards the doors they had entered in on the other side of the church. The trees were gone.

Everything was…gone.

Just a dark, greenish cloud. Moving closer. Reaching inwards.

Swallowing everything up.

"Wha…?" she said, dumfounded that that mist had followed them so quickly. "I thought you said it couldn't come in here!"

"There is no going back that way," Anthony said. "Look around, Paula."

Stained glass windows that lined the sides of the church shattered one by one as the mist billowed through them into the church.

The mist was already moving through the doors to the Cathedral. Its fingers danced in the doorway, slowly feeling its way down the center aisle.

Paula hurriedly followed Anthony into the dressing chambers, and Anthony closed the door. Anthony took all of the vests and robes out of the closet, revealing a door. He opened the door, and there was a set of stairs, leading down into a black abyss.

"Go," he instructed. "I know it is dark as night down there, but it is safe. It's an entire basement level under the church. We will be safe down there."

Paula looked down the stairs uneasily. She couldn't see more than three or four steps down, given the almost total darkness of the room. Looking out the door to the dressing room, she saw the worship area being devoured by the mist.

"You don't want to go in that cloud, Paula. The cloud is certain death. This is our only option."

She descended the steps. Anthony opened a small cabinet that was next to the closet. Inside were stoles, prayer books, and ceremonial candles. With some luck, he also found a pack of matches.

He lit one of the candles and handed it to Paula. She couldn't help but notice the gold strip at the top, and remembered seeing similar candles when she attended church as a child. She outstretched her arm over the first few steps. It cast an eerie yellow glow on the stairwell. She swallowed hard. "Uh…"

The stairs were formed from dirt, as were the walls. It looked as if this were a well carved out cave, right underneath the church. Something, however, didn't feel right. Even with the candle, she could only see a few steps ahead of her, and as she descended the stairs, with Anthony following close behind, she began to feel her skin crawl and develop goose bumps. "Anthony…are you sure about this?"

Out in the worship area, there was a loud, splintering crash.

"Those sound like the pews!" Anthony said. "We have got to go now! Go down the stairs Paula!"

"What's happening to them?" Paula asked, as she snapped her head in the direction of the noise.

But as she turned around she saw, behind Anthony, intense red eyes, peering out from the mist. The cloud was closer now…swirling and entering through the door, only feet behind them.

Paula screamed. Anthony looked back towards the mist.

Seeing the eyes, Anthony's greatest fear was confirmed.

He descended the stairs as fast as his injuries would let him; he still managed to knock Paula down. Both candles went out, and the stairwell was enveloped in total darkness. Anthony got up from where he fell over Paula, and struggled to continue down the stairs.

"Come on Paula!" he said, continuing down, using his hand to feel the wall, falling down the steps again.

Paula looked up and back one more time, and she wished she hadn't. Since the candles went out the mist seemed black, and all she could make out were the intense red eyes, staring from the top of the stairs down at her.

CHAPTER FOURTY-FIVE

Antoine never noticed the Green Mist that overtook the city of Miami.

Even though the time that he spent crossing between the dimensions that he created, even though all those who came in contact with him eventually also came in contact with the mist, Antoine paid it no mind. For him, the coming of the green mist was a regular daily occurrence that happened precisely at the same time every night when the clock struck three hours into the new day, and more often than not, Antoine walked right through the mist, heading to his car and his home, and didn't even care about or look at what the mist contained.

This time, however, Antoine was affected differently.

He saw from his illuminated confines of the bubble, he saw it creeping in and under the doors of the passage that he had been sitting and waiting for hours for his captor to appear. As the time had passed, he lay down, seeing the dark passage outside like looking through a smeared film, each object taking a glossy appearance.

He even thought he fell asleep for a while. Waking up, covered in sweat, reminding him of his mortal days, he paused to remember.

Digging.

His shovel hit the dirt hard, and hoisted it over his shoulder, as he dug and he dug and he dug, deeper and deeper into the moist, caked cool dirt, digging deeper and deeper but not finding anything.

What was he digging for? He stopped for a moment. Leaning against the shovel, he wiped his brow. He couldn't remember. All he knew was that he had to dig. And dig.

He looked up and above, out through the hole he was digging. He hadn't realized how deep he had dug so far. He must have been six or eight feet below the surface, and he was standing so his head was still at least a good foot below the surface.

He looked up and saw stars.

The night sky and moon offered a pale light, and he saw the roots sticking out of the sides of the hole he had dug.

The night was silent. All he heard was his own breathing.

But something wasn't right.

He had been here, digging and working up a sweat, feeling so much more like a mortal, more than he ever had since he had actually been a mortal, he felt small and scared and unsure of himself. He felt tired and weak and hungry and hot.

And then came footsteps. They weren't deep and booming. They were small and determined and methodic, starting far away, that he could tell.

But steadily approaching. As each minute passed, the footsteps came closer and closer.

And stopped.

They stopped just above where he was standing, just above his hole.

But looking up, he saw nothing. He saw no one. But what he heard – what he stopped and stayed silent and strained to hear – was light breathing. Someone was up there, and someone was breathing.

Waiting.

Waiting above, and waiting for him.

Waiting for him to climb out of the hole, to rise above the edge of the earth and reveal himself to the mysterious stranger who stopped and stood above him.

And that's when he didn't have time to think. He didn't have time to look above any longer, because the hand that grabbed his neck and plucked him out of the hole moved too fast for him to see it; and it had him dangling high above the hole, up in the air, and when he looked down at the ground below, he saw. He saw the grave that he had been digging.

But when he turned around, when he craned his neck back to see who or what was dangling him high in the air, he blacked out.

Was I digging my own grave?

And then he saw swirling green; the mist had filled the passage, swirling outside of his bubble, so deep and dark and thick that he could not see through it. But there was something there.

Antoine stopped.

It was time to get out of this confinement. It was time to face what was in the mist; it was time to face what was waiting for him.

He pressed against the edge of the bubble, trying to pierce his fingers through it, but all it did was expand outwards. It seemed to be some sort of gelatinous substance, but very elastic. It would not give, it would not break.

After several attempts at breaking the barrier surrounding him, Antoine sat. He sat and thought, pondering a way out of the bubble. But he didn't have to think long. The mist began to press against the sides of the bubble, and the mist pressed harder and harder, desperately trying to get in.

Antoine darted his head back and forth, running through his mind possible ways of escape as the bubble began to shrink around him – the mist, forceful as it was, starting to crush and press its way closer and closer to Antoine…until the bubble burst.

And there he was, sitting on the floor, the mist devouring him, screaming at him, urging him to get up.

And then his mother spoke to him.

You stupid, silly little boy.

I saw you leave that night. I saw you go out and I saw you leave in the moonlight. I waited for you! I was waiting and waiting but you never came back! I needed you and you left me! I saw you leave and then he was gone, he was dead out in the stables! You left and he died! I waited and waited and nobody came!

Antoine screamed, and covered his ears.

His eyes were shut tight; he dared not look ahead, because he was afraid that he would see the face of his mother, his mother from so many years ago. He shut his eyes tight as long as he could, until he felt the mist pry them open.

And when he opened his eyes, his mother was there.

You left me to rot in that house. I sat in that rocking chair until it fell apart!

But it was not the mother that he remembered; it was not the mother that coddled him as a child or scolded him when he tracked mud inside the kitchen; it was not the mother that he grew to love.

It was she, yes.

He saw her brown hair framing her face. But there was hardly any of her face left. The flesh mostly eaten away, the blood long since dried up, she still had maggots swarming in and out of her eye sockets and crusty dried tendons dangling from her chin.

"You left me to *die!*" she screamed at the top of her lungs, as Antoine screamed, covering his face with his arm, falling backwards as the beast lunged at him.

"It's time!" she screamed, standing up. She was an extremely tall rotted corpse, the skin half rotted and dangling from dry bones. She was still wearing a housedress and apron. "It's time for your punishment! Get over here!" She reached out to grab him.

And then Antoine lunged forward.

Are you going to abandon me again?

He took his arm and swiped his mother to the side, and she was swallowed up in the mist without a sound. And in an instant, she was gone.

But he heard a voice. He heard a voice trying to speak through the mist in broken syllables.

"Annnnntoooоiiinnneeee….." it called to him, faintly.

It was far away. But it continued to call his name, and each time, the voice was closer.

When it got quiet, he listened again for the voice, but heard nothing. The swirl of the mist retained its silence and kept his blindness persistent. He felt like a vulnerable mortal, like he had never transformed and never gained any power; the feeling of being a troubled youth overtook his being.

And then he heard the voice of Darius. Calling to him. That was it. That was the voice. He knew that he'd detected a familiarity in the voice that was off in the distance. But now, as the voice continued, much closer, he knew it was Darius. No one possessed the distinct tone that Darius did.

"…*Antoine*…"

Darius sang out to him, but as Antoine strained to see, as he tried with every effort he had, all he could see was the green mist. And then the voice moved, this time it came from his left. And then it called him from behind.

"Antoine," this time he spoke, mere inches from him. But Antoine still could not see him. The mist was far too dense.

And then suddenly he was there. His face projected through the mist, his loving face.

"Antoine, have you been so naive? Do you not know where you are now?"

Antoine got onto his knees, preparing to stand. "I know this, Darius. I have seen this before."

"That is true," Darius replied, "but did you not know that tonight the mist seems to have a directive towards you?" Darius smiled, his eyes looking around them, and chuckled softly to himself. "Oh, Antoine. Close your eyes for me. Do it, please."

Antoine sat back for a moment, feeling for the edge of the passage, leaned back, and closed his eyes.

"Do you remember the night you came for me? I want you to think Antoine, I want you to remember. Think hard and remember even harder."

How couldn't he remember? It's been a night that he could never forget. Antoine remembered entering the graveyard, he remembered digging the first shovelful of dirt, and he remembered being trapped in a cave filled with crystals.

"Now think, afterwards – the next day. Do you remember that?"

Yes, it was still all with him. He had not forgotten.

Antoine had stepped outside of the casket he was using at the Chateau quietly and walked over to the dressing area. It was an elaborate stone room – stone floors and walls with large picture windows that overlooked a well manicured lawn. On the windows hung massive dark maroon colored drapes with gold cords tying the fabric back. It was dark and black outside, and Antoine could see his reflection in the windowpane as he peered out into the garden.

He had run his fingers over the healing wound in the center of his chest, and studied it in the reflection on the windowpane. It would most definitely leave a scar, a branding of sorts – like a tattoo signifying that he was the property of Asmodai.

The deal was sealed. There was a body in the next room which Antoine had gingerly placed in a casket for rest, and when Darius was ready to rise he would be ready – and then Antoine would have some explaining to do.

He had washed himself, and pulled a clean shirt over his muscular torso. After pulling up a pair of pants and slipping on some black boots, he had ventured out the door into the hallway.

Antoine's door was in the center of the hallway – at one end the hallway spilled out into a gigantic foyer, while at the other end was the library. On the wall opposite of Antoine's door was another door leading to a spare room with a casket in the center. Antoine carefully turned the doorknob – carefully to not make a single noise.

The door opened slowly, revealing the silver casket. It was the only item in the room – the room was cold, stone and windowless, and the casket almost blended into the stone surroundings.

The casket rested on a stone slab, which was just large enough to hold the coffin and nothing else.

And the coffin was closed.

Antoine stood at the door for a moment, replaying the events of the night before in his mind. He did not get a good look at the corpse that Asmodai had chosen for Darius' resurrection. At that point in the ritual, Antoine had surrendered, accepted his fate and handed the heart to Asmodai. Antoine surrendered to the fact that Asmodai owned him now and would place demands on him and expectations on his actions.

Darius was another story.

After placing him in the ground so many years before, after burning him and leaving only his heart and ashes, would there still be malice and ill-will? Antoine peered through the doorway at the closed silver casket.

Darius was inside.

In a new, healed human form.

But he wouldn't be human. He would still be Darius, still be immortal, and still be a killer. Dare he open the lid now?

He thought it be best not to.

He turned around, he quietly closed the door, carefully like a father who had just checked on his sleeping son, and slowly walked down the hallway to the foyer. He slipped through the front door - out quietly and undetected, and when he closed the front door to the chateau behind him, it didn't even make a sound.

"But you didn't leave undetected, Antoine, you didn't."

Antoine snapped out of his daze. He could see Darius more clearly now, and it seemed as though the mist had lifted a little. As he scanned the area, he saw the earthen black walls, the stone floor with the puddles of water, and Darius, bent over in front of him at eye level.

"You most certainly didn't," Darius added.

Antoine started to get up, but Darius stopped him.

"You are not going anywhere," he said, as Antoine fell back onto the floor uncontrollably from a simple wave of Darius' hand.

Antoine looked back up at Darius with a perplexed look on his face.

"You don't think I have been holding you here just so I would let you go did you?"

Darius stood and laughed. "You are showing me, Antoine, that you still have much to learn. I command this mist!" He rose up to his feet, a sinister scowl on his face. "Look and see here!" he pointed over to his right.

The mist swirled back in, heavy and thick like a muscular arm, grabbing Antoine and hoisting him off the floor. Antoine was paralyzed to move, no matter how hard he struggled and tried to break free.

"No!" Antoine screamed. "The mist commands *you!*"

~~*

Paula was now alone. She ran her hands along the walls of the earthen stairway below the cathedral, her eyes shifting to the red eyes that still stared through the dark, swirling mist above.

She felt it.

In the intense blackness, she had fallen down the stairs. But she could not find Anthony. It's like he vanished into thin air. And up above, at the top of the stairs, it was waiting for her. She did not know who it was or what it wanted – but she was not about to find out.

"Anthony!" she cried out. She looked around in the darkness, seeing nothing. She lay on the stairs where she fell, face down, she reached her hands in front of her to feel her way down the remainder of the stairs.

The steps were made of earth – it felt cool and rough, like moss. Some spots were soft. She felt the light stringy feel of weeds growing up in the moss cracks as well. Feeling further down, running her hands down the steps, she slithered down, remaining on her torso, until she came to a large flat area – earthen and mossy as well; it appeared to be a landing of some sort.

"There will be no returning!" Asmodai yelled down to Paula. "The door will close for eternity!"

Paula looked up in the direction of Asmodai's booming, grating voice. She could see the silhouette of the demon for the mist was starting glow an eerie luminescent green. It was now a pale, brighter green.

"What are you?!" Paula screamed.

But the door slammed.

It was a thunderous sound, shaking the hallway; bits of dirt from the walls fell to the steps, and she closed her eyes. Once the door closed, there was laughter.

There was someone – or something – below…laughing. A high pitched wail, further down the stairs.

And she had no choice but to go further down, for the door to above was now closed.

CHAPTER FOURTY-SIX

Paula was trapped.

She weighed the two options in her mind: she could run up the stairs, most likely tripping and falling flat on her face in the darkness, bang on the door as loud as she could, and scream until she lost her voice to unhearing ears.

But that wasn't necessarily the best option. Was the beast still out there? Had she imagined the whole thing?

Or, she could venture further down into the unknown, closer to the source of the demonic laughter. When the beast closed the door, a thunderous bolt rang into the blackness, like that of a massive security bar being drawn over a door. She doubted that wasting her almost spent energy banging on the door would be very fruitful.

In the temporary but welcomed calm, her focus returned to the pain in her ankle. Forgotten for a bit while she was consumed with the beast and escaping the mist, the pain returned, but it was not throbbing as it was before.

She ran her hands across the landing, searching for the candle. She was still unable to find it. Deciding to press on and find Anthony, she struggled to her feet.

She steadied herself against the wall in front of her also comprised of moss and dirt. She ran her hands along the wall, and stuck her foot out in front of her, feeling with her feet for the first step. Once she was comfortable that she had found it, she began her descent.

Very carefully and cautiously she ventured below, step by step, never taking her hands off the wall. About four or five steps down, she began to feel stone. Running her hands higher, she felt the stones curve around, like they were surrounding a window. A window in the shape of a traditional gravestone – flat on the bottom and rounded on top.

Paula stopped in front of the mysterious window. It definitely had the rounded top, squared off bottom, and was lined with large, rough stones. Bringing her hands to the center, expecting to feel glass, she felt only air. And the air was hot.

The heat blew out of the opening with such a force it knocked Paula back on the opposite wall, but she remained on her feet. Bright, hot flames were roared out of the window.

A monstrous demon appeared in the window, standing in the flames and appeared instantly and was only a few feet in front of her! The face had a long snout and razor sharp teeth, dripping saliva to the floor in acrid smoke.

The demon cursed and thrashed, crashed up against the wall so hard that it shook and sent the moss and dirt falling to the steps below. Paula could not understand what dialect was being spoken, but it felt to her like a command. This demon was angry, and this demon wanted her.

Now able to see thanks to the raging flames, she turned to exit. She was going to do her best to break down that door. Or at least die trying.

But when she turned, all she saw was a wall.

A stone wall of moss and dirt. She distinctly remembered a landing being there just minutes ago.

She had no choice but to go down.

The wall shook where the demon heaved his weight against it, and it looked like it was about to give way and crash down at any moment.

She broke into a run down the stairs.

They led further and further down, deep into the earth, until the steps finally ended in a dark hallway.

She heard a crash above, like giant stones falling down steps.

Paula looked up the stairs.

She heard the stones falling out of the wall with each thunderous shake. She heard the mountains of dirt cascade to down the steps like a breach in safety.

The demon was out.

The steps and the walls shook methodically, for the booming footsteps of the demon were getting ever closer.

She turned her head back to the hallway, away from the steps.

At the end of the hallway was a dark steel door. It seemed to be the only thing in this odd place that was not made of the earth. She did not know what lie behind the door, but she had no choice but to attempt to go through it. Returning from where she came was no longer an option. She would have to face the raging muscular demon beast racing for her. She knew her time was limited as the thunderous, booming footsteps started getting louder and the monster descended the steps.

There was a door handle was in the center of the strange steel door, a giant round disc in the center of the door that looked like it belonged on a deep sea submarine rather than in a dank hallway under a church.

She hurried towards the door and wrapped her arms around the disc.

"Fuck!" she said, struggling to turn it, hoping that it would give and open the door. "Open! *Fucking door*!"

But it was too late.

She felt a hot, brawny arm reach around her shoulders, as piercing nails dug into her arm.

She cried out.

She was yanked away from the door so fast that she blacked out momentarily, and came to just a minute later, with the demons arms wrapped around her in a perverted embrace – breathing it's humid, noxious breath directly into her face.

"I have been waiting for her," he spoke, eyes glaring. The man-beast in front of her looked similar to Asmodai – powerful, roping muscles pulled tightly under taught greenish brown skin, covered in lesions and sores; wings on the back that looked drawn together; but slightly smaller in stature and not quite so big and imposing as Asmodai. The face was that of a dog or wolf – the face of a beast with razor sharp teeth - the body like that of a man but very muscular, tall and large. She looked down, and noticed that his green brown skin was exposed – there was no sheet of armor or covering like that of Asmodai. All this beast was wearing was a small loincloth – a brown, primitive type material like what would be worn by cavemen.

She struggled to get free, only making the demon hold her tighter in his fierce grip.

"No!" she cried, throwing her head back, attempting to squirm out of his grip like a caught fish.

But she was no match.

Holding her still with one powerful arm, as the veins protruded and pumped beneath the greenish brown skin. Throwing her to the floor, the demon held her and pinned her to the ground. She felt as if she were being split in two. She screamed. It was a pain like no other, she felt as if she were ripping into shreds.

She passed out briefly.

The demon took advantage of her brief intoxication to lower her to the ground on her back. His grip never loosened, his nails remained dug into her, deep and profound. She awoke to the demon on top of her, face to face.

She screamed and tried to thrash beneath him but couldn't budge under the weight of his massive, muscular body, being held in place by his powerful hands and roping muscular arms. His wings opened and expanded and crashed into the walls, and the hallway began to change around them.

The mossy, dirt caked walls around them crumbled. The room filled with the green mist, surrounding them, swirling above them as if on cue, as if celebrating. The hallway caved away and opened to a large, vast underground chamber. The walls became stone, the floor turned to marble. Torches appeared on the walls, igniting in flames and casting an orange hued glow against the green mist, building around them.

She raised her arms up off the ground and wrapped them around the demon's massive back and pulled the beast closer to her. The wings, now open and free, flapped through the room and carried them upwards into the mist, displacing it around them, and they landed again in the center of the room.

PART FOUR

NESMARON'S EGG AND THE CASKET FULL OF ASHES

The casket.

So soft.

Supple.

Comfortable.

I'm in you. I feel you.

But you won't feel me.

CHAPTER FOURTY-SEVEN

Jonas Mayer hardly remembered the night he died.

He didn't remember being whisked away in a racing ambulance, or the bright lights above as he was being wheeled down the halls of the South Shore ER as he barely clung to life, and he certainly didn't remember when he first left his body and had a conversation with his killer, right in the hallway outside the trauma room that his body was crashing in.

Jonas remembered getting up off the examination table, still wearing the clothes he was wearing earlier, a yellow short sleeved button down shirt and dirty, faded jeans – now splattered in bright red blood. He could recall the cold linoleum floor on his bare feet, thanks to the loss of his sandals, as he hoisted himself off the table as the doctors were still frantically trying to revive him.

But what stood most clearly out in his mind, the memory that he knew that as long as he existed that he would never forget – was the face of his killer, standing in the hallway in his dark blue glasses and long black hair and coat, his dark skin and mysterious looks – gazing in on the activity in Trauma-4 as if waiting.

Waiting for Jonas to rise from his body.

And the strange thing, Jonas thought as he was staring at his killer through the glass, was that no one noticed his killer, and no one noticed him. There he was, standing over his mauled and bloody body – and there was his killer, facing each other in the midst of chaos and bedlam.

But no one seemed to notice them.

And then his killer walked casually through the doors, right up to the side of the table. He looked down at the body, and then up at Jonas.

"You are most certainly better looking in this form," he said, gesturing his hand over to the standing Jonas, with a small smile. "I really must speak to you. I have to make you understand why I have called you here."

Jonas had a look of despair on his face, looking for a moment like an abandoned puppy. "You killed me!" he cried, tears starting to well up in his eyes. "I had a life!"

The killer put his hands up, quieting Jonas. "Wait, wait. Don't jump to conclusions. I have not killed you. Please do not misunderstand that. But I need you to come with me. Somewhere quiet that we can talk. Even though no one here can see us or hear us, we need some peace and quiet so you can focus on what I am about to tell you. Come with me."

The killer took his hand, and grabbed Jonas' hand over the table just as the doctors had given up, drawing a white sheet over his body. Jonas couldn't help but stare at his body for a moment, standing at the end of the table, looking down and staring in disbelief.

"Come on," the killer insisted. "You will have plenty of opportunities later to re-enter your body."

And that is all that Jonas had remembered, no matter how hard he tried. After he had left Trauma-4, his mind drew a blank.

As he stood at the top of the stairs leading to The Astral's offices, fumbling with the lock, he turned back to Uriel who had been patiently waiting on the stairs just a few steps below. He stopped with the lock for a moment. "You know, Uriel, I honestly cannot remember much before I came here."

"To where?"

Jonas began to fumble with the rusted lock again, which a key that looked equally rusted. The door was located at the top of the steps, in the ceiling, making it look like the steps disappeared – and they did, at least they would until Jonas would get the lock open.

"Here…this dimension. I try and I try, yet all I can remember is the few short minutes after I died. After that, I draw a blank. I don't even know who my killer was."

"I see. I am the same way…I barely remember much."

"But he wanted to tell me something. He seemed very insistent on it. I intend to find out his purpose for killing me. He was saying that he selected me…that he called me. There!" The lock finally gave, and crumbled in Jonas' hand, a dry and rusted version of its former self.

The door opened, and the green mist spilled through like steam and smoke, billowing through the door. Uriel looked up expectantly with wide eyes. "What is that?" he asked.

But Jonas did not answer.

He simply waved his hand to come, moved forward, and was swallowed up by the mist.

Uriel stood at the top steps for a moment, not exactly eager to jump into this mist at a moment's notice. He peered his head as close to the mist as possible. "Jonas?" he called, being as quiet as possible and desperately trying to hear his footsteps. But looking ahead, all he saw was swirling dark green, and heard nothing. It was eerily silent.

"Are you there?" he called again.

He felt he needed to follow Jonas into the mist. He felt that a job needed to be done, and that he was the one to take care of it – at least that is what Jonas had been explaining to him since he knocked on his quarters door earlier that evening. He looked down the stairs. About ten steps below, there was a small landing lit by a small light bulb that hung from the ceiling. It cast a yellowish glow on the small, dusty walls and stairs.

He considered running back down, away from the cold mist, back down into the catacombs. But where would he go? Back to his quarters?

His mind has been bombarded since he got here with information, names, places and expectations – he wondered if he would even remember which door was his.

And what would Jonas think of him if he retreated in fear? What would the punishment be?

And so he started to climb the few remaining steps, and looked once again up above him at the mist, and the mist seemed to call him – to beckon him.

Enter me.

He stopped at the last step.

This was it. There was nothing else to tell, it was now or never. And then thoughts raced through is mind. Thoughts of the past, thoughts of death.

And then he was lying again. On his back. And it was dark. Too dark to see.

But he was awake. He knew that much. It felt like he was moving; it felt like he was being lifted. But he was lying down, in a bed. But it wasn't a bed.

Enter me!

He was not lying in a bed.

But it was pitch black dark, and cold. And constricted. He could not move far beyond where he was lying. On either side of him, there was a wall of some sort. But it was a soft wall. Covered in some sort of sheet, or it might have been a pillow. But when he rubbed his elbows against it, it was soft yet firm at the same time. And the pillow was firm and cold too, but it wasn't big and overstuffed like his pillow that was on his bed at home – it was just large enough to rest his head upon and not much larger. And it was much firmer.

His hands were clasped together, and he had a hard time moving them, but he managed to pry them apart. Something rubbed his hands that felt like a necklace with many beads, but he heard it fall to his side.

Reaching his hand up, it stopped. It stopped on some sort of low padded ceiling that was only inches above him.

And then he stopped.

Enter me now, Jean Carlo! Come inside and make me feel so good like you made all those gays feel through all of your miserable fucking life!

Curiosity took the best of him. It was now or never. He opted to find Jonas, who he had not heard a sound from since he had entered the mist. There was nowhere for him to go. Heading back down the stairs would only trap him.

He still didn't understand this strange society that existed below the city. He felt like he could trust Jonas, but then again, the society just seemed so odd. And the Metatron – what were those contraptions? The mist was the unknown, and he sensed evil – an uneasy sensation which overtook him the closer he got to it.

His stomach felt uneasy.

But at least the mist offered something that going back downstairs didn't seem to – a possible way out.

CHAPTER FOURTY-EIGHT

The last thing that Roberto could remember was the flaming stone room. The hot bright flames and the silver casket.

Running.

Where was he?

Why, Roberto? Why do you ask such a question? Certainly you don't know where you are? Or where you have been?

Or what you have done…

The room that he found himself in, the room that collapsed towards him was where he was; the flames that were trying to reach for him and burn him alive, which would boil the skin off his body, as it bubbled and dripped off his bones.

But did it really happen?

There he was. Once again.

But the halls were no longer made of the earth.

At least, from what he felt, he did not believe that to be the case. The floor felt hard, like he was standing on wood or concrete. But it was black, pitch dark black, the kind of black that you would open your eyes as wide as they can be opened, but see to no avail. He could not see a thing in front of him. Not a sliver of light.

He turned his head around, in the direction that he thought was the stone chamber with the casket, but he could not tell for sure.

He heard something. A grating, like stone moving against stone. And in his mind, he saw a vision.

Hernan.

Lying dead in that coffin.

And then he closed his eyes. He saw the silver casket as is he were observing from standing in the corner of the room, just feet away; he saw the casket being placed on the stone slab by two tall, broad shouldered men in dark black suits, but when they turned towards him, they had no faces.

Just skin.

Plain, flat skin.

Once the casket was in place, the two men turned and looked at Roberto. They each cocked their heads to the side. They each took a few steps forward, they came closer and closer to Roberto, to the point where their faces seemed to be right in front of his.

And then they turned back around.

They returned to the casket, and stood over it. One of them gestured for Roberto to come over and to come closer.

He did.

Roberto felt himself moving forward, like he could not control it. He felt himself gravitating towards the casket, as one of the men opened the lid. He opened it just ever so slightly, just enough to let some light in and see the reflection of flesh…

And then stopped.

Roberto opened his eyes, still only seeing the blackness and blueness of the dark surrounding him. He was breathing heavily. He mopped his forehead with the side of his forearm.

Who was in that casket?

He leaned up against the wall, and exhaled. But when he was running possible solutions through his mind, how to get himself out of the situation he was in, as he dropped ever so slowly down into a sitting position with his back pressed to the wall, he felt a hard, round object jutting out from the wall.

It didn't erect itself from the wall and prod into his back. Roberto felt that the door handle had been there all along, but he did not notice it until he had slinked back onto the wall and started to ease himself down. And then he felt it.

A door.

Instantly turning around to face this mysterious door, he felt out with his hands and determined that, yes, there was a door. He couldn't remember if it had been there before and he didn't care.

Was the building beckoning him in farther? Or was this the door that he originally entered through?

It was too dark to tell.

All he could do was feel the mysterious surfaces with his hands, and when he ran his hands out in front of him, he felt the smooth grainy surface of the wooden door; he caressed the cusp of the woodworking on the frame, and the sharp transition to a rough rocky mountain range, where the stone wall fought against the streamlined woodworking and reached outwards.

He drew his hands back downwards, and rested his right hand on the cool, smooth and rounded knob. He paused for a moment. He clicked the knob to the left.

He turned his head back once more, straining his eyesight to see anything, anyone that might have been back in the stone room, but he saw nothing.

But it was what he felt…and what he heard…that said otherwise. There was definitely someone or something there in the room with him.

~~*

Roberto heard a faint cry – not like a scream, but more like a squeal. Far off in the distance, but moving closer.

And then Roberto could make out what the woman was saying. The moans – so methodic and mesmerizing – started to sound familiar. And then he realized.

He saw that night again.

Roberto…oh, Roberto? Where have you gone? What have you done to me?

And then standing there dead still with his hand still clutching the doorknob, he heard it. Right in front of him.

"Roberto! Listen to your mother!"

He closed his eyes, as tight as he could shut them. So tight they ached. Tighter than he could ever remember, since he was a little kid sitting up in bed with the covers drawn up to his chin thinking there was a monster in the closet – so tight that his face wrinkled up.

"*Roberto! Look at me! You abandoned me! You left me…and my face was smashed against the cabinets! And now here I am, I am the demon-seed whoring myself in hell! You sentenced me to this! You fucking bastard!*"

He didn't look. He didn't want to. "No!" he screamed.

But she didn't have to speak.

It didn't matter what she said. *Oh Roberto! You are so much better than your father! Such a strong young man taking care of me!*

Oh I love you Roberto!

He turned the handle and the walls started to crumble. He could not see it, but he felt crumbling rocks assaulting his arm. Wincing at the pain, he tried the knob again. The whole hallway shook, like an earthquake.

Roberto! Open your eyes! Come and save me!

The door wasn't budging. So he turned and opened his eyes.

There was his mother, just as he remembered her; the shoulder length brunette hair, the pretty youthful face; the glistening smile. She even had all of her teeth. So this must have been from years ago.

But something was different.

"You've been dead and gone for years!" he screamed to her.

That's no way to speak to your mother. You see I have all my teeth, right? Remember when I had to get the dental implants? And what did we tell the dentist? I am trying to remember.

Her smile faded. "Is this the kind of welcome that I get? I have been waiting here for years now, watching the world and waiting, waiting for you to come and join me, and now here you are!"

She jumped forward and put her arms around Roberto in a motherly embrace. She took her hand and caressed his cheek.

"Yes…" she said, "You see this? Look around. Try to ignore the rumbling and falling rock."

Roberto looked around and could see. He saw the crumbling stone was falling around them, like a crumbling city. The hallway began to glow white, bright white and upon looking outwards, he saw the stone crumble and fall to reveal the same stone room with the casket.

"Don't think about going back there," she said, snapping his chin back in position to look at her face dead on. "You're not dead yet. That is your father's destiny. Not yours. Yes, *that* is your destiny." She pointed to the door behind him, which would not budge.

"What is my destiny?"

"You go through that door," she said, "you will have made your choice. Look around you. The walls have crumbled. It's like a cave. This place is a sentence! But that door…is what can save you."

He turned around, now seeing the door clearly outlined in a wall that was a mixture of moss and earth and leftover fragments of stone. But the door looked perfectly wooden; it actually looked out of place, like it was intentionally built just for him.

Roberto.

Roberto! You were never like this when you were my son! You loved me, yes you did. I never doubted that. But when I got the cancer, when I began to submit to my punishment and my destiny, you deserted me. You slimy little faggot! You took it up the ass every night! What happened to you?

And then I died.

I remember dying, lying in my hospital bed, alone. I could barely open my eyes and look around the room; I saw the bright lights filtering through from the hallway.

But the room was dark.

I saw shadows in the ceiling. They moved across the ceiling and hovered over my bed. In the corners where the wall met the ceiling and another wall…there was a laughing demon waiting for me. They seemed to say, 'That's right Eva, come on girl! We know in just a few short minutes you will be ours! We're here waiting for you! It's just a matter of time now!'

And then I died.

And you were out somewhere getting fucked. And who knows where Hernan was.

As soon as I died, I got up out of bed. I rose out of bed like I would any other time that I rose out of bed, but this time I did not feel tired or weak or needing a few minutes extra of sleep.

I felt nothing.

As I stood up, I looked back down.

There I was, lying in the bed, eyes closed, a look of peace on my face. But I knew that peace would not last into this realm. That's right Roberto.

Those demons that were waiting for me in the dark corners of the room – guess what they did? They came up and stood in front of the door. I couldn't see them. They were out of focus like silhouettes – but they made it clear that they had come for me.

I knew what I had done. My guilt has consumed me. And now, here I am, sentenced to eternity to this hell! I cannot forgive and I cannot forgive myself!

She stood in front of Roberto, smiling like she always did as his mother. She gazed upon him with love and affection. "You see, my son, I have many regrets. And I believe, that perhaps…just perhaps…that we shouldn't always regret what we do in life. Because we are all imperfect. But they came for me my son. They came for me because I of what I didn't do in my life."

"What didn't you do?"

"I wasn't there for you…as your mother. I expected so much from you…to protect me from the poor choices I had made. And even so, I never regret marrying your father, even despite what he did to me, because he gave me you."

Roberto felt his face twitch for a brief moment.

"And what I regret most is what I forgot," Eva said as her gaze fell downwards.

"What was that?"

"I forgot that you were my son. And I should have never lost sight of that."

She smiled wanly, for a fleeting moment, as her youthful face contorted in pain and distress; her hands tightened their grip on Roberto's forearms, squeezing them until the flesh turned red, causing him to cry out.

The skin on her face began to drop off and liquefy, revealing the muscle and bone beneath. That began to rot and fall away as she cried in defeat. "I'm sorry Roberto…"

Each exposed patch of skin on her body shrived and dried and began to fall off, and then her head dropped back and her grip loosened on Roberto's arms. He dropped her rotted corpse down to the floor.

It was time to go through the door. Wherever it led, he was meant to go there.

It was time.

CHAPTER FOURTY-NINE

Dawn.

As Sheldon stood in front of his small bedroom window overlooking Ponce De Leon, the sunlight crept through the rust colored cross-hatched pattern in the glass, warmly casting small yellowish squares on the cranberry colored rug.

Today was the day.

He had lost Anthony to Antoine and Darius, and did not know of his fate. Paula was long gone. But that did not matter to Sheldon. Antoine had sunk into the underworld of Demons – somehow he managed to embroil himself in their evildoings. But Sheldon could not put his finger on it – on how he got involved with Asmodai.

When he first had discovered Antoine, he was still a student in Boston, studying theology at Boston College. The year was 1965. Antoine had kept a relatively low profile throughout most of the twentieth century; he did emerge into the public eye as a spiritual leader and healer until the 1990's, during the end of the century when the world began filling with hate and chaos.

During the period that Sheldon attended school in Boston, he read of Antoine one evening while at the campus library, stumbling upon

Les Livre Des Vampires. Sheldon always held a deep fascination with immortals.

The young, twenty-something Sheldon Wilkes was a much leaner and trimmer, athletically built man with a full, thick head of dark brown hair and a trimmed beard covering most of the bottom half of his face - contrasting greatly to the round and paunchy older man with the silver-haired receding hairline, horn-rimmed glasses and three-piece suits he was destined to become. He was wearing large, round rimless glasses framing his face and making him look rather scholarly – and in Boston, he pretty much blended into the scholarly crowd.

There it was, staring at him through the columns of books of varying degrees of thickness and height, it was standing on the shelf, as if it appeared brighter than the others – like it was highlighted by some unknown aerial light source.

LES LIVRE DES VAMPIRES:

THE BOOK OF THE IMMORTALS,

the spine read. He slowly and reverently pulled the book from the shelf. It was the first time he had laid his eyes on the volume, not knowing then that it would be a great part of his life for the remainder of his days, and not knowing that the book before him would develop into an obsession.

Holding the book respectfully as if it were the Bible, he slowly padded over to the closest table in the library. He sat down next to a large picture window, overlooking a well-kept garden. He placed his backpack in the center of the table, and sat in the wooden chair. Setting the book gently down on the table, he sat upright in the chair and settled himself. He opened the binding carefully, for the book seemed to be quite old.

Parchman's Press

Boston, MA

1864

the title page read, at the bottom. Above it, it bore the title again, in the center of the page.

He leaned forward, reached for his backpack, unzipped it and fished out a yellow legal pad and pen.

This is perfect, he thought, folding back the first few pages with scribbling on them in blue and black ink. *This can be a topic for my thesis.* Sheldon had long been toiling with the decision of what topic to address for his senior thesis, and he was already behind on his research. The book of the vampires was an impressive find. Although his professor may or may not accept a paper that presented the mysteries of the immortals, Sheldon could certainly conjure the question that he would pose in the dissertation: how can immortals integrate themselves into everyday society? He jotted down the question on the yellow legal pad, at the top of the page, underlining it twice for clarity.

He began to read, and he read and he read – page after page of detailed accounts of immortals – revealing their vampire origins hundreds and thousands of years ago to modern-day immortals who posed, sometimes, as public figures. He read about Claret, a young girl in the times of Christ that was rumored to be an immortal. Several drawings accompanied her story – one of her in her apparent mortal form, looking like an innocent girl of no more than ten or twelve.

According to the synopsis, Claret disappeared from her bed one night. There was no noise made, no evidence of a scuffle – and it was apparent the next morning when her parents arose to see her bunk empty.

Claret was gone.

She had gone off wandering into the night. Perhaps wandering the streets of Jerusalem searching for Jesus Christ – she was always infatuated with Him – but then again, why would she do it? Her mother shook her head, crying on her husbands shoulder unaware of where her child went.

But the truth was never revealed, except in the excerpt that Sheldon was reading before him, all while taking notes furiously. Claret never wandered off. She was taken, right under the sleeping noses of her parents and siblings. In a one-room clay hut on the outskirts of Jerusalem, through the doorframe covered simply by sheepskin, Claret could see a spiny hand pull the covering back from the doorframe, slowly.

Like any child would, she lay in her bunk frozen still and unable to move, covering her eyes with her fingers – watching through her fingers the sheepskin curtain pull back from the door and reveal a man with long, flowing black hair, wearing a black hooded robe. He entered silently, and headed towards Claret. She pulled her blanket over her head in a childish hope for protection and lay there motionless with a racing heart until she felt a hand grab her arm, pulling her out of bed.

No one woke – not her mother or father, and not her brothers or sisters. During the entire abduction, they slept with a depth like death and no one arose to her aid or even made move. Claret rose out of bed when she felt the gruff, strong commanding hand raising her up. She arose without protest, as if she wanted to.

Removing the hood, the man smiled down at Claret, looking on her like an adult would an obedient child. Claret had never seen this man before – his dark hair framed his chiseled face, and he had a long and full beard which looked like a mane growing from his chin. And the eyes. Deep blue and intense.

He extended his hand, and as if on cue, Claret took it. The two headed through the sheepskin door, and disappeared into the night. Claret's family never saw or heard from her again.

~~*

Sheldon closed the library that night. Reading of Claret, he saw that she was rumored to be the center of immortality. Fascinated by the detailed account of how she became immortal, he continued his scribbling.

Claret.

He wrote her name down in the center of the page, circling it. It stood out amongst the sea of jotted shorthand notes, names and dates.

How can I find Claret? He thought.

He pulled the book closer to him, setting it on top of his notepad. Reading on, he learned that none of the immortals knew who captured Claret's attention so significantly that she left with him in the middle of the night. The next page had a crude drawing of Claret drinking out of some sort of goblet. Underneath, was the inscription:

Claret drinking from The Cup of Christ.

Sheldon sat back in his chair for a moment, exhaling a deep breath from the depths of his torso. He leaned forward again, and studied the picture. It was a crudely drawn pencil drawing. The figures representing Claret and what appeared to be the hooded man looked to be similar to demonic cartoon characters.

He sat at that same, small wooden table near the large picture window overlooking the well-kept garden full of springtime flowers, and jotted notes furiously. The book of the immortals was proving to be a perfect source for Sheldon for his thesis, and when he turned to page 212, that was when he glimpsed Antoine for the first time.

There was a spread with a rather flattering picture of Antoine in the center of the page proclaiming how this immortal "financed solely expeditions to unearth ancient Egyptian relics". Sheldon sat back in his seat for a moment, wondering how the author got that information. In the 1800's as well. How would Antoine know of relics in Cairo? Weren't they discovered in the 1900's? He rubbed his bearded chin, and removed his glasses.

This is a mysterious man, he thought to himself. *How did he finance those expeditions? How did he keep it a secret from the Egyptian authorities? And how did he know that the relics were there?*

Some of the lights shut off.

Sheldon looked through the stacks, noticing that the library appeared to be closing. He desperately had to have this book. He closed the book for a moment, and looked at the bottom of the spine, where it indicated that the book was a reference book. He could not risk stealing the book from the library – his education and future would have been at stake, and he did not want to tarnish his stellar record. But he was determined to come back tomorrow to continue his note-taking, and he *had* to get a copy of that book for his own!

~~*

"You have been following me for the better part of your life now," Antoine had said, in his living room amidst the popping and crackling fire, to Sheldon, the same misty night that he had come to talk to Antoine. The same night that Anthony and Paula had followed him.

"Yes," Sheldon replied, tipping the glass of whiskey towards his view, examining the ice cubes for no apparent reason but to search for a better answer.

Antoine smiled, walked from the fireplace over to the sofa, sat down gracefully and crossed his legs; he raised his eyebrows to Sheldon, as if signaling him to continue speaking.

"I first saw you in a reference book I stumbled across in a library in Boston in 1965," he said with a slight slur in his speech. He set his empty glass down on the reading table next to his chair. As always the gracious host, Antoine arose and walked to the bar to refill Sheldon's drink as the circumstances of how Sheldon discovered Antoine was revealed.

"I took notes furiously that night, hoping that I could use the book for my senior thesis. I studied Theology, you see, and my specialty was the paranormal."

"I see."

Sheldon eagerly sipped the whiskey that was poured before him, and Antoine set a platter of caviar and crackers on the small table as well, which Sheldon attacked like he was in a bar. He leaned back in his chair and continued. "I have become obsessed with you, I will not lie. That very night that I first saw the article written on you – in the *eighteen hundreds* no less – I pledged to myself that I would find you and meet you. Anyone that could have known about the ancient buried treasures in Egypt – and keep it a secret from all of humanity – I had to discover."

"So you became obsessed with me because I had an inner sense and appreciation for the Pharaohs?" Antoine asked as he again glided to the sofa, sitting across from Sheldon.

"Not exactly," he replied. "What intrigued me was the fact that you knew of the tombs that had the treasure, before it was discovered. *And* you didn't announce it to the world. You left it for humanity to find, years later."

"That's it?" Antoine pressed, leaning forward. Sheldon polished off the last of the caviar and crackers, and took a large sip of his drink.

"No," Sheldon replied. "My interest in you goes much deeper than that. My interest revolves around your immortality. That article explained how you financed the excavations by yourself to unearth artifacts – to search for something, I suppose. But what intrigues me is that you managed to keep this a secret from the Egyptian authorities, from the entire *world* as a matter of fact, and then you covered your tracks like you weren't even there!"

Antoine looked straight ahead, but saw nothing. His faced lacked expression as his mind foraged ahead behind unseeing eyes. He replayed the events in his mind, he replayed the night that the excavations took place. He saw himself, leading a group of immortals, digging and pressing into the tombs in the Valley of the Kings. He saw himself unearthing the precious treasure, the treasure that no one knew was there, the treasure from thousands of years ago, the cup that Jesus Christ Himself drank from.

The Holy Grail.

Antoine snapped out of his musing and shook his head. Sheldon was missing the point.

It seemed as if the silly old man was assuming that he was simply excavating the tombs because he was looking to find some mythical buried treasure, or to get some ancient artifacts to support his extravagant lifestyle. Or perhaps to add to his personal, private collection. But Sheldon was indeed misguided. He didn't even know how Antoine managed to excavate the tombs without alerting the authorities. Silly, simple old man.

"Sheldon," Antoine said, rising from the sofa. The fire was slowly dying. "Stop speaking of things that you do not know of. I work in many realms that you are not aware of, and you will never *be* aware of unless you become one of us."

Antoine walked over to Sheldon's chair. The old man looked up at him with a slightly drunken stare. Antoine extended his arm for the man.

"Come with me," Antoine said. "I have to show you something."

Sheldon got up from the chair on his own, and once standing, gave Antoine a pat on the back, as if he were an old friend. "So now you are finally warming up to me!"

The two headed out of the sitting room to the foyer, and through the dining room that led to the kitchen, where Paula would eventually stand behind the swinging door and spy on Antoine and Anthony. There was also a second door, next to the swinging door, that led to the unknown.

"Do you know how I got this house?" Antoine asked as they paused in the kitchen before the door.

Sheldon shook his head. Antoine nodded, expecting that answer.

"I acquired this house from a family that I become very well acquainted with over the past few years. The owner's name was Hernan. Hernan Perez. He had a son named Roberto. Roberto and I met on Miami Beach, and that is when I was drunken with his beauty."

He crossed the kitchen to a rack of keys that was hanging on the wall near the stove, and drew a key from the rack.

"When I first saw Roberto, he was the most beautiful specimen of a mortal I had ever laid eyes on. But I saw much deeper than that. Roberto had a dark past. But I chose him. I chose him to become immortal like me, but I didn't act fast enough. I just couldn't bear to turn him into what I am." He placed the key in the door.

"The ironic thing is – he is physically older than I am." Antoine threw his head back and laughed, and opened the door to darkness.

"As you can see," he said, "I appear rather young. I am. If I were a mortal, I would be nineteen. But, in actuality, I am hundreds of years old." He flipped the light on, revealing a set of dark wooden stairs heading to a mysterious, dark lower level, stale looking white walls and a few electrical outlets. But that was all. At the end of the stairs, the light faded, and the blackness took over once again.

"Anyway," Antoine continued, "Hernan proved to be a domineering man who beat and controlled Roberto to the point where Roberto surrendered himself to me, giving up on his life. I killed Hernan for what he did to his son."

Antoine started to descend the stairs, and Sheldon cautiously followed.

"Sometimes", Antoine said, peering into the darkness below the stairs, "if you listen carefully and the house is silent, you can hear him. Hernan calls sometimes…sometimes I think he is looking for me."

"Hear him?"

"Deep in the night…when the house is dark…I can hear him."

"You hear him speak to you like he is still living?"

"Oh you think that he is dead?" Antoine questioned with a chuckle. "Anyone I touch becomes immortal! Have you done your homework dear sir?" He reached around to Sheldon with a smile and patted him sharply on the back. "Apparently not!"

Antoine continued. "I killed Hernan, but he still walks the earth. He is immortal, but not in the same way that myself or Darius are.

Hernan is a crossover. Confused. When I drained him of his blood, I took him to the edge of death. And then something else took over. I think it was a demon."

"And what do you mean?" Sheldon asked. "When you said you didn't act fast enough?"

"It's the rules of Tartarus," Antoine replied. "I can stake a claim, but there is a fine line that must not be crossed. I crossed it, and Hernan died. I could no longer claim him at that point."

Antoine stopped at the end of the stairs.

"Here we are," he said. He extended out his arm towards the darkness, as if he were on a game show displaying a brand new car. "This is what I was going to show you."

"But all I see is darkness," Sheldon said.

"That's true. You will have to trust me. The bowels of this house are part of the other realm that I was talking to you about. The other realm – remember Sheldon? When I was in Egypt? The other realm."

Sheldon looked around like the inspector that he was, and Antoine took the clue.

"If you are looking for a light switch, there aren't any. There is no basement beneath this house. Living in Florida, you should have known that. The water table here is too high."

"So what is this then?" Sheldon asked. He reached his hand out in an attempt to touch the thick blackness before them.

"Like I told you," Antoine explained, as the two stood at the base of the stairs, in the small remainder of light that instantly was swallowed up before them. "This is not a basement. I can't just flick a switch, I can't just proclaim 'Let there be light' like God did. I can't control this dimension. But I can guide you through it."

Sheldon paused, and turned to Antoine.

"You meant to take me here?" he asked.

"Yes."

"And what if I don't want to go?"

"Oh you will. You are too obsessed with me to say no. You still have whiskey running through your veins, which has lowered your inhibitions, and I know that you will say yes, or I would not have taken you down these stairs. This will answer all of your questions."

"I thought I had answered my questions when I spoke to you these last few days," Sheldon replied.

"Like I said, it goes much deeper than that. Do you really think that I am simply an immortal? Do you not think that there is a darker force at work?"

Sheldon scratched his head for a moment.

"So shall we proceed?" Antoine asked.

"Yes," Sheldon said. "I want to see this. But can I get my recorder first? I left it up in the living room."

"No. You will have no need for it where we are going."

Sheldon looked up the stairs for a moment, seeing the warm glow of the kitchen light shining down, seeming so far away this moment.

"So shall we go?"

"Yes."

Antoine looked at Sheldon expectantly.

"Will you come with me?" Antoine asked, inviting him into the blackness. And the two proceeded, quickly becoming enveloped into a wall of blackness so dark that as soon as they entered it, it was if they never were there.

~~*

Anthony caressed the back of Antoine's neck as he showed the new member to the door. Anthony was an Inductee.

What Paula didn't see when she had been spying in the other room was Antoine sinking his teeth deeper and deeper into Anthony's neck – sending a stream of bright red blood cascading down his back, bleeding through his shirt and spilling bright red drops to the white carpet below.

"So you will come?" Antoine asked, expectantly, gazing into Anthony's eyes. Antoine wiped a drop of blood that oozed from the corner of his mouth, and smiled with blood stained teeth. "I would most certainly like to have you there when I exhume him. No. I need you there."

"Yes, I will come."

"Good then," Antoine said. "Go and rest. You will be transforming soon. Once you do, come back to me. I will take us to Lyon."

Anthony left the estate, and staggered down the front path; he walked quickly across the street in bloodstained clothes to his car, all while being watched from afar by Paula.

CHAPTER FIFTY

It was Antoine who saw the events in the cemetery playing in his mind – he saw himself stand before Asmodai, surrendering the heart; he saw himself looking at his own heart beat in his chest; he could feel the warmth of his flesh as he touched the wound. He saw himself later, with Darius, after the ritual. And he even imagined himself, much later, examining the healed wound.

But that is only what he saw.

For Anthony was always there. And what happened is his mind was just how he imagined that it would be. But Anthony was there…and, that part, he did not take into consideration.

From a safe vantage point, Anthony had watched the events in the cemetery unfold before him. Like Antoine, he had heard the rustling in the woods, he had heard the tree come crashing down, and he had felt the rumbling of the footsteps. He had seen the demon come out of the woods as if on cue, and he had watched Antoine duck into the grave. But what was different now, from before, was that Antoine never made it to resurrect Darius; for Anthony had been present the entire time. He was perched up in a mature oak tree; huddled in a large, thick branch on the opposite end of the graveyard, and through the shroud of foliage and brushes he could see the entire scene unfold before his eyes, to the point where Antoine had been dodging giant fireballs from the glowing eyes of a corpse – and then seeming to be overtaken by a pack of demons.

He climbed down the tree he had been watching from effortlessly like an athlete.

His newly acquired powers assisted him with speed and agility, and when he hit the ground he didn't even make a sound. All attention was focused Antoine, on the opposite side, as his arm was slowly devoured by a corpse.

Springing into action, he darted into the cemetery silently and ducked behind a large tombstone, running through his mind the events and what he might be able to do to help. He would be no match against Asmodai. And if he intruded, Asmodai would certainly dispose of him.

Antoine turned and jumped away from the corpse, and Anthony took the cue and sprinted at superhuman speed across the graveyard, darting from grave to grave, taking refuge behind the periodic large stone.

Asmodai drew his sword. Not speaking, he charged towards Anthony, swinging his flaming sword back and forth.

Anthony sprinted and began dodging demons – for a moment, he stopped behind a large marker, catching his breath. Despite being immortal, he was still newly changed. He still clung to a bit of mortality, and the powers have not been fully bestowed upon him yet. He was still partially human, and therefore still experienced the mortal shortcomings.

He rested his hand on the edge of the stone. Looking forward, he saw Antoine perched back up in the tree.

"Anthony!" he called, looking over towards his partner. "Take this!" He threw the heart down, and Anthony caught it. He looked down upon the organ, he paused for a moment, noticing its freshness; the blood was still bright red and the muscle was pumping methodically. The blood copiously coated it; it still flowed and covered his hands. He clutched the heart close to his chest, and darted to the other end of the cemetery, further away from the action.

Asmodai followed the heart with his eyes and came up to the stone where Anthony was standing, swinging his sword against the mortar, ushering a loud clank and a spray of sparks to the ground below. Anthony had left just in time.

But Asmodai continued, and several other demons followed, swords drawn and aimed towards Anthony. Getting closer to where Antoine was perched in the tree, Anthony stopped behind another large stone, catching his breath for a moment. He looked up.

"I am coming for you Anthony!" Antoine said, jumping down, and again the corpse attacked. Antoine reached out, fending off the attacking rotted human, and grabbed the heart from Anthony. The demons stopped in their tracks, as if commanded by some unseen force.

The thunder rumbled, followed by bright flashes of lighting, and Antoine threw the thrashing body onto the ground, stepping on its legs to hold it down. Anthony knelt down to assist, holding down the thrashing arms.

Asmodai stood in the clearing of the cemetery, about ten feet away from them. His anger mounted and grew, grunting and groaning – appearing as if trying to get out of an unseen force field, which trapped him in a giant unseen bubble.

Yes, this is the way it was written. Darius shall rise again. Darius shall walk the earth again.

"Take the heart!" Antoine yelled, over the winds, which began to roar again, this time much stronger than before. Both immortals had to shield their eyes from soaring debris.

Antoine mustered all of his strength, all of his powers, drew them together from the pit of his stomach and struck the chest of the body, ripping out the heart in a shower of decayed, rotted and dried out flesh, grayish and spoiled, dusty and old. He threw the heart on the ground.

"Place the heart in the chest Anthony! Do it quickly!"

Anthony did as he was told, shoving the heart into the chest. The organ spun around in circles inside the chest, and emitted a bright, white light – so bright that they had to shield their eyes in pain. The corpse levitated above the ground, with a renewed energy flowing through it.

Antoine rose to his feet, grabbing Anthony's hand and pulling him up. Anthony stared at the body dumbfounded, as it began to hover several feet off the ground, spin and drop again to the grass. "Come on! Grab it!" Antoine said, straining through the winds. "I don't know how much longer they will be held!"

Anthony looked back towards the clearing, and Asmodai was furious, thrashing around inside his bubble. He was about to break out.

The storm stopped and Asmodai broke free – his entire body tripling in size and glowing orange. His eyes slanted and he stood over ten feet tall, his muscles bulged to an enormous size – ripping his armor right from his body.

Asmodai raised his arms to the sky, drawing giant wands of fire that dropped down from the clouds into his hands. He held each of these wands like swords, turning around and ripping each bubble trapping the demons behind him with one thrash.

"Grab it, go!" Antoine yelled.

The two each took an arm over their shoulders and drug the body into the woods. They ran. They ran as fast as their legs would take them, dodging fallen tree branches, shrubs and thick foliage, deeper and deeper into the dark woods.

Asmodai was right behind them, swinging swords of fire, igniting all of the trees around them, turning the woods into a blazing inferno.

"Stay away from the fire, Anthony! That is the one thing that we can't survive!" Antoine said, looking over his shoulder. "It's not much farther!"

"Where are we going?" Anthony asked, amidst explosions of burning trees.

"Just follow me! You will see!"

There was another clearing in the woods behind the graveyard, and in the clearing was a cave with an entrance so small the giant demons would not be able to enter. Antoine ducked into it, dragging Anthony and the corpse with him. “Go in, come on, deeper inside!”

The cave was pitch black, and continued, through muddy and murky waters, into the bowels of the earth. They could hear the sizzling and roaring of the fire outside the cave walls, the rumbling thunder and the army of demons surrounding the cave attempting to enter.

But the cave did not offer a sanctuary yet. Asmodai was right outside in the clearing, shooting flames into the cave, which lit the cavern in a yellowish orange glow of fire, sending searing heat that stung their faces.

“Keep going deeper!” Antoine yelled from the front.

The fire shot through the cave entrance like flames from a gas line, boiling the water on floor. Anthony screamed out in pain, wincing at the heat in the water and noticing steam rising to the cave ceiling. “Don’t think about it! That will not hurt you!”

Then the entire cave shook, as if there was an earthquake. Rocks and small boulders broke free from the ceiling, cascading to the floor one landing on Antoine’s back, sending him face first into the water. “Antoine!” Anthony exclaimed, temporarily forgetting the boiling water and flames, dropping the body and rushing to Antoine’s aid.

Antoine pulled his face out of the water, letting out a deep breath, coughing up some water. “We need to go deeper,” he said.

The cave continued to shake. There was a crash from the entrance. “Come on!” Antoine said. “He is breaking into the cave!”

CHAPTER FIFTY-ONE

Opening her eyes gradually and wincing at the pain between her legs, Paula gradually began to make out her surroundings. She felt the cold, hard marble beneath her on the floor, and she even felt the heat resonating from the flames of the torch above her. Feeling like she just woke up from a night of restless sleep, she struggled up to a sitting position, feeling the ache in her muscles and the fuzziness still veiling her thoughts.

Opening her eyes gradually, she scanned her surroundings.

She was in a mysterious stone room – but she did not recall how she got there. Looking around and trying to recall the events that brought her here, it started to gradually come to her in bits and pieces, as if a television picture was gradually clearing. She remembered a set of stairs made from dirt – and she remembered being with Anthony. And she remembered losing Anthony – calling out his name in desperation from the landing on the stairs. But then after she fell down the stairs, she remembered nothing. The veil still shrouded her thoughts.

Making a feeble attempt to stand, she felt an ache that reached her inner thighs. She winced at the sharpness of the pain.

"Get up."

A voice spoke from the opposite end of the room, encouraging her in her actions. In the dim, flickering light Paula could not clearly see the figure standing in the corner. The figure moved closer. When she looked over in the direction of the voice, it seemed like a giant, blurred bright light. It was so bright in that corner that she could not focus her eyes. "Get up Paula."

She struggled to her feet, wincing at the pain in her groin, and screamed.

She fainted, but did not hit the floor.

Someone caught her. She could feel powerful arms grasping her waist, holding her from the floor. Whatever it was laid her back on the floor, and she felt cool air blowing across her face. Slowly opening her eyes, she saw a bright glowing hand gradually moving back and forth above her face, creating the much needed flow of air. The glowing being above her emitted a white, aural luminescence.

"I am Verkai," it said. "I am here to lead you through this dark, sinister world."

"Where am I?" she asked. She still could not see his face, but she could tell that the voice was masculine. And it seemed friendly as well. Loving.

The being waved its arm across the chamber, and Paula's eyes followed it, revealing the stone chamber that loosely resembled a mortuary or crematorium, but without the cold ceramic tile that generally pastes the walls of the lower chambers of earthly funeral parlors. This room was stone – from floor to ceiling, and the floors were made of marble. "You are trapped in the quantum realm. This is the plane of existence that is close to yours physically, but you do not see it. But despite its closeness, the difference between the two dimensions is quite vast. It is going to be a challenge to get you back to your dimension, given what has happened to you."

"What has happened to me?" Paula looked over at the blood.

"There is a demon seed growing inside of you, Paula. It won't be much longer before you bear child."

She touched her stomach, which already appeared larger than before.

"You were raped by an Incubus, Paula, and that Incubus injected its demon seed into you. You can see it is growing very fast. We do not have much time."

Paula glanced again down at her midsection, which appeared even larger in just that short moment.

"Why can't I be taken back to my dimension? I don't even know how I got here!" Paula pleaded. "All I know is I was on Anastasia, and then all of a sudden, it stormed, I looked up, and the place looked like it was deserted! Like all of the houses were abandoned and unkempt for years! And then…I started getting chased by these *monsters!*"

"Monsters, yes, they are monsters. They are far worse than that. They are directly from Hell. For you crossed over, Paula. You were chosen. And you have been here since you crossed."

The figure rose, casting a warm white glow throughout the chamber. Paula instinctively followed.

"You are carrying Nesmaron." Verkai glided across the room to a door on the opposite wall that looked to be of steel like on that of a submarine. "We must carry you deeper into the Netherworld so Nesmaron can be birthed without corruption to society. If he gets out of this realm, he will most certainly bring all of humanity under his control. He is the ultimate of demons."

"How did I get bestowed the honor of birthing this being?"

"I can explain to you, but you may not like what you hear. You are more involved in this sinister plot to raise damnation than you may think."

"How so?"

"You have been to Sacrafice, the nightclub that Antoine and Darius have opened on Miami Beach."

"Didn't that place just open? And no, I was not there."

"Yes you were, Paula. You were there for opening night. You have been an integral part of the process. And the fact that you are here with me now shows that there is some hope for saving you."

Verkai opened the door into blackness, as a swirling white mist flowed out like smoke.

He continued. "Time means nothing here. Events can happen in this realm that parallel events that happen in reality – meaning, in a sense, that people who are in this realm could, in theory, bilocate."

"Bilocate?"

"Meaning you could be in two different places at once, doing two different things at exactly the same time."

"*Bilocate?!* You must be kidding right?"

He raised his hand, as if in protest to Paula's response.

"Bilocation is possible because you have interests in reality. You are Paula Tandy, and you are you who say you are. But in the Netherworld…" his voice trailed off.

Paula scoffed ."The Netherworld-"

"- is beyond there," Verkai pointed out, gesturing a glowing, muscular arm towards the darkness of the unknown. "We are in the fourth dimension right now. But beyond there…there is no help. Beyond there, you will no longer be Paula Tandy."

"And I have crossed that line before?" she asked.

"Yes you have," Verkai said.

Paula stopped for a moment to consider what he was saying to her. Who was she and what had she become?

"As I was saying," he continued. "Time means nothing here in comparison with reality. Since you crossed to this dimension from reality during the storm, you have crossed over many times. You have had many recollections of your past, ran from many demons in your present, and are destined to a hellish future if we do not get you back to your reality. But all that is normal for this dimension. Demons run free here. It's not like your reality, where they must be controlled by a super demon or conjured by humans."

Paula collapsed to the floor and shook her head. "When will this nightmare be over?" Verkai knelt beside her and placed a strong hand on her shoulder, squeezing it softly. She closed her eyes and leaned on his aura, feeling held and supported despite his transparency.

"Through that door, you will become your alter-ego. It's someone that you created, that you have wanted to be your whole life."

She sat and imagined, for a moment, who she had wanted to be. It was clear to her, watching the super models on tv as child and as a teen – there was one in particular, who had long, flowing dark brown hair, and bright red lips. She looked so naughty, so much like a vixen. That was her. That's who she wanted to be. Not the plain-Jane frumpy investigator she had become.

Mustering up the strength to go through the door, she started to transform, right on the floor. Crawling through the threshold to hell like a spider, she entered through the door and got swallowed up by the darkness. As she crossed the threshold she felt a searing pain through her body causing her a moment to cry out, reverberating and echoing around her.

Something dropped to the floor, with a soft, mushy feeling followed by a splash. She felt as though she had been cleaned. She felt as though her body had just gotten rid of load of toxins; she felt lighter and refreshed. Verkai was closely following, and his aura provided some light where he was standing in the chamber, but the light stopped at the threshold. So did the light of the torches. It seemed as though all light stopped at that line.

But it didn't matter.

Paula looked down at what dropped from her body. Looking like a glowing alien egg, it was translucent and pulsating in a repeated fashion like a beating heart. It seemed as if it were gestating. Looking closer, she saw something dark inside. Something that looked like it could be something waiting to be birthed.

"*What the fuck is THAT?!*" Paula screamed.

She looked for a moment back at Verkai. He was still standing at the door, and he glanced at her with a knowing glance.

She knew.

She bent down to touch the glowing egg. Her fingertips hovered close to it, her fingers almost touching the clear, thick skin. She stopped just short.

"Should I touch it?" she asked Verkai, looking up at him expectantly.

"I wouldn't, but it *was* just inside you. So go ahead. Might be alright."

She paused for a moment. "But…but I feel cleansed. I just feel lighter and clean…so…I wonder…but…"

She bent down again and brought her hand just next to the object. Her finger touched the substance. It felt gelatinous like a jellyfish – slimy, cool, wet and spongy. But then the dark figure inside moved suddenly, noticing her touch. She screamed sharply and jumped back.

"Shit!" she exclaimed, running back to the door, closer to the apparent safety of Verkai.

"Nesmaron…" Verkai said slowly, shaking his head and moving back into the darkness. "That egg contains the most powerful and most evil of demons next to Lucifer."

Paula shuddered and took a few steps further back from the pulsating egg.

"It is too late, I'm afraid," Verkai stated with a touch of despair in his voice. "I didn't expect it to mature so fast inside you. Certainly you were an open portal." Verkai looked down at Paula, suddenly looking human. His face was painted with worry, like that of a concerned father. He closed his eyes and shook his head slightly. "We are going to have to get you out of here. But I am afraid that the only way out is to go farther in."

Paula looked up at Verkai, wondering what he truly looked like. Before her now, all he seemed to be was an aural presence exhibiting a masculine face and presence. But he seemed too comforting, and he seemed…like an old friend.

He moved closer to Paula and put his arm around her, pulling her tighter to him, as she felt herself becoming enveloped by his aura. The closer she got to him, the more refreshing coolness she felt. Not the damp, musty cold of the darkness that they were on the threshold of, but rather a fresh, calming feeling taking over; like fresh spring air.

His calming luminescent aura glowed all around her as she was hugging his body tightly, his brightness reaching out and surrounding her like a blanket.

She looked up at his face. That's who it was! She knew it all along. He came to her, he came to her out on Andelusia, where she was hiding. The demons were chasing her, and he came to save her. She didn't know how he got to be in this form – or how he got here after disappearing in the first place – but she was glad that he was here.

He looked down at her and smiled. "I came for you girl," he said, gently pulling strands of her hair from her eyes and smoothing it back over her head. "You called me to come."

Paula looked ahead and said nothing, she just closed her eyes and smiled. For a moment, she felt safe in all of the terror. She felt like maybe – just maybe – everything would turn out okay. A familiar face in all of the madness is just what she needed. Too much has happened over the past twenty four hours – the intensity of the storm and her falling into the quantum, running from Asmodai, and reliving the horrors of losing her child; she was glad to have a minute to lay her head back, breath out a deep sigh, a rest for a moment in loving and familiar arms.

Lost in her moment of relaxation and displacement, neither of them noticed the egg until it gurgled and stopped pulsating. Paula lifted her head from Verkai's shoulder, and looked over at her offspring.

It had indeed stopped.

Looking like it was lying in a pool of some sort of ectoplasmic substance, she saw that the being inside was much larger, this time almost taking up the entire confines of the inside of the egg.

"It's almost time, Paula. We have to get you out of here. He is about to birth, and since he wasn't deep in the Netherworld, he may get out of the quantum."

Paula broke free of Verkai's grasp and stood next to him, staring at the egg. Something was moving inside. Paula ducked behind Verkai for safety, but still kept her eyes trained on the egg. It began to ooze a clear, thick liquid. It began to seep out of the entire skin of the egg, emitting a hiss and a foul odor from the porous object.

The monster inside started to thrash in its confines. It was dark and black; the arms were long a spiny with sharp pointed fingers. As the hand – or what looked like a hand – started to open, revealing the bony digits and pointed nails, the egg burst, sending a cascade of clear liquids throughout the room, and the foul odor started to overpower Paula with the smell of human excrement.

Paula screamed as Verkai held her tightly.

The demon still sat hunched in a crouched position, with its arm extended, as if exhausted.

"Do not say a word or make a move," Verkai whispered to her, as she continued to look on, paralyzed like a statue – admittedly too fearful to make a move for fear of disturbing the Hellspawn. "Very few have witnessed such an event as this," he continued, hugging her closer.

Nesmaron.

Once the demon stood and started to drip free of the plasma juices, he turned his head to their direction. He reached his arm closer to where Paula was standing. He was crouched across the blackness, across from Paula, the black armor on his arm stretched and extended out to her.

The monster pulled her free from Verkai's grasp, and Verkai was frozen cold and still. He could do nothing to stop the power from Nesmaron. Paula gravitated towards the demon as it stood even higher, getting taller the more its limbs stretched out.

The arms and legs were lined with black fins that looked more amphibian gills than anything else. When he stood up completely, he towered over Verkai and Paula to more than double their height.

He was the demon incarnate.

A long, thick tail grew from his back, and the limbs and body filled from the spiny appendages from gestation to gargantuan, treelike muscular trunks. His chest broadened; his arms grew with muscle and veins. His fingers spiked as did his face – his face was elongated and spiked at the chin and the forehead.

Paula stared at the monster, walking up to him, and hugged him tightly around the torso. He put one hand on her back, tapping his spiny fingers, rubbing her back as her dirty blonde hair lengthened and darkened, and her form and figure began to fill out – her bosoms grew, and so did her height.

Nesmaron turned his gaze to Verkai.

Verkai instantly spilled to the floor in a heaped mess, writhing in pain, as smoke hissed and seeped from his body. The acid that was eating his aura from the inside out was searing through his inner being and left him piled on the floor in a darkened smoking mess.

And the door slammed shut, closing out all light as the blackness overtook and the monster bore his teeth and flames ignited in the walls. The monster held his creator in lengthy arms, holding her tighter and tighter as he screamed and dripped acidic saliva, and the two fell – they fell down deeper and deeper into the darkness as blood red shone through the darkness coating them in thick viscous bright red blood.

CHAPTER FIFTY-TWO

Jonas felt like he was floating.

He felt like he was floating down the bright white hallways of the sterile South Shore hospital, following his killer, just steps ahead. The mysterious dark-cloaked figure glided through the halls and around nurses, doctors and orderlies that were harried and full of chaotic activity.

And Jonas most certainly was floating. For when he looked down, he saw that he was not standing on the hard tile floor, but levitating above and down the hall. He was drifting forward, in a motion that he felt he could not control and didn't want to stop.

He wanted to know this killer. He wanted to feel what he felt.

But there was too much pain, too much heartache that he still felt clinging to; he didn't feel as though a transition would have been easy.

The killer turned and faced him, with a darkened face and smiled; the killer stood waiting at the door for his follower to catch up.

"Come with me," he said. "Through these doors. Out there, that is where we will go and beyond…it has just begun, my dear child, just begun. You will see. Follow me, and you will see."

But when the doors open the green mist poured in like a giant toxic cloud and filled the hallway, destroying all light and the darkness quickly overtook the hospital. It was eerily silent, and he could not see in front of him. The mist was so dense and dark, when he brought he arm up in front of his face, he could not see it. But he assumed it was there.

"Are you there?" he asked quietly into the mist. It swirled in front of him, as if mocking him. There was no sign of his killer. Just the tease of the mist. He continued his search for the mysterious man. "Hello? Are you there?"

He squinted his eyes and tried to get his bearings, but all he saw was the mist. He tried moving forward, but couldn't feel the floor. He extended his arm to search for the wall, but nothing was there – just the gaseous swirling cloud.

Off in the distance, there was a clanking. It was a shrill, methodic sound, like a wrench being rapped against a steel pipe. It started quietly and slowly, but then got increasingly louder and more determined, until it deepened to a deafening boom.

"Who is out there?!" he called into the darkness. He lunged forward and lost his footing, falling into the mist but not reaching the floor. Instead he felt like he was floating.

The banging persisted, but he did not attempt to venture closer to the source. It kept on increasing in intensity.

And it sounded like it was getting closer to him.

The mist cleared somewhat, at least enough so Jonas could make out his surroundings. He was now able to return to standing, and felt the reassuring solidity of the floor once again.

He was no longer at the South Shore Hospital, he could tell that much. Where he stood was now vast and open and dark.

He tried to remember, as best as he could, what his killer had done. He closed his eyes and saw the hospital hallway, right before the mist came. He saw his killer open the door and then turn to him and smile. And then the mist quickly entered and overtook him – killing his senses.

And that had been it.

But recalling his movement down where the hospital hallway had been, as he remembered looking in the direction of Trauma-4, he now saw nothing that resembled a hallway filled with racing doctors and nurses pushing patients on gurneys. He saw a large, vast open space. When he looked up, the darkness seemed as though it went on forever, into some unknown distance, like the heavens in space, but without stars.

Just a deep, dark black.

Peering ahead, what he assumed must have been quite a distance, he saw an flickering orange light that looked like it might be a fire. And surrounding that fire, he thought he saw movement. It also sounded like the banging was coming from there. His curiosity getting the best of him, he started to move forward towards the fire. When he reached his foot in front of him, he felt for the floor; it was there, but he did not move across it like one might normally. He glided, hovering and moving – not because his brain told his feet to reach forward, but rather as he was willed to come to the new location. As the flicker became larger in his view, he confirmed that it definitely was a large fire of some sort, like a bonfire. There were dark figures which appeared to be dancing around the flames.

And then he stopped moving.

He crouched down, in an attempt to conceal his presence.

While still at a distance, he was much closer to the fire, and saw something being carried in by two muscular figures. The figures moved several feet apart, and appeared to separated by what could have a been a body laid out between them on some sort of transportation device like a stretcher.

The figures set it down next to the fire, and Jonas felt strong winds start to blow. They came instantly and rapidly increased to such velocity that Jonas fell to his knees, and only then did he realize that whatever the ground was – was not grass, nor was it dirt.

It felt soft and spongy.

And warm.

He brought his hand up closer to his face and sniffed the slimy substance that slowly dripped from his fingers. Grimacing, he wiped his hands on his pants, and made a feeble attempt to stand against the winds. He sought something to hold on to and steady himself, finding nothing and falling once again.

He found that he could steady himself in a kneeling position, and saw that even with the intensity of the winds, the fire had gotten larger and was raging. The flames reached and fingered against a darkness that held steady; he could feel their searing heat and the intensity of their roar.

But the flames now highlighted a third figure, standing in front of the fire. A giant beastly silhouette. Expansive wings stretched out from the center figure wide and far. The winged beast stood above the body lain on the stretcher.

The two smaller figures held the stretcher in front of the largest beast; they lifted it up several feet off the ground, and placed it on a stone slab which held the fire.

Jonas watched, mesmerized and glued to the action in front of him. He did not notice his killer was there too; he had return next to where Jonas was, and Jonas didn't hear his killer's cry for help until he felt a tight grip on his arm, pulling him forward and almost pulling him over.

The he was, the same mysterious man who had smiled to him in the hospital hallway, reaching up for him from a pool of blood. His eyes were deep yellow, and his hair was covered in blood in a dark, sticky mess.

"Help me!" he cried to Jonas, collapsing back onto the ground in a bloody mess. "Help me and help him!" He pointed to the fire, and Jonas saw the largest beast draw a sword, and touched the tip to the fire; the sword ignited in flames.

The figure on the table started to writhe and squirm.

"They're alive?" Jonas asked, focused on the writhing man. "That man is *alive*?"

"You need to help him!" the killer cried, fervently pointing towards the fire. The sword was held high over the squirming body, and all three figures had their wings spread.

"What happened to you?!" Jonas called to his killer over the winds. "Where *are* we?!"

A storm raged above them as the sky turned red and lightning crashed as the thunder raged.

"He is all I have!" the killer pleaded. "He is the one I created! He is the one that resurrected me! I must have him alive!"

"How do we stop them?"

"You don't understand! I no longer can! I tried to save him, I tried, for when the mist came, I saw! I saw that his only son betrayed him! He has been running from this demon for so many years, so *many years* and I am the cause of it!"

The flaming sword crashed down against the slab; the storm swelled and the fire spread on the writhing figure.

"No!" the killer cried. He tried to move closer to the fire, but Jonas saw that he was seriously injured. Jonas saw the greyish bone jutting out from the torn flesh of his killer's leg.

The killer collapsed on the ground and sobbed as the fire swelled, burning the figure on the stone table. The three muscular figures flapped their wings and flew away, leaving the fire to burn.

"Take me to him!" the killer pleaded through tears. "Carry me over there, I must see him!"

"Is it safe?"

The winds died down, and from the distance they could hear the cracking of the fire. They even felt the heat.

The killer wiped his eyes, smearing his cheeks with blood. "Yes. They are gone. The deed is done. They will not return."

Jonas bent down to pick him up. He tried as gently and gingerly as he could, easing his arms under the man. His killer winced in pain, but continued to stare at the fire. "Please hurry!" he said.

Carrying the man to the fire proved to be easy, and he quickly set the man down and helped him steady his feet. The man screamed in pain again, as the protruding bone moved. Shortly Jonas was standing right in front of the stone slab, staring at a body burning down to ash, in front of an altar of flames. His killer stood as close to the fire as he could, and extended his hand towards the fire.

He covered his eyes and sobbed.

"Who…is this…this is someone very dear to you is it not?"

He shook his head in affirmation, wiping his eyes once again. It remained silent save the crackle of the fire.

"I knew this would happen," the killer started. "I knew this would happen but I did nothing to stop it. I tried. I tried and now look at me. A pitiful excuse of my former self. What I once was…what I once did…with him!" He looked down at the body and shook his head. "I didn't choose him, he chose *me*," he continued.

"Who was he?" Jonas asked.

"He was a brilliant and loving immortal. He was a sinful demon. And here he met his destiny. A destiny that was determined when he came for me. A destiny that was determined when he killed me. He killed me, but he came back for me. He knew what he was doing when he came for me. He knew, that I can tell you for certain."

"And what happened of those monsters that were here?"

"Those were no monsters," the killer said. "They were demons settling a debt. He was destined to pay for what he did, for coming for me, and that is how he met this fate. And now, trying to save him, I have mine. For I used to be what he was."

"What he was?"

"Yes. I sit here before you in pain and destined to die. I do not know how much time I will have left or if I will be able to be saved. The clock has begun, and if I don't find a way to raise him up I am destined to die and spend and eternity in Hell. And I will not be able to be resurrected again."

Jonas looked at the body in the fire before them. It was breaking down quickly into ash, the skin was dripping off the bones and the bones were splitting and cracking in the heat. He stared, mesmerized.

"It won't be much longer now. Once the fire dies down and he is only ash, I must take him and bury him. But I need him to be resurrected. I need him to survive."

"Who is he?"

"He is my creation, Jonas. I killed him like I killed you, but I did so very many years ago. And he came here, and was betrayed by his only creation…"

Jonas held his killer more tightly, and looked down at his broken leg. "Maybe we should get that taken care of," he said. But the killer paid him no mind.

"His only creation put him right into the hands of Asmodai. You, on the other hand, left your protégé alone and scared in the mist, outside the offices looking for you, where this beloved immortal used to go so many times. You left him there because I entered your thoughts."

"Uriel?"

"Yes, Jean Carlo. The one you stole from me. But how do you think you remembered the hospital? You remembered because I called you here. I needed you here to help me. I know because I killed you."

"How did I steal Jean Carlo from you?"

"I took his life, Jonas. He ran to you. I let him run. But now he is scared and alone and waiting for you, but you are here with me. I know where your loyalty lies."

"So you are saying that this is Jean Carlo!?" Jonas stared down at the body with wide eyes.

The killer shook his head. "No," he said. "This is the one who resurrected me, and now has paid the price for it. All because of his the one he created. I tried to protect him. I tried my hardest, but Asmodai won. He always does."

"And who are you?"

"I used to be just like him, but now I am going to die," he said. He paused smoothed his dark hair, and stared down at the body before them, a tear streaking through the blood on his cheek. He looked over at Jonas, and stared him in the eye. The flicker of the flame caught his face, and he seemed to glow.

"My name is Darius," he said, as tears weaved their way down blood stained cheeks.

CHAPTER FIFTY-THREE

Jonas couldn't hear Jean Carlo calling his name out, over and over again through the green swirling mist that overtook the offices of The Astral. Neither did Sheldon, but Sheldon was close by and would be making his appearance soon. No one heard Jean Carlo stumbling over the coffee table in the waiting room, or crashing into the glass door and spilling out onto Ponce De Leon in a shower of broken glass.

But what Jean Carlo could hear – above all else – were the sounds of feet. Many feet that were taking steps in unison, like the sound of a military regimen.

He waved his arms in front of him in a feeble attempt to part the mist and see the source of the commotion, but all he did was move the mist around and it seemed like it got denser and angrier.

"Run!" a mystery voice screamed, right in front of him, startling him until he fell backwards through the broken window. A bloodied female face matted with stringy yellowed hair, appeared from the mist and warned him with wide eyes. "Get out as fast as you can! It's them! They are here!"

She screamed, and a phantom arm grabbed her face around from the side, and pulled her back into the mist.

The army sounded closer now. So close, in fact, it sounded like the soldiers were marching right on the street in front of where Jean Carlo lay.

He struggled back onto his feet, gingerly brushing the glass from his pants, and stopped when he heard a voice.

"Good Evening, Mr. Castillo."

Standing in front of him was a short, fat paunchy old man. He couldn't quite remember where he had seen this man before, but he knew he looked familiar. Where did he know this man from?

"What have you done here to my door?" he asked, stepping forward as the glass crisped and crunched under the man's heavy shoes. The man stopped and scanned the doorway, observing shards of glass still hanging from the edges of the frame. He glared down at Jean Carlo sternly. "Sir, let me pass!"

Jean Carlo stood aside, and the man squeezed by, seemingly un-phased by the blinding vapor. The old man crept further into the offices, and snapped around to see where Jean Carlo was standing. "And another thing," the man said. "*Don't snoop in my fucking office again!*" The man screamed at the top of his lungs, and his head detached from his body as his did so, fireballs shot from his eye sockets as the skin and fat bubbled up in the searing heat; it slowly dripped and melted off his body into a steaming lake of melted skin on the floor. His skeleton tried to open the office door.

Jean Carlo turned to run from the boiling mess and was stopped by a hulking beast standing in the doorway. The beast reached behind his back and drew a giant steel weapon which had a long barrel like a cannon and fired it at the screaming skeleton.

A giant fireball exploded in the office and engulfed it in flames as the mist turned black. The skeleton screamed in agony, pleading over and over again to quell the fire.

The beast looked down at Jean Carlo.

Jean Carlo shuddered at the thought of what was standing above him. There were angry lines reaching under a black steel faceplate which covered the eyes. Those angry eyes. But what Jean Carlo shuddered at was the size of the beast. He looked like a combination of a powerful beast and machine.

"Come with me," the deep voice commanded. The beast extended his massive arm. "We have been waiting for you."

Jean Carlo followed the beast, as he didn't seem to have much of a choice, sticking close to him. The mist seemed to be laughing at him; taunting the poor little man.

The beast dragged him through the streets ignoring the mist. He could tell they were walking through the city streets but he still saw nothing. What he heard was vastly different.

He heard voices, but most were muffled and distorted and he could not decipher what they were saying. Most of the voices he could tell sounded rushed and urgent, and every so often he could make out a word or two – *"stop! Damn fools gonna - !"*

"Who was that man back there?" Jean Carlo finally called out up to the beast over the chaos. They continued walking and the beast at first did not answer. Then suddenly they stopped. The beast turned to face him.

"That was a lost soul. He wandered too far. He was caught by the serpent."

The beast turned around and started pressing forward again. Jean Carlo tugged at his arm, attempting to stop his heft.

"Wait!" Jean Carlo insisted. "What am I doing here? Where is Jonas?"

The beast stopped again, and once again turned to face him. "Jonas is waiting for you Uriel. You seemed to have gotten lost back there, and he sent me for you."

The beast turned around and again they pressed on.

And then there were screams. What sounded like thousands upon thousands of screams of agony, and the sound of burning fire and many explosions.

And he could feel the heat.

"We are here," the beast said, as the mist cleared. "Welcome to Tartarus."

Jean Carlo stared at the scene before him. What had felt to him like a short walk down a city street revealed a fiery destination.

The sky burned red with flames, hovering over black clouds; and below, a sea of screaming souls. They seemed human – they even looked human; but they each had several things in common. Their terror was all equal; they fought the same fight in the same lake of fire; they each screamed in search of something less than terror; but their wide eyes, plastered open against their pale skin, never able to close, confirmed one thing. That there was nothing but terror where they were…and that their search proved fruitless. Each screamed and writhed over the other, the limbs spilling on to one another in a mass of a tangling mess.

In the center rose a giant, impending dark black figure; it stood over the fiery lake as if cloaked in black; it reached out over the screaming souls with spiny arms over the sea like a governor.

Jean Carlo returned his attention to the beast.

"Come with me," it said as it grabbed his arm and yanked him behind a giant rock. They stood out of view for the moment.

Scanning the area, Jonas noticed a steel door at the end of the rock structure.

"They will come from that door when the battle begins," the beast explained.

Jean Carlo stopped and looked at the beast. "Who are you?" he asked. "What battle?"

"The battle that *you* ordered. It's about to begin. That is why you are here. Nesmaron must be stopped. *Per your orders.*"

Jean Carlo tried as hard as he could to remember that meeting. He remembered walking through the door – he remembered the Metatron lining the table, he remembered the sea of papers and Jonas explaining to him…

"Yes! I remember!"

The steel door crashed open, so hard that rocks broke off and crumbled from the wall of stone that they were hovering behind and fell to the ground.

Giant armored beasts came through the door, heading out towards the clearing in front of the sea of souls. Each soldier lined up in front of a giant cliff that dropped down to the fiery sea, and as Jean Carlo turned his head to see the cavalry prepare themselves, he saw the beast who led him here leave his side and join the others.

Feeling a tap on his left shoulder, he snapped his head around to see who was requiring his attention and saw Jonas standing with another man, about the same height but far younger.

"Hello Uriel," Jonas said, smiling warmly. He hooked his silver hair to the side of one ear.

"Where did you go?!" Jean Carlo rushed towards Jonas. "You left me and a crazed lunatic exploded in front of me!"

"I know, Uriel," Jonas said. "There are still going to be many things here which we do not understand. But I assure you, they all happen for a reason." He turned to introduce the man that he was standing with. "This is Darius. This is the man who took my life."

Jean Carlo stopped for a minute. He stared at the man before him and saw the face of his killer. He turned to run, but Jonas stopped him.

"Wait! Jean Carlo stop!" Jonas grabbed Jean Carlo by the arm, keeping him there.

And then Darius stepped forward, caressing the cheek of his former victim. "Don't worry, my precious," he said. "My motives right now are not to reclaim you. I called Jonas because I needed to reveal to him what would happen, what would happen to the one I created."

Jean Carlo stopped struggling from Jonas' grip.

But Jean Carlo glared at Darius. His eyes pierced outwards to Darius; and his face was outlined with contempt; every line and crevice stood standing and forthright as he clenched his fists.

Darius gently placed his hand on Jean Carlo's shoulder. "Please. Stop. I know what I have done. But I did that as a monster that I formerly was, not as the man that is standing before you." Darius squeezed his shoulder. He smiled wanly while placing his other palm on Jean Carlo's cheek. "I wanted so much for you to be my creation, a son, a warrior that I could mold," he continued. "But things went differently. Everything has changed now."

All three men looked towards the Metatron patiently standing guard and awaiting battle.

"It's going to happen soon Darius," Jonas said.

"I know. But I must finish." He turned back to Jean Carlo. "I killed Jonas, at first, for the sport of the kill. He has *every right* to be angry with me because I did not kill him for a reason. But here he is standing before you next to me because I revealed a reason to him. I stand before you not as the monster who took your life or raised you out of your casket, but as a man. I am here because I need your help."

"But the Metatron are not on your side Darius," Jean Carlo pointed out. "They are here to combat this evil. They are here to set things right again."

"I know," Darius said. "But you must understand. I am no longer a part of that realm. It was taken from me."

"Taken from you?" Jean Carlo asked.

"Yes," Darius replied. "I am no longer immortal."

Jonas nodded in agreement. "And we need to save Antoine," he added. "Because he is…"

"- he is the only hope that I have for survival," Darius interrupted. "Only he can make me immortal again. And only he knows where the Chalice is."

"What chalice?" Jean Carlo asked.

"The Cup of Christ," Jonas offered. "It offers renewed immortality."

"So you are saying with that cup you will become immortal again?" Jean Carlo asked.

"Not exactly," Darius said. "Only Antoine knows where the cup is located. We found it together several hundreds of years ago in Egypt. But since then, and since Antoine and I had become estranged due to our differences in running Sacrafice, the cup has been lost. And, to make matters worse, there is another. Claret."

"Claret?" both men asked Darius in unison.

"Yes, Claret. Please don't say that name loudly here. She might hear you. She has been showing her face lately. And she is one of the reasons that Antoine will be destroyed here today. Antoine took the cup and the cup was a gift from Claret to King Tutankhamen. She lived during the times of Jesus Christ. Some say that she took the cup directly after the Last Supper had ended."

"And she gave it to Tut? Didn't he live thousands of years before Christ walked the earth?" Jonas asked.

"One of the great unsolved mysteries," Darius offered, shrugging his shoulders. "Some say she can time travel, others say she is the Devil. All I know at this point is that I need that cup, I need to save Antoine – or I will die a rapid death."

"And it won't be easy," Jonas said. "Nesmaron is the most powerful of demons. Even Asmodai kneels before him. They have been gathering. The Metatron there are waiting, protecting reality, but they won't wait for long. Soon they will attack. You will see. They are just waiting for your command."

CHAPTER FIFTY-FOUR

Before Jean Carlo had been told that he was the leader of a spiritual rebellion against evil, there was the mist. And before that, there was the bubble.

It was Antoine that had remembered.

Antoine remembered taking the money into the door behind the stage in the club, and then that was it. But he felt something had brought him there.

Coming to, Antoine sat chained to the wall in a misty, greenish dungeon. The walls above him towered over his head, so high that when Antoine looked up he could not see the ceiling – just darkness, as if it were a night sky devoid of stars. The walls were made of stone blocks covered with a layer of greenish brown moss; it was scattered about the walls like small continents in a sea of stone.

Looking back to his torso, Antoine brought his damaged right hand and delicately touched the gash across his abdomen, wincing as he did so. He brought his hand back to his side abruptly when he heard a heavy, grating door open in the darkness before him. The chains clanked as he did so. The door sounded far away, yet he could feel the grating in the stony, earthen floor.

Antoine knew that his time had come. It was the moment when he would pay for his mortal sins, and it was the time that he would pay for his immortal sins as well. No matter what he did in his immortal life to correct and undo what he had done, it was too late. Payment must be rendered, and it must be rendered now. The determined deep footsteps that grew closer told him that.

When Antoine was put in the dungeon, he was in a state of unconsciousness, but was still semi-aware of what was around him. He had heard Nesmaron. That he knew for sure. He felt the clasps forced over his wrists, that he knew for sure too. And he heard Gizelle. Both mortals that he had saved, turned on him in immortality.

As Antoine peered into the darkness before him, he saw a long hallway, and even further, what seemed like a faint orange glow. That was certain death, but he was not bothered. He knew this moment would come, and knew that it must play out as it should.

As the glow came closer and brighter, he could see the end of the hallway, and a wall on the far end, which revealed another hallway branching off to the left. On that far wall the orange glow was the brightest. It was not bright and steady, it was moving and fluid like the liquid like glow cast from a flame. To the right the orange glow flowed, like a faint, distant sun, when he saw the long, spiny fingers silhouetted in the luminosity…Nesmaron.

Hello, father.

I am coming for you. I hope you enjoy your stay.

Certainly you didn't think that I would stay playing second fiddle to you forever, did you? I found my own portal; I found my own way.

And now you are here, sitting in shackles. Waiting for your destiny.

It could only be Nesmaron. Only Nesmaron had a hand like that. With six spiny fingers jutting from a muscular forearm, Nesmaron was the epitome of the demoniac hierarchy.

And he was spawned from Antoine.

Closing his eyes a sighing a deep breath into the dark, damp air of the dungeon, Antoine lay back on the wall, exhausted, preparing to accept his fate. He knew that Nesmaron has come to claim his throne of the earthly realm, and now it was time to pass the torch.

Which is what Darius had done many years before.

~~*

The cave of crystals.

Antoine remembered it very clearly. A secret room, offering a sanctuary and safety from Asmodai, he remembered and drifted off…

~~*

…Peering intently at the body before him, Anthony recognized the facial features starting to take form. Gradually, the body was starting to transform into Darius. Right now, it looked like a cross between and old, rotted corpse and Darius – but the face was gradually starting to show the facial structure and look that Darius had possessed.

Antoine crawled up to the pile of rocks where the hole had once been, pressing against them, checking for their solidity.

"This will only keep Asmodai from us for so long," Antoine said, as the room shook once again with the waves of the earthquakes and falling boulders. The entire floor moved as if on a seismic roll. "He is going to get in here…unless…"

Antoine's attention was diverted from the rocking of the earth. Anthony was extending his arms out over the corpse. The corpse was glowing white, taking in Anthony's luminescent aura.

"Come over here Antoine," Anthony commanded while closing his eyes. "We have to leave. This cave is going to collapse around us!"

Antoine crawled over piles of rock, ducking below jutting stalagmites, down the pile to where Anthony was. Anthony was hovering over the corpse now, levitating on what seemed to be a translucent could of gas.

But Antoine knew that it wasn't a gas. The cave was almost airtight, and despite the earth's movements, the cloud was expanding. Whatever it was, and whatever it seemed to be, it was aural and it was other dimensional. Whatever Asmodai did to Anthony certainly bestowed many powers upon him.

What many powers? Antoine thought, descending the rock pile. Looking at Anthony's levitation – while not that impressive of a power for netherworldy beings, was certainly remarkable for a mortal who was so recently transformed. It was apparent, if not from anything else that Anthony had exhibited but for the glaringly apparent aura – and the levitation – that Anthony somehow advanced to a much higher level than Antoine in the moments that he had disappeared from the graveyard.

Stepping into the brightness Antoine immediately felt swallowed up by a force with a great magnitude like he was being gravitationally pulled into the center of the force. When it overtook his face, his vision was blocked by a brightness so intense that all he could see was whiteness, all he could see was purity.

The sounds of the earth and the sounds of Asmodai were swallowed up and faded away; faded to a beautiful, clean, crisp silence like that of death – but the brightness indicated life and prosperity – washing away the sadness and despair of the cave of crystals.

Anthony did not speak, but Antoine did not have to ask anything.

He felt a wind against his face, a wind as though they were moving. But it still felt like he was kneeling on the cave floor.

But they were safe.

Antoine felt the security envelop him; Asmodai could not go here – the sanctity of the situation greatly overpowered the forces of the darkness.

Antoine began to get a sense that they had traveled quite far. Holding on to Anthony's torso – of which his grip had never loosed since he ventured into the brightness – he opened his eyes and looked into the wild and dazzling beyond.

~~*

"What?!" Antoine exclaimed. He was jolted out of a state of dreamlike existence by a pair of strong hands on either shoulder. Nesmaron was standing above him in all of his glory, accentuated by his tall, slender body, pointed head and flowing robe.

"It is you I have come for," Nesmaron said flatly. He leaned in close to Antoine's face, so close that his nose was almost touching Antoine's and their eyes were at the same level. "I have come for you, Antoine. You have failed me. Uriel is rebelling and forming a legion with an army of angels!"

The hatred in Nesmaron's eyes was apparent. He was furious that his plan was not going like clockwork. He backed away from Antoine's face, and stood up, folding his arms over his chest. He started swinging the stole from around his neck, round and round.

"What a waste," he said, shaking his head and looking down at Antoine. "You could have joined me. We could have controlled every dimension together. Damn Hell! *Damn God*!" He raised his arms up to the darkness, and a crash of thunder sounded as a flash of lightning illuminated the room for a split second. In that split second, Antoine thought he saw Roberto, if just for a split second.

Antoine looked up after the room went dark again. "I made you…" He clenched his teeth and growled.

Nesmaron threw his head back and laughed. "You! Made me? What do you mean? When you were fucking me senseless in my father's house? No wait! It had to have been when you told me that you loved me! Certainly it was *then*!"

Antoine glared at Nesmaron.

"I am Nesmaron, and I was made this way by the demons you see before you."

Antoine looked up in each direction at the two demons that were still holding his shoulders, and they pulled him from the floor gruffly, like the prisoner he was.

"You will be damned to hell," Antoine said, staring up at Nesmaron, directly in the face.

"I already am there! What do you think this place is?" Nesmaron looked at the two soldier demons. "Take him away," he commanded.

~~*

The beasts hauled Antoine to his death.

"Get on your knees!" Nesmaron shouted, standing over Antoine on a stone altar.

Antoine obeyed, the shackles on his neck and arms clinking as he did so.

Nesmaron first looked down before him, seeing Antoine looking up to his eyes like a child kneeling before his father asking for forgiveness. But Nesmaron was not forgiving. It did not matter that Antoine created him.

Nesmaron was standing in front of the stone altar, which was atop a terrace, also made of stone, which sprouted four wide steps leading down to a platform where Antoine was kneeling. Behind Antoine was a legion of Demons, and they were standing in a sea of writhing lost souls.

The sky turned blood red as the thunder sounded in the distance, getting closer with each passing moment. Nesmaron turned to the legion behind Antoine.

"It is time my brethren," he began, bringing his arms to his chest, folding his hands in front of his stomach. "All of you know Antoine." He gestured down to Antoine as he spoke his name.

"And all of you know that Antoine committed the ultimate betrayal to Tartarus," he continued. "And now he will be laid to rest! Asmodai will come! Claret will come! They both will come and take you straight to hell!" He pointed with a flaming sword to Antoine, the pointed tip of the sword just inches away from his face.

The sky opened up in fire, flames shooting from out of the dark red clouds, swirling with fury above the stone altar. The two demons closest to Antoine stepped forward and grabbed each of his arms, and two more came around to the front of Antoine and began to shred his clothes with their swords, taking the tips and catching the bottom of his shirt and ripping it to pieces, until just small bits of fabric clung to his battered and bloodied frame. They held him standing, nude, in front of Nesmaron.

"Lay him down on the altar," he commanded. "It is time."

The demons were not gentle as they drug Antoine to the altar, his face now hanging in defeat, looking towards the stone floor, his long locks shielding his face from torment. And the winds began to increase in velocity with great intensity the closer he came to the altar.

Getting ever closer to the stone slab, Antoine closed his eyes. How had he gotten here?

The first shovelful of dirt.

The coffin.

In his mind, he saw it again, playing over and over. He saw himself, standing over a rotted, muddy coffin, tearing the lid away piece at a time. He could hear the splintering of the wood, feel the dustiness and dried wood fall apart in his hands.

And Darius.

Darius had spoken to him that night. Before the demons came, before Asmodai called the winds…Antoine had spoken. But what replayed in Antoine's mind, was a night many, many years ago…

…"You enjoy your bloodlust!" Antoine had screamed at Darius, so many nights ago. The two were standing in the foyer of the chateau, about to head out for the evening. Antoine stammered. "I can't – I can't…" he had continued but didn't finish his sentence. He collapsed for a moment at the foot of the stairs, exhausted and spent. Darius had approached him and placed his hand on Antoine's shoulder.

"You are still clinging to your mortal life, Antoine," Darius explained. "This is where your grief comes from." Darius took his hand and ran the back lovingly on Antoine's cheek. "You need to find some definition as an immortal – a purpose. I took you into this world for a reason. And that reason was not to cause you grief."

"And for what reason was that then?" Antoine looked up at him desperately, his cheeks stained with fresh tears.

"You were a lover in life. There is no reason why you can't be in your immortal life. And that is why I must do this."

Darius reached to his pocket, and removed a shiny dagger. It gleamed in the warm glow of the light. Antoine stared at the dagger.

"Do it Antoine. You need to find your way. I cannot force you to choose mine. Let go of your mortal life, and find definition for yourself. *Shed your skin.*"

Antoine took the dagger from Darius' hand gingerly, never taking his eyes from the piece. He knew what Darius meant. But could he do it?

Darius stood up slowly and removed his shirt. "Do it," he said. He stood in the center of the foyer, under a giant hanging candelabra, the faint glow of the light making his skin seem warm and like that of a mortal. "Just remember to bury me quickly. *Do it now!*"

Antoine lurched forward and plunged the dagger into his neck; instantly blood spurted out of the wound like a geyser – spraying into his face.

Darius clutched his neck and fell to the floor. Antoine must have hit a central artery, as the blood was spurting out at high speed, causing Darius to fade quickly.

"Just…" Darius coughed, "- take – *cough!* Take my heart – *cough!* – and burn me!"

~~*

Antoine opened his eyes and saw the altar before him.

Just a simple stone slab.

The winds…he thought. *The winds have started.* Antoine raised his head to the sky, and through strands of hair covering his face, he saw the flames in the sky.

Asmodai is coming…

He hung his head back down, but it got whipped back as the demons lifted him swiftly off the ground and laid him on the stone slab.

He closed his eyes slowly.

The legion of demons that stood at the base of the steps parted, revealing a long wide open path, at the end of which stood Asmodai. He stood there staring with his canine snout, his muscular frame, and his long tail curled around in front of him. Behind him, he extended a pair of pointed wings; the wings started to flap and he carried himself up above the army and promptly over to the altar.

He looked down towards the altar, where Antoine lay with his eyes closed, awaiting his fate. Asmodai drew his sword, and held it at his side.

"Nesmaron," he said quietly. "Have you brought this sinner to me?"

"Yes," he replied.

CHAPTER FIFTY-FIVE

Nesmaron had landed earlier on the Sea of Souls with Gizelle in his hands. She was a far cry from her former self; now she was a vixen, formerly fucked by a studly monster demon; now she possessed all that she physically desired for herself. Her long brunette hair framed her supple face and pouty, red lips; the tips and curls of her hair played with her gigantic breasts. All of her was sexy; all of her spelled desire.

Nesmaron pointed to the top of a cliff that led towards the city. "Go," he said. "Go out into the city and do what I have instructed."

She obediently left, climbing the edge of the cliff. In the meantime, Antoine had been carried closer to the Altar.

Gizelle stopped at a large stone wall and backed towards it, ducking around the side and stopped suddenly.

A grey hair older man stopped suddenly in her path, his eyes widened and he froze. "Shit!" he said.

She bore her teeth, elongated out of her dark snout, reaching through acidic saliva toward the man's throat, ripping his skin and showering the ground with deep red blood.

The man fell to the ground, shaking and dying.

The other two men ran to his aid.

"Jonas!" Jean Carlo screamed, falling to his knees and grabbing Jonas' shaking body in a desperate attempt to pull him away from the demon girl and save him.

But it was too late.

She tore through Jonas' neck once again, ripping off his head and throwing it into the pit of flames.

"Who the *fuck* are you two?!" She stood tall and stamped her feet on the ground. Jean Carlo almost lost his footing. He tried to speak, but Darius stopped him. He reached for Jean Carlo's shoulder, and pulled him back. Both of their eyes were trained on Gizelle, watching as she doubled in size.

She sprouted black wings, her long black spiny legs lunged forward.

Jean Carlo snapped his head in the direction from whence they came. "*Metatron*! I am Uriel and I command you!"

Darius looked at Jean Carlo quizzically.

The army of Metatron lurched forward in unison, all drawing swords that burst into flames. They surrounded Jean Carlo and Darius.

Gizelle hissed and spit, snapping her wings but advancing no further.

Darius and Jean Carlo crouched backwards towards the protection of the squadron.

Several of the Metatron drew flaming swords towards Gizelle, as she snapped her claws, closer and closer to Jean Carlo.

~~*

The rocks that surrounded the Sea of Souls shook away from their foundation and crumbled away as a giant earthquake shook everyone off of their feet. The winds grew, pinning everyone to the ground.

Darius knew who was coming.

Looking up, both men saw the super demon riding down on a blanket of black clouds in a blood red sky. But the demon did not seek them, nor the Metatron or Gizelle. He was coasting slowly towards where Nesmaron was posted.

"No!" Darius called out, trying to get to his feet. He crawled towards the edge of the Sea. "I am coming Antoine! This time, I will! I will not let you burn!"

Nesmaron snapped his attention towards the other side of the sea, watching Darius as he fell into the lake. Countless bodies grabbed him as he fell into the sea, smothering him, carrying him below, pinning him down.

Darius felt the stirring in the pit of his stomach, the power of the stench overwhelming. He thought he was going to vomit. He tried to climb to the surface, but so many rotting limbs were holding him down.

Nesmaron threw his head back and laughed. "You silly, stupid mortal! You can't stop what is already written to be done!"

But Darius fought for a gap and managed to surface.

"Come forth!" Nesmaron offered. Darius was able to navigate through the bodies. He kept his eye on the altar across the sea, his focus never broken.

But he was too late.

With a chorus of thunder and a shower of lightning, Asmodai's sword called the flames down to the altar and Antoine burst into flames.

"No!" Darius screamed, reached the edge of the lake. But several guarding demons prevented him from getting any closer.

I am sorry love. I have failed you. I am sorry that it had to end this way. I am sorry that you had to see this, Darius.

"You have not failed me," Darius said, watching the flames intensify as the storm grew. "I have failed you."

Darius collapsed at the edge of the lake.

~~*

The storm intensified as increasingly violent bursts of lightning struck, closer and closer to Jean Carlo and the Metatron.

"They are attacking us!" Jean Carlo called.

One of the Metatron caught a bolt of lightning, and as his sword ignited he drew it towards Gizelle, still frozen.

Gizelle called out across the sea. "Look what you have done to me!" she hissed. "I have served you!"

The Metatron lunged his sword into Gizelle and the flames engulfed her.

Asmodai called across the sea, watching Gizelle flail like a giant impaled insect. "I never promised sparing you!"

And he rode the clouds away.

~~*

"Darius!" Jean Carlo called out across the sea. "Darius! Come back! There is no saving him now!"

But Darius held steady.

The guard demons retreated once Asmodai left, and Darius crawled towards the altar, collapsing in a fetal position on the ground, looking up at the plume of smoke rising from where Antoine had lay. He managed to find the strength to stand, and hoisted himself up, and looked down at Antoine's remains. He ignored the ashes and focused on the beating heart.

There you are, my friend.

"Darius!" Jean Carlo called again, still from a distance, but this time much closer. Darius turned around and saw that Jean Carlo was navigating the Sea of Souls, dodging Nesmaron's fireballs, gradually getting closer.

But Jean Carlo succeeded.

"He is gone," he said quietly to Darius, once the two men were standing together next to the altar.

"Give me the urn," Darius said. "It's time to go. We don't have much time."

Darius looked behind them, hearing the methodic deep rumblings of monstrous footsteps.

Nesmaron was coming.

Jean Carlo reached into his backpack and produced the small stone urn that they had brought with them for the worst-case scenario.

"Hurry!" Darius said, scooping up the ashes and throwing them into the urn hurriedly. Jean Carlo stepped in to help.

"Let's go!" Darius said, placing the urn in Jean Carlos' backpack.

They ran down the edge of the sand to the lake and stopped dead in their tracks.

Nesmaron was patiently waiting for them in the center of the sea, rising from the multitude of writhing bodies like a giant, commanding black serpentine insect.

The demon did not wait, but immediately called on the fires again, sending fireballs towards the two men.

"Follow me!" Darius said, diving into the bodies. Jean Carlo followed quickly behind him, holding his backpack and precious cargo tightly.

The two men surfaced. Nesmaron was still a ways away, still in the center of the sea. He lunged forward.

"Take this!" Jean Carlo said, giving Darius the backpack. "And move away from me! I have never done this before!"

Jean Carlo looked towards the sky. *Tell me how, Jonas. Tell me how!*

Jean Carlo closed his eyes, looking down, and let himself sink deep into the bodies. Darius looked on, and then snapped his head in the other direction, and froze, watching Nesmaron get closer and closer.

~~*

The sea turned a brilliant bright white, as if glowing. The brilliance of the light illuminated the entire area, and was so mystical that Nesmaron stopped his advances, and Darius simply stared in disbelief.

And then what rose from the waters was so beautiful, majestic and glowing that Nesmaron was dumbfounded as well.

"Go now Darius," the presence commanded. "I am holding him. It is safe to cross the sea."

Darius proceeded, slowly and carefully walking past the retreating bodies, never taking his eyes off of Nesmaron until he was safely on the other side of the sea. Darius looked out into the sea, shielding his eyes from the glowing luminescence, calling out to Jean Carlo.

"I cannot hold him much longer, Darius," it said. "Go to a safe distance and I will join you shortly."

Darius obeyed and waited at the entrance. He sat down for a minute, caught his breath, and waited for Jean Carlo.

But almost no time had passed when Jean Carlo came running around the corner, furiously screaming and panting. "Let's go! Now!"

Darius got up and the two ran out to the streets as the ground opened up and fireballs charged past time, igniting everything.

They approached the wall of the green mist, and Darius hesitated for a moment.

"Go!" Jean Carlo said, pulling Darius' arm and dragging him into the mist.

Getting closer to the offices of The Astral, Darius looked back towards the Sea of Souls.

The mist had devoured everything. Buildings, rocks, the altar, the sea itself.

They ran through the offices, just as the mist was demolishing everything. They flew down the stairs below, slamming the door shut behind them.

CHAPTER FIFTY-SIX

Manhattan at night –

The hustle-bustle of the city never stopped and never quieted. The crowds never thinned. Despite the cold and bundled up citizens huddling at each corner, chit chatting with each other which caused their hot breath to puff like smoke, Darius was dressed in a much lighter fare.

He walked slowly and surely towards his hotel, ignoring the crowds around him. In his arm, he carried an urn. He passed a red haired woman, dressed in a long black leather coat, smoking at a small café table…sitting outdoors despite the cold. When he passed, her eyes followed his moves, but she quickly returned to her steaming cup of coffee.

~~*

Later that night, Darius fell asleep next to Antoine's urn. The urn had lay with Darius in his coffin for three days and three nights; and for those days Darius did not move or open the casket lid, nor did he open his eyes, think, or speak.

For those days, Darius was just as dead as Antoine. But the two were together again, side by side, together as one inside the casket.

"No matter what, Antoine, I will keep you near me," Darius had pledged, upon scraping up his ashes off the altar and carrying them back into the present dimension. "I will bury you as you have buried me, and I will let you rest and I will raise you one day. That I promise to you."

Upon waking after the third day, Darius felt the steel, hard cold of the urn in the pit of his right arm. There he was.

Antoine.

Safe and sound as he should be.

What Darius didn't know is how long Antoine would be dead. To raise him now, of course, would be foolish and impossible. Asmodai has too much power in the fourth dimension, Miami is in chaos, and Nesmaron has become the world leader – guiding all of humanity and immortals alike into darkness.

"One day, my friend, one day," Darius spoke, while rising out of the coffin and gingerly placing the ashes on the mantle in his chambers. One day Antoine would rise again.

Darius started to dress.

He dressed in a two-piece dark suit that was customary to the early twenty first century, white shirt and black tie. He tucked his long brown hair behind his ears, tying it back into a ponytail and slipping it under his jacket.

It was quarter past ten p.m. when he looked at his wristwatch.

He was going to catch a red eye flight to Frankfurt, head back to the Chateau, and stay there for a while. But first he was going to bury Antoine.

Surrendering to renewed mortality, but not giving up the ways he has been accustomed, he glanced over at the casket. *I don't need that anymore,* he thought. *I should be looking at beds.*

And then he opened his brown leather travel bag, waiting for him on top of the dresser. Inside, he drew out the ticket, one way from New York to Frankfurt.

And now I am cursed to fly the old-fashioned way…in a plane.

Mortal.

A two-syllable word that rang in his ears, over and over. No longer immortal. Life would be very different from this point forward.

And he could die.

Permanently.

And soon.

Darius came to that realization, knowing that he would have to lie low for a while, until he could find a way to become immortal once again.

In the world since the Metatron, much has changed. Asmodai sits at his throne in Hell, and Nesmaron is the ruler of Evil on Earth. Was there a place for Darius in that equation?

Gathering his bags, he closed his eyes and pictured Antoine's estate.

It was not the palatial surroundings that it was when he first arrived to Miami. All of the furniture has been covered in dust cloths, the windows shuttered and doors closed and locked. The house looked like it would be empty for many years.

But the deed would still read Antoine Nagevesh, and would remain that way, for as long as Darius could see to it.

Walking out the door, Darius made a mental commitment to locate the Chalice and retransform. He had to. He had no choice. If not, it would be certain death. He wanted to raise Antoine himself, but could not. Nesmaron – no Roberto – must do it. And how would that happen?

But perhaps…perhaps…*perhaps I could do it. Perhaps I could raise you, old friend. I remember that day, the day I first saw you, under the full moon in Badulla, as if it were yesterday. And I remember that day, when I woke in a new body, when you raised me. And I remember the deal you made with Asmodai, and I know that it is why you are closed up inside this urn today.*

I am sorry, Antoine. I am sorry.

As the hotel door shut behind him, he shuddered and thought of Antoine's parlor one last time, picturing it empty with the dust cloths covering everything in a field of white.

But it did not matter.

~~*

Darius decided to wait until evening to bury Antoine, although as newly mortal again he was starting to become more accustomed to being about during the day, seeing sunrises, sunsets, lying out by the water in the afternoon sun, and relishing all the mortal pleasures that immortals can no longer partake of.

Although he could have easily buried him in the afternoon, the fading sunlight in the desolate location kept somewhat of a veil of secrecy.

He laid down the same brown tarp bag on the grass that Antoine had used before to unearth him before. He felt the knees of his pants grow cool and then wet, as the grass was already saturated with nighttime dewdrops.

This was the spot.

Exactly where Darius had been buried.

He reverently stood the urn next to the tarp of clanking tools, dug for the shovel, lined it up perpendicular to the ground, and forced it into the earth.

Antoine's grave.

Antoine, the fierce leader and healer, the corrupt and the just, the merciless and the forgiving. Now, before him, sealed in an urn.

As Darius continued to dig, the warmth of his tears started to wet his cheeks. No more arguments, no more tears, no more killing together. No more plays in Paris.

I am burying you, my son. I am digging your grave for you. I am putting closure to all of this madness. I am calling on Asmodai to see that you are paying your dues for bringing me back into this world, the sacrifice that you made, the determination that you showed – in standing up to the demons.

You tried.

And now, it is my turn. It is my turn to dig, it is my turn to put the six nails in your coffin, it is my turn to let you rest while I fight – while I find a way, that I promise to you, I will find a way to make myself immortal again, to regain the power, and to raise you from these confines. The madness is over. Or is it? The madness, really, is just beginning.

Evil reigns.

The shovel clanked, hitting the grave liner in the dirt, sending bright sparks into the air as it touched the cement and iron.

The coffin would be just underneath.

The wind picked up slightly, causing Darius to raise his head, peering out of the grave, raising himself up from the edges of the grave liner that he was standing on.

He looked over to the woods, the urn in the foreground.

The leaves to the trees were rustling in the light winds.

Somewhere in the distance, a tree branch snapped.

Darius did not care what happened. At this point, all he wanted to do was bury Antoine, and go home and go to bed. If demons came and made an appearance, so be it. He was at the point of giving up.

Antoine has paid his dues.

He has fulfilled his end of the bargain and will wait in this casket until Roberto chooses to raise him.

If that might ever happen.

The wind picked up again slightly, causing a rustling in the woods, but Darius continued preparing the grave. He used the shovel to scrape the last of the caked dirt off of the liner, which caused a sharp grating sound, reverberating against the silent, still night air. He removed the lid to the liner, and hoisted it up topside with a thud.

The coffin.

There it was, sitting down below, in the darkness. One could barely make out the brass handles on one side, the lid was in pieces from when Antoine had torn it apart.

But it would do.

He would just fit the pieces of the lid together like a puzzle, and pound each nail in, as deep as they would go, to hold the lid in place and keep Antoine safe.

Darius grabbed the plastic bag with the six nails, bringing it down into the grave with him. He looked down again at the coffin. The satin lining looked so comfortable. Antoine would rest well, as he did on that very satin.

Darius stood on the side of the grave liner again to reach topside out of the grave, and grabbed the urn. Holding it close to his chest for a moment, he opened the lid slowly.

There they were.

Antoine's ashes.

All that was left of him.

Ashes.

A deep, dark, greyish dust.

He took the urn, and turned it over so the ashes fell out onto the satin bedding. He spread them out, so that they lay along the entire length of the casket.

Turning the urn back up, he drew it closer to his chest once again, and reached inside for the heart. This, truly, was Antoine. An over two hundred year old heart, still fleshy and beating, and would remain fleshy and beating for all of eternity.

Antoine….

He closed his eyes for a moment, holding the beating heart to the side of his face.

Setting the heart reverently in the center of the casket, roughly where it would have been if Antoine's entire body were lying in the casket, he reached in the bag for the six nails.

The first nail in the coffin.

Antoine, there you were. When we first spotted each other, before we met. I sat at my table, making it look to you like I was nursing a drink and listening to the owner chat, but all I really was thinking about was you.

You had such an alluring look, such a way that you drew me to you. I chose you, you chose me. We chose each other.

The hammering rapped loudly like steel against steel, in sharp contrast to the quiet as Darius finished with the first nail; he continued driving each nail deeper and deeper, getting one step closer to sealing Antoine's coffin.

Do you remember floating in the clouds? Do you remember the lust and the ecstasy that we felt together? Do you remember the first time that I woke you?

Wake up, sleepyhead.

Darius placed the second nail in the center side of the coffin.

You were so kind when you raised me from the dead. You put me in that grave, yes, but you raised me from it. You raised me from where I stayed for years, waiting for you, my son, waiting for the day I would walk the earth again. And now I am here.

A mortal again.

What am I going to do? How can I raise you? How can I do this – without getting killed?

So many things, Antoine, that I must consider now. Now, being very, very mortal. My fragility has returned. I need to find another way to raise you. I need to raise you and resurrect you before I die. You need to transform me back to immortality! I need the Chalice! Damn Claret!

Darius put his head in his hands for a moment, pausing on the fourth nail. He cried softly, overwhelmed by the fact that he may very well die before Antoine is resurrected. And then he would be dead forever, unable to rise again until the Lord's Judgment Day. He would certainly be damned to Hell for all of his dastardly deeds in his brief mortal life, and, most certainly, for his evildoings in his life since Tramos transformed him.

Oh Antoine, why did you raise me? Why did you sell your soul to Asmodai? Why are you putting yourself through all of this torment and suffering at his will? And because of what you did, what you did not initially out of love but out of your own personal needs, the needs for a corporation of immortals that were going to rise up and make a place in society – all went in vain, and the visionary is now lying beneath me, being slowly sealed into this coffin.

And your revelations to The Astral – that was to be the best venture yet! The Astral would have been key. I understand your purpose.

We are not human, Antoine. Wait a minute – I *am human, but you are not. I once wasn't. I'm sorry my dear old friend, sometimes I start thinking like I am still an immortal. This is going to take some getting used to, that's for sure.*

I am going to make a pledge to you, Antoine, as I hold this last nail in my hand, it's the last nail in your coffin, the last nail that will seal you from society. The last nail until I can raise you. What I pledge to you, my friend, is to find a way. To find a way and bring you back to life, before I die.

My time is short, dear child. I am already starting the aging process, the mortal process where humans die a little bit, day by day, until their bodies give up. A process I have been researching lately, with a new friend that I have made, Dora. She is like me, so she understands. I also have been seeing a lovely counselor named Claire.

Still with all that, I promise you to find Nesmaron. I promise to you to be immortal once again, to be newly transformed again, before I die.

Once I find Nesmaron, I will try to find a way to convince him to resurrect you, as it was written, he is your child. He must raise you.

Darius stood and looked at the last nail for a moment .The last nail in the coffin, the last nail that would seal Antoine from life.

He looked down at the casket, the pieces of the puzzle all placed together to form an adequate coffin lid, now held in place by five nails digging deep into the sides.

"Goodbye, Antoine," he said softly, looking down at his child's resting place. "I will miss you, my friend."

He took the last nail, and drove it down into the side of the box, using the greatest force that he had used for any of the nails he pounded. The banging reverberated so loudly against the stillness of the night, the dirt on the sides of the grave crumbled down above him, sending a light cascade of dirt on top of the lid.

He brushed it away, and reached up out of the grave again for the liner.

He placed the liner on top of the casket, sealing Antoine away from life.

Darius lifted himself out of the grave, dusting the dirt off of his jeans after he was on the grass again. Grabbing the shovel, he began to fill the grave back with dirt.

Goodbye, my friend.

"I will see you again one day, Antoine. You will not be in that grave forever, I promise you that. I will put an end to all of this mess."

The grave, once filled, made a small mound of freshly packed earth in the graveyard. Darius could not help from looking at the pile of dirt while he was gathering his equipment and placing it back in the brown tarp.

Afterwards, he blew the grave a kiss as he exited the cemetery in the fading, fiery sun.

I know you will, Darius, I know. But you can't possibly know, can you? Being the mortal that you now are? You can't possibly know or even fathom…

That I am still alive.

THE END

The Story Continues In BOOK TWO: The Quest for Immortality

In Memory of Author John Woodley, my uncle and an influential writer in my life.

Visit www.almengel.com for updates on all of A.L. Mengel's novels.
Visit www.eatlivewrite.blogspot.com for more writing by A.L. Mengel.
Visit www.facebook.com/authoralmengel

...Turn the page for one more surprise...

THE

QUEST FOR IMMORTALITY

I kill.

Everyday. Perhaps not in the traditional sense. Every day, I stare at a lifeless body beneath me, lying on the ground in a hapless mess, sometimes covered in blood and other times already cold and rigid and in the beginning stages of rigor mortis. Sometimes the bodies I am standing over don't even seem like human bodies anymore. Sometimes they are so mauled and mutilated and bloodied beyond recognition that I look down and see someone that looks like they could be someone familiar or perhaps someone that I do not know.

But I feel like a killer. I brush the feelings of uncertainty off. I look at the body lying beneath where I stand, and a feeling of contentment passes over me. I reach into my right pocket and fumble with the pack of cigarettes and lighter; the sweet, intoxicating smell of the cigarette smoke wafts through the still, humid summer air as I exhale slowly, closing my eyes and concentrating on the hum of the cicadas.

The body was found lying in a thick of trees at the side of Dixie. It was perhaps one of the worst messes I had come across in years. Totally drained and dried, like a grayish prune. There was a pool of blood beneath the corpse, but it had long since dried up by the time I had stood over the body.

"Ned," a voice called from behind me. I slowly turned to face a short, balding middle aged man holding a steaming cup of coffee in his right hand and a manila folder in his left. "Here is the case file." He held it out to me, casting a square-ish shadow over the body in the bright afternoon sun.

"How can you drink that on such a hot day like this?" I asked him, grabbing the folder from his hand. I fumbled with the clasp as he continued: "They found him a couple hours ago. The offices are destroyed – I have never seen such a fucking mess! The place looks like a bomb went off!"

He examined the file and saw a photo. Antoine Nagevesh.

"Now why is his picture in here?" I asked myself out loud, thumbing through the papers and news clippings, searching for an answer. I didn't find one. But I knew who that was. No one in Miami could *not* know who that was – he has always been such a glutton for the media and the spotlight. But, where has he been lately?

My assistant Pat rolled up a gurney, guzzling a cola right out of the can. "This is a nasty one," he commented, tossing the can in the woods. "Never seen one like this before!"

"Let's just get him back to town," I said, bending over above the head, placing my hands beneath the shoulders, positioning myself to hoist the dead weight onto the gurney. Now, closer than ever, I was hit by the stench of the rotting flesh. I brought my hand up to my face pocket of dead air hit me in the face with full force, almost knocking me back off my feet.

The body was dry and dusty, but heavy. Dead weight. So dry and so dead yet so heavy. Like his body was freshly gone but almost completely decomposed at the same time. Pat and I strained at the weight of the once overweight man despite his current dried out state and hoisted him on the gurney.

We were both out of breath, and I took a white handkerchief out of my shirt pocket and mopped my sweaty brow.

Yes, I feel like a killer. This is the type of scene that I am subjected to on a daily basis.

The drive back to town took roughly thirty minutes. Pat and I did not speak the entire way. I just smoked a steady stream of Newports, one right after another, and Pat drank another two colas. We had to drive with the windows rolled all the way down so our hair was blowing back and forth in the wind to keep the stench from overpowering us.

And this is the fun part. Box up the body, slide it in. Turn the bitch on! And then reduced to ashes. So many times I light a cigarette and exhale, closing my eyes and listening to the cracking of the flames, the gas. Sometimes I have to interrupt it and reposition the body so the chest remains on the hottest part of the flame, but I have become numb to the half burned bodies of rotted flesh that was bubbling and boiling off of the bones in heat of the chamber.

The cold, pale green tiles – with their crusty old dead mosquito carcasses and dried spots of rusty colored blood and bright florescent lights always remind me of where I am. I am not in the bowels of hell, I am here working – earning my living. And damn I'm good at it.

The Blood Decanter

A Novel

A.L. MENGEL

In the beginning there was a great war between the angels and the demons. It was a war that had waged and continued since before time had existed, and before man had walked the earth. But this war, this unholy and unearthly battle, this war during which beasts would draw flaming swords, and angels would chorus through the skies surrounded by legions of light and dive downwards to cast the demons away, was taking place through space and history and time, in a dimension that was very little known to those who did not live in it; this enduring battle would cause earthquakes and fires and explosions, but essentially was undetected by those whose perception did not create an awareness of the spiritual beings.

But the war did, at a certain time in a certain city on the earth, make its presence known with humanity. For the war was not always just that of the beasts, or the angels.

Others would join the battle.

There had been a point when the humans would come. They would stand on the edge of the angry sea, standing pale, naked, and staring straight ahead, with expressionless, blank stares, as if stripped of their life force.

And, in a sense they had been.

For the war was taking place in the place – or, as many have argued, in the space, or dimension outside of the reality that these humans had once been accustomed to.

There eventually were these humans which would involve themselves – the souls of the formerly living that would be cast into a dark, burning sea; in an ocean of sorrow, burning with flames of despair and torment.

There was much turmoil and a constant veil of sadness; there was an eternal fire that burned in the sea of souls; the flames covered the water and burned, seemingly without a source, but strong and commanding, a leash of insanity, pulling on the crying, filled with despair, sadness and loss.

In a sea filled with faces, desperate souls looking upwards with unseeing eyes, limbs reached upwards from icy waters in search of air, but finding none. Wide eyes saw nothing, bleeding ears heard nothing, and skin, which was pasty white and covered with ulcers felt nothing.

The bodies did not feel the frigidness, nor the chill of the waters.

Their numbness was benign.

Their black fingertips, rotted with gangrene, some to the point where fingernails had fallen off and skin cracked and bled, did not feel the cold, nor the pain that would have normally been associated with failing skin.

The waters of the sea were always frigid, always writhing with bodies, always agitated and screaming.

And the war waged on, for what seems like years, but there was no sense of time. There was no eternity; no hourglass with sand tipping from one globe to the other; no sun, no clocks or anything indicating that the war should stop.

Just a red sky painted with black clouds.

And on the shores of the sea, the rocks were assaulting, rising through the sands like pointed mountains, which dug into the unprotected feet of those who stood on the sand, waiting to be banished into the sea.

And it was the monstrous demon who stood on the edge of the shoreline that cast the evil sinners into the sea, to be swallowed by thrashing limbs and screaming. He held a pointed spire, shooting flames into the sky, a sky from which only drops of blood would fall.

"Do not pass here!" The demon raised a muscular arm, pointing his spire towards the sky. A small group of people huddled together on the beach, not far from the demon; they all looked in horror over towards the waterline, saw the angry sea and the white foam crests of the waves, revealing the thrashing limbs and arms climbing and grabbing and pulling.

But despite the order of Hades, despite that the new arrivals at the shore of the sea that was very consistent and steady, the war waged on. And during that war, there was a focus, and that was one particular demon.

It was a demon who looked that of a man who knelt on the shore, his head hung low, his arms in shackles. He was not monstrous, muscular nor did he have wings or horns.

He was a man who had long, dark hair, twisted locks that hung down from his shoulders. He was dragged from a group of towering rocks towards an altar in the center of the sea, which stood in the center of the waters upon giant boulders that rose upwards towards the swirling, angry clouds.

He was dragged along the sand by two muscular men, his feet bloodied, broken and limp.

Coming Soon from Parchman's Press

www.ingramcontent.com/pod-product-compliance
Lightning Source LLC
Chambersburg PA
CBHW030821310726
48980CB00006B/586/J
* 9 7 8 0 9 8 9 3 7 7 3 8 6 *